Experts Praise

Thriller

DIE AGAIN TOMORROW

"*Die Again Tomorrow* held me captive me from the opening chapter—in which a murdered woman is subjected to a secret medical procedure that brings her back to life. From there the story takes off like a rocket, full of surprises, fascinating science, and vivid characters. If you enjoy the medical thrillers of Crichton and Cook, this book is for you. I can't recommend it highly enough."
—Douglas Preston

"Peikoff's thrillers are really scary and scarily real."
—Taylor Stevens

NO TIME TO DIE

"Breathless thrills and pace, but real substance too: a perfect mix of nail-biter and thought-provoker, from a writer to watch. Highly recommended."
—Lee Child

"*No Time to Die* is an intelligent, exciting tour de force; the story is tight, the characters are fascinating, and the twists are terrific and totally unexpected . . . A crackling good read. . . . Has the magic touch."
—Michael Palmer

DIE
AGAIN
TOMORROW

KIRA
PEIKOFF

Kensington Publishing Corp.

www.kensingtonbooks.com

PINNACLE BOOKS are published by

Kensington Publishing Corp.
119 West 40th Street
New York, NY 10018

All Kensington titles, imprints, and distributed lines are available at special quantity discounts for bulk purchases for sales promotions, premiums, fund-raising, educational, or institutional use. Special book excerpts or customized printings can also be created to fit specific needs. For details, write or phone the office of the Kensington sales manager: Kensington Publishing Corp., 119 West 40th Street, New York, NY 10018, attn: Sales Department; phone 1-800-221-2647.

ISBN-13: 978-0-7860-3491-8
ISBN-10: 0-7860-3491-2

First printing: October 2015

10 9 8 7 6 5 4 3 2 1

Printed in the United States of America

First electronic edition: October 2015

ISBN-13: 978-0-7860-3492-5
ISBN-10: 0-7860-3492-0

For Matt

PART ONE

Numberless are the world's wonders, but none
*   more wonderful than man . . .*
From every wind, he has made himself secure—
*   from all but one:*
In the late wind of death he cannot stand.

—Sophocles' *Antigone*, 5th century BC

Contrary to popular belief, death is not a moment
in time, such as when the heart stops beating,
respiration ceases, or the brain stops functioning.
Death, rather, is a process—
a process that can be interrupted well after
it has begun.

—Sam Parnia, MD, PhD,
Director of Resuscitation Research at
Stony Brook University
School of Medicine, 2013

1 minute dead

Her body undulated in the sea. It swayed with the waves, rising and falling, a rag doll in the froth. Seaweed clung to the dark tangle of her hair. Facedown, she floated on the crest of a swell, then plummeted with the breaker. Her slender limbs splayed out, strangers to pain. She was nothing now but a marionette at the mercy of the tide. White foam engulfed her body and carried it express to the shore.

It washed up on the beach. The tide receded. Her cheek lay against the sand, her eyes swollen closed. Her mouth hung open. Salt water trickled out.

The first person to notice was a little boy digging for crabs. He scooted over and squatted in front of her face.

"Time for wakey," he said. He planted his chubby thumb and forefinger on her eyelid, pried it open, and gazed into her unseeing pupil.

"Wakey," he said, frowning. He poked her limp arm. Nothing happened.

He started to cry. A woman jogged toward him but stopped short.

Then she screamed.

7 minutes dead

Two ambulances arrived at the same time. A pair of emergency medical techs jumped out of the first one and raced to her body, where a crowd of about ten sunbathers had gathered. Some were taking turns trying to deliver chest compressions while others stood to block the view of nearby children. The second ambulance waited at the curb; its purpose was to preserve the organs of a corpse for harvesting and donation in case attempts at resuscitation failed. With Key West's popular opt-out program, everyone who died in the city was assumed to be a consenting donor unless otherwise indicated.

As the two EMTs approached the body, they saw right away that her skin was waterlogged and turning bluish. Frothy salt water spewed out of her mouth as if from an erratic hose.

"Out of the way," the older one commanded. His voice carried an air of authority that matched his jaded expression. The younger tech followed on his heels with a case of equipment slung over his shoulder. He was in his late twenties, about the same age as the drowned woman.

The crowd parted and stepped back.

The first EMT dropped to his knees and grabbed her wrist. No pulse. He flung her disheveled hair off her face and opened her eyelids. Despite the bright morning sunlight, her pupils were fixed and dilated.

The younger tech covered her body with defibrillator pads and attempted to shock her heart. When nothing happened, he switched to giving her chest compressions, hard and fast, about one hundred per minute. Salt water tainted with blood kept dribbling out of her mouth.

"She's flatlined," the older tech said after two minutes. "We should just declare her."

The other man kept on pushing, though his arms were tiring. "No, let's—give her a—chance," he sputtered. "She's so young."

His colleague looked skeptical, but nodded. "Let's switch, you do the line."

The young tech rolled off her chest and tried to inject a peripheral line with epinephrine into her arm, but her skin was so mottled that he couldn't find the vein. He cursed under his breath and moved on to the next last-ditch step.

As the older man continued to deliver fast compressions, grunting and sweating, the other hauled a canister of oxygen and a plastic breathing tube out of the supply bag. Using an L-shaped laryngoscope, he pushed up the roof of her mouth to see down into her throat.

That was when he noticed a piece of what looked like black neoprene cloth lodged inside her cheek. *That's weird,* he thought, and tried to pull it out, but it wouldn't easily dislodge, so he bypassed it. Her throat was extremely swollen and he had to work hard to shove the breathing tube all the way in.

"Should I just put the epinephrine down the tube?" he asked.

"You know—there's—controversy about that," the other man huffed, still doing compressions. "It doesn't—necessarily—help survival."

"What does she have to lose?"

He seized the drug and pushed 2 milligrams into her tube. Then he connected her to the oxygen tank, and the men switched positions again so neither tired for too long.

Every two or three minutes, they switched, while one checked her pulse on her neck, her groin. Nothing. Her skin was now a frightening shade of blue.

After twenty-one minutes, the older man pushed on

her chest for the last time and rolled off her, sweating profusely.

"We should just stop, I don't know why you want to save the world all the time."

The young man glared, but didn't rush to perform any further compressions. "She had her whole life ahead of her."

It didn't help that she was beautiful: he imagined how her cascade of black hair might have draped across her tanned shoulders, how her green eyes might have lit up when she laughed. She had the athletic figure of a swimmer—flat abs, toned biceps, defined calves. With a body like that, he wondered how she could have succumbed to the waves, even in high tide. Some things would forever be a mystery.

"We have to accept it. She's gone. I'm calling it." The older tech glanced at his watch. "Time of death: 10:12 A.M."

A few of the onlookers turned away. One made the sign of a cross over his chest and bowed his head.

The young EMT sighed and radioed to the waiting ambulance to come claim her body. Then he removed her breathing tube and packed up all the equipment. He tried to think of the bright side: a young, otherwise healthy person was a prime candidate for cadaver organ donation; as many as fifty lives could be saved or improved from her body alone.

Within seconds, two more bored-looking EMTs arrived with a stretcher and nodded at the pair who had failed.

"We can take it from here. Thanks."

They lifted her corpse and strapped it in, wasting no time hauling it to their own ambulance. As they tipped the stretcher to load it, her drying hair fell over the edge and glinted in the warm November sun.

Inside, a white-haired doctor was waiting. He beckoned to the EMTs to hurry. They scrambled in after loading the stretcher, just as the doctor pulled the door shut behind them. Exhilaration radiated from his flushed cheeks, but his demeanor was steady.

He was the famed—some would say infamous—Dr. Horatio Quinn, who had vanished from the public eye seven years prior. Now approaching eighty, his back was stooped, his arthritic fingers gnarled, his messy brows furrowed. But behind his tortoiseshell glasses shone an insatiable hunger for truth that kept him as young as the first day he ever walked into a lab.

He placed one hand on the woman's lifeless forehead and smiled.

"Gentlemen," he said, "close the blinds. This is when the fun begins."

33 minutes dead

Dr. Quinn lifted a corner of the rubber floor pad and pressed his index finger to a tiny sensor. Together, he and the two EMTs turned to stare at a blank white area on the wall a few inches below the ceiling, near the head of the corpse. They heard a click, followed by a whirring sound. Then four cracks materialized in the shape of a square about two feet across and two feet wide. It was a door. The edges popped out and slid to the left, revealing a secret compartment in the depth.

"Never gets old," muttered Chris, the tech with the best poker face around.

His new apprentice, Theo, rubbed his hands together in anticipation.

The doctor reached inside the hole and extracted an automatic CPR device—a small round machine the size of a helmet. He put it on the dead woman's sternum, securing it around her chest with a band pulled tight. Right away the machine started to deliver perfect chest compressions to the highest standards of timing and force—with no chance of tiring. Next, the doctor opened her mouth and inserted a laryngoscope attached to a camera so he could visualize her trachea.

He frowned; a piece of shredded black cloth was stuck between her teeth and cheek. It had a fraying string wrapped around her tooth. *What the hell is that?* he thought. He yanked it out and flicked it away, then slipped in a breathing tube connected to a ventilator and a portable oxygen tank. He set the CPR device at ten breaths per minute.

"Game on," he whispered near her ear.

At the same time, while Theo connected her arm to a standard blood pressure cuff, Chris retrieved a black circular pad from the secret hole. It looked like an eye patch, but with a narrow blue tube connecting to a digital display: it was a cerebral oximeter that used near-infrared light to measure the amount of oxygen getting to her brain. He stuck it on her forehead above her right eye. The display quickly lit up with a red number: 5 percent.

"Why is it still so low?" Ty asked at her left side. "Shouldn't it be coming up already?"

"It will." Dr. Quinn was standing at her head, twisting his frail body to reach up into the hole. "You'll see."

What he took out next looked like a red gun, but with a long needle in place of a barrel. It was an intraosseous device that could shoot drugs directly into bone, bypassing veins.

"My favorite toy," he declared. He leaned over the corpse, pressed the gun against her left shoulder, and fired. It recoiled as a pin lodged itself in her bone. He shot three more pins—one into her other shoulder and just below each knee. The techs watched with a mixture of awe and envy at his precision. Then he attached a line into each pin that would serve as a conduit for the drugs.

Chris and Theo moved aside in the cramped space as he positioned himself next to her left shoulder. "Now," he said with relish, "for the moment of truth. I want the X101 first."

"Got it." Chris handed him a tube of chilled clear fluid that had been stored in a container inside the hole.

Dr. Quinn cradled it in his hands with the affection of a father. It was his life's work in a vial—the culmination of decades, the reason he had once been celebrated and then viciously destroyed, accused of intellectual theft by a jealous colleague, driven out of research, driven almost to suicide. If not for the Network's rescue seven years ago, he might very well have been as dead as the corpse before him.

He had designed the drug to exploit the critical time between a person's death and the death of their brain cells—roughly a four- to eight-hour window, maybe even longer. But by injecting an inhibitor of the calpain enzyme—the signal to brain cells that it was time to die—the process could be slowed down, the window expanded, and the brain temporarily protected from damage. One dose of X101 had bought an additional ten hours of brain cell preservation in animal trials, and now, at last, he was secretly testing it in humans.

He injected a single dose into the woman's left shoulder. Working quickly, the other men addressed her remaining lines: Chris injected her right shoulder with an icy slurry of water to chill her down rapidly from the inside out. Into her left knee, Theo injected an experimental solution filled with billions of microglobules of fat, each of which contained a dose of oxygen. When released into her body, it would provide a welcome gush to her brain and other organs. In the last line, her right knee, the doctor injected one final drug: coenzyme Q. It was meant to protect mitochondria, the energy-producing part of cells. But the oxygen slurry and the coenzyme Q, both commercially available, were worthless without the X101 to prevent neurons from dying.

Next Theo got to work using the ultrasound machine installed in the ambulance to locate the carotid artery in her neck, then he inserted a thick catheter with two separate tracks, pushing it down near her heart.

"Nice work, Theo," the doctor commented.

He took over and connected the catheter to a portable machine called an ECMO that pumped blood in a loop outside the body, infusing it with oxygen and cleansing it of carbon dioxide, before cycling it back into the dead woman.

At the same time, Chris inserted a catheter into her groin to start a drip of epinephrine to bring up her blood pressure.

"Hey!" Theo exclaimed, pointing at the cerebral oximeter on her forehead. "It's already up to forty-five percent."

"Told you," the doctor said. "But it's still got a ways to go. We want it at seventy percent. Now ice her."

Maneuvering around the stretcher in the tight space, Theo reached into the secret hole and loaded his arms with nearly a dozen artificial ice packs. Together, he and Chris covered her arms, legs, and stomach to cool her down quickly from the outside, in addition to the inside. A thermometer indicated that her current temperature was 95 degrees, but the ice would bring it down to 70. Cold was key: it slowed down decay, snatching back time from the impending claws of irreversible death.

"Excellent, gentlemen," the doctor announced. "Let's hit the road."

Chris hopped out and took his place up front in the driver's seat. The curtains remained closed, the sirens off. As the ambulance started to roll out of the beach's parking lot, Dr. Quinn fitted an EEG skullcap over her head to measure her brain waves. The monitor lit up with a low, sustained beep.

Theo's freckled nose wrinkled. "Shit. She's still totally flatlined."

"Because we shut her down," the doctor said. "We've hibernated her."

The engine whirred and the ambulance sped up. He and Theo settled into straight-backed seats with their knees butting up against the stretcher, holding the black straps dangling from the ceiling. With each turn, the woman's head lolled from side to side. Her bluish lips were slack around the breathing tube and her puffy eyelids were sealed shut.

Dr. Quinn inched aside a curtain to peek outside. He saw the hospital and morgue pass by, a cluster of old beige buildings as desperately outdated as the medicine that was practiced there.

"What about her organs?" Theo asked. "Isn't the hospital waiting on the body?"

"Not for long. Chris should be calling it in now—he'll tell the morgue that we were able to resuscitate her after all, and he'll tell the hospital that her organs were too damaged for donation. A junkie or something."

Theo smirked. "Way to honor the dead."

"The trick is to get her lost in the system. The hospital will think we're taking her to the morgue and vice versa. Trust me, once organs are out of the question, no one cares about a corpse."

"What about her family?"

"We don't know who she is—yet. Let's hope we get the chance to find out."

2 hours, 6 minutes dead

The ambulance approached a port where a 440-foot cruise ship was docked. On its side in flowery script were the words *Retirement at Sea.* It was a stately white vessel with five decks, all but the top one lined with rows of circular windows.

Chris navigated onto a wooden pier parallel to the ship and drove several yards until he reached a certain threshold. As soon as he crossed it, a loading ramp yawned out of the side of the ship and flattened onto the pier. It was lined with seven-foot-tall opaque white panels, ensuring the privacy of all who came and went.

Chris backed up to the ramp and killed the engine. That was their cue: Dr. Quinn and Theo popped open the back door, now shielded from onlookers, and quickly hoisted the dead woman's stretcher up the ramp and aboard the ship, accompanied by the equipment on poles: the blood-pumping ECMO device, the cerebral oximeter, the still flatlined EEG monitor.

A tall, square-jawed man in his fifties was waiting for them on the deck, where a dozen people were bustling about carrying charts, conferring with one another, striding purposefully in and out of adjacent doors. All were clad in medical scrubs. Though the tall man was the odd one out in black sweatpants and a gray T-shirt, his erect posture lent him an air of dignity. He had the sculpted muscles and wavy dark hair of someone half his age, but the no-nonsense face of a commanding officer. Yet there was a hint of mischief in his blue eyes that softened his intensity. One felt in his presence that nothing could faze him, nor should it.

"Galileo." Dr. Quinn greeted him with a respectful lift of his chin. "We need an OR."

"It's ready and waiting." Galileo stared at the corpse with the resolve of a doctor confronting the world's sickest patient. "What's the prognosis?"

"Iffy. Her lungs are a mess, still no pulse. But the good news is she's cooled, brain oxygen's up to seventy percent, and the drugs should have bought us some time."

"She looks too young to die." He pressed his lips together, staring at her bone-white face. The black hair plastered to her cheeks made the contrast even starker. "Go. The nurses are already scrubbed in."

After also scrubbing in at a station of sterile sinks, the doctor and his two techs took the elevator down to the lowest deck. The wide open space that was once a luxurious restaurant with seating for 120 had been entirely transformed. Three plastic partitions separated it into several state-of-the-art operating rooms, each stocked with the surgical tools of a world-class hospital. The only hint of the deck's past life was a gold, crystal-encrusted chandelier still hanging from the ceiling.

They hurried into OR 1, where two gray-haired intensive-care nurses were gloved, masked, and standing by. Though only their eyes were visible, Dr. Quinn was pleased to recognize Annie and Corinne, the Network's most experienced gems. They flashed him smiles with their eyes, while Chris and Theo laid the corpse flat on the table. The techs were careful not to disrupt any of the tools tethered to her, including the ice packs keeping her cool and the CPR device that was still delivering compressions to her chest in quick bursts.

Then the two men got out of the way while the others converged around the dead woman in choreographed posts: the doctor standing behind her head, the nurses on either side of him, extending his reach to the various shiny tools on trays nearby.

They responded rapid-fire to his commands, and Dr. Quinn was soon gripping a heavy silver drill with both hands. Steadily he punctured a bolt into the back of the woman's skull. The noise of grinding through bone always made him wince, though he knew she could feel no pain. A sensor attached to the bolt sat on the surface of her brain to measure intracranial pressure.

"Good to go," he said. "Next up, a bronchoscope, please."

The nurses moved with the swiftness and grace of dancers. Within minutes, the doctor had inserted a smaller tube with a camera into her breathing tube, sucked out salt water, washed out her lungs with a sterile solution, and given her a dose of antibiotics.

All along the nurses took turns reading out numbers to keep him informed of her oxygen, carbon dioxide, brain pressure, and blood pressure. It was no simple task to maintain the ideal balance of each number: to maintain the goal of 70 percent brain oxygen, they had to pump it into the bloodstream at 95 percent and no further. Oxygen itself was toxic to cells if too concentrated, and dangerously deficient if not enough. Right now she was at a perfect 70 percent and 40 mmHg of carbon dioxide; they just had to keep her there.

"Okay, now bring her blood pressure up, up, up!" the doctor commanded, lifting his hands. The key was to maintain a higher than usual arterial pressure—90 instead of the usual 65—to pump the blood back into her brain. Careful monitoring of the bolt sensor would ensure that the brain wasn't getting crushed by the pressure.

Annie was leaning down to check on the bolt when she caught sight of something odd: a bald patch the size of a thumbprint on the woman's head, near her right ear.

"Did you see this?" she asked the doctor. He shifted his gaze from the blood pressure monitor to the patch and shrugged.

"No, but she's got more to worry about than a bad hair day right now."

"But isn't it—"

Annie was cut off by the sudden angry beeping of a monitor.

"O2's spiking!" Corinne yelled. The cerebral oximeter was jumping up—80 percent, 85 percent, 87 percent.

Dr. Quinn leaped to the ECMO machine that was pumping oxygen into her blood through the tube in her neck and adjusted the output. When the percentages started dropping back down, he exhaled a breath. He didn't look away until she was stable again at 70 percent.

"Okay," he said at last. "Lungs are clean. The numbers look good. You know what to do."

The nurses removed the ice packs lining her arms, stomach, and legs, as the doctor set the temperature regulator on the ECMO to gradually rewarm her body at a rate of 0.25 degrees Celsius per hour. The thaw out of the cold state was precisely calibrated—if it happened too quickly, intracranial pressure could spike and cause permanent death.

When there was nothing left to do, the doctor gazed down at the intubated, catheterized, machine-addled corpse on the table. It was difficult not to think of her as his *patient,* even though—by definition—she was still as dead as ever. No heartbeat, no respiration, no brain waves.

He looked up at the nurses with a hopeful smile.

"Now," he said, "we wait."

15 hours, 20 minutes dead

"Quinn!" yelled a familiar husky voice into the inter-com. It was Annie. Her words blasted through his wall and woke him with a start. It was after 1 A.M. His fitful dream evaporated like vapor as reality hardened around him: he was in his compact box of a room on deck two, gently rocking with the ocean's waves. Frustration nettled him. Where was his patient? Why was he in bed?

Then he recalled keeping vigil next to her body for nearly twelve hours before falling asleep on the floor. Someone must have moved him here.

He jumped up and crossed the three steps to his inter-com. "What did I miss?"

"Come fast. There's a flicker on the heart monitor."

He felt a joyous bubble rise in his throat, somewhere between a laugh and a sob. Ten seconds later, he was back by her side in the operating room. Her pulse was erratic, to be sure. A shy beep could be heard at jagged intervals, persisting for several seconds and then disappearing altogether. Her temperature had climbed to 86 degrees Fahrenheit. A pinkish smudge was returning to her ashen cheeks.

"Come on," he muttered. "Come on."

Within minutes the flicker became a sustained line and the beep, a steady rhythm.

"Atta girl!" he cried. "Isn't that the most beautiful music you ever heard?"

Annie stood behind him, her hazel eyes bloodshot and weary. "But she's still flatlined. What if her brain doesn't come back?"

"It will. Give her time. I'll take over. You go to bed."

For three more hours, he waited. As the rest of the ship

slept, he kept an obsessive eye on every number that could be measured. No matter how many times he had gone through this process—she was the twenty-second patient in his clinical trial—he was awestruck witnessing the retreat of death. It was the stuff of the supernatural, the Holy Grail sought across all of time—yet it was real. It was happening in front of him.

Only in the last decade had pioneers in cardiac resuscitation made it possible to revive people hours after they'd drawn their last breath, and now his drug X101 was lengthening that window. So far it had worked every time to limit brain damage and restore patients to their full selves, even up to twenty-four hours after their deaths. He was confident it would work again on this Jane Doe, yet he still felt a desperate yearning bordering on despair with each minute that ticked by.

What would he do if he actually did bring her back to life, but brain-dead? Could he ethically just pull the plug without consent, if he didn't know her identity or her family? Or was he bound to keep her on life support indefinitely? It was a dilemma he had never faced, but he tortured himself with its plausibility as the night wore on.

At last, when her temperature reached 91 degrees, he saw it: a spasm of electricity on the EEG. He jumped from his chair and stared, captivated, at the monitor. The previously flat line transformed into spiky bursts of peaks and valleys. They stabilized over the next six hours as her temperature rose to 98 degrees. The doctor oversaw every moment, talking to her gently in case she could hear him. She was in a deep coma, but she wasn't brain-dead. Now she wasn't dead at all.

1 minute awake

Her eyes opened. They roamed back and forth, squinting under the fluorescent lights. Her face scrunched up as if she were about to cry. Instead she groaned past her breathing tube and thrashed her legs, her heart rate skyrocketing: 132, 140, 147.

A petite young nurse, who was covering the morning shift, cupped a hand over her mouth and gasped. At the bedside, Dr. Quinn clutched the woman's warm left hand in both of his. He had been awaiting this moment all night.

"You're okay," he said softly. "You're just waking up from a bad accident."

Her head rolled back and forth. An involuntary moan escaped her.

"I'm going to take out your tube now. This'll be quick. There we go, see, no problem, easy does it—and it's out."

She immediately coughed. "Wa—" she started, then choked and coughed again. Her hand flew to her throat.

"Right here." The doctor lifted a white paper cup to her lips. He cradled her head and she sipped greedily, spilling much of it down her neck. When he pulled back her paper drape to blot her collarbone dry, he noticed a row of deep purple bruises. How could he not have seen them at first? But then he realized that would have been impossible; they could have shown up only after blood was recirculated through into her body.

"Boy," he said, "you really got tossed around in those waves."

"Won't . . . pay," she mumbled, her eyes blinking rapidly but failing to focus on anything. "Not got. Me no."

"What's she saying?" the nurse asked under her breath.

"She's just confused," the doctor whispered. "It's the drugs. Don't worry—it's normal at first."

"Me!" the woman exclaimed with a sudden loopy grin. Her tone was gleeful. "Me! Mama." Her eyes darted around the room, then closed. In a minute she was asleep again.

The nurse raised her eyebrows. "Imagine what her family must be going through, wherever they are."

"We'll get her back to them soon enough." The doctor stroked his patient's clammy forehead. "Once her delirium wears off and she's stable, we'll give her a mild tranquilizer and transport her to the real hospital. She'll think she was there the whole time, in a coma, and the staff will conclude that some embarrassing miscommunication caused her to get lost in their system. They'll do everything to cover it up, but if any investigation is opened, our ally on the Board will shut it down. All that counts is that she's reunited with her family alive and well. Her death will be nothing but a forgotten footnote in her life."

48 hours awake

She spent two days in a blur of intravenous feedings, babbling, sleep, and agitation. Once her vitals stabilized, she was moved up to deck three into her own private recovery room, with a porthole that let in abundant sunshine. Its morning rays now bathed her skin in a healthy glow, no signs of her earlier pallor. She was sleeping, but Dr. Quinn knew that when she awoke this time, the effects of the drugs would be over. She'd be herself again—whoever she was.

He grinned at the report in his hand from the recent MRI of her brain: normal. Completely, beautifully normal. The X101 had once again proved its efficacy, in combination with the oxygenated fat globules and the mitochondria-protecting enzymes. Part of him wanted to just call off the clinical trial and make the whole protocol available stat to every hospital in the country, hell, in the world—but he knew it was too risky to blow the Network's cover over such preliminary results. If they got to five hundred patients and the percentages held, then he and Galileo would have some serious decisions to make. Would the U.S. government forgive their transgressions of illegal human experimentation if the peace offering was a way to reverse death? He liked to think so. But if not . . .

He brushed those concerns aside, gazing down at the woman's face—her sloped nose, her chapped pink lips, her arched brows. Each steady breath she inhaled was an affirmation of his own reason for being. He memorized the moment, knowing she would soon be leaving his care. It was hard not to get attached to the patients whose lives he had saved, even if they were mysteries as human beings.

"We did good," he said, standing over her. "It was rough for a while there, but you pulled through."

Her lids twitched at his voice, then fluttered open. She stared up at him blankly.

"Well, look who's awake! Hello there," he said, watching her expression transform into curiosity as she took in his white coat, wrinkled hands, and kindly face. "What's your name?"

She cleared her throat, keeping her intelligent eyes on him. "Isabel. Where am I?"

"Nice to meet you, Isabel. I'm Dr. Quinn, and you're in a hospital. You had a bad accident a few days ago in the ocean. Do you remember?"

"*No.*" She shook her head with surprising exertion.

"You don't remember?"

"No, I do." A fierce glare narrowed her eyes.

"You do? Then what's no?"

"It wasn't an accident." She fingered the bruises at the base of her neck. "I was murdered."

CHAPTER 1
The Day of Isabel

Key West

Her death happened fast.

When the ferocious wave slammed her and her fellow surfers off their boards, she plummeted to the bottom, but didn't panic. Not at first. She held her breath as she tumbled through the chaos, waiting for the sea to straighten itself out. The light of dawn struck the water, transforming its surface into a glittering kaleidoscope above her. She pushed her way up, greedy for air.

That was when a mysterious hand yanked her ponytail down. Her head snapped back, her lips parted, a nauseating flood of salt water rushed in. She choked and gagged and grew furious. Her arms and legs thrashed, but the hand was as firm as an anchor chaining her to death. She kicked harder, clawing and biting at her tormentor: a wet-suited scuba diver whose lips were wrapped around a breathing tube. It enraged her that this monster was feasting on air while she drowned. Her lungs felt like pressure tanks about to explode. He clamped down on either side of her neck with both hands and squeezed.

Soon a realization came that she had no choice but to

confront: she wasn't going to make it. Yet in spite of her rage and despair, she clung to an absurd optimism that persisted until the very end.

She never wondered why she was being killed. She understood perfectly. Her only surprise was that she, of all people, had succumbed—in the one place she thought she was safe. She didn't even get to say good-bye. Her final thought was of Richard Barnett—and how, like a typical man, he had failed her, having vanished from her life without ever making good on his promise.

Despite everything, death itself was peaceful. In the final split second came acceptance—then the absence of pain, followed by an all-encompassing blackness. She encountered no light or universal warmth. Instead, she simply ceased to exist, along with the secret of the violence she almost carried to her grave.

Six months before

The Brazilian Amazon was no place for wimps. But Isabel Leon believed she could survive anything. The Arctic tundra in the winter, where she sought warmth inside a bear's carcass. The shark-infested waters of Australia, where she fashioned a raft of bamboo. The scorching dryness of the Sahara with nothing but her own sweat to drink.

Those were only the first three episodes of *Wild Woman,* the new reality show that was going to redefine what it meant to be a lady in the twenty-first century. She was brainy, with a master's degree in exercise science, and just as tough as any man: she'd participated in three triathlons alongside her army vet father. Yet her toughness didn't negate her femininity. The camera adored her lithe figure, green eyes, and cascading dark hair; it was television, after all.

To the producers, she was a star in the making. Little did they know she was as vulnerable as any other twenty-eight-year-old woman running empty on heartache. In the last year, her father had passed away of a sudden heart attack, and her fiancé had admitted to cheating on her with his ex. So the show was a way to reconnect with her own strength rather than a vehicle for fame. But if fortune came her way, she wasn't about to deny it. Then her widowed mother wouldn't have to work anymore, and her little brother could quit worrying about whether their family's struggling indie bookstore back home in Key West was going to make it. Her mom and Andy were the loves of her life; they were all she had left.

She was thinking of them—not death—when the producers dropped her by helicopter into the middle of the rainforest. She didn't pay much attention to her own mortality. The concept was about as real as an outer galaxy; it existed, but only in the abstract, light-years away.

She had no idea that the very moment she jumped to the ground, a fateful e-mail was whooshing into her inbox. An e-mail that would trigger the events leading to her murder.

But in the midst of the jungle, the canopy of trees was so dense that she barely had access to sunlight, let alone e-mail. So she wasn't too worried about anything other than getting through the next week. Snakes, vermin, insects, and birds thrived in such quantity that it was enough to make Manhattan look sparse. The constant buzzing and hissing, plus the smothering humidity at 97 degrees, forced her into high alert against predators and heatstroke. Hydration was key: you could survive only three days without water.

Yet even with all the rain, uncontaminated water was nearly impossible to come by. Plan A was to find some bromeliad plants—a relative of the pineapple, its broad waxy leaves could act like a bowl for catching rainwater. Yet her luck ran dry, as it were. Instead of bromeliads, she came across benign-looking heart-shaped leaves that she recognized as the deadly curare, a plant used by natives to poison arrow tips. Giving it a wide berth, she stumbled onto a small pool of clear standing water—so delectably tempting—but likely chock full of parasites. She knew she had to boil it, but all all the potential kindling she could gather was slick with moisture, so fire wouldn't take.

While looking for dry twigs, she kept her eyes peeled for food sources like berries, recalling a mnemonic from her days in Girl Scouts: *White and yellow, kill a fellow. Purple and blue, good for you. Red . . . could be good, could be dead.* At least back then she'd had a troop and a leader to guide her. Even on her most difficult survivalist adventures, working as a white-water rafting guide during the summers, she'd never really been alone. Once, while leading a group of six tourists on the Middle Fork of the Salmon River in Idaho, she and her charges had gotten stranded after a jagged underwater rock tore apart their raft. While they waited three days for help to reach them in the dense woods, she launched into cool survival mode—collecting water from the dew on plant leaves, foraging for pine nuts and cattail stalks, using one man's glasses to start a fire. Once they were finally rescued by helicopter, the story of her heroism landed her several local prime-time television interviews, both in Idaho and back home in Florida. It was through one of those charismatic appearances that the producers of *Wild Woman* noticed her and invited her to a casting call. And now, quite astonishingly since she'd never aspired to fortune or stardom, she had her very own television show.

Back in the Amazon, with the camera crew watching her every failed attempt to find a suitable drinking source, she felt increasingly distressed for reasons they would never know. The producers wanted to intervene after her second dehydrated day, but she refused. It was the last episode of the season, and so far, she hadn't required any assistance. She was determined not to spoil her pristine record, as though doing so would constitute a betrayal of her promise to the viewers—that she was "alone in the wild." After what her ex-fiancé put her through, she was extremely conscious of betrayals. So: not a drop. It was maddening to watch the camera guys tipping back canteens, but it was also galvanizing.

Deep down, though, she knew her motivation had nothing to do with the viewers or her bastard ex. It was about trying to prove to herself that she really was the independent survivalist she played on TV, and not the helpless girl who had failed her father so horribly at the end of his life that she stumbled around shrink-wrapped in guilt.

But her determination to survive on her own in the rainforest proved futile. After three days, her dehydration grew severe enough for producers to call off the shoot and fly her to the nearest hospital in a remote village. There she spent six hours hooked up to an IV with fluids, berating herself for failing, until a doctor who spoke no English pronounced her "*volta ao normal*." Finally she could go back and finish the job. She hoped the producers would edit out the past few days like they'd never happened; if only they could do the same with the past year.

But first, since she was near a computer for the first time in days, she rushed to check her e-mail. It was the

only way she'd been communicating with her mother between breaks in filming.

Now that her dad was gone, Isabel worried daily about
her mom, who'd already endured enough for any lifetime.
Thirty years ago, she escaped from the tyranny of Cas-
tro's Cuba on a raft with nothing but a few days of water
and bread. When she reached Florida, she fought to build
a life as a bookseller away from the sharp eyes of the immigration patrollers. Isabel was born after her mom met
and married an American soldier whose ruggedness belied the softness of his heart. Their home life was cheerfully modest, filled with frequent camping trips, nature
excursions, and quiet nights reading together in the family room.

Then, when Isabel was eighteen, her mom's younger
sister—who had gotten detained in Cuba years before—
tried again to escape, this time with her husband and their
one-year-old son. The worst happened. The aunt and
uncle she'd never met drowned in a storm, but her young
cousin survived the crossing. Upon arriving in Key West,
he was sheltered by her parents, raised as her brother, and
called Andy instead of Andrés. Ever since, her family had
lived with the omnipresent tension that he was at risk for
deportation if the authorities ever figured out the truth.

When Isabel was off shooting *Wild Woman,* her mom's
e-mails were her only reassurance that they were okay. A
week had passed since her last log-in, so she was hoping
for several messages of pretty pictures, lighthearted gos-
sip, and new book recommendations—the usual fare.

When she logged in, just one e-mail was waiting.

The subject line was in all caps: CALL ASAP.

The message in its entirety read: "This isn't something
to discuss over e-mail. I love you."

It was dated four days earlier.

Without wasting a minute, she tracked down the crew's satellite phone and dialed home. To hell with the expense and permission.

"Mom?" she said as soon the line picked up. Her heart was firing bullets.

"Izz?" It was Andy. He sounded small and scared, not at all his unsentimental thirteen-year-old self.

"What's wrong? Are you okay? Where's Mom?"

"She's in the hospital. She found a lump . . ."

Isabel felt a rush of heat to her face. "How bad?"

"Stage four. Spread to lymph nodes under her armpit. She had surgery yesterday and the doctor said something about good margins. I just . . . I wish you were here."

"I'm coming." The calmness of her voice barely masked the strain she was trying her best to hide. "Don't worry about a thing until I get there."

As soon as she got home, she learned that the situation was both reassuring and dire. Her mother's prognosis was shockingly good: 90 percent chance of complete remission. But that was only if she went on a sophisticated new chemotherapy drug, Braxa, that specifically targeted diseased cells, rather than wiping out her whole immune system. Her recovery would be easier, faster, and practically guaranteed.

Yet Braxa was only available through the one pharmaceutical company that had developed it. Since the drug's recent FDA approval, intense global demand had caused the price to skyrocket. For the required three months of her mother's treatment, it was going to cost upward of $300,000. Of course, she needed to start immediately.

But her cheap health insurance refused to cover it, claiming that the standard regimen with the older drugs was the only approved treatment. If she went that route, according to her doctors, her prognosis would drop to 15 percent, given how aggressively her breast cancer had developed and spread.

An 85 percent chance of death; Isabel couldn't even contemplate it. This was her mother, the indomitable woman who had risked her life for freedom, who had taught her that any goal was attainable with enough creativity and discipline. There was no way Isabel could walk away from her predicament, especially not after what had happened with her father.

But how could she come up with three hundred grand right away? Her mom took a salary of $50,000 a year from the bookstore if she was lucky. Isabel was getting paid a flat fee of $120,000 from the network, and the show wasn't going to air for months, so any royalties or commercial offers would be too little, too late. The network itself was struggling in the ratings, so they weren't willing to advance her any cash. Her father's death benefits from the army had gone toward paying off her college loans. Their outdated two-bedroom house wasn't worth that much. Isabel even contemplated selling the family bookstore, The Thumbed Page, but who in their right mind would buy it? It would be like asking for bids on a mule in the era of the steam engine.

She shielded her mother and Andy from the impossibility of the situation. Her mom's job was to recover from her mastectomy; his was to be a kid; hers was to raise the money. But when she confessed her hopelessness to the chief oncologist, his stern eyes narrowed over the bridge of his spectacles, and she could tell he was a man not often denied.

"She needs this drug," he said. They were standing in

the hallway outside the hospital room, where her mother's groans were softly audible. "And she needs it now. It's the only way. I don't care if you have to sell your soul to get it."

Neither of them knew then how prescient his words would be.

CHAPTER 2
The Diary of Richard Barnett

5 months, 2 weeks before, Key West

Thursday, May 18. I'll never forget the date we met. Oh, Isabel. I know how jaded I must have seemed to you that day. After all, I sell death for a living. When I said it with a dry chuckle, you eyed me like I was the Grim Reaper himself. Most people do. I don't take it personally.

"I promise not to bite," I said, waving you past the doorway into my office. Your sweeping glance took in my drab carpet, the coffee stains on my desk, the window behind me overlooking the parking lot. Then you plopped into the tired old chair where my desperate clients laid out their need for instant cash. I'd heard it all. Nothing affected me much at that point except for people who wasted my time—the too young and too healthy. You were both.

When you first walked in, with your slender, athletic body and your silky dark hair, I groaned to myself. I had become inured to beauty. You looked more like a pro fitness model than a normal woman, let alone a sick one. Unlike most other clients, you radiated liveliness. If you *had just come from running a marathon, I wouldn't have been surprised.*

I thought you might be one of the hypochondriacs who sometimes come to my brokerage. Convinced of their approaching deaths, they want to sell their existing life insurance policies for a quick buck. What an annoying bunch. Don't they realize that their medical records speak for themselves? I can never haggle a good deal when my buyers see perfect blood counts and hormone levels and not a single diseased cell, not even a rash. Go home, I tell them. Get a life. Like the one you already have.

But you didn't have a bone of self-pity and that's how I knew you were something else entirely. You told me about your mother's illness and why you needed serious cash now. I tried not to let on that I admired the way you looked me in the eye without flinching. Most women I see break down in tears by the second sentence.

"How much is her policy worth?" I asked, lighting a cigarette. By force of habit, I was already running calculations in my head. Typically I could negotiate around 12 percent to 25 percent of the death benefits for an instant cash settlement, and possibly up to 60 percent if your mother was terminal and paid low premiums. Then I'd net 10 percent of her settlement. So, if she was worth at least a million bucks dead, I could walk away with sixty grand if I was lucky. I admit I was hoping for this best-case scenario; I was saving up for a new BMW.

"Her policy would pay $250,000," you said, "but—"

I cut you off, glancing at the door. "You know I'm not running a charity."

"Mine's two mil."

I paused. "What?"

You flashed me a triumphant smile. Your teeth were a

dentist's dream—straight, white, clean. "I work in television for one of those reality survival shows. Before I signed up, I made sure I got one hell of a life insurance policy for my family in case I didn't make it."

That explains the teeth, I thought. You proceeded to tell me that in your quest to raise money, your financial adviser informed you that you were sitting on a pot of gold with your policy. You'd never heard of the secondary market for life insurance before, but were fascinated to find out that it was a thriving trade. You could sell it like any other asset for major cash to a buyer who would take over paying the premiums until your death, when that person would receive your benefits. It was morbid, yes, but it was exactly the solution you needed. You were so proud of yourself for figuring it out that I hated to deflate your enthusiasm.

"There's just one little problem," I said, twisting my cigarette stub into my frosted glass ashtray. "You're not dying."

You raised an eyebrow. "As if that's a bad thing?"

I sighed. Your innocence was charming, but tedious. I was around fifteen years older than you, but the gap in our levels of cynicism couldn't have been wider.

"Every investor wants to make a profit as fast as possible. This is a business of quick turnarounds. But you could live another sixty years."

"So you're saying no one will want it?"

"I'm sure I could find a buyer. But you won't get the settlement you want."

"How much?"

I shrugged. In truth, you were a terrible client. "At best maybe a hundred and fifty grand."

"That's only half of what I need! You have to do better. Who are these buyers, anyway?"

"Hedge funds. A few specialize in buying up old and

sick 'lives' so their risk is minimized in this shitty economy. These guys are making a killing." I smirked. "Pun
intended."

You rolled your eyes without the consolation of a
smile.

"The only guarantees in life—" I started.

You sighed. "Are death and taxes, I know."

"And the former has no loopholes."

"Very funny." Your curled upper lip revealed your disgust. "What's it like to get such a kick out of other people's misery?"

"Lucrative." I knew I was being a jerk, but I was so
numb then that I didn't care. "What's it like to be humorless?"

"Ugh." You stood up, your nostrils flaring. "I'll find
someone decent to help me."

"I'm the only life settlement broker in the Keys," I said,
lighting another cigarette and drawing a deep puff.
"You're stuck with me." I coughed on the exhale, failing
to cover my mouth because it happened so often I didn't
even notice. At least smoking quashed my appetite and
kept me as thin as a gym rat (which I was absolutely not).

You threw me one last revolted look. "Then I'll drive to
the mainland."

Your shoulders slumped as you walked away, and I felt
a momentary pang. As tough as you seemed, even you
couldn't hide your pain.

You grabbed the doorknob.

"Wait," I called. "I'm sorry. I didn't mean to insult
you."

You turned around to glare. Your wispy bangs fell over
your eyes and you pushed them to the side. I knew I had
only that moment to make peace or you'd be gone for
good.

"Can we start over?" I said, my own warmth surprising me. *"You don't have any time to waste. Let me help you."*

"No thanks, I prefer dealing with human beings."

"I could halve my commission," I heard myself say. *"Five percent instead of ten."*

Your brow softened, but your voice remained harsh. *"What does that matter when I need double the offer you predicted?"*

"I have an idea." I put my elbows on my faux wood desk and steepled my fingers.

"What," you said, *"fake my own terminal illness?"*

"Yeah, right. Would you buy a house without an inspection?"

"What then?" Your tone was sarcastic, but I had your attention.

"Your said your mother has hereditary breast cancer."

"Yeah. A mutation on BRCA1."

"Have you thought about what that means for you?"

"I don't want to know," you said quickly. *"This isn't the time for me to worry about myself."*

"What if I told you I could more than double your payout if you have the same mutation? The higher your risk, the better."

Your mouth twisted into a scowl. *"This is a screwed-up business."*

"My ex-wife would agree. But I'm helping people out of very tight spots. It's win-win." I leaned back in my cushy leather chair, knowing you were hooked—even if you didn't know it yet.

"But if I have the gene, then I have to live with that knowledge for the rest of my life. I can't un-know it."

"Is that too high a price to pay for your mother's life?"

Your green eyes narrowed. "And what if I don't have it?"

"First get tested. Come back as soon as you know the results."

A queasy look crossed your face, but you nodded and stepped out without another word.

Despite your mother, I hoped for your sake that the news was good. After you left, I reached into my desk drawer and pulled out my scrapbook of newspaper obituaries. It was bound in handsome brown leather with gold trim, a fitting record to commemorate my past clients. I liked to read their life stories, to remember that I had helped them in their final months or years, so my self-loathing wasn't totally justified. But most of all, I liked to remind myself that I knew better than to get attached to anyone who was mortal.

CHAPTER 3
Joan

5 months, 2 weeks before, New York

Joan Hughes felt her husband's dry lips brush against her forehead. She pulled the goose-down comforter up to her chin and kept her eyes closed against the early morning sun. He was standing beside the bed in a navy suit, his briefcase slung over his shoulder.

"Have a good day," he whispered.

She murmured something inaudible into her pillow, burying her face so it wouldn't give her away. Underneath the covers, the sheet was sweaty where she was gripping it. His dress shoes clomped over the wood floor out into the living room, through the foyer, out the front door. It closed behind him and she heard his key turn in the lock.

Her eyes snapped open. In one fluid gesture, she threw off the comforter and jumped to the floor. She was already dressed, having risen at 4 A.M. to throw on her secret new clothes: hot pink nylon shorts, a sports bra, and a hot pink tank top. She hated the color, but it was well hidden underneath her long-sleeved black nightgown. Now she yanked its silky fabric over her head, kicked her feet into sneakers, and pinned her short blond curls into a Yankees baseball cap she'd bought the day before. She also hated the Yankees. Flying out the front door, she caught sight of her outfit in the hall mirror. It was revolting. Revoltingly perfect.

She rode the express elevator down twenty-five floors and hurried through the co-op's grand marble lobby, avoiding the gaze of the friendly doorman so he couldn't stop her with small talk. She made it outside in time to see Greg walking two blocks south. Her heart quickened at the sight of him from afar—it was hard not to admire his effortless elegance, his confident posture and purposeful stride.

Was she really the kind of wife who spied on her husband, after thirty years of loyal marriage? But he had left her no other option. Week after week over dinner they hashed out variations of the same exasperating dialogue:

Her warm touch on his arm. "Sweetheart, what's wrong?"

His almost imperceptible flinch. "Nothing. I told you."

"But you've been so . . . distant."

"My patients—"

"I know, I know. But you've always had tough patients. That's never stopped you from . . ."

From wanting me, she would think. All their lives he had been a passionate, affectionate partner, his libido barely slowing down over the years. But in the last few months, his interest had dropped off. He greeted her with dry pecks instead of kisses, failed to seek her out in the shower, kept his hands to himself in bed.

Yet her inquisitions always failed. Across from her at the dinner table, he would shrug, his hazel eyes shifting to that faraway state that reminded her of glass hardening. Even in his withdrawn state, he was attractive—six feet tall with a slender athleticism honed by years of running marathons. His salt-and-pepper hair was thick, his features chiseled, his lips expressive.

"You're sure there's nothing else bothering you?" she would press. "Just work?"

"You're doing it again," he would tell her gently, despite the tightness in his voice. "Trolling for a story."

Oh, why did she even try?

Ever since she'd left her beloved career as an investigative reporter twenty years before to become a full-time mom to Adam, their only child, she would gravitate to what she called "little icebergs"—hints of possible stories submerged beneath the surface. If there was anything she had learned from her decade as a journalist, it was that she had a nose for sniffing out stories, though she did sometimes get carried away with dead-end leads.

Of course, that was all well behind her, since Greg's work as an ER doctor and his lucrative consulting gigs had made a luxuriously idle life possible for her. It would be ridiculous to think of going back to work in her midfifties, when she had all the money she could ever hope to spend. So her days were filled with social outings, shopping, fund-raising for Greg's medical charity, and babysitting their two-year-old granddaughter Sophia, the light of her life. Meanwhile her investigative instinct remained, like a phantom limb that sometimes needed scratching.

But this time, the itch wasn't just in her mind. She was sure of it.

She kept safe distance behind him on the sidewalk, following him another three blocks south on Riverside Drive and east two blocks to Broadway. He walked fast, as though he were late. She pulled the baseball cap low over her face when he turned the corner, not that it mattered; he would never think of her if he noticed a woman in an obnoxious pink sweat suit. Her colors were classy whites, beiges, blacks.

His charity office was on the third floor of a walk-up building on the corner of 80th and Broadway, right across from their gym. Across the street, shielded under the arched doorway of a brownstone, she held her breath. If he walked past his office, that would be her first real proof that he was hiding something.

His steps slowed—her heart caught—and then she saw his hand reach into his pocket for his keys. When he stopped at the right door and opened it, she realized the depth of her relief. How badly did she want to be wrong! He disappeared inside, and she turned to go back home, feeling like an inane stalker.

But at the intersection of West End and 80th Street, she stopped. Her reporter's nose for news was rarely this far off. She decided to take her investigation one step further, just for the hell of it.

She checked into the gym and went up to the third-floor weight room, with its floor-to-ceiling windows that looked across the street directly at Greg's corner office. If he was truly in there, she could observe him from afar.

She grabbed a five-pound barbell in each hand and planted her feet squarely in front of the window, away from the blue mat where the other patrons were lifting.

"It's easier to face the mirror," came a deep voice a few feet away.

She looked over her shoulder to see a burly young guy curling barbells she probably couldn't have picked up. He tilted his head at the wide mirror that ran along the side wall.

"Thanks," she said shyly. "But I don't like looking at myself."

Greg would have laughed at that; she could spend up

to two hours getting ready before dinner reservations. Keeping up one's looks was important for any decades-long marriage, but especially when one's husband aged so well.

She turned back to squint outside, pumping her weights. Her eyes took a moment to adjust to the glare of the sun, but soon she oriented to his redbrick building across the way and counted up three flights. There, through the corner window, she spotted him. He was not alone.

Sitting at his desk, his handsome nose in profile, he seemed to be studying something on his computer screen. Next to him stood a young busty woman in a tight pencil skirt and low-cut blouse that emphasized her curves. Joan recognized her short pixie haircut from the description Greg had given of his new executive assistant, Alaina.

He had described her as *efficient.* Was she pretty? Joan had asked. All he said was, *That hairstyle doesn't do her any favors.*

He hadn't mentioned that she would ooze sex appeal if she were bald. Even from this distance, that much was obvious.

Alaina lay her hand on the back of his chair. Not touching his neck, but close. Joan felt her own neck prickle. What she would have given at that moment to hear what they were saying.

Greg swiveled in his chair to face his assistant. He must have said something funny or teasing, because she tossed her head back with a laugh. Then she flicked her wrist at him and sashayed toward the door. Joan watched Greg eye her shapely butt until it was out of sight.

A harmless flirtation, Joan thought. *He's a red-blooded man. No harm in looking.* But the voice of reason didn't match her body's reaction. Sweat pooled under her armpits. She ceased to feel the weights in her hands, pumping them fast up and down.

Just when she thought the show was over, Greg's posture transformed. As soon as the door closed behind Alaina, his shoulders hunched forward. He put an elbow on his desk and picked up his landline. He stared at the dial pad for at least ten seconds, the phone cradled in his hand. Then he made a call.

It was short, less than a minute, but his gestures were telling: he sliced the air with his hand and waved furiously. He appeared to shout before pulling the phone away from his ear and staring at it, openmouthed.

The steel-nerved Greg she knew prided himself on his composure; he almost never raised his voice.

Then he shocked her once more.

Alone in his office, he leaned forward and buried his head in his arms. His body shook in little spasms that took her breath away.

He never, ever cried.

CHAPTER 4
Isabel

5 months, 1 week before, Key West

The envelope arrived a week after her visit to Richard
Barnett. She had kept her promise and gone to the
nearest lab right away for expedited genetic testing. One
blood draw and several anxious days later, the results
landed in her mailbox. The return address was stamped
MYRIAD GENETICS, SALT LAKE CITY, UTAH. It was strange to
believe that her fate was contained in something so thin
and plain, so indifferent to the magnitude of what lay inside it.

Her mother was home from the hospital by then and
knew nothing of her quest to raise money for the radically
better treatment; Isabel didn't want to get her hopes up
only to crush them if the plan failed. In the meantime, her
mom had accepted the standard chemotherapy regimen
and was already suffering its hazardous effects.

Of course, Isabel acted as if she would be in the lucky
15 percent who made it. The number acquired an outsize
significance. She bloated it any chance she could, especially for the sake of her frantic little brother. A 15 per-

cent chance of rain? Better find the umbrella. A 15 percent tip? Plenty high. Fifteen percent battery on the cell?
It'll last.

Andy became obsessed with statistics, to the point that
he was compulsively guessing the odds of mundane events:
baseball games, his grade on a history test, his chance of
catching a cold.

"Odds, schmodds," their mom was telling him as Isabel walked in with the fateful envelope. Andy was hugging his knobby knees to his chest near the sofa, where
she was curled up under a knitted wool blanket. Her long
black tresses were already falling out in clumps, but she
pretended not to notice. "What were the odds you would
survive the crossing on that broken raft, alone? Zero? But
you're here, aren't you?"

That was Mom—the standard-bearer of reassurance.

Isabel stashed the envelope into her purse before either of
them could notice. Her palms were clammy with dread.
Most confusing was that she didn't know what she wanted—
a positive or a negative result.

She promised herself she would open it later. There
was work to do first.

In the last eleven days, she'd gotten more up close and
personal with survival than she ever had been on television. There was no question which role was the more gru-
eling, now that she was a home nurse, bookstore manager,
cook, maid, and substitute mother. The setting wasn't
glamorous—a wood-slatted bungalow instead of a Brazilian rainforest—but staying alive here actually counted.
Not as a bauble for bored viewers, but as a matter of life
and death. No safety net. No edits. No do-overs.

After making sure her mom had enough water and dry
toast, a wastebasket, and the remote, Isabel kissed her

cheek, gave Andy a playful slug, and headed out for a shift at the store. The letter remained at the bottom of her purse, unopened.

As she walked down the porch steps, Andy's voice caught up with her. "Izz!"

She turned around to see him closing the front door so their mother couldn't hear. When he looked up at her, his dark brown eyes seemed laden with the weight of the world. His red Miami Heat jersey hung off his scrawny frame.

"What's up, dude?"

He crossed his arms. "I have to ask you a question."

"Yeah?"

"But you have to tell the truth, okay? I'm not a little kid anymore."

She inhaled the scent of the coconut palm trees that shaded their porch. The air was hot and sweet, but the hair on her arms prickled.

"What is it?"

"Is Mom gonna die?"

She leaned back against the porch railing, ignoring a splinter that dug into her palm. "Of course not." The words sounded shrill even to her.

His face scrunched up. "You promised not to lie!"

She crouched down to his eye level, swallowing hard. "I'm doing everything I can to help her. I promise you that much."

"You swear?"

She extended her pinky and he interlocked his own. They squeezed on it.

After he trudged back inside, she knew she couldn't wait any longer.

She sunk to the steps and pulled the envelope out of her bag. Her name taunted her in bold black ink.

Holding her breath, she ripped the seam. Her hands fumbled as she pulled out the thin piece of paper. It was on formal letterhead and began with a preamble she was sure no one had ever paused to read:

The BRCA 1 and 2 mutations can greatly increase a woman's risk of developing breast and ovarian cancer. . . . Finding out your genetic predisposition gives you the knowledge you need to make informed decisions. . . .

She skimmed as fast as she could, looking for only one word.

At the bottom of the page, it assaulted her: *Positive.*

CHAPTER 5
Joan

5 months, 1 week before, New York

Joan heard the front door close behind Greg with a thud. It was time. She had only ten minutes while he ran out to buy wine for the Saturday-night feast she had cooked. Then their son, his wife, and toddler would arrive, and there would be no time left to accomplish the task that she had once scolded herself for even contemplating, but today, at last, had decided to do.

Seeing him cry from afar was the tipping point. She could no longer abide the tacit rules of computer privacy that existed between a husband and wife.

She raced into their living room, her bare feet sliding over the polished wood. There, on the marble coffee table, was his silver laptop. It was already propped open. With her fingers inches away from the keys, she froze. Her red manicured fingers hovered in the purgatory between truth and betrayal.

Outside, through the floor-to-ceiling windows, the egg yolk sun was sinking down to meet the green foliage of Riverside Park. The sunset usually calmed her, but now her heart kicked in her chest. She glanced around at her home's treasured objects—the ornate rug from Thailand, the six-piece black leather sofa set, the Renoir and Degas prints collected from trips to Paris—but even their familiarity failed to comfort her.

The clock above the mantelpiece was ticking. In five minutes, Greg would return.

Her hands descended on his keyboard. The screen lit up. Under his full name, Gregory David Hughes, was a box waiting for his password. That was easy. He'd had the same password for years. She typed it in: "JemAdam41685." The initials of her maiden name, Joan Eve Miller, their son's name, and their wedding anniversary.

The box wiggled, rejecting the password.

She frowned and typed it in again. Rejection. Her fingers trembled. She tried multiple permutations of capital letters, to no avail.

The one and only time he'd hidden a secret from her was eight years ago, when he'd coped with a frustrating string of career disappointments by escaping into the numbing haze of Vicodin. He grew increasingly withdrawn, and one day Joan caught him writing himself prescriptions to feed his addiction. Together they found help in a twelve-step program; he got clean, founded a charity to help other doctors with addiction, and life returned to normal.

Or had it? After all these years, had he gotten sucked back into that dark place? Or was it something else? Perhaps his flirtation with his assistant wasn't as harmless as she wanted to believe . . .

So far there was no evidence in his drawers, cabinets, or closets. If only she could get on his computer and poke around. But him changing his password wasn't tantamount to hiding something. Was it?

His key jangled in the lock. She yanked back her hands as if from a hot stove. As the door opened, she jumped to her feet and tugged on her beige silk dress. Several voices echoed in the foyer—Greg's, and also Adam's, his wife, Emily's, and the high-pitched giggles of Sophia.

The little girl led the charge into the living room, squealing when she saw Joan. A toothy grin spread across her face. "Grammy!" She leaped into Joan's arms, blond ringlets bouncing, and wrapped her chubby legs around her waist. Joan laughed, stumbling back a step, and hugged her tightly. All worry was momentarily dissolved by the scent of baby shampoo and the soft cheek on her shoulder.

"Gentle, kitty cat," Adam called after her, following behind with Emily. "Hi, Mom."

"Hi, guys." Joan set down Sophia and kissed her son and daughter-in-law on the cheek. Adam was a young doppelgänger of Greg, tall and slender, with a full head of wavy brown hair and her own lively blue eyes. Emily was petite, blond, curvy, and just as sweet as her dimpled smile implied. Seeing them, Joan felt reassured. How lucky she was! Many of her friends' kids had moved far away to raise children, relegating their relationships to weekly Skype chats. But you couldn't have tickle wars through a screen, or teach a toddler to walk, or feel the weight of a small body sleeping in your arms. No matter what was happening with Greg, these three were always there; they lived in a darling one-bedroom apartment just ten blocks away.

"Where did your father go?" she asked Adam.

Just then, Greg walked out of the kitchen carrying a tray of wineglasses and an uncorked bottle of Merlot. He briefly acknowledged her with a peck on the cheek before turning to the others.

"Sit, sit," he said. "The night is young. I thought we could start with an aperitif."

The breeziness in his voice sounded forced, but if anyone besides Joan noticed, they didn't show it.

"Sounds good," Adam said. They all settled into the comfortable L-shaped leather sofa. As Greg set down the tray on the coffee table, Joan moved his laptop to the nearby desk. She noticed with relief that there was no evidence on the screen of her attempted log-ins. Then she opened a drawer in the coffee table and handed Sophia a coloring book and crayons, while he poured wine for the adults.

"Hey, so can you guys believe what the Dow did this week?" Adam shifted in his seat. "I feel like maybe we should pull out of our stocks. Things are getting kind of crazy."

"Nah, it could still turn around," Greg said, pouring himself an ample amount of wine. "Just give it more time. I think all the talk of a crash is premature."

Joan felt a tightening in her stomach. According to Greg's recovery program, he was supposed to stay away from all narcotics, but enough years had passed that he occasionally indulged in a few ounces of alcohol. She cast a disapproving glance his way, but he avoided her gaze and took a sip.

"For now," Adam allowed. "But if banks start going under, then we're really in trouble."

"Oh, forget all that," Joan said, waving off the topic like an annoying fly. "It's the weekend. Stock market's closed. Can't we all just relax?" She tried to trade a look with Emily—*men and their money worries*—but her daughter-in-law just smiled feebly and smoothed a wrinkle on her blue cotton dress.

Adam cleared his throat and took Emily's hand. Her face was a shade too white, Joan noticed, but a small smile was tickling her lips.

"The thing is," he said, "we actually can't afford to ignore it." He took a breath.

"We're moving," Emily blurted.

Joan's gaze darted to Sophia, who was scribbling happily on the floor, then back to Adam and Emily. "You can't be serious."

He pursed his lips in apology. "I'm afraid so."

No more mornings with Sophia visiting the park jungle gym. Joan lived for those mornings. Now she would have to take a train to some far-flung place. The Hudson River Valley, or maybe Jersey City. That was where the young people flocked these days.

"Why?" Greg asked. "Where?"

Adam hesitated, biting his lip. "Kansas."

"Like the Wizard of Oz!" Sophia piped up with glee.

Joan stared at her son. Greg set down his glass. He looked as shaken as she felt.

"It's so much cheaper there," Adam went on, "and Emily's parents will be nearby, so we'll still have some family at least . . ." he trailed off, seeing his mother's crestfallen face.

"I don't understand," she said. "Why do you have to go that far?"

"You get so much more for your money," Emily said. "With the way the economy is going, it makes sense to get out of the city . . ."

"But we have plenty of money," Joan said, not caring if she sounded tactless. She turned to her husband. "We can help them out, right, honey?"

Greg ignored her. "Adam, you have a degree from Harvard Law. Why don't you take a job you were trained to do, not mess around all day in a music studio? I'm sorry, but it needs to be said. You have to make sacrifices for your family."

Adam refused to be rattled. "I'm following my dream, Dad. It would be nice to be near you guys, but right now, this is the best solution for us."

"And I fully support him," Emily added. "Trust me, I don't want some dead-eyed corporate lawyer coming home at eleven every night."

Joan shook her head. The idealism of youth was galling; that was one thing she and Greg could agree on. Here was their son, highly educated, with every opportunity to make a big success of his life, and he was going to throw it away for some penny-pinching middle-class existence. It reminded her of her own naïveté when she was in her late twenties, with that same dreamy-eyed determination to conquer the journalism world, practicalities be damned. But Greg had come along and saved her the struggle, and now she would try to do the same for him.

"But would you stay if you could?" she pressed. "If you could have it all?"

"Well, of course," Adam said. "New York will always be home."

She let out a breath she didn't know she was holding. So there was hope. She would just have to get Greg to agree to an early release of Adam's inheritance. It was absurd to think that money could wrench her family apart, when they had so much. There was something else, too—a desperation she couldn't share with her son, but that she tried to impart with her eyes. *Don't leave me,* she thought. *Not right now, don't take Sophia away.* If Greg left her in spirit, and they in body, what of her life would remain?

"There's no rush," she said, too calmly. "Let's just slow down and think this through."

"There's no time to think." Adam exchanged a meaningful look with Emily, right as Joan noticed that she hadn't touched her glass of wine. "We're actually flying out tomorrow to look at houses, because—"

"Sophia's going to be a big sister," Emily announced, breaking into a grin. Adam patted her belly. "Three months along. With all the time it will take to find a place and move and get settled, we can't start looking soon enough."

Joan's hand flew to her lips. Elation and despair mounted in equal measure. She reached instinctively for Greg's hand, but he was raising his glass in a toast. The edge in his voice was not lost on her.

"To a healthy baby!" he declared.

Joan raised her own glass, miming celebration. Hers clinked against his. A crystal note rang out, sharp and shrill. It was the sound of her heart breaking.

CHAPTER 6
Victim

5 months before, Key West

The ring of the doorbell on Monday night caught Mrs. Ruth Bernstein by surprise. She had forgotten the sound. No one visited her anymore, not that she minded. At eighty-three years old, widowed and blind, she had grown pleasantly accustomed to solitude. Except for Autumn, her golden retriever guide dog, she spent her days at home alone, in a cozy studio apartment that was small enough to navigate without feeling lost.

She counted the eleven steps from her recliner to the front door, Autumn's soft head under her fingertips. The dog and she were like a single organism, rising and walking everywhere in tandem.

"Who is it?" she called.

"Mike," came a man's voice. "I work for the landlord."

She unlocked the bottom and top locks and opened the door. The sensation of light beyond her eyelids was all she could detect—no shadows or forms.

"Hello, ma'am," the man said in a polite voice. Sounded young, in his twenties, though she couldn't be sure. "I came to check the batteries on your smoke detector and carbon monoxide alarm. Florida law says we gotta check it once a year."

"Oh! Of course, come on in. It's—" She hesitated, realizing she had no idea where the alarm was. She hadn't thought of it when she rented the apartment the year before; it had a balcony overlooking the beach in Key West, and just smelling the salt air was enough to sell her on the place, no questions asked. Thanks to her life settlement payout, she could afford to live out her days in such luxury.

She felt a swish of air as the man marched past her into the apartment.

"Right over here," he said kindly. His voice came from the kitchen area, about fourteen steps away. "Directly above your dining room table."

"You're a dear. Do you need a stepladder?"

"Nah, I'm good. I can reach it if I just climb up on this chair here . . . all right, hang on, it's gonna make a loud beep when I check it."

Ruth knelt to cup her hands over Autumn's ears. The dog whimpered anyway when the shrill note pierced the room.

Then she heard the man's feet hop to the floor and walk back through the kitchen, toward her. He paused to cough—a dry, noisy hack. What she couldn't see was that he was turning on the burners of her gas range.

His footsteps resumed.

"All done," he said, heading past her. "You have a good night now."

"Thanks very much." She wondered if she should tip him, but he was already opening the front door.

She closed it behind him and locked the locks.

Within an hour, she began to feel sleepy, though it was only 8:30 P.M. She changed into her nightgown and climbed into bed. Autumn curled up next to her so their backs were touching.

She knew something was wrong before she could articulate the thought. Compelled beyond her control, she felt the need to gasp for air. She sucked in each breath with rising desperation, despite telling herself that there was plenty of air in the room. It was probably one of those panic attacks that used to sneak up on her after her husband died.

She rolled over to spoon Autumn. Her heart was beating frantically. The dog lay beside her, oblivious. She buried her face in its soft furry neck and stroked its chest. But her symptoms only escalated.

If she turned her head an inch, a tidal wave of dizziness smacked her. She thought of trying to reach for her phone, three steps away on her dresser, but knew she would fall over first. The balance she depended on was gone.

Autumn was trained for emergencies. She knew how to press a special large button on the landline that went straight to the police. It was time. Ruth shook her.

The dog remained motionless.

"Autumn," she choked out. "Go call 911. Nine-one-one!"

The dizziness was unbearable, accompanied now by a paralyzing nausea. But what was wrong with the dog?

She shoved her ear against Autumn's chest. There was a heartbeat, but it was faint. Very faint.

"No," she whispered. "Oh God, no."

That's when she realized: it was something in the air. A tasteless, odorless poison seeping into their lungs. She needed to get them outside, onto the balcony, as fast as possible. The idea of going alone never crossed her mind.

She squeezed her arms around all seventy-five pounds

of Autumn and hauled her toward the edge of the bed. The dog barely budged.

After a minute she realized the task would be impossible. She was choking and coughing, too dizzy and disoriented to figure out what direction to go. Her strength was fleeting along with her consciousness.

She fell back against the bed, still loosely hugging Autumn to her chest. In her last bid for strength, she pressed her lips against the dog's velvety ears.

Of all the parting words she wanted to say, none were enough.

But it didn't matter.

None came.

CHAPTER 7
The Diary of Richard Barnett

4 months, 3 weeks before, Key West

I know you think I'm the bad guy, Isabel, and you're not completely wrong. But there's more to it than you think. I'm writing this account to tell you the truth—the whole truth—behind our relationship, because by the time you know enough to demand answers, I'll be gone.

The good news for us both is that I won't be around to squirm at your reaction.

In the spirit of openness—nothing to lose—I'll admit that when you walked through my door the second time, I was delighted.

You, considerably less so.

Your hair was tied in a bun at the nape of your neck, and I remember thinking how slender and breakable it looked. Despite your tough girl act, you were just as vulnerable as my sick and dying clients.

Vulnerability was my currency. I could spot it like a shark a mile away. I'm not proud to tell you that I swooped in for the kill. (Sorry, too soon?)

"I have the mutation," you announced, marching into my office and plunking down into the chair across from me. "Eighty-seven percent odds of getting my mom's cancer."

Your expression was part horror, part boast. It was a strange combination to behold.

But even stranger was my own gut reaction. Normally I would have launched into transaction mode without a second thought. A positive BRCA mutation was a value-added proposition, a welcome bargaining chip to any life settlement broker. Like jaded surgeons, we came to see bodies as parts, not persons; but in our trade, the faultier, the better.

That's why I was surprised when I felt my stomach clench. Your type of mutation was particularly lethal in young women.

"I'm sorry," I said. I meant it.

"Yeah, yeah." You waved me off like my politeness was a charade. "I know I'm worth more to you now."

"I'll be able to help you more now," I corrected.

It wasn't fair of me to take offense. All you saw was a greedy, heartless asshole. I had given you no reason to think otherwise.

"Do you believe your own spin?" you asked. "Or do you just spout that crap to make people feel better?"

"Look, I know you're angry and scared. But I'm going to help you save your mother's life. Our incentives are aligned, okay? I get paid only when you do."

Any trace of vulnerability disappeared when your green eyes locked on mine: Your stare was unshakable. I had mistaken you for a damsel in distress, but really you were Prince Charming coming to the lady's rescue.

"Three hundred thousand," you said. "Not a penny less."

"I have just the buyer in mind."

"The buyer of my death?"

I cocked my head. You were a no-BS type, unlike most other clients who preferred reassurance to reality.

"Yes," I said. "He'll pay your premiums until your death, then take the two-mil cash payout when the time comes."

You looked off into space, then back at me. "Who is this person?"

"A fine investor. Robbie Merriman of SkyBridge Asset Management."

"What if I outlive him?"

"His fund will be the official beneficiary, not him personally."

"Oh." *You pressed your lips together in disappointment.*

"Nice try," I said. "There's no escape clause in this deal."

I can't help cringing now as I remember telling you that. I know it sounds nefarious, but I swear I didn't mean it that way.

Your face took on a shade of worry. "Is he, you know, ethical?"

Everyone always asked that, and I always gave the same pat answer.

"The business of death is a gentlemanly one. It's all reputation. If some buyer had even a whiff of corruption, all of us brokers would gallop away like spooked horses."

"So you know this guy?"

"Seriously, you couldn't be in better hands."

I had never met him in person, but we'd done many deals on the phone over the years. I pulled out my heavy leather scrapbook of obits and slid it across the table into your hands. You opened it and scanned the black-and-white clippings; I watched your face change from surprise to revulsion as you connected the dots.

"Your past clients?"

"Clients who were very grateful for my help," I said. "You won't find a single horror story of some violent death. Go ahead and look."

You flipped through a few pages, reading out the causes of death: "Heart attack, stroke, cancer, natural causes."

"No murders," I said. "In fact, there has never been a single record of someone dying because they sold their policy."

You hesitated, twirling a lock of hair around your finger. "What does it even matter? We both know I have no other options."

I wanted to reassure you even though you weren't asking for it. I reached for the local newspaper I'd been reading that morning, the Key West Daily, and spread it out before you.

"Look right there." I pointed to the last page of section B, an obit in the upper right corner. "See Mrs. Ruth Bernstein, age eighty-three? She just died the other day, poor lady. I had helped her out when her savings ran dry, so she could live in a luxury apartment instead of some crappy old folks' home. She was thrilled with her settlement from Robbie."

You squinted at her obit, which I had already flagged for the scrapbook. "Her death was ruled accidental," you read aloud. "She left her burner on by mistake and it leaked carbon monoxide. How sad."

"I know. Nice lady, but she was blind and getting on. Doesn't surprise me one bit."

You pushed the newspaper and the scrapbook away, and reached into your backpack at your feet. You handed me a manila envelope: your genetic test results and your medical records.

"Thanks in advance," you said, standing up. *"I'm count-ing on you."* You turned to leave after we shook hands. No limp fish there; your handshake was solid.

"Wait," I heard myself call.

You stopped to look back at me, an eyebrow raised. You were eager to get out of there, but I wanted to postpone the inevitable. After you walked out, you would never come back. I'd make the deal, I'd cut your check, and I'd wait to see your obit in the Key West Daily one day, hope-fully not anytime soon. Then you'd be nothing but another clipping for the book.

But at that moment you were still alive—and impossi-bly beautiful.

I opened my mouth, having no idea what would come out. *"You're doing the right thing,"* I said. *"Your mother is lucky to have you."*

You were listening for cynicism, but there wasn't any. You rewarded me with a small smile. Then you stepped out without a word.

That smile drove me to get Robbie Merriman on the phone the minute you left. I laid it out for him nice and simple:

"Twenty-eight-year-old female, worth two mil, carries BRCA1 at eighty-seven percent, plus her mom's already got stage four. I'm talking an aggressive family history. You can get in on the ground floor of a real cash cow right now."

(Forgive me, will you? You're the furthest thing from a cow.)

"Interesting," he said in his typical unenthusiastic voice. Nothing seemed to impress him. *"But she doesn't have cancer yet?"*

"Not yet." But I quickly added: *"Eighty-seven percent, Robbie. It's practically a shoo-in."*

"What about the time value of money?" he shot back. "She might not pay off for a decade or more."

"Isn't your portfolio short on cancer, though? And I don't have to tell you that the mutation she has is especially common—and fatal—in young women. Very difficult to treat."

SkyBridge Asset Management balanced its investments by expected causes of death: specific portions of the portfolio were devoted to cancer victims, heart patients, AIDS, terminal illnesses, et cetera, so that payouts would occur at strategically anticipated intervals.

I heard silence on his end, which meant I was getting closer.

"She'll settle for three hundred and seventy-five thousand today," I said. I drove him up a bit because I liked you. "Her future valuation is thirteen times that. Honestly, it's a frickin' steal."

"Send her records," he snapped. The line clicked off.

That was Robbie-speak for "We have a deal."

You want the whole truth. Here it is: I pumped my fist in the air. I entertained a vision of us celebrating with a drink.

I had no idea what was coming next.

CHAPTER 8
Joan

4 months, 3 weeks before, New York

To Joan, the matter was simple. Adam and his family were moving far away because they couldn't afford to raise two kids in New York City. Greg had so much money that he flung it everywhere—at his charity, at her Bergdorf habit, at the mortgage for their penthouse, at vacations to Bora Bora. The solution was obvious.

But Greg hadn't volunteered it, and the fragile state of their relationship made her resist bringing it up right away. It was his money after all, but didn't she have just as much a say over how he spent it? Wasn't that a perk of marriage? Her difficulty in confronting him made her realize just how far apart they had grown in a few months' time. She found her courage during their evening stroll around the neighborhood, two weeks after Adam's announcement. They were holding hands as usual, but the wall between them seemed like solid brick.

"I can't stop thinking about this whole thing," she said. "I mean, we're both devastated, right?" She heard the nervousness in her voice.

His quizzical glance told her he did, too. "Of course."

"Babysitting Sophia is what I most look forward to," she went on, talking quickly. "I wish you could see how much fun we have. The park swings, catching potato bugs in the grass, reading *Goodnight Moon* . . . and then the weekends with Adam and Emily . . . and now the new baby we're never going to know. How can we just stand by and watch them *leave*?"

Greg kept his eyes ahead, on the stop-and-go traffic crawling down Broadway. She wasn't the only one stuck trying to get somewhere.

"Adam's an adult, Joan," he said. "We need to respect his decisions."

She winced at his use of her name, which he invoked only when he was annoyed. Otherwise, she was *darling* or *sweetheart*.

"But that's not what you told him! You wanted him to stay, go back into law—"

"Well, he's not going to, is he? He's as stubborn as a rock, you know that."

I wonder where he gets it, she almost retorted.

"There's still a way he could stay here and do music and raise the kids close by . . ." She took a deep breath. "We could help them out."

"I can't do that," he said.

The pronoun change from *we* to *I* enraged her—as if she had no say in it, just because she was the partner who didn't work! Just because she had given up her career to raise *their* child.

"Why not?" she demanded. "You have no trouble being generous in a million other ways."

"It would be bad for Adam's character."

She laughed out loud. "You're joking."

He withdrew his hand from hers and folded his arms, walking faster. "I'm serious. He's grown up with everything, and now he needs to learn what it means to be a man. A man has to sink or swim by the choices he makes, not come crawling to his father when it's time to face the consequences."

She pulled herself up straight, almost jogging to keep up with him. "Don't make this about you. Just because you grew up poor doesn't mean you should punish him."

It was acid on his sore spot.

He stopped dead his tracks, glaring at her. "This conversation is over."

There was nothing more she could say.

For the rest of the walk, they silently stewed. Why was Greg suddenly worried about their son's integrity, when Adam was as hardworking and independent as they had raised him to be? All she could think was something wasn't adding up. There were given reasons, and then there were real reasons.

Once she had a lead, nothing could stop her from tracking down the truth.

CHAPTER 9
Isabel

13 days before, Key West

It had taken four months, but Isabel was finally feeling good again. Going to Richard Barnett and selling her life insurance policy had proved to be the best decision she'd ever made. The stress of her mother's illness and her own dire genetic forecast—all that was behind her now.

The balmy October sun caressed her bare skin as she walked toward the beach, her surfboard under her arm. Half naked in a red string bikini, she dared the world to look. She didn't care. She was proud. She was a survivor.

It was her first day in a bathing suit since her double mastectomy.

Her mother—who was in remission thanks to the miracle drug Braxa—insisted that Isabel take the money left over from the settlement to invest in her own health. Her ensuing preventive surgery and months-long recovery was an agony she wouldn't wish on anyone, but in losing her breasts, she'd restored her future.

Her cancer risk had shrunk from 87 percent to just 4 percent. And the fake breasts the doctors reconstructed weren't half bad. They were a tad bigger than her natural

B cup, so she could fill out her bikini without puffing up her chest.

As for the permanent gash across it? Her father used to say that a battle scar was a story with a happy ending. A scar was courage made visible. His most prominent one, from combat in Vietnam, had been right smack on his face—a raised white mark that stretched from his left ear to his lip. Far from considering himself disfigured, he wore it as proudly as his Purple Heart.

Isabel traced her finger along her own fresh scar under her breasts. Its smooth contour was a welcome reminder of him, despite the guilt that still bubbled to the surface every time she thought of his final day on earth. During his heroic life, he'd shown her that staying alive was not a given, but a prize that required a fight to win. And winning demanded celebration.

So today she was taking her first surfing trip in months. There was much to be grateful for: her mother was healthy, she was safe, her brother was happy, and *Wild Woman*, her reality TV show, was a hit. The eight episodes had aired over the summer to much enthusiasm. As soon as she was ready, the show runners wanted her back for season two. Her doctors wanted her to wait another few months, but she was feeling better than ever: in fact, she'd written to the executive producer and told him she wanted to return next month—plus a raise. Despite the horrible economy and the financial stress of pretty much everyone she knew, her family was going to make it through okay.

Palm trees fanned out overhead and cast lazy diagonal shadows across the street. On the main drag, Duval, patrons were sitting at sidewalk cafés drinking coffee and reading. She smiled at them on her way to the beach. When they smiled back, she wondered if anyone recognized her.

The glittering blue expanse of the ocean lay five blocks

ahead. She walked fast, eager to let the waves wash away
the disturbing thought intruding on her good mood: A
man named Robbie Merriman was counting on her cancer diagnosis.

Every quarter, he requested an update of her medical
records, just like he did for every other "life" he owned.
According to Richard Barnett, that was standard practice.
Merriman kept tabs so he could update his death fore-
casts. Business as usual.

But how would he react when he learned about her
surgery? The report with the news had gone out to him a
week ago—and she hadn't slept well since.

By circumventing her genetic fate, was she ripping
him off?

It wasn't like she had signed a contract promising not
to seek medical treatment. No one could blame her. Yet he
was no longer going to get what he paid handsomely
for—and she wasn't about to offer a refund.

Maybe it was all in her mind, but in the last few days,
she'd gotten the creepy sense that someone was watching
her. A strange tingling crept over her at random moments,
when she was sitting in her mother's backyard hammock,
or ringing up a customer at the bookstore, or picking out
apples at the grocery store. But when she looked over her
shoulder, no one was there.

She hadn't told anyone because there was nothing to
tell. She just needed to shake it off, hit the waves. She
quickened her step and turned off Duval Street, down a
narrow alley that was a popular shortcut to the sea. The
walls of adjacent buildings towered on either side of her,
leaving a footpath about eighteen inches wide. Her sandals slapped the dusty asphalt as her arms began to wilt
from the heavy board. She paused to let it drop for a second—and that was when the light dimmed.

A shadow behind her blocked the entrance to the alley.

Her heart lurched. She turned around to see an imposing man in his forties standing four feet away, smiling at
her. He was wearing khaki shorts and a wifebeater that
did little to conceal his hairy chest. His gaze lowered
from her face to her ample cleavage. He kept one hand in
his pocket.

She lifted her surfboard to block her chest. "Can I help
you?"

His smile widened. He stepped toward her. "You're the
girl."

She backed away, her sandals scraping the ground.
"No, I don't think so."

A hit man wouldn't come right up in broad daylight.

"Yes, you are," he said, rummaging in his pocket. "I'd
recognize you anywhere."

Would he?

When he pulled his hand out, something silver glinted,
and in a split second she found herself running, sprinting
as fast as possible with her surfboard toward the other end
of the alley. The bright sunshine and open road beckoned.

"Hey!" he called, approaching fast behind her. "Wait!
Isabel!"

Her name coming out of his mouth sent a shock through
her, but she kept running. When she reached the public
street near the ocean's crowded boardwalk, she was surprised to hear his footsteps still closing in on her.

"What do you want?" she screamed, whirling around
to face him. Several people nearby turned to stare. She
raised her surfboard like a shield.

He can't stab me in front of witnesses.

A flustered look crossed his face as he stopped short.
He held up his palms as though he didn't mean any harm,

and she got a better look at the threatening silver thing in his hand. It was a pen. He held it out like a peace offering.

"Sorry, I just wanted an autograph."

"Oh." She slowly lowered her board, feeling her cheeks flush. The realization solidified into a relief that left her shaky and drained. Around them, the gawkers lost interest and resumed their conversations.

"Is that cool?" he said, after a pause.

"Uh, sure."

He produced a napkin from his pocket and handed her the pen. She signed her name a little unsteadily and added the logo of interlocking *W*'s that stood for *Wild Woman*.

"Awesome. My kids will love it. Your show was the best thing on all summer."

She managed a smile. "Thanks."

Life was fine. All she had was a slight case of fame. No reason to be paranoid.

Right?

CHAPTER 10
Joan

12 days before, New York

After four months of spying on her husband, Joan was no closer to answers. Greg from afar seemed no different than Greg at home. He remained tense, distracted, edgy. *It's work,* he would tell her. *Work is killing me.*

When he wasn't in the ER, he was at his charity office putting in fourteen-hour days. Through the gym's windows, she might watch him pacing on the phone, or talking to his sexy assistant, but nothing damning enough to constitute betrayal. Mostly he sat and stared at his computer. She never saw him cry again. That mysterious episode disturbed her, but she couldn't confront him without admitting her own duplicity.

One thing she *could* do was help out their struggling son, whether or not Greg approved. Time was running out. In the last few months, the economy had full-on crashed—just as the doomsayers predicted. In August, a major bank collapsed. In September, Adam's investment account—his future down payment—went up in smoke in the stock market, just as he was trying to close on a house in Kansas.

Now it was an unseasonably hot October, and her poor son was confined to a six-hundred-square-foot apartment with his very pregnant wife and their rambunctious toddler.

But that wasn't even the worst of it.

Just this week, she'd been babysitting at Adam's place, half distracted by an entertaining new reality show called *Wild Woman,* when Sophia tripped over a doll house cluttering the small living room and broke her ankle. She would be fine when the cast came off, but all Joan could think was: *that place has got to go.*

She didn't care anymore about Greg's rigid stance. They still lived like kings, and their son's family was hurting. Nothing else mattered.

Greg didn't know what she was planning. She was going to surprise him after it was too late to back out.

If you can have secrets, she thought, *then so can I.*

A gust of cool air-conditioning welcomed her as she stepped inside the office of Corcoran, a real estate agency on 80th and Broadway. The sleepy receptionist perked up, taking in Joan's three-carat diamond ring, her silk chiffon white dress, and her red-soled Louboutin heels. Her blond hair was curled in loose waves around her face.

The receptionist smiled at her. "Hi, how can I help you?"

"I'd like to speak with an agent," Joan said. "About buying an apartment."

"Of course, right this way."

Joan followed her down a hall lined with pictures of extravagant apartments—floor-to-ceiling windows, magnificent city views, marble Jacuzzi tubs. They turned into a corner office where a woman about her own age was at a computer, clicking the keys with long manicured fingernails. When she smiled, her thick foundation broke into tiny cracks around her lips.

After introducing herself, Joan sat across from her and explained what she was looking for—a two- or three-bedroom apartment in the neighborhood for her son's growing family, preferably in a doorman building with an elevator, very bright, and kid-friendly.

"Oh," she added, "and not more than fifteen blocks from Eighty-sixth Street. I don't want to have to take a cab to get there."

The agent's first question rolled off her lips. "And your budget?"

Joan ran a quick calculation in her head: If she could put one hundred fifty thousand dollars toward a ten percent down payment, then . . .

"Not more than one point five," she said. What was one and a half million when Adam's inheritance was bound to be at least double that? Greg had been storing it in a private trust account for years. It didn't make sense not to touch it now, when he needed it most.

"That sounds reasonable." The agent looked pleased. "As you probably know, it's a buyer's market. We have amazing apartments that have been sitting for months, so it's a good time to look. Why don't I pull up some listings for you right now?"

Joan felt a little thrill zip through her. There was no question she was doing the right thing. "Please do."

The agent brought up a website, then tiled the screen toward her. A long list of available apartments showed up, ranging from the most expensive—$48 million—to the least.

"I have a darling place in mind," the agent said as she clicked through the pages, getting to the lower-end apartments. "It's a two-bed on Eighty-second and Columbus, newly renovated with a cook's kitchen, oak hardwood—"

"Stop!" Joan suddenly cried.

The agent's hands froze over her keyboard. "What?"

Before she knew it, Joan had sprung to her feet and was leaning over the agent's chair to stare at the screen.

"Show me that," she demanded, pointing to a listing of an apartment for sale in the $5 million range. The picture on the screen showed a spacious living room refinished in dark cherrywood, with a vast window overlooking the Hudson.

"Oh, that's a bit out of your range," the agent said delicately. "I was thinking more of—"

"No, please," Joan said, her voice bordering on desperation. "Click that."

The woman obeyed.

Up popped more pictures: a kitchen with rare blue-black Italian granite; a master bathroom with a steam room and six showerheads; a dining room sun-drenched from a wall of windows, outfitted with a crystal chandelier and seating for six.

"That's the dream, right?" The agent cocked her head. "The perfect apartment."

Joan's voice came out strangled. "How long has it been on the market?"

"About two months."

"You're joking."

"It's not really that long. As I said, inventory's just been sitting."

Joan stared at the pictures, unable to speak or move.

"Ma'am . . . are you okay?"

"No," was all she could manage. Her mind was blank. A sense of surreal devastation penetrated the edges of her being.

Her hand flew to her throat, where a sob was fighting to escape.

The agent touched her arm. "What's wrong?"

"That apartment—" she broke off.

"Yes?"

"That apartment is mine."

CHAPTER 11
Isabel

12 days before, Key West

What Isabel was looking at made no sense: the sea stretched endlessly around her. She squinted into the setting sun, but there was no promising speck on the horizon. Only the distant shore, no larger than a sandbox.

Her kayak was gone.

Kicking her plastic fins, she held her brother's arm and tried not to show panic. They were alone, about to return home after two hours of snorkeling out on the reef. Now the water was getting cold, the tide choppy.

Andy bobbed up and down in the rippling current, held upright by his life jacket. His plastic air tube hung near his mouth. "Where's the boat?"

Her gaze swept the surface with increasing urgency. Surely it was somewhere close. It had to be.

"Izz." Andy was watching her through his goggles, his brown eyes unnaturally magnified. "Where'd it go?"

Just a few hours before, they had dropped anchor near a certain rock outcropping that served as an orientation point for snorkelers. Spending time there was her and

Andy's favorite shared hobby on weekends. Key West locals knew it as the best destination to spot sea turtles, and all afternoon, the area was crowded with other marine sightseers. But they had outlasted everyone else, swimming out farther and farther to follow a playful turtle that kept eluding them. By the time they returned to the rock, it was already getting dark and no one was left.

"It can't have just disappeared," she said matter-of-factly. "That's impossible."

Andy hugged his elbows to his skinny naked chest. He was starting to shiver. "Then where is it?"

"I'd love to know."

"Maybe someone else thought our kayak was theirs?"

"But we had stuff in it. Mom's red cooler, remember?"

"Oh yeah. She's gonna be pissed if we lose that."

"I know." That was the least of it, but ever since their mother's illness, he became upset easily; the last thing she needed was to stoke an anxiety attack. She didn't add that his prescription Xanax, which he carried everywhere in case of emergency, was also in the missing cooler.

"What should we do?" he asked. "You're the Wild Woman, right?" His teasing nickname—which he'd goaded her with all summer—had lost its edge.

"Yep," she said. "That's me."

It was one thing to be a survival expert with a backup crew, on-site medical help, and multiple contingency plans. It was quite another to be alone, truly alone, in the wild.

She shielded her eyes from the vanishing sun, which was level with her gaze on the horizon. The restless ocean was a mirror of pink and orange clouds. Within minutes, it would turn as black as the sky. No matter how far she strained to see, there was no sign of the boat.

Survival rule number one: assess the facts. Rule two: Act accordingly. No hoping, pitying, or praying. That was time wasted, which meant death.

"Guess what?" She tried to spread her lips into an impish smile. "I just realized what's going on."

"What?"

"This is for the show. The producers said they might surprise me with a survival stunt to kick off the new season. You know, raising the bar for the viewers."

Andy's mouth fell open. "No way." He paused. "But why bring me into it?"

"Who cares, you get to be on TV! How freakin' cool is that? All your friends will be so jealous."

She could tell he was starting to buy in, and that was all that mattered.

Survival rule three: attitude was everything.

"So there's cameras secretly watching us?" he said, looking up. A helicopter was some distance away and he raised his eyebrows meaningfully.

"Yup. But right now, we have to start swimming like our lives depend on it, or else they'll cut the episode. Race you to the shore?"

He was already extending his arms to get a head start.

"Go!" he shouted, then plunged himself into the surf, thrashing and kicking his small body for all it was worth.

She glided easily past him, calling out in her wake: "You can do better than that!"

He redoubled his efforts, purposefully splashing her as he caught up. They continued to one-up each other for about twenty minutes, as the sky deepened from violet dusk to navy blue.

"Come on, slowpoke," Isabel shouted, when she noticed he had fallen behind.

"I'm tired," he whimpered, shivering. "And numb. I can't feel my arms."

"You can do it," she said, though she couldn't have agreed more. Her own body was weak from hunger and exhaustion; too much more exposure would put them at risk of hypothermia. "I know you can. Look, we're almost there."

"No, we're not! It's still so far . . ."

"It just looks far. I promise it's not that bad. Come on, you gonna let me win?"

"I don't care," he pouted. "I'm over it. Hey, up there!" he waved his arms wildly. "Come and get me, I give up!"

A pang of guilt shot through her—and fear. A prickling chill told her this was no accident. She paddled back to him and wrapped him in a hug, rubbing his arms in a futile attempt to pass on warmth.

"We can't give up. If you're tired, take off your fins and wrap your legs around my waist."

She had no idea how she could find the strength to swim on her own, let alone with him on her back, but he complied without hesitation. She sank under his weight as though she'd gained a hundred pounds.

"You okay?" he said, holding on to her shoulders.

"Fine. Let's go."

Gasping, she pushed through, one stroke after another, kick after kick. The waves grew hostile and rocked them around like a blender, but she went into a trance, heeding nothing but the goal. After she could no longer sense her limbs, the muscle memory of swimming directed her forward. Her eyes and throat burned from the salt, and soon she realized she was slowing down—still too far away for anyone on land to see them in the dark.

"Can't your stupid producers see we're practically drowning?" Andy screamed. "Hello, where are you, come get us!"

She had no strength to explain, but struggled on, well past the point that she would have believed possible. On the show, she would have tapped out long ago, and then the shoot would be over. The truth was that she was sorely unaccustomed to actual survival situations, without a crew backing her up every step of the way. Except for that one time getting stranded with her white-water rafting group, but even then, she didn't have to fight to breathe.

Her chest tightened in a familiar prelude to grief and she tried to push away the memory, but it bubbled up anyway: the recollection of her only other encounter with a real-life survival situation. It was in, of all places, her family's quaint indie bookstore, The Thumbed Page, a place she had always considered as safe as home. She and her dad had been alone unpacking a new shipment of glossy hardcovers, when, without warning, he let out a strange groan, clutched his chest, and fell hard on his knees. A terrified look contorted his face—his mouth opened but no words came out—and then his eyes had rolled into his head as he toppled face-first to the floor, like one of Andy's toy soldiers.

Every time she recalled the moment, she wanted to scream at the mental image of herself to run, call 911, do CPR—anything but the big fat zero she had done to help him. Instead she'd stood perfectly still, lips dumbly parted, staring at his limp body. It had all happened so fast, one minute they were trading fiction recommendations and the next—

She remembered thinking one useless thought: *But he never even caught colds.* As if pointing out logic would convince fate of its mistake. She had no idea how long she stood there, clutching the spine of a thick blue hardcover, gaping at the back of his head. What did she expect, for him to get up and dust himself off? All the survival skills he'd taught her about CPR and doing chest compressions to the tune of "Stayin' Alive" totally vanished. It didn't matter that she knew continued circulation was key to survival after cardiac arrest. Or that the bookstore had a defibrillator on the wall behind a glass case. Still she froze. Her brain was fumbling to grasp the reality of his collapse when a customer stepped into the store, ran at once to his side, and called 911—but by then it was too late. He was gone.

As the freezing water sloshed into her face now, one thought sparked out of the ashes of her guilt: she would not fail Andy like she had failed their dad.

Almost there, she thought, even though she knew it was a lie. The dark blur of the shore remained at a seemingly fixed distance. *One more minute, and then that's it, I'm done. I'll just float, let the current do the work.* Every time she felt her willpower diminishing, she told herself: *One more minute. One more yard. One more stroke.* The trick of imminent rest coaxed her ahead, at an ever slowing pace. Each minute stretched into its own hellish infinity.

You can do this, she kept urging herself, but after twenty more minutes, letting go became viciously enticing. She finally let her muscles relax and felt the icy water slide over her neck, her cheeks, her forehead. Fully submerged, she resigned her body to the whim of the current. *Just for a moment.* She was so numb she could barely feel or think. Andy's legs unlocked around her waist, his weight lifted, and then she felt his hand clamp around her elbow and yank her up. Cold air rushed into her lungs. Her memory of her father's face started to blur along with her vision.

"Come on, Izz." Andy's voice cracked. "You can't drown."

Someone wants me to drown. Someone doesn't care if my brother does, too.

As she stared at his terrified face and quivering lips, a new energy source clicked on inside her: Rage.

"Let's go," she declared. "Get back on."

He obeyed. She pumped one arm in front of the other, running on nothing but the pure hatred of evil—a form of fuel more potent than food. With every stroke, it kicked up a notch, and her leaden body felt lighter, electric, as she lashed out at the invisible enemy. *You picked the wrong girl, bastard. No one messes with my family.*

As if in validation, the shore at last approached. The dark and barren strip had never looked so beautiful.

They floated the final stretch on the crest of a wave that left them tumbling onto the sand, crying out in triumphant relief.

The rest of the journey home was a blur—flagging down the nearest car, getting driven home to their distraught mother, collapsing into steamy baths. By then Andy had figured out her lie about the show, but he was safe and warm thanks to her, and he knew it. When he told their mother about her "badass" feat, his eyes shone with a new respect, and she suspected that his teasing taunts of *Wild Woman* were over for good.

Despite being limp with fatigue the next morning, she wasted no time driving to Richard Barnett's office and storming inside without so much as a knock.

She found him at his desk smoking a cigarette. He blinked several times before standing to greet her with a grin. His slim six-foot-four figure, neat blond hair, and intelligent hazel eyes added up to a man who could have been dignified, she thought. A man who could have been good for the world. But instead, he had chosen to capitalize on the pain and suffering of others.

"Isabel!" He walked around the desk to welcome her. "What a surprise."

Keeping her feet planted, she scowled at him from the doorway. "I don't know what sick game you're playing, but you're not going to get away with it."

He pulled back his hand as if she'd bitten it. "Excuse me?"

"Don't play dumb."

He shook his head slowly. "I have no idea what you're talking about."

"Oh no? Because I'm pretty sure your investor is trying to kill me. And you set the whole thing up."

CHAPTER 12
Joan

11 days before, New York

"**W**e *need to talk.*"

Alone in her bedroom, Joan tested the words aloud. They sounded ominous, a surefire way to put Greg on the defensive the second he walked in the door. He'd been away on business since her discovery of the apartment's on-sale status the day before. Now, any minute, he was set to arrive home, and she still hadn't figured out how to start off the most significant conversation of their marriage.

Having such a talk over the phone was unthinkable. Maybe Adam's generation could do that, but they could also have entire relationships over text.

No, she needed to confront her husband face-to-face. But nothing could be more terrifying. She rose from the illusory safety of her satin bedspread and went to wait by the window that overlooked the building's entrance, fifteen floors below.

She felt like she were standing on the edge of a precipice, staring down the past thirty years of their relationship. He had never deceived her before, except for the slipup with the prescription pill addiction. That he was capable of a lie on this scale—

The thought ended there, for its implications were too staggering to bear.

It wasn't cold, but she was quivering. The muscles in her arms twitched. She pressed her hand against the window. Her French manicured nails were chipped, her cuticles torn from hours of absentminded abuse.

She couldn't help recognizing the irony of her situation: for five months, she had been trying to discover some elusive truth he seemed to be hiding. Now, on the verge of forcing it out, she wanted nothing more than to retreat into a shell of ignorance.

Down at street level, a familiar stride caught her attention. There were those long legs, that lean torso, that proud posture. His effortless dignity was one of the things she loved most about him. *A real class act,* her friends used to tell her enviously. *You got to marry not just a doctor, but a gentleman.*

She watched him disappear inside their lobby, imagined him heading to the express elevator—just ten more seconds—what was she going to say?

"Hi, what the hell is going on?"

That wouldn't do. She fled to the bathroom to buy time. Any second now. Was she prepared to leave him? Were these the dying moments of their marriage—one that had, until recently, been filled with mutual love and respect?

And then it was upon her, his key inside the lock, the turning of the door. It swung open and his voice called out, kind and welcoming—

"Sweetie, I'm home!"

"Hi!" she yelled back, too harshly. Her tone was all wrong. There was no way he would miss it. She heard his footsteps approach the bathroom door, then his gentle knock.

"You okay in there?"

She was sitting on the toilet lid, about to cry, when a sudden calm came over her. The facts stood out in sharp relief: He had lied. She needed the truth. Like any trained journalist, she knew she had to separate her emotions from the reporting if she wanted the whole story.

Neither polite questioning nor covert stalking had done the trick. The only strategy left was a bold play.

After splashing some water on her face, she opened the door. Standing there in his dapper suit, his brow furrowed, Greg broke into a grin at the sight of her. A cold drop trickled down her forehead. He leaned in to kiss it away.

Even then, she wanted to yield to him, to feel his lips on her skin, to be held and reassured and protected and loved. Just for a little longer.

"No," she said. The firmness in her own voice surprised her. "No more."

He pulled back, confused. "What?"

She stepped past without letting him touch her. "I think you know what." She perched on the edge of the bed, her arms crossed. "No more playing dumb. No more lies. No more bullshit."

He stood completely still, as though one slight move might prompt an explosion. When he spoke after a moment, his voice sounded tired. "Please tell me what's going on."

Her eyes never left his. "You put our house up for sale without telling me."

His eyebrows shot up. He glanced to the floor, swallowed. Still no gestures. Like other ER doctors, he'd automatized repression during a crisis. He always had.

"Well?" she said acidly. "Aren't you at least going to own up to it?"

"How did you find out?"

"That's what you care about? Not that I'm two seconds away from walking out of here?"

His features scrunched into an expression she almost never saw: fear.

"No! Don't leave. Just give me a chance to explain. I'm sorry you found out however you did, and not from me. But you have to realize I was only trying to protect you."

The torment in his eyes seemed sincere, and she almost felt sorry for him. She recognized the same look from when he'd finally told her about his addiction all those years ago—guilt, sadness, panic. But never evil. Never betrayal.

She took a deep breath. If he bore any resemblance to the man she married, then there was a damn good explanation. Maybe even a redeeming one.

"I'll stay," she said, "on one condition: You tell me absolutely everything. Or we're done."

"Deal. God, I've wanted to tell you for so long, but I didn't want you to get hurt . . ." he trailed off. "I thought I could fix everything without bringing you into it."

She refused to let herself soften—yet. "Spit it out."

He walked over and sat next to her on the bed. "You're not going to like this, but please just hear me out. Because I love you more than anything on God's green Earth and I need you now more than ever."

The intensity of her dread left her speechless.

He picked up her trembling hand and bowed his head. "I have a confession."

CHAPTER 13
The Diary of Richard Barnett

11 days before, Key West

I can't say I blame you for accusing me of a malicious setup, Isabel. When you stormed into my office that day, you were pretty shaken up. A perma-wrinkle cut a deep groove between your brows. Your long dark locks hung in limp waves, bluish circles underscored your eyes, and your yellow sundress did little to counteract the blackness of your fury.

Will you forgive me for thinking you were still beautiful?

"Undo the deal," you demanded from the doorway, after describing your near-drowning incident. "Undo everything. I don't care what it costs. I want nothing to do with you and your psycho investor."

I listened calmly. Your experience, while no doubt frightening, was less a testament to my guilt than your own. On some level, you clearly felt bad about your double mastectomy and it was manifesting in paranoia.

"No one is out to get you," I said. "I've been in this business a long time. Relax."

My failure to buy into your version of events irked you

even more. You marched up to me and for a moment I thought you were going to slap me. I think you considered it. But then you crossed your arms and glared.

"I want it undone. Today."

"Sorry, lives are nonrefundable."

"But I can pay back every cent! My show was a hit and I've signed on for a second season."

"Doesn't matter. A deal's a deal."

You whipped your head in frustration. "But someone is trying to kill me!"

"That's where you're wrong." I gently put my hand on your shoulder. You shook it off. I was undeterred. "It's quite common for clients to have second thoughts later, then rush to me freaking out. You probably didn't drop anchor properly and your boat got swept out by the current. I really don't think you have anything to worry about."

Your scowl persisted. "What about my mastectomy? I ripped him off and now it's payback."

There was something to that line of reasoning, I had to admit. Usually, the investors knew what they were getting and the deal paid off in a straightforward way. I'd never encountered such a twist before, but I couldn't conceive of murder as a real possibility. I also didn't understand who we were up against—and how desperate he might become.

"I'll talk to Robbie," I said to reassure you. "He has tons of other lives, so if one doesn't mature for many years, it's no big deal. The fund will still come out ahead in the long run."

You uttered a disgusted snort. "Your euphemisms are killing me."

I smiled at your unintentional pun, hoping to lighten the mood. It didn't work. You turned your back on me and headed for the door. What else could you do? I hadn't given you much choice.

"I'll let you know what he says," I called. "You'll see there's nothing to it."

"Just like there's nothing to your new Beamer outside," you shot back. "Hope your blood money drives well."

"I earned that fair and square," I snapped. But you were already out the door. I didn't have time to explain that the crash of the economy in recent months had rocketed my brokerage into the stratosphere. Business was up over 200 percent, thanks to all the people who suddenly needed fast cash and ran to me to sell their policies. I was getting rich off of honest work, nothing sinister.

With anyone else, I wouldn't have been so insulted. I would have had a smoke and laughed it off. But with you, it was different. I needed you to know I wasn't the slimy jerk you believed. Proving you wrong would also give me an excuse to contact you again. Maybe even see you one last time.

I set up the record function on my phone so I could play you the call later. Then I dialed Robbie. I couldn't wait to show you that the corruption you pinned on me— and him—was purely imaginary.

His tough nasal voice came on the line. I detected a dash of blue-collar Midwesterner in his otherwise accent-free speech. Later I would realize this was all I had to go on.

"This is Robbie."

"Barnett here," I said. "Just a quick follow-up about my client Isabel Leon. Did you get her updated medical records I sent last week?"

"I did." His tone was ice.

"Everything okay?"

"What do you think? Do you think it's okay that she cut off her breasts?" His voice turned outright hostile. *"What the hell did I pay for?"*

This was not at all what I was expecting. I switched to a harder tone to match his. *"That was a risk you were taking. You knew this surgery existed for cases like hers."*

"She should have said something if that's what she was planning!"

"Maybe she didn't know then! You can't blame her for wanting to stay alive."

"Like hell I can't."

Was that a threat? Was it just hot air? I wanted to know desperately for your sake, but I had to be careful. Accusing him of stalking you would get me nowhere. I had no evidence to connect him to your missing boat. And if I had any hope of going to the authorities, I needed some kernel of evidence. So I tried a different tactic.

My voice turned sympathetic. *"I get you. Let's find a solution."*

At the same time, I was doing a quick Google search on SkyBridge Asset Management. For years, Robbie Merriman been nothing to me but a voice on the phone, a reliable buyer who paid well and on time. But who was he? And where was he? I had never cared to find out until now.

"There is no solution," he snarled. *"She screwed me over."*

His checks were issued from a bank in the Caymans. His cell phone was an area code from Connecticut, and his fund had a PO box in Manhattan. That was all.

He could be anyone, anywhere.

"Maybe we could meet in person to figure something out?" I asked, hoping to glean useful information.

"*My time's been wasted enough.*" He sounded like he was about to hang up, so I rushed to stop him.

"*Wait!*" I said. "*She'll pay you back her settlement fee. I know there's no precedent for it, but then you'll have nothing against her.*"

There was a pause. "*It's not enough. I was counting on two mil long-term.*"

I blurted out my next thought, however reckless. "*What if I find a fall guy then? Some other client who will pay off so fast and so big, you'll forget all about her?*"

He shot back an impossible bargain: "*Only if you can net me at least a million.*"

Or else what? I didn't know, but I didn't want you to find out.

"*Oh,*" he added, "*and I'd need it by the end of next week.*"

"*Done,*" I said. My heart was thudding against my ribs—what was I agreeing to? Yet did I have a choice? This was your life at stake, Isabel. There was nothing the police or the FBI could do to find him before it was too late, especially given the lack of hard evidence linking him to your missing boat. But I shared your suspicions now. I was the only one who could help you.

I needed to track down somebody who was on the verge of death, with a huge policy, willing to sell it at a cut rate.

"*Ten days,*" he said. "*Make it happen.*"

My voice shook only a little. "*I have just the right person in mind.*"

CHAPTER 14
Joan

11 days before, New York

Joan braced herself. "What is it?"

Beside her on the bed, Greg was bowing his head and refusing to make eye contact. Possible catastrophes hurtled through her mind: he wasn't just having an affair, but a baby. He wasn't just doing drugs, but dealing them. He wasn't just getting fired from the hospital, but losing his license. Anything but what he whispered next:

"We're going broke."

She heard the words but didn't comprehend them. She was surrounded by luxury—her bare feet rested on a heated wood floor. She was sitting on a ten-thousand-dollar memory foam mattress. Her arm hair was prickling against the sleeve of his Prada suit.

His forehead was lined with pained wrinkles. "I screwed up really bad. I didn't want to tell you, I thought I could fix it—"

"How?" she interrupted. "What? When?"

He heaved a sigh. "When the economy started going to hell about six months ago, I got nervous. We were heavily exposed—"

"Were? Or are?" As far as she knew, most of their money was invested in either stocks or real estate holdings that paid regular dividends. Greg thought it was a waste to let cash sit in safer places like banks or bonds.

"Were," he said. "As the market got worse and worse, we lost an insane amount—but I was scared to pull out. I thought it would come back . . ."

"You should have told me."

"You hate dealing with money. That's always been my job."

It was true; their marriage was very traditional that way. She rarely asked about their finances, and he didn't often volunteer. She just assumed he had it under control. But there'd never been such a downturn in their lifetimes. It was only getting worse still.

"I don't care." She felt heat radiating from her face. "You should have told me! What were you thinking?"

He stood and began pacing at the foot of the bed, his hands clasped behind his head. "Honestly I couldn't bear to see you get as panicked as I was. I just wanted to fix it. But then our condos in Hawaii and Florida went vacant practically overnight and I was stuck with the bill, plus the mortgage on this apartment, and *then* the hospital furloughed our shifts—and on top of it you wanted us to help Adam. I knew we couldn't swing it, but I didn't want to disappoint you or him. I couldn't take it anymore, so I had to do something. I had to get our money back."

"Oh God." If she was sure of anything, it was that Greg hated to lose. Once, on a family vacation to Las Vegas, he'd parked himself at the blackjack table for six volatile hours, doubling each bet to recoup what he'd already lost. Only when he was victorious did he finally walk away, jittery and drained, a measly two hundred dollars richer.

Before he even said the words, she pressed her fingertips to her temples. "Tell me you didn't."

He spoke in a rush, as if to gloss over the ugliest bits. "I cashed out a lot of our remaining stocks, borrowed some additional money from the charity, and started playing online poker. I got really good, and for a while, I was making thousands a week, keeping us going. But then I got arrogant, made a few bad calls, and needed more capital again, so I pawned off a few things—my Rolex watch, my father's collection of gold coins. But the money wasn't growing fast enough, and the bills were piling up like crazy—so I put the apartment up for sale just to see what kind of offer we could get. I still was hoping the market would come back up, or our properties would start paying off again, or I would hit it really big so we wouldn't need to sell. So you would be spared any involvement in this crisis."

He paused to gulp short bursts of air, as though his throat was closing. He gnawed on his bottom lip, snatching nervous glances at her reaction. She was glaring at him, her arms crossed tightly over her chest. Her mind flashed back to the three or four times over the last few months that he'd asked her to join him for lunch somewhere, usually at the last minute; now she realized that his desire to get her out of the house had probably been due to a Realtor coming around to show their place.

"There's more, isn't there?" Her flat tone lacked inflection. "I can tell."

In tacit assent, he resumed pacing, keeping his eyes on the floor. "We never got an offer on the apartment, and the creditors were starting to call, so I had to do something else to raise money right away—"

She jumped to her feet, cutting him off. "You better not have touched Adam's inheritance!"

"No! Never. I'd rather be out on the street than bring him into it."

Her pulse was racing all the way down to her fingertips. A mistake that hurt their son could never be forgiven. There was a fine line between a screwup and a savage. "You swear to God?"

"Absolutely," he declared, holding his hands up. "It's ironclad."

"Then why didn't you want to give him access to it before? All that talk about him needing to be independent—that was crap, wasn't it?"

He nodded. "I was trying to protect him, too. No one can touch his trust until I die." He paused gravely. "But if I were to grant permission now, my creditors could seize it as one of my assets."

"Jesus. They're already after you?"

"They were, until . . ." he rubbed his neck, glancing out the window. The words seemed difficult to get out. "A few weeks ago, I sold my life insurance policy for cash."

She felt her stomach tense as if she were dropping from a great height. Of course he would think of doing that. For some years, he'd leveraged his medical knowledge into a lucrative consulting gig for one of the many hedge funds that specialized in buying up life insurance policies and that needed a doctor's expertise in predicting patient mortality. By the time the side gig eventually dried up, Greg had become inured to the creepiness of the industry in a way she never had. She knew he considered it as professional as any other sector of finance.

He still wouldn't look at her, and that's when she knew there was something more, a dagger at the bottom waiting to break her fall.

"My settlement was enough to cover our immediate bills," he went on, "but at what cost?" He turned toward her again, and she was startled to see that his blue eyes were clouded with tears. "There's an auction website where you can put your policy up for sale. I accepted the highest bidder, a fantastic offer from some faceless hedge fund I'd never heard of, and thought that was the end of it. But I don't think it was. I know I always told you this business wasn't sketchy, but I might've been wrong."

"What do you mean?" she asked, not sure she had the capacity to take any more.

"I started to feel like someone might be following me, or watching me. Then the other day, on my way to the hospital, some guy on the corner of Sixty-third and West End bumped into me so hard I fell into the street, right in front of a cab that had to slam on its brakes."

"You never told me that."

"I told Yardley"—his doctor colleague who also worked in the ER—"and mentioned my recent sale. Did he think I was being totally paranoid? I just wanted reassurance. But I couldn't believe what he said. Apparently there's been talk at the hospital of one or two patients dying from weird accidents after selling their policies, but no one can prove the connection. So far it's just quiet rumors. The targets seem to be people like me—idiots who accept offers way above market rates, so they think they got a deal."

"You can't be serious," she said, even as she could see a distressed vein popping out on his forehead. "Why doesn't anyone go to the police?"

"What could they do? There's no evidence of foul play. Whoever is behind this is careful and slick." He stared at her with naked dread. "And I think I'm next."

CHAPTER 15
Isabel

10 days before, Key West

Isabel stayed away from crowds. She disliked being jostled and bumped, elbowing her way through layers of people, shouting to be heard above competing voices. But today, she insisted on visiting the tourist trap of Mallory Square—the waterfront gathering of Key West's nightly sunset celebration.

Richard Barnett had demanded to see her in person for some kind of emergency meeting. But now that he knew of her suspicions, she didn't trust him enough to return to his office, alone. This was the most public place she could think of.

When she arrived at 6:30 P.M., the jugglers, unicyclists, and fire-breathers were in full entertainer mode, taking turns hopping into the center of a captivated circle of onlookers. Behind them, an inimitable performance was playing out in the sky: the sun was sinking to meet the turquoise waters of the Gulf, accompanied by a dramatic palette of pinks, oranges, and purples.

Isabel hung on the outskirts of the cheering crowd.

Dressed in skinny jeans, sandals, and a black tank top, she aimed to blend in. Her colorful dresses and purses were stashed away. Anything that attracted attention made her uncomfortable these days. Thankfully she'd be back on location in two weeks, this time in New Zealand, with a crew surrounding her night and day. Good luck to anyone who wanted to stalk her there. Or maybe, as Richard Barnett suggested, she was just being paranoid. In that case, going back to work soon would serve as a much-needed distraction.

She scanned the strangers around her—sunburned teenagers in board shorts, middle-aged couples snapping pictures, little kids perched on their fathers' shoulders, white-haired retirees licking cones of green key lime ice cream. No one seemed the least bit aware of her, let alone after her. Could Richard be right? She felt herself starting to relax and enjoy the spectacle, until a finger tapped her shoulder. She tensed up and spun around.

He was towering over her, one hand brimming his eyes to shut out the sun. Even with his face in shadow, his heavy brow conveyed distress. She saw that he must have rushed straight from his office to meet her, because he was panting and the armpits of his tan suit were dark with sweat.

He leaned down and spoke into her ear: "We have to talk."

The scent of his cologne poorly masked his cigarette breath.

She stepped back with a grimace. "Hi to you, too."

"Not here. Follow me."

He hurried away from the whooping crowd toward the edge of the plaza, where a bronze dolphin statue was spouting water from its mouth into a shallow coin pond. It was the farthest they could get from everyone else while still remaining in the bounds of Mallory Square.

She followed behind, walking quickly to keep up with his long strides. When they reached the fountain, he turned so they were face-to-face. She kept her distance a foot away and folded her arms. He gazed down at her with concern—and a hint of tenderness. Coming from the sarcastic jerk who lived off death, it didn't seem plausible. Vampires weren't known for their humanity.

"You were right," he blurted out. "You're in trouble."

She squinted up at him. "How do you know?"

"I talked to Robbie." He pulled out an iPhone and tapped it a few times. "Listen, I recorded the whole thing."

As he played it back on speaker, she felt her heart climb into her throat. A gut feeling might be rationalized away, but evidence of it made the danger suddenly real. Instead of a shadowy knife glinting at a sideways angle, here was the blade thrusting out right under her nose. She listened to every nuance, every loaded pause. Robbie Merriman's message could not have been more explicit, even if his words weren't: he wanted her dead.

In ten days or less, someone—somehow—was going to make sure of it.

When the recording clicked off, Richard didn't waste a second getting to his point: "He's not going to touch you. I'm going to help you out of this."

She pressed her fingertips to her forehead. "I don't see how." Her mind flashed to her vulnerable mom and brother, and their relaxed bungalow's single lock. Now that her dad was gone, they were more unprotected than ever. "What about my family?"

"You're the only one he wants. It's the money he's after. So as long as I find someone else, he'll let this go."

"Seriously?" She threw her arms out. "You have ten days to find someone who has a big policy *and* is about to die *and* is willing to sell? That probably doesn't even exist!"

He coughed, patting his chest a few times. "Sorry. I understand your skepticism, but . . . what other choice do you have?"

She racked her brain, glancing from the fountain to the darkening sky to the dispersing crowd a few yards away. "I don't know. I could go into hiding, fly to New Zealand early—but I don't feel right leaving my family now, even if you don't think they're in danger. What if he uses them to get to me?"

Richard pursed his lips. "You could try going to the police."

"And do what, get a restraining order for a ghost?"

She had her own additional reason for not involving the authorities. If they found out the truth about Andy's illegal immigrant status, she would never forgive herself. It was why her mother made a point of never calling the cops, even when a homeless man had once tried to break into their home.

Richard glanced toward the remaining onlookers and the street performers, who were packing up. "If only we knew who he really was—and where . . ."

Isabel eyed him suspiciously. "And after all your years of making deals with this guy, you never thought to check him out? You really had no clue?"

"Honest to God, I never had a reason to. He paid well, on time. I deal with so many investors on a daily basis and dozens of clients. You think I have time to become a private investigator?"

"Then how do you have time to help me?"

"Just trust me."

She gave a derisive laugh. "Now I'll sleep well."

He frowned at her. "I'm serious." As if by instinct, he reached into his suit pocket and pulled out a thin white cigarette.

"Don't," she said. "Not around me."

"Fine." With a sigh, he slipped it back into his pocket. "Look, I know I tend to come off as sarcastic, but I'm being real right now."

She shook her head at his cluelessness. "You want to talk about real? My fiancé's loyalty wasn't real. My dad's good heart wasn't real. My mom's good health wasn't real. My own good genes weren't real. And you expect me to take *you* at face value*?*"

He winced. "I'm sorry."

She felt tears prick her eyes. "How am I supposed to trust anything?"

"Because I—" he broke off, clearing his throat. When he glanced away, she noticed that he was clenching his jaw.

"What?"

"I feel responsible." He looked at the ground. "I didn't know who I was dealing with."

"I guess I still find that hard to believe."

The hair on her arms stood up as she realized that she was completely on her own. Anyone around her could be the perp—including Richard Barnett himself.

They were pretty much alone on the plaza. The sky was dark, the crowd thinned to a few remaining stragglers. She hugged her arms as a cool breeze gusted off the water.

"I have to go. Just leave me alone, okay? You've done enough."

"I'm going to take care of this," he said. "I wish you could believe me."

As if to seal the deal, he plucked a shiny penny from his briefcase, rubbed it between two fingers, and tossed it into the pond. It plunked to the bottom. He looked back at her with his eyebrows raised.

"But I know your wish," she said. "So now it won't come true."

She turned on her heel and strode toward Duval Street, where half a dozen pubs promised to keep the carefree island spirit alive long after sunset.

But no matter how much she wedged herself among the patrons, she couldn't escape the feeling of eyes on her back.

CHAPTER 16
Joan

5 days before, New York

Adam sat before Joan and Greg in horrified silence. His eyes narrowed to pinpoints as he glanced back and forth between them. He dug his nails into the armrest of their black leather sofa, an artifact of the home they would soon no longer inhabit. His compact, muscular body was quivering with fury. Joan tore her gaze away from his face and looked at Greg, who was perched on the edge of his recliner. His shoulders were hunched forward and he was holding his elbows as if trying to minimize his own presence in the room.

"Let me get this straight." Adam shook his head, tugging at the collar of his polo shirt. "Dad screwed up, you're going broke, and now you have to move?" He stared at Joan, dumbfounded. "And you're just going along with it?"

She winced at how pathetic the situation sounded aloud. Since Greg's confession five days before, she'd gone through her own stages of anger, grief, and ultimately sympathy for his decision to keep her insulated from his own panic. It was the wrong choice, yes, but Greg was nothing if not an alpha male. She understood that his actions were motivated by a deeply masculine desire to protect her without admitting to weakness. Besides, his life was very possibly in danger, so how could she leave him now? Only a sociopath would be capable of deserting her partner at his most vulnerable moment.

But Adam couldn't sympathize with her decision to stay because he didn't know about the threat. She and Greg had agreed it was better not to upset him more than was strictly necessary.

"It isn't quite that simple," Greg muttered. He barely raised his eyes to his son's. "The economy—"

"You gambled away your money!" Adam flung his palms up. "Who are you? What kind of idiot does that?"

"Adam," Joan cut in. "Your father made a mistake. He had honorable intentions. He was trying to keep our lives afloat."

"This is a betrayal." Adam ran a hand through his hair. "I can't believe you're just going to let him get away with it."

Joan glanced at Greg. Her red-faced husband was squirming in the throes of shame, crossing his legs and sighing. He kept his eyes plastered to the floor. She knew there was only one thing he hated more than admitting defeat: suffering in the presence of others. It was a wonder he was staying put, a testament to the respect he knew they deserved.

"He's punishing himself plenty," she said to Adam. "Can't you tell?"

"It's not enough. Look what he's done to you, Mom. You have to move!"

"Just for the time being," she allowed. "So we can rent out this place for additional income. I'm just sorry we're not in a position to help you and Emily out, but your father thinks there might be some other money on the way."

Adam cocked his head. "Oh, like when you get your royal flush?"

"I've stopped gambling," Greg said softly. "I'm joining a twelve-step program."

Joan raised her eyebrows as if to say *See? He's not all bad.* But Adam wasn't buying it. He rolled his eyes at the ceiling. In his disdain, she recognized something else brimming to the surface: resentment. Greg's focus on success had nearly estranged the two of them in last decade, since Adam graduated from college. Greg had pushed him into law school, doing his best to smother his son's musical passion before it derailed his future. But Adam cared more about happiness than wealth. For years, their argument had been unbridgeable. The chasm between them mirrored the broader one between their two generations: Greg, who'd grown up with nothing as the son of a post-man, saw his son's peers as spoiled and entitled, while Adam thought his dad's crowd mistakenly prioritized financial stability over personal fulfillment, so they were rich, but miserable.

Now, in Adam's self-satisfied little head shake, Joan could see that her son felt validated at last. If money had meant less to Greg, he could have let go of his losses and downsized their life. But Adam was naïve. Joan grasped that money was just a proxy for the real issue: the very core of Greg's identity. As long as she'd known him, he had been driven by the singular ambition to succeed, to give himself and his family the luxurious life he'd always wanted but never had. Without the wealth he'd worked so hard to attain, who was he? How could he face himself?

But he would make it back somehow, she thought. Even if it took a long time. He'd already promised to take on more shifts at the hospital, plus some more freelance consulting. Not that she cared so much if they lived in one modest bedroom or a palatial penthouse. Whatever their address, safety mattered most. Especially now.

"I need to get home," Adam announced, interrupting her worries. He stood up and caught her eye, refusing to look at Greg. "Emily's about to pop. In the meantime, I really hope you're doing the right thing."

His hard tone belied his true meaning: *You're digging yourself in deeper by staying with him.*

His incisive stare contained another message, too—a conversation contained in a glance only she understood. Her mind darted to the unsettling event he was surely trying to resurrect in her memory: The time a few years ago that Adam had stopped by his father's office for an impromptu visit, only to be greeted with Greg's uncharacteristic wrath. Shouting had ensued, a fist slammed on the desk—didn't Adam know how to pick up a phone first? He'd interrupted a very important phone call, et cetera. *I've never seen Dad lose his temper like that,* Adam had told Joan later. *It was like he was a different person.*

Of course, Greg had recovered his senses and apologized afterward for overreacting, so Joan brushed it off. Lack of sleep, long hours in the ER, the pressure to keep up his charity—it all had to catch up with a man once in a while. Just because Adam resented his father for the outburst didn't mean it was significant. In fact, Joan was annoyed that Adam even still thought of it. Her son had a maddening affinity for grudges.

She tried to keep her voice even as she addressed him. "Thanks. We're dying to see the baby the second he's born."

"I'll keep you posted. But I think it's best if Dad doesn't come."

Greg gasped. "You're not going to let me meet my grandson?"

Adam's gaze was steely. "Not until you prove I can trust you again."

"He's not a criminal!" Joan snapped. "He made a mistake!"

"Gross negligence takes victims, too," he retorted. "The punishment's in a different kind of court."

Then he marched out, letting the door slam behind him.

She and Greg stared at it. The heartbreak was plain in his eyes.

"Give him some time," she said. "Just let him calm down."

Greg got up and locked the bolt on the front door. He peered through the peephole, then slid the gold chain lock closed as well. When he returned to the living room, she blurted out the announcement she'd been holding in all day:

"I've decided to go back to investigative reporting."

A look of displeasure crossed his face. "Honey, I'm going to fix this. I'll do whatever it takes. You don't have to do that."

"I want to."

"But you can't make much money. Plus you haven't worked in twenty years."

"It's not about the money. I spent my career fighting to expose corruption and I was damn good at it." She crossed her arms. "You think I'm just going to ignore it now, when the biggest scandal of our life is right under our noses?"

He grimaced, but in a rush of excitement, she sprung from her chair and skipped across the room to clutch his hands. They felt cold and limp.

"I'm going to start today," she said, gazing up at him. "Maybe I'll run into a bunch of dead ends, but I'm going to try, before you and other innocent people get hurt."

"But it's just rumors. How can you do anything if the cops can't?"

"They need a warrant and probable cause. I don't."

He enveloped her in a hug, wrapping his strong arms around her shoulders. "You always were the spunkiest girl in the room."

She leaned into his chest. Beneath his starchy button-down shirt, his heart was thumping fast. She sensed the feeling worming its way through him: Fear. She felt it, too. It was fear of the unknown, of evil that lurked in close quarters waiting to strike. It was too vague to confront head-on—which made it all the more frightening. But that wasn't about to stop her.

They stood embracing for what felt like a long time, united at last by a common goal—and a common enemy.

CHAPTER 17
The Diary of Richard Barnett

1 day before, Key West

I found you a fall guy, Isabel. Just like I promised. A sad
old schmuck whose time is near. He didn't take good
care of himself, physically or otherwise. His ex-wife
thinks him depraved, a description he doesn't dispute.
He's got no kids to leave behind, so no one will miss him
much. Has he lived a good life? Done noble work?
Doubtful. He gave up on all that a long time ago.

He's worth a million bucks dead and has no heirs, so it
wasn't too difficult to persuade him to sell his policy. I
knew I had to act fast, before Robbie made his move on
you.

I called him a few days ago. The deal went down like
any other. Except this time, I was proud. For the first time
in my life, I was doing right.

"Got you a sure thing," I said. "Huge payday right
around the corner. So no funny business, okay? You leave
that woman alone."

"Oh yeah?" His voice was like a snarl. "How sure?"

I reeled off the facts with practiced neutrality, my voice
shaking only a little: "Male, forty-five, family history of

heart attacks, smokes three packs a day. Never exercises. He recently found out he has a massive clot in his pulmonary valve and is refusing surgery."

It was the truth. Unlike some of my competitors, I never exaggerate to make my clients look worse than they are.

And it was perfect timing; my doctor broke the news to me last week.

Robbie gave a low whistle. "Guy must be dying as we speak."

I swallowed, a cold sweat prickling my skin. "No doubt."

Then I let him off easy. As much as I wanted to drive a hard bargain—the prick deserved it—I was more determined to make sure he was satisfied with the deal, so he'll leave you alone. We agreed on a measly $50,000 settlement.

The check just arrived. I'm enclosing it with this diary and mailing both to you today. Don't bother coming to thank me. You'll be too late.

For most of my life, I've known how my death was going to happen. My father and grandfather each collapsed of sudden heart attacks at the ripe old age of forty-five. We were all cursed with pulmonary valve stenosis—a congenital disorder that lessens blood flow to the lungs and gets progressively worse as you get older. When I turned the magic age a few months ago, I knew my time was almost up. I'm just glad that now it won't be for nothing.

You'll never believe me, but I was a nice kid once. Want know why I turned into a cynic? At age eight, I watched my father clutch his chest, crumple to the floor, and die— right as he was scrambling eggs for breakfast. I never ate eggs again. Shortly afterward, a cardiologist checked me out and said I had inherited the same condition. Back then, they didn't have the techniques they do today to fix it. So I grew up with a ticking bomb strapped inside my chest. My life has been spent waiting for the moment it decides to go off.

I never got too invested in any attachment in this world. The closest I came was at age twenty-seven. At my mother's urging, I married the girl I was halfheartedly dating. She was a good girl from a nice Jewish family, but she wanted children desperately. I vowed never to put a kid through growing up without a father the way I did. We split up after a year.

Eventually I got a job selling life insurance for a big company. Then I figured out I could make a better living if I opened my own business as a secondary broker. It was morbid at first, profiting off the sick and dying, but then I grew inured to death. And maybe that was the goal all along—so I would no longer fear my own.

I never did find my true purpose. But you awakened something in me that I didn't know still existed.

Which is why I'm refusing the bypass surgery that could clear out my clot and the balloon dilation procedure that could open the valve. I want to do the honorable thing. I feel responsible; I sold you into this mess and I should be the one to get you out of it. The way I see it, you need my death more than I need to live.

But it might not happen today, or tomorrow, and we don't have the time for me to sit around and wait. So I've gotten a prescription filled for Prozac. Seven days' worth of pills can cause a fatal overdose. (Remember my business, so don't ask how I know.) As soon as I finish this final diary entry, I'm going to mail off your package, get comfortable in my favorite rocking chair, and pour myself a glass of Scotch. That should make those suckers go down easy.

Don't be upset. Mine is not a tragic death, as yours would certainly be.

It's coming up so fast now, the moment I've spent my whole life dreading. I'll admit to being nervous, but I know I can go in peace. I finally feel like a decent man.

The closer I get to the end, my hope for an afterlife intensifies. I've never been able to believe, but on the off chance I'm wrong, maybe we'll meet again someday. One last time, I'd like to see your smile.

I just hope it won't be soon.

Yours Sincerely,
Richard Barnett

Enclosure: Check for $50,000

CHAPTER 18
The Day of Isabel

Key West

Surfing was her one escape. The morning ritual that kept Isabel sane, when every other waking moment was consumed by paranoia or defiance.

She never expected it to be her downfall.

So when the ferocious wave slammed her and her fellow surfers off their boards, she plummeted to the bottom, but didn't panic. Not at first. She held her breath as she tumbled through the chaos, waiting for the sea to straighten itself out. The light of dawn struck the water, transforming its surface into a glittering kaleidoscope above her. She pushed her way up, greedy for air.

That was when a mysterious hand yanked her ponytail down. Her head snapped back, her lips parted, a nauseating flood of salt water rushed in. She choked and gagged and grew furious. Her arms and legs thrashed, but that hand was as firm as an anchor chaining her to death. She kicked harder, clawing and biting at her tormentor: a wetsuited scuba diver whose lips were wrapped around a breathing tube. It enraged her that this monster was feasting on air while she drowned. Her lungs felt like pressure

tanks about to explode. He clamped down on either side
of her neck with both hands and squeezed.

Soon a realization came that she had no choice but to
confront: she wasn't going to make it. Yet in spite of her
rage and despair, she clung to an absurd optimism that
persisted until the very end.

She never wondered why she was being killed. She understood perfectly. Her only surprise was that she, of all people,
had succumbed—in the one place she thought she was safe.
She didn't even get to say good-bye. Her final thought
was of Richard Barnett—and how, like a typical man, he
had failed her, having vanished from her life without ever
making good on his promise.

Despite everything, death itself was peaceful. In the
final split second came acceptance—then the absence of
pain, followed by an all-encompassing blackness. She encountered no light or universal warmth. Instead, she simply ceased to exist, along with the secret of the violence
she almost carried to her grave.

"And now I'm here," she said to her riveted audience.

She was sitting upright in her hospital bed on the
cruise ship, surrounded by a dozen people: the kind old
man who had resuscitated her, Dr. Quinn, plus a group of
wide-eyed nurses in blue scrubs, a couple of male EMTs,
and a tall, stern man with intense blue eyes for whom the
crowd had parted. He was given a few feet of space to
stand by her bed, in the prime spot. Everyone else was
crammed shoulder to shoulder in her small cabin, with
several more people clogging the doorway, all clamoring
to hear her story.

She'd been talking for an hour, describing the details
of how she came to be murdered. It still didn't feel real

that she could possibly be alive. But she was. The scent of salt water permeated her hair. She could almost still taste the squishy cloth of the scuba attacker's suit. The bruises on her neck felt fresh and sore. Her throat was raw and dry from so many hours of intubation.

She paused to sip from a white paper cup that Dr. Quinn handed her. The cool water was a balm to her parched vocal cords. Then she went on.

"Nothing's changed except that I survived. There's still two million dollars at stake."

No one moved or said a word. A heavy dread thickened the air. From all sides, the hospital staff stared at her, fearing the inevitable conclusion. She closed her eyes, delaying the words that had to come next. It was glorious to feel the air pass into her lungs, to feel her chest rise and fall, to feel the sturdy beat of her heart. Each moment was a novelty she wanted never to end.

At last she lifted her eyes to the waiting crowd.

"When I go back home," she said, "whoever wants me dead is bound to find out. And they're going to want to finish the job."

PART TWO

CHAPTER 19
Isabel

Key West

The starchy cotton sheets of her hospital bed were drenched with sweat. She clutched the plastic guardrail of her bed, feeling her own anxiety escalate as she watched it reflected in the faces of the onlookers.

Expressions of horror and sympathy surrounded her. She waited for someone to say a word, to offer support or advice, but they stayed inexplicably silent. Several women wearing blue medical scrubs traded dismayed looks. A cluster of young male doctors in white coats shifted on their feet, but no one spoke. Standing at her elbow, Dr. Quinn regarded her with a frown that deepened the crease between his sparse white brows. In the corners of his lips, his skin was pinched like cracked clay. He, too, remained silent.

A sudden feeling struck her that she was missing something. Something everyone else knew, but wouldn't tell her. She became aware of the floor's gentle rocking motion. A salty warm breeze drifted in from the circular window.

"Why are we on a ship?" she blurted out. "Who are you guys, anyway?"

When Dr. Quinn looked away from her, she noticed the rest of the crowd's attention had also shifted. They were all watching one man.

The tall man with blue eyes the color of glacial ice.

At the foot of her bed, he was standing perfectly still—a contrast with the nervous fidgeting pervading the crammed quarters.

He was watching her with a quiet intensity. Isabel felt that he was seeing more of her than everyone else, taking stock of her every move. She was reminded of an encounter while filming her show in the Sahara desert, when she found herself across a pond from a lion. This man projected a similar mix of vigilance and perceptiveness. At least six feet tall, with symmetrical cheekbones, a square jaw, and a prominent nose, he possessed a formidable majesty. A mane of wavy black hair gave him a youthful aura, though the lines on his face put him around sixty.

She was captive, but felt no fear. Unlike the lion's eyes, his were kind.

"What's going on?" she asked him. "Who are you?"

"I go by Galileo." His gaze swept to the others. "Isabel and I need a few minutes to get acquainted."

The nurses, doctors, EMTs, and lab techs cleared out in a respectful exodus. Even Dr. Quinn rose from his stool by her side, patted her arm, and left.

When they were alone, Galileo closed the door and came to perch on the edge of her bed. Whatever he was about to say carried a gravity that made him draw a deep breath.

Her heart sped up, as though in preparation for important news.

"Have you heard of the Network?" he asked, looking her in the eye.

She shook her head. "I don't think so."

"So you have no preconceived notions then."

"Nope."

"That makes things a little easier. I'm going to be frank. Your situation has never happened in our history. I can't in good conscience deliver you back home into the hands of a killer—but I also can't risk the damage you could do by going public."

Isabel pressed her lips together. "I'm not sure I follow . . ."

"Let me back up. You're in the heart of a world-class research center, maybe the best in the world. Only . . . we're not supposed to exist. So no one on the outside is supposed to know."

"This is a joke, right?" She squeezed her eyes shut to clear any debris from her consciousness. When she opened them, he was still sitting there, deadly serious.

"Should I go on?"

She nodded.

"Our organization, the Network, has been around for twelve years. We started as a group of a few scientists at odds with the establishment, who were eager to accelerate major breakthroughs. The kind that would take decades of regulatory headaches and billions of dollars to happen in the regular world—but our way makes it much faster and cheaper. In the last decade, we've grown to almost forty core members who live and work here on this ship. We've also established safe houses and key allies all over the country to transport supplies and people. I manage the whole operation and handle recruitment—we look for researchers who are frustrated with the system, on the verge of a serious breakthrough, and comfortable working in seclusion without any prestige. We provide the lab space and equipment, and in return, they agree to let the Network share ownership of any discoveries made here."

He paused, studying her face for signs of a negative reaction. But her amazed expression was anything but hostile.

"So this is for real?"

"You're in it. We have a small hospital on deck three, where you were resuscitated, and state-of-the-art labs on deck four. The researchers live in private cabins here, on deck two."

"Wow. Ever since my mom's life was saved by this new drug Braxa, I'm in awe of the people who actually develop that stuff."

"Ah, Braxa." His face lit up as though she'd mentioned a mutual friend. "That was one of our first successes. We developed it a decade ago and licensed it to LifeTech Pharma. It took them all these years just to get FDA approval."

"You're kidding." Her jaw hung open. "You guys are behind Braxa?"

"Yep." He smiled sadly. "There's a reason the public doesn't know."

"It's not legal?"

"Exactly. You need federal approval for clinical experimentation. The U.S. government has been trying to find and shut us down for years now." He paused. "There's even a reward out for my head."

"So you're a criminal?"

"Not just *a* criminal. I'm on the top ten most wanted. At least, the concept of me is. They have no idea what my real name is, and neither does pretty much anyone else—hence my pseudonym."

She chuckled. Grouping this man with murderers and rapists seemed about as logical as grouping Martin Luther King with the KKK.

But he wasn't smiling. His mouth was a thin, grave line. "Now that you've been here," he said, "you could report us."

Her amusement vanished in an instant. "So why are you telling me this?"

"I want you to know all the facts. Because I'm going to offer you a deal in exchange for your discretion."

She frowned. "I don't need to be bribed. You already saved my life."

"I have to take certain precautions. Everyone else inside our headquarters has been vetted. But we don't know you at all."

She hugged her knees to her chest. "I'm listening."

"First, a little history. We recruited Dr. Quinn seven years ago, after he lost his professorship at Harvard to scandal. At the time, he was working to develop a chemical compound to delay the decay of brain cells in recently deceased mammals—blurring the boundary between life and death. A jealous colleague accused him of stealing ideas from her, but in reality he was the victim of her lies.

"After we recruited him and his associate Chris, he finished the rest of the research here, tested it successfully on rats, then dogs, then started human clinical trials using recent corpses. You were the twenty-second one in the trial. All have been successfully revived. In every other case, once the patients woke up, we tranquilized them and immediately sent them back to the outside world, so they would have no memory of their time here. But then you came along."

"Wow." She touched the inside of her wrist. Her pulse was strong and steady. It was mind-boggling to think that only a few days earlier, she'd been cold and lifeless. "I need to get to my family. They must be freaking out."

"But if you go home, you yourself said you're risking your life."

"What else can I do?" She scowled. "That asshole broker, I knew he was setting me up."

Galileo raised his eyebrows. "You think he was part of it?"

"Pretty sure. He was going to help me, then he just disappeared—and look what happened."

"Why didn't you go to the police?"

"What could they do? I couldn't prove it. I still can't." But the truth was more complicated: Andy's immigration status was as illegal as ever. She would never risk bringing the authorities into their lives, not even now.

"I have a background in law enforcement," Galileo said. "I might be able to help you."

She felt herself tense. "What kind of background?"

"Ex-FBI. I know a thing or two about trapping bad guys."

"So what's the deal?"

"You have two choices: you can go home, unprotected, and wait for your killer to come after you again. You can rat us out and try to collect the reward money, but this ship would be long gone. We could be anywhere. Of course, we'd rather not have to go. We stay in harbor whenever we need to transport supplies."

Isabel took a sip of water from the paper cup beside her bed. She noticed her hand was shaking. "Or?"

"Or"—he gestured to her cramped room, filled with nothing more than a standard-issue hospital bed, a wooden dresser, and a bathroom so small she could barely turn around—"you can stay here on the ship, under our protection. You agree to let us monitor you as a continuation of the study. So far, we haven't been able to test our subjects for more than a few days, so you present a unique opportunity to see how a human body reacts to the chemicals over a longer time. In exchange, we'll work to bring your killer to justice."

Immediate protests sprang to her lips: what about her family, her television show? Remaining here would derail her whole life. But then again, her killer had done a pretty good job of that already.

"So?" Galileo raised his eyebrows. "What do you think?"

"Could I leave any time?"

"Of course. We don't hold anyone hostage. But once we part ways, you're on your own."

She touched the sore bruises dotting her collarbone. The dull ache was a reminder that her life wasn't the only one at stake—and her death wasn't the only one to avenge. In Richard Barnett's heavy scrapbook of obituaries, how many were victims? How many unwitting clients were still alive, about to be next?

His existence on earth was like ink stuck to paper, bleeding an ever wider circle of carnage. He and his accomplices needed to be found—and destroyed.

"I'll stay," she said. "But only on one condition. And it's a big one."

CHAPTER 20
The Investor

Location Unknown

The phone in his hand felt like the weight of the world. Any second the call was going to come that would start to fix everything. The door to his office was locked tight. His body was rigid in his chair, his eyes bleary from a sleepless night spent imagining the scene taking place thousands of miles away.

The bitch who cut off her breasts to spite him was going to get what she deserved. Then he was going to collect the hush money that would go a long way toward securing his freedom. The person he'd once trusted with his biggest secret was threatening to go to the feds if his capital wasn't released from the fund ASAP. Polite requests were turning to shouts. Excuses could buy him only so much time.

It was running out fast.

The life he'd worked so hard to create was teetering on the brink. *Create* was an accurate term; he was the star of a most realistic type of performance art. The theater was so elaborately built that the set dissolved into the background for every other character involved. To succeed fully was to intoxicate himself into belief, too. He lived for those moments when even he forgot it was all an illusion.

But the recent economic collapse had shattered his buzz. The spiraling layoffs, the mortgages going unpaid, the houses being foreclosed, entire financial institutions vanishing overnight—all unthinkable a year before. His own debts were piling up frighteningly fast. If his panicked partner wasn't now trying to cash out everything at the same time that he needed all the liquid assets for himself, no "lives" would need to die. That wasn't how he liked to do business. It was messy. He hated leaving any room for error in his carefully constructed world. And it went against everything he believed.

But when you were *alone in the wild*, with your back against a wall, you did what you needed to survive. Surely Isabel Leon, the golden goose of all his "lives," understood that better than most.

The phone vibrated in his hand. He brought it to his ear and spoke softly, so no one outside the door could hear.

"Is it done?"

The gruff voice on the line sounded proud. "Yep. Just as you wanted."

"No witnesses?"

"Impossible. We were underwater."

"She's definitely dead?"

"Some EMTs tried to revive her but they gave up. An ambulance took her body away. I stuck around to make sure."

"Good. I'll transfer the rest of your payment now."

"Pleasure doing business with you, sir."

"Believe me—the pleasure is mine."

CHAPTER 21
Joan

New York

Joan raised her fist to knock on the door of Greg's study. It was their last Sunday afternoon at home for the foreseeable future. In just a few days, they were moving into a one-bedroom rental on a dingy street twenty blocks north. A venture capitalist who'd just gotten divorced was going to sublet their furnished penthouse, easing the burden of their $10,500 monthly mortgage.

Though she acted relieved for Greg's sake, she was crushed. Leaving their home was a major sacrifice for not enough benefit. Sure, it helped to downsize, but they were still responsible for the mortgages on the vacant luxury apartments in Hawaii and Florida that had always brought in so much reliable income. Not to mention the astronomical credit card debt. The interest they owed was replicating every day at a cancerous pace.

Yet none of that was her prime concern. Even Adam's fury was not top of mind. A much more dangerous and timely debt needed to be addressed: Some shadowy investor owned Greg's death.

And there was no one he could turn to for help—except her.

She tapped on his door. "Honey," she called, "I'm going out."

"Okay, bye." From inside the study, his voice sounded tense. "Be careful."

The phrase had become his mantra. His eyes roamed the streets when he left the apartment. He worried about simple errands like grocery shopping—the crowded aisles, the blind corners. His paranoia was swelling like a tumor. It was painful to watch, yet she couldn't blame him.

"I will," she called back lightly. *Oh, I will.* Little did he know the risk she was about to take. If she told him, he would try to stop her. Like any good investigative reporter, she knew when to keep mum.

The cab ride to Roosevelt Hospital was a quick shot down West End Avenue to 63rd Street. The building was an imposing white concrete structure that stretched the length of an entire avenue. Whining ambulances came and went from a side entrance in a loop of perpetual crises. The incessant sirens made her plug her ears as she approached the front sliding glass door. A red sign above it read in all caps: EMERGENCY ROOM.

Despite her apprehension, she felt a burst of pride knowing that Greg saved people's lives here three times a week. She almost wished she could tell the staff who she was, just so she could bask in their respect. After the excruciating mess he'd caused at home, some outside positive reinforcement would be gratifying.

But that wouldn't get her very far.

Instead she clutched her chest and scrunched up her face into a look of agony. Then she trudged inside, purposefully tripping a little over her leather flats. Only a few

people were sitting in the waiting room—a teenager holding a skateboard with a cut above his eye, a drunken
homeless man muttering to himself, and a woman texting
on her cell phone in no obvious distress.

Joan's lingering hesitation evaporated. She wasn't about
to displace any patients in need of immediate care. However questionable her actions, as long as she wasn't hurting
anyone, she could plow full steam ahead.

She stumbled to the receptionist's station, where a sour-
faced woman was sitting behind a shield of Plexiglas.

"I think I'm"—Joan winced, squeezing her eyes shut—
"I'm having chest pains. Please." She lifted the back of her
hand to her forehead. "I need a doctor."

The receptionist perked up and reeled off some code
into a microphone. In what seemed like seconds, two
nurses shot to her side with a crash cart, helped her onto a
stretcher, and wheeled her down a sterile hall into a triage
room filled with medical equipment. She lay on her back,
still clutching the spot above her left breast.

"When did the pain start, ma'am?" one nurse asked as
the other one snapped a black cuff around her upper arm
and a clip on her index finger. A broadcast of steady electronic pings filled the room. The square heart monitor at
her side showed a jagged green line rising and falling.

"Um, about an hour ago," she said. "I was, uh, reading
the paper and I just got a crushing feeling in my chest."

"And you didn't call 911?"

"I live close. My doorman got a cab right away."

"Hmm." The nurse on her right, who was taking mea-
surements, frowned at a dial behind Joan's head. "BP's
normal. Heart rate's 82. I don't think you're in cardiac arrest. Do you ever have panic attacks?"

"No." Joan whimpered as if an unbearable pain was

pulverizing her chest. "It hurts. Please. Can you get me Dr. Yardley?"

Dr. Ellis Yardley, Greg's colleague who often worked nights with him in the emergency room, whom she'd never met. He was the one who had confirmed Greg's fears about a suspicious scam winding up in deaths framed as accidents.

The nurse on her left, who was writing in a chart, raised her eyebrows. "Do you know him?"

"No, just heard he's the best." She gulped a shaky breath. "Is he here today?"

The nurse consulted a chart on the wall. "Looks like it."

Of course he is. Joan had called in advance to make sure of it.

"Thank God." She grabbed the woman's gloved hand as though overcome by another spurt of pain. "Will he come fast?"

"I'll page him now. Do you have anyone else you want us to call? Family?"

"No," she said quickly. "My husband's out of town."

"Okay, well, the doctor should be in soon."

The nurse extricated her hand from Joan's grip to go out and make the call, while the other one remained by her side watching the monitors.

Joan curled into the fetal position and buried her face in her arm so she wouldn't have to keep up interactions. The bleeps of the heart monitor were the only sound for several minutes, until a man's figure darkened the doorway.

She rolled onto her back as she heard his footsteps approach her stretcher. She looked up with a suitably anguished expression when he reached her. He seemed about midfifties, same as her and Greg, but unlike her husband, this man sported a receding hairline and a band of flab under his white coat. Red lines snaked across his corneas from having been on call all night.

"I'm Dr. Yardley," he said. "I understand you're having some chest pains?"

She nodded, squirming for good measure. "Thank you for coming so fast."

"Let's see what's going on." The remaining nurse read off her oxygen saturation, blood pressure, and heart rate, while Joan lifted her silk blouse for the doctor. He placed a cold stethoscope on the skin above her breast and listened. After about five seconds, he moved the stethoscope to other spots on her chest and her upper back.

"Does it hurt more when I do this?" he asked, gently pressing two fingers to her chest.

"I think so. A little bit."

"Well, you can't make heart pain worse by pressing on it. And I don't hear anything wrong. Your vitals are perfect."

Behind him, the was nurse eyeing her with a hint of annoyance.

"Oh, well, what could it be? I mean, it really hurts."

"Probably just a musculoskeletal spasm, nothing serious, but I'll send you for a chest X-ray just in case. You'll want to follow up with your regular internist."

He wrote a comment in her chart, then turned to leave.

"Wait," she said, "can I talk to you for a second? Alone?"

He followed the line of her gaze to the nurse, who was still hovering beside the heart monitor. The woman muttered something under her breath, but bowed out and closed the door behind her.

"You seem better," the doctor noted. "You've stopped writhing."

"It's starting to lessen, I think."

"That's great. See, nothing serious."

"Here's the thing," she said, dropping her voice to a low tone. "I think there *is* something serious going on, besides this."

He frowned. "What do you mean?"

"Well, about a month ago I sold my life insurance policy for cash. I used an auction site, so I don't know anything about who bought it. Ever since, I've been feeling like someone's watching me. Then, the other day when I was crossing the street, some jerk pushed me so hard I almost fell in front of a cab. I don't know if it's connected, but I've been having a lot of anxiety about it—maybe that's where the pain is coming from?"

She watched his face carefully for signs of recognition. After all, it was the same story Greg had confessed to him.

But the only expression he let on was wide-eyed bafflement. "That's bizarre."

"Do you know if—have you heard of anyone else experiencing something similar after selling a policy? I just wonder if I'm not alone . . ."

She cast her eyes down, waiting for his reaction. Now her heart was racing, its frantic pings echoing from the monitor. On the screen, her blood pressure was spiking to 145 over 90.

Was he going to give her a crucial lead? Or leave her in the dark? Only her husband's life hung in the balance.

His blank stare told her the answer.

"I'm sorry," he said. "I've never heard of anything like it."

CHAPTER 22
Isabel

Key West

"I'll only stay," Isabel said to Galileo, "if you agree to put my mom and brother up in one of your safe houses until my killer is found. No way am I leaving them behind alone."

She heard the defiance in her voice and worried it might sound ungrateful—after all, he was offering to take on a dangerous mission to help her. But instead of chiding her, his lips spread into a kind smile.

"Naturally," he said, as though all she'd asked for were fresh clothes. "I have just the place in mind. A condo right near the Key West naval station. It's in a gated community."

"With a security guard?" She knew she was pushing it, but she didn't care.

He chuckled, setting her at ease. "That can be arranged."

"Thank you." She let out a breath she didn't realize she was holding. "They're all I have."

"Not true." He rose from his perch on her bed and brushed off his khaki pants. "Now you have us. Deal?"

So what if she had to become a lab rat in the trade? Her mom and Andy were alone and vulnerable. "Deal."

Galileo's capable hand gripped hers in one firm pump.

"They must be worried sick," she said. "Can I go home for a few minutes to see them and get my things?"

"Of course. I'll have Chris escort you. I don't believe you've properly met."

Galileo pulled a black pager device from his pocket and punched in a code. He held it near his mouth. "Chris to deck five, room twelve."

"He was there when I was dead, right? That's why we haven't met 'properly'?"

An awkward pause ensued. She stared at Galileo, expecting him to offer condolences that were bound to feel stilted. There was no social protocol for responding to someone's temporary death.

Instead, with a straight face, he said: "You made one hell of a first impression."

For the first time since waking up, she laughed. "Fair enough."

His blue eyes shone with amusement. "Chris actually assisted in your resuscitation. He's Dr. Quinn's protégé, and he drives the ambulance, so he can take you home and back."

"Great."

"I think you'll like him. He's very—"

A knock on the door cut him off.

"Competent. And there he is." Galileo took two steps and swung it open. At the threshold stood an attractive bear of a guy about a decade older than her. He wore teal surgical scrubs and a face mask around his neck. He was almost as tall as Galileo, but thicker through the chest and arms, like a bouncer. Blond scruff dotted his chin, lending him an endearing ruggedness.

"Hey," Galileo said to him, "am I interrupting your lab work?"

"Quinn can handle it. We were just synthesizing the X101. Supply's real low."

"Ah." A momentary shadow darkened Galileo's face. "Well, if you can spare a little time, Isabel here needs you to take her on a quick errand." He glanced at her, back to business mode. "I'll make some calls to arrange the safe house so your family can go there today if they want."

"Thanks." Isabel tightened her cloth gown around waist. "Nice to meet you," she said to Chris. She swung her legs over the edge of the bed to stand, but when her feet touched the floor, her knees buckled.

In a flash, Galileo's strong arms caught her. "Easy does it. Your body's been through a lot." He helped her sit back down.

"Sorry." Her face burned with embarrassment. She was the most athletic person she knew—and now she couldn't even get out of bed?

"Take your time," Chris said from the doorway. "No rush. I'm here when you need me."

Their eyes met across the room, and Isabel felt a tingle in her chest that she was pretty sure had nothing to do with exhaustion.

Through sheer determination, she forced herself to walk from her cabin to the side plank that unfurled out of the ship and connected to the wooden loading dock below. Her family was no doubt in agony. She wasn't about to make them wait a minute longer to see her. Wearing a pink cotton dress and Birkenstock sandals on loan from a young nurse, she shuffled down the plank to the ambulance, where Chris was standing next to the passenger door.

When she reached him, he extended a hand to help propel her up the high step.

"No more riding in the back for you, young lady," he mock-scolded her.

She just shook her head weakly. Once she was buckled in, she slumped against the soft leather seat. Her fatigue was more severe than after any weeklong episode of filming her show. She felt almost detached from it, like an observer of a foreign phenomenon. *This body weighs ten times normal,* she would report back to the scientists. *Its muscles are leaden jelly.*

She repressed a surge of anger at what they had done to her without her consent. All those chemicals loaded into her veins—who knew if they had any unknown side effects? But that's what they wanted to find out by keeping her around. If there were hidden costs of reversing death, at least she could still breathe and feel and walk and think. She was alive in the fullest sense of the word— not brain-dead. That, she reminded herself, was what mattered.

Yet a nagging unease persisted. Something about this version of her body felt different, and it wasn't the exhaustion . . . Something else she couldn't quite explain.

Chris gunned the engine and they rolled down the dock to the harbor's parking lot. She had never been in an ambulance before—alive, anyway. The front seats were like thrones, straight-backed and high up. A pane of glass separated their section from the cramped interior, where an empty stretcher was surrounded by emergency medical equipment.

As Chris navigated to the main street with the siren off, she stared through the glass at the place where her lifeless body had lain. She couldn't stop herself from picturing it. Flat on her back. Eyes swollen shut. Stuck with tubes and wires.

Someone still wants me that way.

She whipped her head back around to stare out the windshield. A shiver tore down her spine and her body gave an involuntary jerk.

Chris reached for her hand. The familiarity of the gesture surprised her, but felt appropriate. He had helped to save her life. It was only natural that his care would extend to comforting her now.

"How you doin'?" he asked. "Okay?"

"Kind of," she mumbled.

She was grateful he didn't pry. It was stressful enough to anticipate her mother's reaction. They sat in silence for a while, her clammy hand resting in his warm one. She watched the palm trees go by outside. Lazy beach houses with cheerful blue and yellow shutters lined the narrow streets. The sea in the distance reflected the afternoon sun like a piece of smooth glass. Its tranquility calmed her, until she remembered that it had almost been her grave.

She turned instead to glance sidelong at Chris. Having changed from his blue scrubs into a gray T-shirt and jeans, he seemed less authoritative and more like an equal. His rounded, ruddy face looked more angular in profile—his nose jutted out from the soft plains of his cheeks. His dirty blond hair was trimmed short in military style. Resting on the oversized steering wheel, his fingers were long and bony, with short clean nails. Watching him maneuver around the traffic, Isabel thought of Galileo's word: *competent.*

"So, what's your deal?" she asked him, partly to distract herself, but also out of real curiosity. "How did you end up in this secret network?"

He smiled coyly, keeping his eyes on the road. "I was recruited like everyone else."

"How does that happen? Or can you not say?"

He paused, as if calibrating how much to reveal. "Dr. Quinn got me in," he finally said. "I worked in his lab at Harvard back in the day. We came as a package deal."

"Two for the price of one?"

"Something like that."

The effort of making conversation sapped her scarce energy, but she was intrigued.

"So you guys all live and work on the ship full-time?"

"Pretty much." He pulled his hand away from hers to turn the wheel sharply. Her left palm was sweaty and exposed on the glove box. She didn't want him to think he had to hold it again, so she tucked it under her thigh.

"And no one knows where you are?" she said. "What about your family?"

"I told my parents I had to go away for a special fellowship abroad. It's not like they think I'm dead or something."

"What if you want to, like, get married and have kids one day?"

His tone was noncommittal. "If the time comes, I'll feel it out. I'm a spur-of–the-moment kind of guy."

"Then we're opposites. Before this happened to me, I was on a reality survival show, and I'd always plan my strategy a month ahead."

He raised his eyebrows. "You mean you're a control freak?"

The way he said it was more affectionate than insulting. "Totally," she admitted. "I'm not good at being spontaneous."

"I'll show you." With a roguish smile, he pressed a red button on his dashboard and the siren squealed to life,

howling overhead. It was like being in the belly of a crying wolf. She plugged her ears, but Chris was only getting
started.

He slammed on the gas and accelerated through a con-
gested intersection as the other cars dutifully pulled over.
She gripped the hanging strap near her window as he careened around a corner. They passed a middle school,
where a cluster of cars waiting in line for afternoon pickup
scrambled to get out of their way.

"You're so bad," she yelled over the siren.

"You're in a rush to get home, aren't you?" he shouted
back.

She couldn't argue with that. The ride was exhilarat-
ing, if a bit dizzying. Chris expertly avoided obstacles on
the road, hardly letting up on the gas to swerve around
cars and bikes who didn't pull over fast enough.

Her stomach flipped when she noticed they were pulling
up to her street. He slowed down to scout the addresses on
the houses. She pointed him toward the one-story bungalow
at the end of the block, with its leafy oak tree shading the
porch. Its faded leaves littered the ground as though
someone had forgotten to sweep for a few days.

He turned off the siren as he pulled into the driveway.
She was as breathless as if she'd sprinted a mile.

"Do you want me to come in with you?"

"No thanks, it shouldn't be long."

Already she could see the front door opening and her
mother's face peeking out with a look of concern. Ambulances weren't commonly found roaring down their block.

At the sight of her mother's mostly bald scalp, Isabel's
heart swelled. Thin strands of black hair were growing
back in fuzzy patches, a testament to her recovery, but
also to her fragility. In only two days of being away, Isabel

noticed how gaunt her cheeks had become. Her eyelids were pink and puffy.

"Mom!" she called, jumping out and rushing up to her, forgetting all about her fatigue.

Her mother's fingertips flew to her lips. She sagged against the doorframe, her face draining so fast that Isabel reached out to catch her.

But instead of collapsing, she grabbed her daughter into the tightest embrace possible. "Oh my God, oh my God."

Isabel's innermost organs practically squeezed together, but she was grinning. All she wanted was to breathe in her mother's familiar gardenia perfume and never let go.

"Is it really you?" her mom breathed into her hair.

"It's me. I'm okay."

A shaky whisper came out: "I thought you were dead."

Isabel gently pulled away. "I was . . ."

Her mother's eyes opened so wide that the whites were visible around her green irises. "What? What happened? I couldn't find you at the hospital, the police had no record, you just completely vanished!" Tears spilled over her lids. "Andy and I thought we might never see you again!"

Isabel hugged her frail body. It was quivering. "I'm so sorry. I can explain."

"I know you've been hiding something—Oh God, I didn't want to believe it, but . . . honey, did someone really try to kill you?"

Isabel let out a gasp. "How could you know that?"

Her mother ran into the house and promptly returned with a plain red notebook.

"This came in the mail for you today."

Isabel took it and flipped to the opening page.

In neat cursive, it read: *The Diary of Richard Barnett.*

Her lips curled in revulsion at the sight of his name.

"What is this? Some kind of sick joke?" She flung it to the ground.

"Hey!" Her mother picked it up, wiping off a speck of dirt.

Isabel was so furious she could barely contain her rage. She wanted to pluck the stupid diary out of her mother's hands and hurl it across the street.

"You don't get it, that asshole was playing me the whole time! He has to be found and arrested."

Her mom seemed strangely unconvinced. "Are you sure?"

"He disappeared right when he was supposed to help me. Next thing I know I'm being attacked. Clearly he was in on my death benefits."

"I don't think so."

"How would you know?"

She thrust the diary into Isabel's hands with surprising force. "Because he's dead. He killed himself for you."

CHAPTER 23
Isabel

Key West

Isabel seized the diary and skimmed the pages as fast as she could. Richard Barnett's careful handwriting revealed a more complicated man than she'd understood him to be. A sincere cynic. A caring loner. Hardened by death, but afraid of his own. Unwittingly complicit in a horrific scheme. Racked by guilt. Hoping for redemption through a single-malt Scotch and a bottle of Prozac.

Most shocking, the diary revealed that he'd watched his own father collapse, too. A swell of sympathy rose inside her. All this time she'd dismissed him as a callous villain, they'd shared their deepest tragedies in common without even knowing it.

When she finished reading, she looked up with a sickening feeling of remorse. The final entry was dated November 5—three days earlier.

"See?" Her mother's eyes were glassy. "The poor guy really was trying to help."

But Isabel was already a step ahead. "Where's the package this came in?"

"There." Her mom pointed to a torn manila envelope on the kitchen counter. "How come?"

Isabel made a frantic beeline to it. She flipped it over to see the return address: 307 Olivia Street.

His house was only ten minutes away, right near the famed Ernest Hemingway mansion. She'd passed it a thousand times without realizing it.

Behind her came light footsteps, then a soft hand on her shoulder. "Honey, are you okay? What's going on?"

She whirled around. "I have to go. It might not be too late . . ." She gave her mom a quick kiss on the cheek. "I'll explain everything soon, I promise."

With the envelope in hand, she sprinted for the door.

"Too late for what?" her mom called to her retreating figure.

She glanced over her shoulder as she ran out. "To bring him back."

Chris took one look at her face and turned on the siren without even asking why. The instant she climbed in, he gunned the engine, checked the rearview, and zoomed out of the driveway.

"307 Olivia," she panted. "Go."

Once they were out of her neighborhood, Chris shouted over the blaring noise. "Who's in trouble?"

"This guy . . ." She trailed off, realizing she had no idea how to explain their relationship.

"What guy?"

A man who'd sold her into murder without knowing it? Who was paying the worst possible price to make it up to her?

"A friend," she said at last. "He sent me a suicide note and he's all alone. We might already be too late."

"Oh, man." Chris pumped the gas harder and the ambulance lurched forward, throwing her against her seat belt.

In only five minutes, they reached his street, a cul-de-sac punctuated with palm trees, well-tended gardens, and sleepy pastel-painted cottages. Number 307 was a squat, unremarkable house that seemed half forgotten. The paint was gray and peeling. The lawn was overgrown with tall brown grass. A bed of yellow roses was wilting in the sun. The navy shutters over the front window were closed, except for one broken slat that didn't turn sideways like the rest.

As soon as they pulled up to the curb, they hopped out and raced to the door. Isabel knocked loudly. Nothing happened. Turned the knob. It was locked.

"I know he's in there!"

Chris approached the front window and peered with both hands into the spot left uncovered by the broken slat. When he turned to her, his face was solemn.

"Oh God." Her throat tightened. "You can see him?"

"I'm sorry."

"We have to get in!"

He tried to slide the window up but it wouldn't budge.

She edged past him to a wooden side door that led to the backyard. It was easy to reach her finger up over the latch to unlock it. She mustered all her energy to follow Chris down a narrow concrete path along the side of the house, which opened up to a fenced-in lawn with a patio table and a chaise longue.

He tugged at the obviously locked back door, but she stopped him with a whisper.

"Wait! Do you hear that?"

He froze, listening. A few birds were chirping on nearby branches. A car drove by somewhere in the distance. "No, what?"

"A TV." Very faintly, Isabel could make out the hum of voices and dim musical chords—so dim that they could almost be mistaken for the wind.

He cocked his head. "How the hell did you notice that?"

She shrugged and rushed around the side of the house where the sound was coming from. Five feet up the wall, a large window was open an inch. A light ocean breeze billowed out its sheer white curtains. Pressing her palms on the cool glass, she slid it up the rest of the way. Chris hoisted her up inside, then climbed in after her. She found herself in Richard Barnett's bedroom. Navy sheets were crumpled on the floor next to his unmade bed. With Chris on her heels, she followed the increasingly loud television sounds out to a hallway, past a kitchen, a bathroom, and finally to a living room at the front of the house.

Though she knew what was coming, a cry burst out of her when she saw him. Unconscious.

He was lying on his back at the foot of an old rocking chair, clothed in a T-shirt and black mesh shorts. His legs were bent at the knees and one arm was flung up near his head. His face was sallow, his lips dumbly parted. Vomit stuck to his chin. It had pooled on the floor beside him, soaking the neck of his white shirt in bile. The stench filled the room, sour and vaguely alcoholic. On his coffee table, an empty glass tumbler sat next to an empty orange prescription bottle.

Isabel dashed to his side and cupped his cheeks. His hazel eyes were open but unblinking. It was like staring into the face of his wax figure. She almost expected the real him to saunter in, puffing on a cigarette, and call off the horrifying charade.

Chris knelt beside her and pressed two fingers to his wrist.

"Is he really—?"

"I'm afraid so."

"But can you still do something?"

Chris lifted up his shirt to examine his chest and mus-cle tone. "Body's cool but not cold. No signs of rigor mortis yet. I've seen cases like this before—someone tries to OD, passes out, then vomits in their sleep. That probably kept him alive for a couple days but unconscious. Seems like he actually only died within the last few hours."

Her heart gave a hopeful lurch that was immediately tempered by her own knowledge of emergency first aid. Everyone knew that a person without a pulse stood little chance of regaining any brain function after four minutes without oxygen. But what if that was outdated now? She had a sudden flash of her father's crumpled body and her own helplessness—and all at once, she sank to her knees to pump Richard's chest as hard as she could.

"What are you doing?" Chris demanded.

"Not—standing—around," she huffed, as the fatigue of her biceps threatened to derail her efforts.

"What makes you think it's not too late?"

She shot him a pointed glance. "I'm alive."

Chris stared at Richard's body, avoiding her gaze. "His brain cells are dying as we speak, but they're not fully gone until about four to eight hours after death." He paused. "I guess I could give him a dose of the X101 to try to buy time—"

She jumped to her feet, her arms rubbery and limp. "Then what are you waiting for?"

"You said he wanted this!" He glared at her. "We're not supposed to intervene against someone's will."

"Are you kidding me?" Her voice was shaking. "You have the power to bring him back and you're just going to let him *die*?"

"He's already dead."

"You know what I mean!"

Chris pressed two fingers to his temples, blinking fast. "But what if we bring him back and he's brain-damaged? I mean, we don't know exactly how long it's been, and the longer that goes by, the worse the prognosis."

"We have to try. He's a good person, he deserves a chance." She didn't add that she felt partly responsible for his suicide. If she hadn't gotten her mastectomy, then she wouldn't have provoked the investor's ire and Richard's attempts at appeasement. Then he wouldn't have seen his death as a solution.

Chris was still shaking his head, so she squeezed her eyes shut and tried to recall everything Dr. Quinn had explained about her own resuscitation when she'd first woken up. Cooling down the body was key. *Therapeutic hypothermia,* he'd called it.

An image popped into her mind of frozen peas. Didn't everyone have them? She ran to the kitchen and whipped open his freezer. Sure enough, there were two bags of peas, plus a chilled bottle of Ketel One vodka and an ice pack. She piled all of it into her arms and rushed back to his body, dropping to her knees beside his head. She lay the ice pack on his forehead, then the peas on his neck.

Chris stepped aside to get out of her way. "It's no use. He needs the X101, plus chest compressions, an internal ice slurry, oxygenated fat molecules, an ECMO—"

"Then help me!" she screamed. "Don't just stand there!"

He stuck his hands in his jeans pockets. "Do no harm," he muttered.

But she could see his resolve weakening.

"Exactly," she said. "He's dead, you can't make him worse. But if he has any chance at all and you walk away, you're neglecting the one patient who needs you the most!"

"Okay, but if he comes back brain-dead, that's on you."

"I'm not, am I?"

Before he could reply, she marched out the front door to the ambulance and opened the back to get the stretcher. It was light enough for her to carry on her own, though she could feel the rubbery fatigue of her muscles cutting down her strength with each passing minute.

Back in the house, she set it down next to Richard's body, while Chris lugged him under the armpits onto it. She strained to lift his heavy legs as best she could. Once he was flat on his back on the stretcher, Chris single-handedly dragged him outside and hauled him into the ambulance.

The street was deserted, but they wasted no time shutting the doors to any curious onlookers. She squatted on a side seat and held Richard's limp hand as Chris got to work.

After setting a helmet-sized machine on his chest that began to deliver hard and fast compressions, Chris intubated him and connected him to a portable oxygen tank. Then he touched a finger sensor under the rubber floor pad that unlocked a compartment in the roof. Cracks materialized in the white overhead space and a door slid open. Inside was a vial of a clear liquid next to a bag of saline and a plethora of medical devices.

He retrieved a red tool that resembled a handgun, with a long thick needle sticking out the barrel. He was moving so rapidly there was no time to explain anything, so she just watched in fascinated silence as he pressed the gun against Richard's left shoulder and fired a pin into the bone. He repeated the process with the other shoulder and both knees.

Then he reached up into the compartment and care-

fully removed the glass vial, cradling it in both hands like
it was a baby bird.

"This is it," he said. "This is everything."

"The X101?"

"Yes."

She noticed his hands were trembling as he drew about
two ounces of the liquid into a clear plastic dropper, emp-
tying the vial, and injected it straight into Richard's left
shoulder pin. Without further ceremony, he deposited the
empty vial back into the compartment and hastened to the
next step: injecting the right shoulder with a slurry of ice.

"Is there anything I can do?" she asked, desperate to be
useful.

"Yeah." He paused for a split second. "Drive us back to
the ship. And make it fast."

The ambulance shrieked down the street so quickly
that there was no time to notice the silver Toyota Camry
rolling twenty yards behind it.

The driver inside was gaping in disbelief, holding a
cell phone at his ear.

He spoke in a hushed voice as though to soften the
blow:

"I have bad news, sir. She's alive."

"Yeah, right," said the voice on the other end. "That's
impossible."

"It's her. I'm sure of it."

There was a pause. The voice seethed with accusation.
"You saw her dead body with your own damn eyes, didn't
you? Carted off the beach to the morgue?"

"I—I thought so."

"You're losing your mind. Find me her death certificate ASAP. And if you want any cut of the payout, make it today."

"Yes, s—"

But the line clicked off. The phone dropped to his lap.

He wasn't crazy no matter what the boss said.

Isabel Leon, the prime target of all the "lives," had somehow cheated death.

Her ambulance was barreling through a stoplight two blocks ahead, its lights flashing red and blue. He floored his own gas pedal.

No way was he letting it out of his sight.

CHAPTER 24
Joan

New York

The busy hum of the hospital carried on around Joan as if she wasn't even there. Nurses and doctors bustled past her, consulting charts, shouting commands, assisting patients on stretchers who required actual care.

Now that she was no longer in distress from her "chest pains," she was a nonentity. Greg's colleague Dr. Yardley had written her a prescription for a muscle relaxant and pointed her toward the exit. But his odd denial of any familiarity with Greg's near-death experience piqued her suspicion. What was he hiding? Did any of the other staff know?

She stood in the hallway outside the triage room, thinking fast. This was her only conceivable opportunity to be inside the hospital, behind the scenes, without anyone tending to her. She consulted a map on the wall. To the left, down a hallway, was the reception station and exit. To the right, around a corner, was the on-call room, and next to that, the nurses' locker room.

A plan formed in her mind. Before she had time to iron out the details, she was striding to the on-call room, her chin held high. In her black pants, cream cashmere sweater, and impeccable makeup, she could have been an executive. She knocked on the white door. No one answered.

She went in and locked it behind her. The space resembled a cramped dorm, if the students who lived there were slobs. Next to a closet were a bunk bed and two cots. Sheets were tangled and bed covers kicked to the floor as if the prior occupants had fled in a hurry. In the corner, blue scrubs were overflowing out of a hamper whose top was askew.

She saw her opportunity right away. It would be risky, but she needed to act fast if she was going to do it. Any minute someone else might try to come in. She tore off her sweater and pants and stuffed them into her oversized handbag. Then she pawed through a pile of clean scrubs in the closet, looking for a woman's size medium. When she found a set, she threw it on, along with a fresh pair of hospital-issue shoe covers from a stack in the corner.

She looked at herself in the mirror hanging over the door. Her cheeks were flushed and a few mussed tendrils of blond hair hung around her face. Her red lipstick was all wrong, though. What nurse had time for that? She rubbed it off with the back of her hand. *Not bad,* she thought. She removed her pearl stud earrings for good measure.

Then she stuffed her purse under a heap of clothes in the closet and slipped out, heading to the adjacent door down the hall: the nurses' locker room. Here she didn't bother to knock, just walked right in like she belonged.

This room was larger, like the locker room at her gym. Two nurses around Joan's age were chatting near a row of sinks with their backs to her—from the sound of it, not just chatting, but gossiping.

"Well, that's not what I heard," said one, a plump woman with tortoiseshell glasses. "I heard that he—"

Joan coughed. They turned to stare blankly at her. Before any skepticism set in, she plastered on a bright smile and stuck out her hand, walking toward them.

"Hi," she said, "I'm Jane. I don't think we've met yet. I'm from Presbyterian uptown. Just started here in the ER."

"Welcome," said the other nurse, a raven-haired woman with judgmental brown eyes. "I'm Louisa, from OB." They shook hands.

"And I'm Sharon, from peds," the matronly nurse said in a friendlier tone. "Whose service are you usually on?"

"Dr. Hughes," she said. It felt oddly formal to refer to Greg that way, but the other women didn't seem to notice her self-consciousness.

"Oh!" Sharon exclaimed with a knowing look. "Lucky you."

Joan raised her eyebrows in real curiosity. "Yeah?"

"He's kind of a rock star around here. We all have a little crush on him," Sharon admitted. She sighed, pushing away her bangs, and Joan saw that her left finger was bare.

"He's a total professional, though," Louisa said, as though this annoyed her. "He'll barely flirt with anyone."

"We're used to it." Sharon shrugged. "He must have one hot wife."

Louisa smirked. "Or at least a talented one."

Joan gave her a tight smile. "I'll bet." Then she lowered her voice in a conspiratorial manner. "Hey, can you ladies keep a secret?"

They nodded and moved in closer, even though no one else was around. "You can trust us," Sharon soothed. "What's up?"

"Well." Joan bit her lip, as if deciding whether to tell them. "I overheard something kind of scary actually . . ."

They stared at her with open intrigue. Louisa crossed her arms. "Go on . . ."

"I happened to hear Hughes and Yardley talking. Apparently Hughes sold his life insurance policy and then almost got hit by a car after some stranger pushed him."

Their mouths fell open.

"Wait." Joan held up a hand. "It gets creepier. Then Yardley told him one or two patients *at this hospital* died in weird accidents after selling their life policies . . . And he wondered if maybe the incidents are all somehow connected . . . ?"

They both recoiled with looks of horror. Joan couldn't quite read the glance they exchanged.

"Jesus," Sharon breathed. Louisa said nothing.

"Could that be true?" Joan said. "Have you heard anything?"

Sharon shook her head firmly. "I haven't."

"And she would," Louisa said. "She always has the inside scoop."

"Weird." Joan couldn't press further without giving herself away, so she just lifted one shoulder as if to say *Who knows?*

"Well," she said, "I've got to get back to a patient, but it was nice meeting you guys."

She turned around before they could see the extent of her disappointment—and her mistrust. Why was the staff denying rumors that Greg said were swirling around the entire hospital? Were they scared to talk?

No matter how tough, she was going to dig up the truth before it was too late. Before Greg was next.

CHAPTER 25
Isabel

Key West

Isabel stared at the contours of Richard's face. His skin was no longer tinted gray. Signs of life had returned in his pink lips, the black stubble pricking his chin, the twitching of his closed eyelids. She felt his forehead. It was warm. Anyone else might have mistaken his state for a peaceful sleep. The crisp bedsheets were pulled up to his chin, and his head had fallen to its right side on the pillow. His breathing was deep and even through his nose. But no matter how normal he looked, Isabel knew not to be deceived. If his mind was gone, then he was still just a body, albeit a living one.

In the three days since his emergency resuscitation procedure, she'd kept vigil near his body with competing sensations of awe and terror. The events over the last seventy-two hours were remarkable to witness. Even though she knew that reversing death was possible—that she, herself, was proof—she was still astonished to watch firsthand how far science had advanced in this hidden corner of the world.

When they first arrived on the ship, Dr. Quinn immediately took his corpse into surgery, pumping his stomach of toxins and clearing the clogged artery near his heart. Over the first twenty-four hours, as Quinn raised his temperature by a quarter of a degree Celsius every hour, Richard's pulse had returned—followed by faint brain waves. He briefly opened his eyes and let out inarticulate moans. Isabel panicked about his mental capacity, but Dr. Quinn reassured her that the drugs caused incoherence at first, and would wear off in two days.

Then it would become clear if he was doomed to a minimally conscious state—not dead, but not properly alive either. Isabel hadn't slept since, fearing Chris might have been right all along. She was grateful to him for cooperating with her pleas, but his warning echoed in her mind with the frightening ring of truth: *If he comes back brain-dead, that's on you.* How could she forgive herself if that was his future—one she had insisted upon against his will?

Would the Network be forced to support a shell of a man indefinitely? Would he have to suffer for the rest of his days? That would be intolerable, especially since he wanted to die in the first place. If he *was* brain-damaged, maybe they could withdraw life-sustaining nutrients from his IV, allowing him to die passively. But starving him seemed cruel. Maybe they could euthanize him with a painless injection? But then they would be killing him like an animal.

Each thought made her squirm more than the last. From her perch on a stool beside his bed, Isabel glanced at the clock on the wall. The time marked 4:35 P.M., almost exactly forty-eight hours since his initial awakening. If he was ever going to come out of his stupor, it would happen any minute now. The longer it took, the lower his likelihood of ever regaining normal brain function.

She tried to distract herself from the ticking clock on the wall by thinking about her mom and Andy. With Galileo's help, she had called them from the ship using a satellite phone and explained everything. Incredulous at first, but at last accepting, her mother agreed to Galileo's offer to move to the safe house until the mastermind behind her murder was found. As soon as the plan was made, her family packed up their things, closed up their house, and drove straight to their new address. From there, her mom would take every safety precaution—pulling Andy out of school, bringing him to work with her at the bookstore—until Isabel had an update to share. Her mom also did her the favor of contacting her television agent and the producers of *Wild Woman* to let them know she was extending her medical leave until further notice.

It was torturous on her family to be separated. But her mother complied without argument, since Isabel's only other strategy was to leave the Network and go to the official authorities, which risked Andy being found out and deported back to Cuba—his worst nightmare. At least at their temporary house, they were out of harm's way, so Isabel could worry about her other problems: Richard, her killer, and her own disturbing new symptom that she hadn't told anyone about yet.

A knock on the door startled her. Galileo and Dr. Quinn walked in, both wearing drawstring shorts and T-shirts, but their concerned expressions were far from casual. She greeted them with a nod as they somberly approached Richard's bed. They came to a stop on either side of her stool.

"No change?" Dr. Quinn asked her.

"None." She sighed. "I've been watching him like a hawk."

Galileo put a hand on her shoulder. "How are you holding up? Remember, you have your own recovery to focus on."

"Your body's in a delicate state right now," Dr. Quinn added. "We want you to cut down on stress as much as possible."

She gave a snort. "Why not run a marathon while I'm at it?"

"I know it's hard," Galileo said, looking from Richard to her. "But you're not alone. Don't think I've forgotten our deal."

"That's great, but how can you find someone who doesn't want to be found?" She shook her head. "It's impossible." *And I can't hide out here forever,* she thought.

Plain and simple, she was screwed. Staying here was only buying time until her inevitable return to the outside world. Even if she and her family permanently relocated somewhere—easier said than done—she'd always look behind her shoulder, wondering when the next hit was coming.

"I'm working out a strategy," Galileo assured her. And then, without irony: "Trust me."

She almost snorted again. That was like commanding a blind person to look. But she didn't expect him to understand how deeply she'd been scarred. Even the most brilliant scientist couldn't change the fact that the world was a dark place, crammed with disease and heartbreak and evil. Things didn't work out just because you wanted them to.

"Okay," she said anyway, to humor him. "When will you start?"

"As soon as I've figured out the best approach. But in the meantime, we're worried about you. You've been holed up here for two days. Have you even slept?"

She said nothing, just kept her eye on Richard's chest rising and falling under the blanket. The clock read 4:51 P.M. *Any minute now,* she thought. *Come on.*

Dr. Quinn cleared his throat. "Isabel, as much as we want to learn from your recovery, we're also here to help guide you through it."

"I'm not exactly thinking about myself right now."

"Understandable," Galileo said, "but you should be. If you're having any side effects besides generalized weakness, it's important to tell us. Especially if something doesn't feel right."

She hesitated. The symptom she'd started to notice was so strange and unexpected that she wondered if she was hallucinating it. The possibility terrified her—was she losing her mind? If so, she didn't want confirmation from the doctors. But she had to uphold her end of the deal, too.

"There might be one," she began. She kept her eyes on Richard's sleeping face.

Dr. Quinn's white eyebrows shot almost to his hairline. "What?"

"I have this, like, sudden hyperawareness. Like my senses are on overdrive."

Copping to it made her face burn; she felt like a freak.

"How so?" Galileo asked.

"Well, when we went to Richard's house, we couldn't get in at first, and then I heard the sound of his TV through a side window that was barely open. Chris didn't notice at all, but I did without trying. That's just one example. Even now, it's happening. I can't turn it off."

The intrigue was palpable in Dr. Quinn's tone. "What are you sensing now?"

"You had a tuna sandwich for lunch," she said, "before you brushed your teeth with peppermint toothpaste."

He sank to the edge of Richard's bed. "How could you know that?"

"I smell it on your breath. And you think I didn't catch the look on your face just now, but I did."

"What look?"

"Validation. You expected this, didn't you?"

Dr. Quinn exchanged a rueful glance with Galileo, who was still standing at her side. "You're right. I'm not surprised. In the dog trials, the X101 strengthened parts of the cerebral cortex involved with sensory perception."

"So I'm not imagining it," she said.

"Not at all. It shouldn't do any damage, but I can understand if it's unsettling."

She let out a breath. "Will it ever go away?"

"It should, once your body metabolizes the drug."

"How long?"

He rubbed his nose as a distant look came into his eyes. "We don't exactly know. We'll keep testing its concentration in your blood every day. My best guess is about two weeks."

"I think some car was following the ambulance the

other day," she blurted out. As long as she was telling them her symptom, she might as well disclose all her fears.

Galileo's reaction was swift and fierce. "Why didn't you tell me?"

"I thought the hyperaware thing might be making me paranoid. Anyway, I got rid of it pretty fast driving through red lights."

"So no one saw you pull into the harbor?"

"I don't think so. But I can't go back out there anytime soon. Someone's definitely still after me."

"Well, we can't stay here anymore," he said, heading for the door. "Time for the open ocean."

"I'm sorry." She looked down at her hands folded tightly in her lap. "I don't want to complicate your whole operation . . ."

She saw by his grimace that it was already too late for that. But just as he opened his mouth to speak, another voice filled the room. It was hoarse, rasping—and utterly familiar:

"Where am I?"

Her head whipped around. To her astonishment, Richard's eyes were fluttering open. He was struggling to raise himself up on his elbows. She leaped off the stool to his side, with Dr. Quinn and Galileo right behind her.

"Oh my God," she breathed. "Richard?"

After a hazy moment, his eyes focused on hers. Then a grin of recognition spread across his face. "Isabel? Are we in heaven?"

Her eyes watered as immense gratitude overwhelmed her. "No, you were saved. We both were."

His grin vanished. "No." His head sank back on the pillow as if in defeat.

"You're alive," she tried again. "It worked. You made it."

"We're both alive?"

She smiled. "Yes. Thanks to these men." She gestured to Quinn and Galileo.

Richard regarded them with a bewildered frown. "But I was supposed to die." His tone grew panicked as he glanced back at her. "Or else you will."

"She was never admitted to the morgue, sir." The man spoke timidly into the phone. "There is no death certificate. No trace of her anywhere."

"But you saw her *dead body* wash up on the beach!" snapped the voice on the other end.

"Then she must have come back to life."

"Do you hear how idiotic you sound?"

"She's still alive," the man insisted. "I told you, I saw her the other day, driving an ambulance for some reason." He didn't add that he tried to trail her and was thrown off by her ability to speed through every goddamn intersection.

"Oh yeah?" The voice was a snarl. "I want hard proof. Your eyes don't count."

"I—I don't have that, sir. She hasn't returned home since."

"Then find her. If this is true, I want to find out exactly how the hell she survived."

Just before the phone clicked off, the man cried out. "Wait! I do have something else you might find useful. Not about her."

An exasperated sigh came over the line. "What?"

"Her family. After she disappeared, I went back to

watch her house, and saw a woman and a boy leave with a couple of suitcases. But they didn't see me follow."

"So you know where they went?"

"I'm watching their new house as we speak."

There was a pause. "Get me intel on them. Maybe you're not so useless after all."

CHAPTER 26
Isabel

The Atlantic Ocean

"You know, you don't look half bad." Isabel smiled. "For a recently dead guy."

She was sitting at Richard's bedside in his cabin on the ship, two days after his return to coherence. He lay with his head propped up on two fluffy white pillows, his bandaged chest rising and falling with his breath. Though he seemed as fatigued as she'd been at first, she could tell his mind was razor sharp. He threw her a withering glance, despite the twinkle in his eye.

"You're looking a little gray yourself."

"You've just never seen me without makeup."

"Oh, is that all?" He cracked a smile. "We're in the same boat, babe. Literally."

"Very funny."

She cringed when she remembered that only a few days earlier, she'd been convinced that he was culpable for her murder. How badly she'd misjudged him! Now there could no longer be any question that he was an ally. He had died for her. It was such an extreme gesture that she almost felt embarrassed, especially given the feelings he'd laid bare in his diary. When she thought about what he'd written, in light of everything, she was struck with admiration. How many men these days were that committed to honor at any cost? The only other one she'd known like that had been her dad. She wished she could make it up to him somehow—or at least refrain from upsetting him. She was glad that since he was still mostly bedridden, he hadn't yet seen her and Chris flirting.

In the several days since his awakening, she'd filled him in on her murder, the Network, and the deal she and Galileo had struck. Richard was amazed by the drug and the doctors who had saved both their lives, and offered to give back however he could. So he was going to stay on the ship while they monitored his recovery as well as hers; two longer-term patients in the clinical trial were better than one.

He also insisted on helping Galileo track down the mysterious investor known as Robbie Merriman. His own guilt ran deep. He admitted that he'd been duped for years—selling his clients' "lives" to a professional voice over the phone, receiving prompt checks in return, never thinking twice. He was appalled to think of how many victims he might have sold to the man he'd believed was his best customer. And to think that his own suicide would have been a wasted attempt at appeasement; the sociopath was ruthless enough to target Isabel anyway.

Now she was trying to distract him from his anger, since there was nothing he could do at present but focus on his own recovery. But there was a niggling confession she felt she owed him. It slipped out before she could stop herself.

"It was my fault," she said. "Your resuscitation. I made them do it."

His eyes locked on hers. "Fault?"

"I mean, my . . . doing. I've been terrified you might end up brain-dead because I forced Chris to give you the X101, even though you wanted to die. I made him go against your wishes."

Richard drew a long breath, and she feared he was angry. Then he spoke, slowly, as if to convey his deliberateness. His gaze never wavered from her face.

"I never wanted to die. You deserved to live, and I thought it was one or the other."

"So you don't hold it against me?"

"Are you crazy? I have my life back. And this time, I don't intend to live it lying down." He struggled to push himself up on his elbows.

"Hey, you don't have to—"

"Mark my words," he interrupted. "I will fight to destroy that psycho if it's the last thing I do."

When Galileo called her and Richard up to the top deck for a private meeting the next day, Isabel felt privileged. In less than a week on the ship, she'd learned how in demand Galileo was—every researcher wanted his ear. In a few words, he explained his master plan. It was ready. Now he just needed their help to execute it.

She excitedly rolled Richard in a wheelchair from his cabin to the elevator. He was gritting his teeth from the effort of simply holding up his head. A paper hospital gown clung to his bony figure, covering his bandages, and a white chenille blanket lay draped across his lap. Despite his obvious infirmity, she couldn't help thinking that he looked manly. Maybe it was the sheer determination in his eyes, or his complete lack of self-pity.

"You okay?" she asked. "Do you want to delay this a few days?"

He glanced up at her, and she knew there was nothing he wanted more than to go on with the show. He didn't have to say anything for her to nod and wheel him out of the elevator and onto the top deck.

While she was feeling stronger every day, he was recovering more slowly because of the additional surgery to correct his heart blockage and stenosis, performed by a cardiothoracic surgeon on board named Dr. Powell. The good news was that his prognosis was excellent. When he learned he had a future beyond age forty-five, unlike his father and grandfather, he'd turned to Isabel with glassy eyes.

Did you hear that? I'm going to get old!

If he could walk, she was sure there would be a hop in his step. So it was no wonder he couldn't stand to lie in bed, especially given their vendetta against a mysterious—and lethal—criminal.

Through the glass walls of the deck, they could see the gleaming blue sea stretching for miles in every direction. The ship had sailed far enough out that the island of Key West appeared no larger than a coffee bean on the western horizon.

They greeted Galileo, who was sitting at a white leather booth around a table that had once been part of a cocktail lounge in the ship's former life. A polished white bar a few feet away had been converted to storage space for lab equipment—microscopes lined the shelves instead of martini glasses; bottles held hard chemicals instead of hard alcohol. Empty leather booths next to theirs formed a perimeter around a parquet dance floor. A disco ball still hung above it, sprinkling silver flashes like confetti around the expansive room. Once Isabel and Richard took their seats at the table, Galileo gave them a mischievous grin.

"Check this out." He opened his clenched palm.

In it, a breathtaking oval ruby in a gold band glowed like a drop of deep red Merlot. It was rimmed by what seemed to be tiny twinkling diamonds.

"It's certainly flashy." Isabel snatched it, inspecting its perfectly cut edges. "Looks real. Feels real."

Galileo smiled. "Good sign if a woman approves."

Richard plucked it out of her palm and turned it around with two fingers. "Do you think it will work?"

"I think it's our best shot," Galileo said. "As long as you're willing to do your part."

"I'm all in," Richard declared, setting the ruby ring on the table. His elbow brushed against hers as he reached for the cell phone in Galileo's other hand.

"You sure you're up for this?" Galileo eyed the paper hospital gown draped over his bandaged chest. "We can wait—"

Richard shot him a look as if to say *Are you kidding?*

"Fine," Galileo said, surrendering the phone. "I had to make sure."

"I'm ready." There was no trace of his typical cynicism—only steely resolve.

Sitting beside him, Isabel realized how lucky she was that he had made it. Before his arrival, there'd been practically nothing to go on: The shred of black cloth lodged in her mouth from a scuba diver's suit—certainly not enough to ID whoever had drowned her, or who that person might have been working for. Then there was the mastermind's voice on the phone. He could be anyone, anywhere. But Richard had dialed him so often to make deals, he knew the number by heart.

Even with the Network helping her, she shuddered to think where she would be without Richard. Together they were real survivors, hell-bent on justice.

Galileo's blue eyes were laser-focused on him. "You're good with the script?"

"I got this." His voice was firm, but Isabel wondered whether he could actually pull off such a bold scheme, which Galileo had described moments before.

She watched Richard punch in the number for the man who called himself Robbie Merriman—though there were hundreds of people named that, and no way to differentiate among them.

Richard clicked on the speakerphone as it rang. Once, twice. She gritted her teeth. If no one answered, they'd be back to square one. Three rings. Four. Five. She traded a dismayed look with Galileo—right before a gravelly voice barked into the silence:

"Who is this? I don't appreciate blocked calls."

"Robbie," Richard said. "It's me. Richard Barnett."

"Well. Look who's still kicking. So much for our last deal."

"The one where you promised not to touch Isabel? Yeah, so much for that."

"What are you talking about?"

Richard sighed. "Cut the crap, Robbie. I get it. She screwed you over. You just want to collect."

Static came over the line—and the sound of quiet breathing. Isabel stared at the phone, as if that could help her decipher the man's reaction. How badly they needed him to cooperate!

"Look," Richard said smoothly. "I know what happened, but I'm not interested in justice."

"I still don't know what you mean."

"Sure you do. It's my fault for making you a shit deal in the first place, so I've put together a better offer to make it up to you."

Robbie's sarcasm was thick with hostility. "A new fall guy?"

"No one has to die this time. I have two million bucks in hand as we speak."

There was an ugly snort. "You don't have a rat's ass."

"*I* don't. But I'm close with a wealthy entrepreneur in Silicon Valley, we grew up together in Florida. He's a hardware guy, has a patent on a chip in Apple computers. I told him about your fund's solid returns. He wants to invest long-term, but doesn't want his money traced. You know, capital gains and all that."

A pause. Was it hesitation? Then: "I don't do business with outsiders."

"You'd be doing business with me. And I'm sitting here holding a rare Vietnamese ruby, three carats, worth two-point-one million. Take it or leave it."

"What do you get out of it?"

"You agree never to touch any of the 'lives' I sold you again."

"How could you think I would do such a thing?" Robbie's voice was a singsong of deliberate irony. Isabel steamed, biting her lip to keep silent. A string of curses blared through her mind.

"So it's a deal?" Richard pressed.

Robbie's tone abruptly grew severe. "With one contingency."

"What?"

Now he sounded as though he were smiling. "Your precious Isabel has to deliver the ruby in person. Alone."

A cold tingle bristled over her arms. This was not part of the plan.

She looked at Galileo, who nodded once. His mouth was a hard line, his expression inscrutable. What mess was he getting her into? Did she really trust this man she barely knew, even if his Network had saved her life? But there was no time to ponder. Richard was already closing the deal . . .

"Fine," he was saying. "Where should she meet you?"

Robbie gave a humorless chuckle. "Not me. I'm not an idiot, Richard. She'll leave it at a drop-off point in Manhattan. There's a couple old cannons at the Soldiers and Sailors Monument in Riverside Park. She can put it inside the mouth of the northernmost one."

Galileo wrote something on a piece of paper and slid it to Richard.

"She can be there in three days," Richard said.

"Make it five p.m. sharp. Once I receive it, and I know you aren't bullshitting me, I'll call to confirm the transaction." His voice was cold. "You already have your receipt."

After Richard gave him a call-back number for Galileo's untraceable satellite phone, the line cut off without a good-bye.

Isabel stared at the phone. *You already have your receipt.* Robbie's subtext was chilling. The receipt was her life. She dug her front teeth into her bottom lip.

"This guy is seriously disturbed," she said. "I'm not sure if I want to put myself out there like that . . ."

A sharp yearning struck her like a physical ache. How she longed for the simple problems of her old life, before

her mother fell ill, before she met Richard, when all she
had to worry about was surviving a week in one harsh cli-
mate or another. With a camera crew of tough guys watching her back, she knew she was protected, no matter how
threatening nature could be. But nothing about this crisis
was natural. Where was her safety net now that she had to
do the bidding of a homicidal maniac?

"We won't let anything bad happen to you," Galileo
said, inserting the ring into a snug black box that snapped
closed. "Once you're part of the Network, you're family."

"But what happens when he realizes it's a fake?" she
cried. "What's he going to do to me then?"

Richard covered her hand with his own. The confidence
of the gesture took her aback. They had never touched before, not in any meaningful way. But what surprised her
even more was that she liked it, the way his agile fingers
squeezed hers. Or maybe she was just frightened out of
her mind and desperate for human contact.

"It will be okay," Galileo said, unfazed. "We'll watch
out for you."

"But why have me deliver it? What does he want
from me?"

He shrugged. "It doesn't matter. We're one step ahead
of him. Trust me."

There it was again—the command that triggered her
bitter resistance.

Before she could reply, a faint sound out in the hallway
distracted her. From the tilt of Richard's head, she saw
that he heard it, too. Like her, he was experiencing the
X101's powerful side effect of increased sensory awareness. Both of them turned to see a fluffy white dog
padding into the room, his small body swaying with the
ship's motion. He kept his black nose to the floor and

steered himself toward their booth, then jumped up and crawled over Galileo to snuggle into her lap.

Galileo shook his head with a smile. "And here I thought he was my dog."

In fact, Captain, a twelve-pound bichon, belonged to the whole ship; he was one of the first survivors from Dr. Quinn's initial animal experiments with the X101. Galileo had grown attached and let the dog stay on as a pet, but ever since Isabel had arrived, he'd taken to following her around. He had once exhibited signs of being highly sensitive, too, thanks to the drug. She wondered if in its aftermath, he could tell who needed comfort the most.

"Hey, Cap," she murmured, stroking his floppy ears. He gazed up at her with tender brown eyes that looked impossibly wise. His muscular little body radiated warmth. She leaned down to kiss his head, wishing she could bury herself in his curly cotton fur and forget everything.

Richard was regarding Galileo with a look of respect. "Your plan is genius. I just hope it works."

Galileo opened the box and lifted up the ring. It wasn't the petite, elegant kind Isabel preferred. It was gaudy and oversized—a statement piece for an older, snobbier woman. "Like I was saying," he said, "we're one step ahead."

With an impish smile, he turned it upside down so they could see the wide gold band. "You can't tell, can you?"

Isabel plucked it out of his grip and inspected it. He was right. There was no way to tell that one of the material scientists on board had melted a heat-resistant GPS chip into the metal.

"So you'll track the ring," Richard said. "And see where it ends up."

"You got it." Galileo pulled a laptop out of the briefcase at his feet and flipped it open. He navigated to a map program, where a red dot was glowing in the southern Atlantic Ocean. His cursor hovered over it. Two numbers popped up: 24.2476° N and 81.1915° W.

"Here's us now," he said. Then he clicked a few times on the map, bringing the northern East Coast into view.

Isabel hugged the dog close to her pounding heart, knowing and hating what was coming next.

"Next stop," Galileo said, "New York."

CHAPTER 27
Joan

New York

"Listen to me." Greg spoke in the stern voice he reserved for recalcitrant patients. "Joan."

Instead of paying attention to her husband, she stared out the window of their taxi. On the other side of the avenue, white headlights of oncoming cars flashed by like comets in the dark. An unfamiliar pang quickened her breath. She realized it was envy. Those people in those cars were headed away from the place she was dreading. The place she now had to call home.

"I know what you're going to say," she said, "and I don't care." She flicked a piece of lint off her silk black dress to show her indifference.

"It needs to be said. Sweetheart, please."

The affectionate term persuaded her to face him. That evening, he'd gone straight from his shift in the ER to a fund-raising dinner for his charity, Doctors on the Mend. Now, in spite of his crisp suit and tie, he looked haggard. The skin under his eyes was sunken and bluish. His lips, tired from smiling for potential donors all night, were pursed in frustration.

No one knew the extent of their financial meltdown. No one understood how close they were to total collapse, how desperately they were keeping up appearances. The irony didn't escape Joan that while they were out cheerfully soliciting thousands for charity that night, the prospect of their own bankruptcy loomed. Yet she insisted on holding the long-scheduled gala dinner, chatting up wealthy guests, leaving the event by cab instead of walking to the nearest subway. Anything to make their lives seem normal, just for a night. But between her and Greg, a schism was widening.

She'd told him about her charade at the hospital and her suspicion that there might be a conspiracy among the staff.

"Isn't it strange," she'd blurted at home the night before, "that your colleagues pretended not to know anything about a creepy pattern of deaths related to life insurance? Even Dr. Yardley, who was the very person who told you about the rumors in the first place?"

Greg squinted at her. "They don't know you from a hole in the wall."

"So?"

"So they were being understandably discreet," he said. "They're afraid. You think they're gonna talk to an outsider?"

"I don't buy it," she snapped. "They seemed like they really didn't know what I was talking about."

"You don't know them. I do. And how dare you try to deceive them for information? Do you realize how much trouble you could have gotten into—I mean, Jesus. Trespassing on the locker room? Stealing a nurse's *uniform*?"

"I put it back after," she offered. But she didn't say anything else.

The truth became clear to her: Greg had a blind spot

for the people he knew and liked. But she didn't. And she didn't trust them one bit. Not when his life was at stake, on top of everything else—their son's fury, their dwindling cash, their crappy new apartment that was serving as a stopgap.

Now, in the cab, he was attempting a truce.

"Sweetheart," he said again. He reached out across the empty middle seat and offered his hand. She took it grudgingly. His fingers were cold, his skin rough and dry.

"I know you want to be some investigative hero," he said, "but I think you should just back off. It's not worth it."

"Really? Some investor literally owns your life. You already had one close call. I'm not going to sit around and wait for another."

Greg took a deep breath, as if reaching the limit of his patience. "You're not going to find him. It's that simple. This person doesn't want to be found."

Her lips parted in disbelief. His passivity was maddening. "So—that's it, then? You're going to pretend everything's fine?"

"No, I just don't want you getting mixed up in the mess I made." He looked her in the eye. "I would never survive if something happened to you."

"I'm fine," she retorted, but then softened her tone. "I appreciate your concern, but I can take care of myself."

"*I appreciate your concern?* I'm your goddamn husband, not a business letter."

Greg rarely cursed. The stress must have been affecting him more than he let on. It unsettled her whenever she glimpsed his inner turmoil, since most of the time, his medical training kept him painstakingly composed.

His gaze didn't waver. "I know how bad I screwed up, but I love you more than anything. I hope you know that."

She gave him a small smile. "I know."

They sat in silence for the rest of the ride. If he was hurt that she didn't return the sentiment, he didn't say so. She did feel the same way, of course—but it was complicated. Her love was entangled in a braid of resentment, anger, and misery. It didn't help that just then, they were driving past their stately former apartment building.

She pressed her nose to the window to drink in the sight of the grand glass lobby, the doorman standing by in his double-breasted tux. On the top floor—their penthouse—the lights were on. The new tenant was no doubt enjoying every handcrafted detail she'd worked so hard to perfect. Would they ever return home again? Could they possibly make it through this nightmare intact?

Twenty blocks later, when they pulled up to their new building—a squat, six-story townhouse wedged between a noisy bar and a smoke shop—she was struggling to contain the lump in her throat.

There was no doorman, only a black front door leading to a hallway that reeked of cigarettes. She followed Greg inside to their first-floor apartment.

"I'm going to take a bath," she said as he opened the door to a dark living room that was still crowded with moving boxes. She walked in first and turned on the light. "I need a few minutes to—"

She broke off with a gasp.

Their front window had been smashed in. Jagged glass shards littered the room. Pieces big and small covered the wood floor, glittered on the sofa fabric, poked out from cardboard boxes. In what was left of the window, a starburst of cracks spread outward from the hole in its center.

She heard Greg's sharp inhale as he came up behind her. They both stood gaping at the mess in a daze.

"I don't get it," she said after a few moments. "The bars on that window are solid steel. It's not like anyone could actually get in."

Greg's voice was grim. "It must be a warning. That's all I can think of."

"Not random violence? This neighborhood isn't the best . . ."

He was shaking his head. "I think someone did this to scare us. You or me, I don't know, but one thing is for sure."

"What?"

His arms tightened around her. "We need to watch our backs."

CHAPTER 28
Isabel

The Atlantic Ocean

It was past midnight when the storm hit. Isabel lay awake in her narrow cabin, clutching the bed's guardrails so she wouldn't tumble out. Waves pummeled the ship, one slap after another. Thunder rumbled overhead. All she could see outside her porthole was thick fog, illuminated every few minutes by flashes of lightning. The churning of the sea mirrored exactly how her stomach was reacting to the voyage north. Even if the ship wasn't pitching up and down like a shoddy carnival ride, her anxiety about New York made sleep impossible.

In just two and a half days, she would have to leave the nest of the boat—alone—to try to bait a maniac. But why did he insist on luring her out into the open? Who was really running the show? Would Galileo come through for her as promised? And when would she get to reunite with her family?

That was the hardest part—not knowing when she would see them again. God, what she wouldn't give for an hour at home to bask in the glow of normalcy: baking banana bread with her mom, teasing Andy about his latest crush, relaxing out on the porch under the coconut palm—

A soft knock interrupted her fantasy. She glanced at the alarm clock bolted to her nightstand: 1:14 A.M. Oddly late for a visitor. She rolled out of bed and staggered to the door. Since she wasn't wearing a bra under her spaghetti strap nightshirt, she used the door to shield her chest as she opened it.

Chris was standing there, gazing down at her with a crooked grin. In dark jeans, a button-down, and gray Chuck Taylors, he looked cuter than any other physician-researcher on board. She noticed the blond stubble on his chin was gone. Now that his face was smooth, his jaw seemed sharper, more masculine. He smelled of after-shave and musk. There was a gleam in his eye, as if they were both in on some private joke.

"Hey." She could feel a smile spreading across her face. He was a welcome distraction. "Pretty late, isn't it?"

"I knew you weren't sleeping through this." He swept his arm toward the floor rocking beneath them. "So I came by to take you out."

She lifted an eyebrow. "Right, 'cause there's so many places to go."

"Yeah, I thought we could catch a movie."

"Very funny."

"No, I'm serious. Come with me." He grabbed her hand, but she stiffened.

"I'm barely dressed . . ."

His smile widened. "Even better. Come on."

He pulled her out from behind her door and stared at her tight shirt and boxer shorts. At first she covered her chest with her elbow. No man had seen her new breasts since her mastectomy and reconstructive surgery. What would he think of their unnatural perkiness? The slightly uneven nipples? The purple-yellowish bruises still dotting her collarbone? But then she realized she didn't care. She let her arm drop. She had a right to be proud of her body, no matter how much of a beating it had taken. It was strong. And that made it beautiful.

Given his admiring once-over, Chris appeared to agree.

"Where are we going?" she whispered as he pulled her down the dark hallway, past a dozen other cabins, to the stairwell.

He closed the door behind them and descended the concrete stairs, winding around and down. She trailed behind, barefoot.

"There's an old movie theater on deck one," he said, his voice reverberating in the closed space. "And I just so happen to know where the projector is."

"Are we allowed to?"

"Who's going to stop us?"

She shrugged. She usually wasn't one to break rules—not that there was a specific rule against watching a movie in the middle of the night, half naked. That wouldn't violate anyone's research projects. But life on the ship had a certain rigid order—set times to eat, work, and sleep. Everyone followed the pattern. So she couldn't help feeling like they were getting away with something.

He stopped so abruptly that she bumped into him.

"First," he said, "why not a little detour? There's something cool I want to show you."

"What?"

"You'll see."

They exited the stairwell on the second lowest deck and found themselves in another narrow, dark corridor lined by doors on either side. Chris approached a certain door labeled QUINN on a gold plaque. There was a silver number keypad under the handle. He pressed in a code. Two beeps sounded and the lock clicked open.

"Why is there a special lock on this one?" she asked. Walking past the other doors, she'd seen that none of the others had a number pad.

Chris gritted his teeth. "'Cause Quinn's nuts."

His derisive tone surprised her. She was even a bit offended on the doctor's behalf. Dr. Quinn was her savior. She felt extremely loyal to him: He occupied a glorified pedestal in her mind. When she passed him on the residential deck or in the dining area, a thrill surged through her, like he were a celebrity. One day, of course, his name would be legend. He was the developer of the X101. Only no one knew it yet.

Chris pushed open the door. It opened onto a lab about the size of a cozy living room. To the right, several microscopes sat on a high counter next to two sinks, along with an array of scientific equipment that she couldn't identify—bulky rectangular hoods, a heavy-duty circular machine that looked like it spun at high speeds. To the left stood two supply closets, plus a floor-to-ceiling subzero fridge and freezer. On a long table at the back, various chemical bottles were stacked next to rows of glass slides. The whole room seemed precisely ordered. Just how she would have imagined Quinn's lab.

"So," she said, "this is where the magic happens?"

"Yup, check this out." He swung open the refrigerator door and pulled out a frosty glass vial containing a clear fluid. "This is what saved you and your friend. We just synthesized a brand-new dose."

Her eyes widened. How could something so ordinary-looking be so extraordinary? "That's awesome," she said. "Literally awesome."

"Pretty sick, huh?" He put it back in the fridge and quickly shut the door before the vial warmed to room temperature. "But it's a pain in the ass to make. Each dose takes a week of full-time work."

"For you and Quinn both?"

"Yeah. And he only lets me work with him."

"'Cause you're such a rock star?" Isabel sidled closer to him, smiling at herself for stumbling with the ship's seesawing floor.

Chris chuckled. "That, and he's freakin' paranoid."

She rested a hand on his chest, conscious of her breasts pressing against his torso. As she opened her mouth to ask what he meant, he leaned down and kissed her. She tipped her head back and wrapped her arms around his neck. It had been ages since her last romantic encounter, with the fiancé who'd cheated on her. For months afterward, she'd been so intent on getting over him—focusing on her television show, then on her mother's survival, then on her own—that she'd all but forgotten the pleasures of intimacy. Now she relished Chris's hungry mouth on hers, but when he slipped a hand into her boxer shorts, she grabbed his wrist.

"What's wrong?"

"Can we take it slow?"

He pulled his hand back. Their eyes locked, and she felt her face flush. "I mean," she said, "I don't even really know you."

He flipped his palms up casually, but she detected annoyance in his voice. "What do you want to know?"

"I don't know," she said, aiming for levity, "your life story in a nutshell? Sixty seconds, go."

"Um, okay." He ticked facts off his fingers. "Born and raised in Southern California, boring suburb, one of five kids. My mom's a homemaker, my dad teaches high school physics. I was a super nerdy science geek. What else?" He paused. "There was a phase when I dealt drugs, got in some trouble. But I got into Harvard anyway, 'cause my grades were perfect. Then I studied my ass off, got a couple degrees, worked for Quinn, we got recruited . . . and now we're here."

"Impressive," she said. "Bad boy makes good?"

"Something like that." His eyes seemed amused, but there was a hardness in them she didn't understand. He cocked his head. "Your turn."

That was when she heard the sound—and stiffened. Soon Chris heard it, too. Footsteps out in the hallway. Plodding steps coming closer. And men's low voices.

Her feet felt rooted to the ground. The voices were getting louder, approaching the door to Quinn's lab. Her heart somersaulted into her throat. The footsteps stopped right outside the door. She stared at Chris, her mouth forming a silent O. Then came two unmistakable beeps—the number pad unlocking.

Chris grabbed her arm and dragged her into the supply closet, pulling the door closed just before they heard two people walk in. Underneath a shelf sagging with textbooks, she and Chris crouched into the smallest versions of themselves. They held their knees tight against their chests, keeping their chins low, their breaths quiet.

Through a slim crack where the door didn't fully close, they could see Dr. Quinn and Galileo passing by. Isabel caught sight of them for only a split second, but it was enough to make out the distress on both their faces.

"No one is out to get you, Horatio," Galileo was saying. His voice was gentle but firm. "You're safe here. Please, be reasonable."

"But you can never be sure, can you?" The old scientist's tone was prickly. "You know what I think. The human psyche is a mysterious black hole, impossible for anyone outside of it to grasp. Even yours."

"I can't believe you. After all these years, still."

"Every relationship is a leap of faith. And faith is not my strong suit."

"I get it, you've been burned—"

"You have no idea!"

"I know, I know. But that was a long time ago. Don't you realize how irresponsible it is to keep everything in your head now? What you've done—it's the biggest breakthrough we've ever seen. But you're seventy-seven. God forbid something happens . . ."

Quinn's voice was stubborn. "As long as I alone know the formula, I can't be gotten rid of."

"That's ridiculous and you know it."

Their footsteps approached the refrigerator. It opened with a whoosh. Isabel couldn't see what was happening, but she heard the clink of glass against metal.

"I will guard your secret with my life. You have my word."

"Careful," Quinn muttered. "We haven't had time to make more yet."

"Even more reason to do this right now. Tonight. Come on. You talk, I'll take notes. Then I'll encrypt every word. You don't have to trust anyone but me."

"Do you think I don't know how much money I'm sitting on? I mean, why *wouldn't* you want to get rid of me? Then you wouldn't have to share the proceeds when you license it for a billion dollars. The world already thinks I'm long dead, so I'm at your mercy. For all I know, you've been working up to this since the day we met."

"Jesus Christ! Do you hear yourself?"

There was a sigh. "Maybe I am just a paranoid old crank. I don't know. You have been good to me over the—"

At that moment, the ship jerked so violently that Isabel cupped a hand over her mouth to suppress a cry. At the same time, a violent crack sounded overhead, like a heavy branch snapping. The shelf above her and Chris groaned under the weight of textbooks sliding. She squeezed her eyes shut, hoping the door wouldn't pop open. That was when she caught the first whiff. With her senses on high alert, the smell was unmistakable.

Smoke.

CHAPTER 29
Isabel

The Atlantic Ocean

Isabel charged out of the closet with a shout.

"Fire! We have to get out!"

Galileo and Quinn spun around to her in shock. The faint scent of smoke was getting stronger by the second.

Galileo stared back and forth between her and the closet as if trying to make sense of the inexplicable. Quinn's wizened face scrunched up as he looked past Isabel to regard his protégé. Behind her, Chris was reluctantly rising out of his crouched position underneath the shelf.

"Chris?" Quinn said tentatively. "What in God's name—?"

"No time," Isabel cut him off. "Don't you guys smell that? Let's go!"

She dashed out of the lab. Where was the smoke coming from? The hall looked fine. It had to be on another deck. That crack, the ship's shudder, the smoke—it could only have been lightning. She recognized the pattern too well. While filming one episode of *Wild Woman*, during an electrical storm in Fiji, she'd watched a crooked white beam strike the tallest tree. Its branch had snapped off in flames.

The mast, she realized. It had to be the mast.

She bounded into the stairwell, racing up three flights until she reached the top deck. The men followed on her heels. Then she hurried as fast as she could through the glass-enclosed former nightclub to the open-air prow. It was an exposed triangle of about 150 square feet at the very front of the ship. Out here, the smoke hung thick and heavy on the salt air. She looked up, fearing the worst.

The mast was ablaze. Crackling yellow flames shimmied down its wooden beam toward the ship. Isabel threw her arm over her face as black ashes fluttered down. Heat stung her eyes and the inside of her throat.

She was bent over, coughing, when Galileo, Quinn, and Chris caught up to her. Half a dozen other people streamed out of the stairwell with them, their voices pitching and shouting over the roar of the thunder and the sea.

They all stared in horror at the fire, many dropping to their knees as the ship teetered precariously up and down. Only a waist-high metal railing around the perimeter separated them from being flung overboard into the crashing waves below. Freezing cold water splashed up over the sides, spraying droplets everywhere. Isabel shivered, trying to keep calm amid the panicked yells around her. If she knew one thing, it was that survival depended on a clear head.

She squinted through the chaos of ashes and rain and lurching bodies to scan for Galileo by the light of the fire. Surely he would know what to do. But she couldn't spot his tall form anywhere. The violent swaying of the ship dizzied her. It was hard to walk straight, let alone think straight. All the while, aggressive flames were devouring the mast at a frightening pace, inching ever closer to the deck itself.

Coughing fits erupted all around. Orange embers rained down, singeing hair and skin. Isabel sank to all fours and crawled on the slippery wet floor back toward the stairs inside, to the captain's quarters just one deck below. There had to be a fire extinguisher there.

But just when she reached the door, Galileo burst out of the stairwell, holding up a bright red extinguisher like a trophy. His expression reminded her of a warrior's—fervent and resolute. He brushed past her, cutting a path through the crowd as close to the mast as he could. Isabel ran interference for him.

"Back up!" she yelled. "Everyone inside!" If they went beneath the deck to where the air was uncontaminated, it would help the coughing and prevent injuries from smoke inhalation.

But it was impossible to order the chaos, not when the flames were close enough to blister skin and the ship swayed relentlessly and the thunder drowned out her screams anyway.

Galileo ignored it all. He kept his balance like a pro, spraying a powerful stream at the fire. The kickback of the extinguisher wasn't strong enough to deter his aim. Illuminated by the flames, his figure stood silhouetted against the sky. Isabel could see the tense knot of his shoulders, the ropy muscles of his arms, the way his drenched hair clung to his forehead with rain and sweat.

The extinguisher's forceful torrent at first seemed no match for the hissing fire, but soon she saw that Galileo's determination was winning out. The flames curled in on themselves as if trying to escape his spray. The crowd surrounded him, transfixed, shouting encouragements over the wind and waves. When the last orange lick died out and only the blackened mast remained, a cheer rose up. Amid the storm, it sounded weak but triumphant.

Isabel wiped the water off her face and breathed in. The air was still choked with smoke, but it was already starting to dissipate. She searched for Chris among the group of drenched, huddled people, wanting to plant a kiss on his lips right then and there. His thick, burly frame shouldn't have been hard to spot even in the dark, but he was nowhere in sight. Instead, pushing through to the outskirts of the crowd, she found herself face-to-face with Richard. He was clutching his elbows, trembling and pale in the moonlight. A dark smattering of ash stained his cheek. When their eyes met, she felt a fresh stab of fear. He looked not just shaken, but horrified.

"Are you okay?" she said.

"*I* am, but . . ." He trailed off, nodding in the opposite direction of the crowd, toward the very edge of the prow some yards away.

That was when she saw Chris. He was crouched down, leaning over a man's twisted limp body splayed at his feet.

It was Dr. Quinn.

What happened next was a blur—rushing to the scene in disbelief, only to be met with Chris's sobbing moans—*he slipped and hit his head, nothing I could do.* A pool of dark blood was leaking out of the doctor's scalp, staining the deck. His bluish lips were parted, his eyes open and staring. Unblinking.

Richard stood next to her, staring hard at Chris.

"Is he—dead?"

Chris's lowered gaze told them the answer.

"Then do something!" Isabel shrieked. "You know what to do!"

"It doesn't work in all cases," Chris muttered. "He could have a subdural hematoma . . ."

Galileo caught up to them then, the gawking crowd close behind him. When he caught sight of Quinn's body, all color drained from his face. In a split second, he was on his knees, ripping off his shirt and tying it around Quinn's bloody head.

"I can't believe this," Chris was saying over and over. "I just can't believe this."

"Pull yourself together and get him to the OR," Galileo commanded.

"But if he has a brain injury, the protocol might not work . . ."

"Figure out a way." His voice shook. "There has to be a way. You're the best person to know."

"I'll try. We need a neuro consult *stat*."

Together, they lifted the doctor's slight body and staggered through the crowd. Isabel stayed behind, watching them recede into the glass lounge, to the stairwell, down into the bowels of the ship. Richard stood silently beside her. She became aware of an icy feeling on the back of her neck, and not from the rain or the wind.

It was dread.

Her alert senses had picked up on something that only now was breaking through to her consciousness. In her mind she replayed the interaction with Chris from moments before. His face had been scrunched up in distress, the epitome of crying anguish.

But something was wrong. There were no tears in his eyes.

She was about to confess her realization when Richard spoke first.

"I saw what happened." His tone was flat. "With the fire, no one else noticed."

He didn't have to explain; they both shared the same hyperaware side effect of the X101. Just that night, over dinner, they'd commiserated about how pungent and loud and *close* the world now seemed.

"What happened?"

He hesitated. "I don't want to cause trouble."

"Just tell me."

"Quinn didn't slip. He was pushed."

CHAPTER 30
Joan

New York

The call came in the middle of the night, but Joan wasn't sleeping. Since the window-smashing incident, a guardedness kept her and Greg constantly on edge. They'd filed a police report, installed a camera alarm system, and bought a 9 millimeter handgun to keep in the safe, but peace of mind proved elusive. It was impossible to rest when you knew you were targets in your own home—targets of some mysterious psychopath who wasn't afraid to bully you with force.

At night they feigned sleep for the sake of normalcy. And then they lay awake with their eyes closed, listening—to the hum of the fridge, the hiss of the radiator, the rain pounding down overhead—for signs of an intruder.

So when Joan's cell phone trilled at 3:35 A.M., her eyes snapped open before the end of the first ring and Greg shot straight up as if ready to fight someone.

It was Adam. He sounded breathless.

"Baby's coming! Meet us at Roosevelt."

Joan's heart expanded with joy, temporarily nudging worry aside. At last, she and Greg were about to meet their grandson. She sent up a silent prayer of thanks for the one and only benefit of the crashed economy—Adam's depleted savings meant that he couldn't afford a big move out of state, so his family was staying put in New York. That meant Joan got to be a grandmother to little Sophia and now a sweet new boy every day, not just a few times a year.

She grinned at Greg and mouthed: *It's time*. His eyes lit up like hers.

"I can't wait!" she squealed into the phone. "Daddy and I are on our way."

"Um. Actually, I just want you there."

If his words were a sword, she would have doubled over. She knew well enough that Adam hadn't forgiven Greg for his mistakes, but she'd been hoping the bliss of a new baby might smooth over their estrangement.

She leaped off the bed and tiptoed into the bathroom.

"Do you know what this will do to him?" she whispered. Her eyes were already filling with tears. She couldn't bear to look at her husband. "Please, honey. Can't you just let it go?"

"No." Adam's voice was firm. "I told you both before, he has to earn my trust back. And so far he hasn't done a damn thing."

"You don't understand. Your father's been . . ."

She trailed off. How could she explain the stress they were under? Adam knew nothing about Greg's life insurance sale, his close call, the attempted break-in, her suspicions about his colleagues. The last thing she wanted to do was lay all that on him on the eve of his child's birth.

"He's been preoccupied," she said. "Really, you shouldn't be too harsh."

"I'll see you there, Mom. Good-bye."

*   *   *

Eight hours later, after baby Justin emerged into the world with an earsplitting cry, after the cord was cut and he was weighed and swaddled and placed on his mother's chest, Joan was ushered into the delivery room.

The fact didn't escape her that she was at Roosevelt again. Greg's hospital. That maybe she ought to poke around a bit more after seeing the baby—to hell with any warning. If the staff was suppressing information, she wasn't about to ignore an opportunity to dig it up. The intrepid reporter she used to be would never back away from the truth. Before *wife* and *mother*, that was who she was. She had forgotten for too long.

Inside the delivery room, a shiny blue balloon hung from the ceiling above the bed where Adam's wife Emily lay beneath a sheet, disheveled and exhausted. She and Adam were gazing in awe at the tiny red-faced infant curled on her chest. An attentive nurse was hovering nearby, waiting to see if the baby latched on to her nipple.

Joan wasn't prepared for the clashing emotions that overwhelmed her. Tenderness and euphoria—but also devastation. Greg was missing these first precious moments of Justin's life. All because of some bad judgment and a grudge.

Adam gave her a tired, delighted smile when she walked in. After congratulating him and Emily, she settled in an armchair. Adam scooped up the baby, who stretched from his wrist to his elbow, and rested him in her arms.

"This is your Nana," he whispered to the boy. "She loves you very much."

The first thing she noticed was how much the baby resembled Greg. Those long black lashes. The almond-shaped eyes whose corners dipped down ever so slightly.

The shock of dark hair and full pink lips. His translucent white skin was softer than down.

"He's beautiful," she murmured. "Look at that little pout!"

"Isn't he perfect?" Adam's smile was as proud as could be.

Her next words slipped out before she could stop herself. "I wish Daddy could see him."

Her son's face hardened. "Not now."

"He's a good man," she insisted. "All he did was make a mistake."

Adam spoke through clenched teeth, softly enough that their voices would not upset the baby. "He gambled away your money and didn't tell you for months. That's not just *a* mistake."

"He was trying to recover losses that weren't his fault to begin with."

"So you're condoning his lies?"

"No, but sometimes," she said, drawing out her words, "you withhold things to protect the people you love."

"Whatever. I don't want a liar around my kids. And that's that."

Joan leaned down to inhale the baby's sweet scent to prevent her anger from escalating. A vaguely familiar woman's voice cut in.

"I thought I recognized you."

When she looked up, her breath caught. Louisa, the raven-haired OB nurse from the locker room, was staring at her with slit eyes.

Before she could think of anything to say, the nurse put one hand on her hips and marched toward her. Her voice dripped with hostility.

"I tried to look you up and guess what? There is no such nurse. You BS'd us."

Adam glanced between them with a bewildered expression. On the bed, Emily propped herself up on her elbows with a frown.

"I'm here to meet my grandson," she said weakly. "Please."

"Please what?" The nurse aimed a finger at her. "You stole an employee's uniform and trespassed in this hospital. I could have you arrested."

Joan handed the baby carefully back to Adam, then stood up and pulled on her winter coat. "I'm going," she said. "I'm going right now."

"Mom, did you really do those things?"

She planted a quick kiss on her son's cheek, too humiliated to stand there a second longer. It was impossible to explain without telling him everything.

"It's not what it looks like," she told him. "But I better go."

With a longing backward glance at the baby, she headed for the door. The nurse called after her a final good-bye:

"Consider it a warning never to be seen in this hospital again."

CHAPTER 31
Isabel

The Atlantic Ocean

"Galileo?" Isabel knocked on the door to his cabin. It was the morning after the storm. Now the sea was at peace again, and the mast had survived as a charred hunk of wood, but the atmosphere inside the ship was more turbulent than ever. All anyone could speak or think about was Dr. Quinn. Since his collapse, he had been sequestered in the operating room on the lowest deck, tended to by the most senior doctors and nurses aboard, including Chris.

No one else knew what was going on. Was he dead or alive? Did his own drug work to save him? Had he told anyone the formula? What if he didn't make it? The speculation was morbid and all-consuming.

The only question people *weren't* asking was why he allegedly slipped in the first place. He was a feeble old man with poor balance. Of course the violent storm could have caused him to slip and hit his head on the railing. A tragic conflation of circumstances. Only Isabel and Richard harbored suspicions. And she wasn't doing any good by keeping them to herself.

"Come in," Galileo called. His door was unlocked. She

went in. His cabin was as unpretentious as the others, which surprised her. She was expecting a master suite for the man in charge. Instead, in a cursory glance, she noted his narrow white walls, twin bed, plain wooden desk. Not enough floor space to cartwheel.

He was hunched over the desk scrutinizing a piece of paper. A ray of light from the porthole shone on his face. She noticed the wrinkles around his mouth and the heaviness of his eyelids. The mischievous smile in his eyes was gone. He looked bereft.

An uneasy feeling settled over her when she realized the extent of her reliance on this man she barely knew— to protect her family. To protect her. To catch her killer. It was tempting to think of him as almost superhuman, the leader of a powerful Network who could accomplish the unimaginable. But no matter how much confidence he inspired, she saw that he was just as vulnerable as anyone else.

"Isabel," he said wearily. "What can I do for you?"

She struggled to get out her message. Somehow, keeping it to herself made it less threatening, less real.

"How's Dr. Quinn?" she started.

Galileo gave a little shake of his head, his lips tight. She waited for him to elaborate, but he didn't.

"Well," she said, "I don't want to disturb you, but I thought you should know something about his . . . accident." She took a deep breath to slow her palpitating heart. What she was about to say could not be taken back. The strange part was that she actually liked Chris. His rebellious spontaneity excited her. But any romance they might have shared was obviously out of the question now.

"Um, that's the thing," she said. "It wasn't an accident."

Galileo frowned. "What are you talking about?"

"Chris did it," she blurted. "Richard saw the whole

thing. Everyone else was distracted by the fire, but Chris pushed him when the ship was rocking and that's why he hit his head."

Galileo narrowed his eyes. "You've got to be joking."

"I'm not. And then when I went over there, I could tell Chris wasn't really crying."

"First of all, it was dark and pouring rain, so you couldn't have seen much."

"But my senses are heightened! I notice everything."

He lay his large palm flat on the desk. She could tell his patience was thinning. "We agree that your and Richard's perception seem enhanced by the X101, right?"

"That's what I'm saying."

"But we don't yet understand how or why, or what other side effects you might experience. That's partly why you're here. All we know is that certain neuronal pathways are impacted during the metabolic process. Isn't it possible that in your heightened *emotional* state from the fire, you thought you perceived something and jumped to conclusions? More possible, I think, than one of my researchers assaulting his mentor out of the blue?"

"I know what we saw," she said stubbornly. "We weren't hallucinating."

Galileo sighed. "Chris has been here a long time. Years. I assure you I know him a bit better than you do."

"So you trust him?"

"Let me put it this way: Horatio insisted on working with him above anyone else. And he had a pretty hard time with trust."

She flinched at his use of the past tense. Did that mean the doctor was dead?

"Maybe he had a blind spot," she muttered, thinking of her ex-fiancé who had betrayed her when she was least expecting it. "Sometimes that happens with the people closest to you."

But as she said the words, an inkling of doubt crept in. What was the drug doing to her brain? Could she even trust herself anymore?

Galileo ignored her comment. "What were you doing with Chris in the lab last night, anyway?"

She reddened. "He only took me there to show off. We heard you coming and got embarrassed." She hoped he wouldn't remember that she'd been half naked.

"So let me get this straight: last night you guys were, should we say, involved, and now you're turning him in?"

"I didn't know what he was capable of."

"Well, I do." His tone was edgy. "So forget all about it, okay?"

She opened her mouth to protest, but sensed it would be smarter to back off. In just forty-eight hours, they would dock in New York. She couldn't risk him reneging on their deal because she insisted on stirring up trouble.

"Okay." She turned to leave. "I just thought you should know."

"I appreciate that," he said, but he wasn't smiling.

Back in her cabin, Richard was waiting for her. He stood up from her bed when she entered.

"Well?"

Instead of explaining, she trudged toward him and rested her cheek against his chest. His heart thumped under his shirt with reassuring steadiness as he wrapped his arms around her.

Are we going crazy? she wanted to ask him. But deep down she knew the truth. The reality they perceived wasn't a side effect of the drug. A violent criminal was loose on the ship—even if Galileo didn't believe her. But why should he take her seriously? He knew her as scarcely as she knew him.

Terror overwhelmed her—along with an intense longing for the people who supported her and respected her judgment. Her mother. Her brother. And Richard.

Richard had been one of those people all along.

"I'm afraid I have some bad news."

The chatter on the top deck immediately ceased. Galileo looked grim as he surveyed the thirty-seven out of thirty-eight residents aboard—everyone except Dr. Quinn. Everyone stood huddled before him in groups of twos and threes, awaiting the update he had promised to deliver that evening.

In the back row, Isabel squeezed Richard's arm. Her mouth was dry. She saw that Chris was standing a few yards in front of them next to Theo, the young researcher who had also assisted in her resuscitation. Chris's hands were shoved in his pockets. He was staring straight ahead, his expression appropriately somber. Apart from their brief encounter the night before over Quinn's head injury, she had not spoken to him since their rendezvous in the lab. How long ago that seemed!

Galileo leaned against the glass wall as if standing took too much effort. Behind him, the twilight sky was flecked with stars that someone, somewhere might have found beautiful.

He drew a ragged breath. "I'm deeply sorry to report that Dr. Quinn is in a vegetative state. Even though we were able to get his heart back, his head injury was too severe to allow the X101 to restore his brain function."

Isabel was struck by surreal detachment. Was this really happening? She heard the crowd's gasps, felt her entire body clench, saw the devastation all over Galileo's face. But still the news—and its implications—didn't sink in.

"What's gonna happen to him?" someone shouted. A chorus of voices echoed the sentiment.

Galileo grimaced. "As many of you no doubt realize, this is what Horatio himself most feared. He never wanted to resuscitate a patient only to have the drug fail and leave them brain-dead. He and I spoke many times about what to do in such a case, which, fortunately, he never encountered. He was very clear that he considered it an affront to human dignity to keep such a patient alive on machines with no prospect of recovery. During one discussion, he became so adamant that he spelled out his own wishes in writing."

Galileo pulled a folded piece of paper from his jacket pocket. Isabel recognized it as the one he had been examining earlier that day at his desk. He read aloud:

"*I, Horatio L. Quinn, never want to be kept alive on machines in a state of permanent unconsciousness. If it comes to that, then for the love of God, just hasten my death with morphine instead of removing the tubes and waiting for all my organs to shut down. I don't give a damn about a natural exit. Only that it's fast and painless. And please don't make a fuss about a burial. I'd rather swim with the fish than rot underground. Just say something nice and get on with it. Then go back to work.*"

Galileo raised his eyes to the crowd with a pained smile. "He was a bit unorthodox, as we all knew."

Isabel exchanged a troubled glance with Richard. Dr. Quinn was asking to be euthanized. That was illegal in the U.S.—though the Network was, of course, outside the law. Loads of people considered it unethical as well, a form of murder. But was it, if the patient asked for it?

"Since he couldn't have been more explicit," Galileo
went on, "we're going to follow his instructions. I feel it's
only right to honor his wishes. Tomorrow morning, we'll
hold a brief funeral. Then we'll dispose of his body in a
respectful manner in accordance with his instructions."

The researchers murmured their approval. Just then,
Chris glanced over his shoulder in Isabel's direction and
caught her eye. He raised his eyebrows as if to say *You all
right?*

She tried not to appear flustered. It was clear he had no
idea about her suspicions. So she just gave him a weak
nod and shifted her gaze back to Galileo.

"There's one other thing," he was saying, "that I know
many of you are wondering about. The X101. Unfortunately, Horatio never did reveal its formula—and the only
dose we had was used up on him."

Agitated cries broke out. The drug was the Network's
crown jewel. The cash cow they were depending on to
fund other research for decades—and everyone knew it.

Galileo held up a hand. "Wait, before you all panic."
Isabel stifled a noise in her throat when he gestured to—
of all people—Chris.

"We're extremely lucky that Horatio's protégé is such a
diligent student. Chris thinks he's picked up all the complicated elements of the chemical compound and its synthesis from years of observing Horatio in the lab. If he
can replicate it successfully on his own, we're back in
business. As you all know, I can't overstate how crucial
this is.

"And for that reason, I owe you an apology. I feel I've
failed you as a leader. I should have held firm that Horatio hand over the formula long ago. But he refused to work
under any rules but his own, so I always gave in, thinking
he would relax eventually. Just last night, I thought we

might have reached a tipping point." He sighed. "The timing could not have been worse."

It's not a coincidence, Isabel wanted to shout. The only logical explanation lit up in her mind like a flare: Chris must have known he could synthesize the drug the whole time. Then when he overhead Dr. Quinn about to give up the secret, he seized on the soonest possible opportunity to get rid of him. Maybe, she thought, Chris had been planning to get rid of him at some point all along.

Her eyes bore into Chris's back. From her angle, the side of his long face was visible. He was watching Galileo ever so innocently.

"There's just one big challenge in Chris's way," Galileo continued. "Total precision is required for the drug to be synthesized properly. To ensure quality control, Horatio would compare each new dose against a perfect sample. That's why he always made sure to have at least several doses on hand. But the supply got low from the trial, and before he could replenish it, those couple doses unexpectedly went to our new subject Richard, and then to Horatio himself."

"So how can Chris make it right?" one researcher shouted. "We're screwed!"

Isabel frowned, thinking back to the previous night. Chris must not have been expecting to sacrifice that last dose. She remembered how he'd protested at first before using it on Dr. Quinn—some excuse about the severity of his brain injuries. But now his real motive clicked into place. If her hypothesis was right, Chris was no friend of the Network. He was feigning loyalty now to exploit its resources so he could make a new dose, if accuracy was even still possible. Then he'd steal it for himself—and there was no telling what he might do to get away with it.

"Not necessarily," Galileo said. "There's hope yet." He

squinted into the crowd until his gaze rested on Isabel and Richard standing in the back. She glanced behind her to see who he might be looking at, but there was no one else except for the dog, Captain, lying at her feet.

"Isabel, Richard," he said, "you guys are experiencing temporary side effects of the X101 because it's *still in your body.* Chris can use your blood to extract its traces and reverse engineer the perfect sample. It's a tall order, but if anyone can do it, I have confidence in him."

Her lips fell open. All the researchers turned to gawk at them as though they were the last members of some endangered species.

"The thing is," Galileo said, "your bodies will completely metabolize the drug within fourteen days, and it's already been about a week." He ran a hand through his hair and she saw that his nails were bitten raw. "Which means we only have about seven more days before it's gone for good."

CHAPTER 32
Joan

New York

When Joan got home from the hospital, she was so humiliated about the confrontation with the nurse that she didn't notice the distraught look on Greg's face. He was hunched over the kitchen table staring at his laptop.

"I met the baby," she said as she walked in and hung up her coat. "He's absolutely perfect. But you'll never believe what happened."

Greg raised his eyes from the screen. That was when she noticed they were bloodshot, as though he'd stayed up all night. He was clearly heartbroken over missing the birth.

"Oh, sweetie." She raced to his side as he closed his computer. "I'm so sorry. It kills me, too."

Greg shook his head miserably. The corners of his lips were cracked with dryness. Crusts of sleep clung to his eyelashes and stubble pricked his chin. White plaque clogged the spaces between his usually clean teeth. She hadn't really looked at him in days, but now she realized how run-down he'd become.

He rubbed his eyes. "I can't believe it's come to this."

"I know." She plunked onto a chair and told him about the incident at the hospital. "I have no idea how to explain myself to Adam. And now that I can't investigate, I'm at a dead end."

Greg sighed irritably. "I already told you not to poke around there. All we need is you getting arrested."

"I was just trying to help. But now I don't know what to do."

"The warnings are pretty clear: Stop looking for trouble."

"But I can't just give up! Someone out there wants you dead. We can't just ignore that!"

"No, but we also can't ignore our debt." He buried his face in his hands. "It's worse than I thought."

"How so?"

"I tried to refinance the mortgages on the vacant Hawaii and Florida properties. But no one will give us a new loan. It's sucking us dry." He looked down, avoiding her gaze. "Plus I still have forty thousand on the credit cards to pay off."

"Oh, Greg." Neither of them would utter the word *gambling*, as though it were the name of his mistress. *Poker* and *blackjack* were similarly taboo.

"You must hate me," he said flatly.

He looked so pathetic slumped against his chair, searching her face for reassurance. Yet he was still the man she loved. The man she vowed to stand by, for richer or poorer, in good times and in bad. One day, she thought, they would look back on this period and shudder at how close they'd come to the edge. One day, their lives would be safe from poverty and danger, their marriage would be strong, and their family would be whole. Because that was the only acceptable outcome.

She spread out her left hand. Her three-carat round diamond ring glittered a rainbow of light with every twitch of her finger. For thirty years, it had been a permanent fixture on her hand, her most prized possession, a family heirloom passed down from her mother to Greg, so he could propose in style back when he was broke, in medical school. She'd only ever taken it off to clean it and check its prongs. But it was just a symbol. It wasn't love itself.

In one quick pull, like ripping off a Band-Aid, she yanked it off.

Greg gave a startled cry. "What are you doing?"

"Take it." She handed it to him. At the base of her finger was a deep white groove.

He stared at the ring in a panic. "Are you leaving me?"

"Honey," she said, "I'm helping you. Sell it. It's the most expensive thing I own."

CHAPTER 33
Isabel

New York

Thirteen minutes until showtime.

Isabel nervously stared out the window as the yellow taxi zoomed north along the Hudson River. It was 4:47 P.M. on D-day, as she thought of it.

Drop-off day.

Inside the pocket of her Windbreaker, the corners of the ring box pressed into her sweaty palm. She ran her finger along its blunt edges. A hurricane of worries flattened her thoughts. She was on a survival mission, true to her alleged specialty. But real survival was about the art of self-reliance, which she had never needed to perfect. This time, the crew was nowhere to be found. The jungle was concrete. And the danger ahead was the scariest kind, neither nature nor beast. It was human.

The ship docked in New York City right on schedule that morning after the whirlwind three-day voyage. The only consolation of Isabel's current errand was that she got to escape the pressure cooker. Since Dr. Quinn's death and subsequent funeral, the mood on board was swinging between hysteria and despair. The days were ticking down faster than anyone wanted to acknowledge. Chris had less than a week left to reverse engineer the drug from the traces in her and Richard's bloodstreams.

Three times a day, they dutifully sat for blood draws in Chris's lab. Three times a day, they pretended to have a friendly rapport with him, because what other choice did they have? Everyone else was treating him like a hero in the making. Food was delivered to him on request, even in the middle of the night. He leeched whatever he wanted—Galileo's attention, sole use of the gym, extra supplies from other researchers. His suddenly elevated status hovered between boy genius and royal heir, and Isabel suspected he was relishing every minute of it, even under the gun of the deadline.

It was all she could do not to run off the ship the minute it pulled into the harbor, just to distance herself from his subtle smirk and the coldness in his eyes. It sickened her to remember she'd ever been attracted to him, so disembarking had been a kind of relief.

But now that she was in Manhattan for the first time, on her own, over sixteen hundred miles away from her family, the stress of her own task took center stage. The deal with Robbie Merriman seemed straightforward: she would deposit the ring in person, inside an ancient bronze cannon at the Soldiers and Sailors Monument, and then he would agree to leave her alone.

But why did he want her, specifically, to do it? And what would he do once he learned it was fake? Would the GPS chip in the band allow them to home in on his location before he could retaliate?

She drew a deep breath to anchor herself in the present moment. Outside the window, a cluster of skyscrapers reflected the amber light of the setting sun. She recognized the famous silhouettes of the Empire State and the Chrysler, both taller and grander than she'd imagined. But the iconic skyline captured only a sliver of her attention. It was 4:51 P.M.

She had no idea what to expect from the next hour. At least the drop-off point was a public park—hopefully a crowded one. Afterward, Galileo wanted her to stick around to see who came to pick it up. A hidden camera fastened to her front pocket would relay any sightings back to him for further scrutiny. She also wore her own GPS chip, inside the heel of her Nike tennis shoe, so Galileo could remotely keep track of her, and a tiny, beige earpiece that allowed them to communicate in real time.

"Pulling up," she muttered into it now, "with one minute to spare."

"Good." His voice sounded bizarrely close, as if he were inside her head. "Can you move your hair? It's in front of your camera. Better, okay. Now you can get out."

She paid in cash and the cab sped away. It felt like her heart was thumping loud enough for Galileo to hear. A crisp breeze rustled the trees as she stepped into Riverside Park. Its scents and sights and sounds assaulted her. The air smelled like decaying plants. Weeds shriveled in the soil where flowers had once bloomed. A canopy of partly bare branches reached to the sky, the last orange leaves of autumn clinging to life. Their more fragile brethren littered the ground in brown heaps.

A woman strolled by walking a shivering terrier in a cable-knit sweater. Another woman in a tracksuit jabbered into her cell phone as she power walked. Isabel was grateful for the presence of these strangers, however oblivious they were to her. After a few days at sea, her legs wobbled as she walked up the asphalt path toward the monument up ahead. Just off the park, a noisy highway supplied a constant hum of traffic. If she closed her eyes and listened, the whooshing cars sounded almost like ocean waves. Like home.

She clutched the ring box in her pocket as she approached the grand stone columns honoring the fallen warriors from the Civil War. The monument perched about a hundred feet tall on a cliff overlooking the Hudson River far below. Several rows of steps at its base led to a promenade, where three bronze cannons were mounted on concrete pedestals. In between each were wooden benches facing the river.

Some people were already hanging out there: A woman with a bundled-up baby in a stroller, a handsome middle-aged guy typing on an iPhone, an older rotund man smoking a cigar, and two skateboarders flipping tricks on the wide paved walkway.

She ambled past the benches to the cannon nearest the monument. Its mouth was about six inches across. She snuck a glance around to make sure no one was watching. But she couldn't shake the creepy feeling that someone, somewhere, was.

"Now," Galileo instructed in her ear.

She leaned up against the opening and emptied her pocket of the box. Then she squared her shoulders and walked away. There. It was done. Nobody had attacked her. She let out a breath she didn't realize she was holding.

"Good," came his voice. "Now go sit on a bench. Look casual."

She obeyed. It was 5:07 P.M. For half an hour, she waited. The people in the vicinity came and went. She pulled her jacket tight against the biting wind and watched the arc of the sun sinking into the river. It was only getting colder and darker. She wasn't sure how much longer she wanted to sit there, exposed, as the park's patrons emptied out.

And then, when she was starting to fidget, a skinny guy who couldn't have been older than eighteen marched up to the cannon, snatched the ring box, and walked away. Isabel was on her feet running after him before she had time to think.

"Hey!" she called.

The guy turned around. He was tall and bony, with a beautiful coffee complexion and guileless brown eyes. "Yeah?"

"What are you doing?" Galileo demanded in her ear. "You're not supposed to get involved."

She ignored him. She couldn't face returning to the ship, to passive confinement, without more information than she started with. Not when her own life hung in the balance. Plus, the kid's youthfulness emboldened her.

"Do you know what's in there?" she asked, pointing to the box in his hand.

"A ring, I guess. Why, what's it to you?"

She matched his nonchalant tone. "Just curious." Then she lowered her voice. "My friends sometimes use that spot to, you know, trade stuff. I thought only we used it."

He flashed her an amused grin. "That's your drug drop?"

She smiled coyly. *Whatever you want to think, dude.*

He raised his palms. "Well, I don't know nothin' about that. I'm just doing my job."

"Oh?" She racked her brain for a cool follow-up that wouldn't sound too interested. But while she stood there, he turned to leave.

"Hang on," she called. In a desperate rush, she whipped out most of the wad of cash Galileo had given her in case of emergency, leaving a few bills behind in her pocket just in case. The kid stopped and stared.

She counted out two hundred bucks in twenties. His eyes fixed on the crisp green bills. She fanned them out for maximum effect.

"Humor me," she said. "Who do you work for?"

"No one really. I just picked up this gig on Task-Rabbit."

"Oh." She tried not to show her disappointment. That site allowed anyone to assign one-off errands to anyone else. "Well, can you show me the ad?"

"Um, sure." He pulled out a crumpled sheet of paper from his jeans pocket. She held it up in full view of her camera. It was a printout from the TaskRabbit website.

Task: Pick up a ring at the Soldiers and Sailors Monument, 88th and Riverside, inside the northernmost cannon at 5:30 P.M. sharp on Nov. 15. Deliver promptly to 255 Canal Street.
Payment: A woman waiting at the delivery address will pay $100 cash.
Estimated Total Time: Less than one hour
Additional Comments: Don't bother stealing the ring. It's fake.

Isabel stared, flabbergasted, at the last two words. If Robbie Merriman had seen through their bribe all along, he probably suspected some kind of tracking device, too. So why did he agree to take the stupid ring? Why have it brought to Chinatown? There was nothing in it for him. And most unsettling of all: why demand that *she* drop it off?

A sickened feeling pummeled her. She was definitely being watched. But by whom? A few scattered people were nearby, sitting on benches or walking past. A young couple holding hands. A little boy and his dad. No one seemed remotely aware of her.

She handed the boy back the paper, along with the cash, and smoothed her features into an indifferent expression.

"Thanks," he said. He stuffed the wad into his pocket, baffled but pleased.

"Thank you. I was just headed downtown myself. Hey, there's a cab." She waved down an empty taxi rolling down Riverside Drive. "You can hitch a ride if you like. I'm passing Canal on my way to, ah, Tribeca."

Thank God for the city map posted in the back of her first cab. She'd studied it on her way up to orient herself to Manhattan.

The taxi pulled over. She got inside without turning to see if the kid followed, as though his coming along were inconsequential.

He hopped in beside her. "You sure?"

"No biggie." She crossed her arms over her jacket in case he noticed the little camera eye and got spooked. *Sorry, Galileo.*

"All right. I hate the subway at rush hour."

"Who doesn't?" she said like she rode it every day. The cab jerked ahead and sped onto the West Side Highway headed south.

"What are you doing?" Galileo screeched in her ear. "You don't need to chase this down. We have the GPS going!"

She pushed her long black locks over her ear so the device was obscured.

"Isabel, come back," he said. "Your job's done. This isn't part of the plan."

It wasn't like she could argue with him in front of the

boy. She couldn't explain her repulsion toward being on the ship now, given all the anxious reverence surrounding Chris. She couldn't explain her fury over Dr. Quinn's wrongful death and her frustration that Galileo had dismissed her suspicions. And she couldn't explain her rattled faith in his leadership, now that he'd proven himself capable of such a mistake.

If she could talk, she might admit that she felt more alone than ever. That she longed for her intrepid crew in lockstep behind her, but in their absence, she was forced to depend on herself. And so she was taking a risk, going against the plan, to learn anything that could lead back to her killer. Because out in the wild, you had to do whatever it took to survive.

"Come back," Galileo repeated. "You're safer here."

Am I? she wanted to retort. *With a murderer on board?*

But all she could do was clear her throat in defiance.

When the cab pulled up to 255 Canal Street twenty minutes later, the kid repeated his thanks and jumped out onto the busy sidewalk. Once he disappeared behind a glass storefront, Isabel paid the driver, got out, and slipped into the crowd. The sky was mostly dark now, but the streets of Chinatown were thriving. Cramped hole-in-the-wall stores lined the block, jammed with cheap handbags, sunglasses, and cologne bottles. Some items were stuffed under black plastic bags, attended by shady men who hissed designer names as she passed. The air reeked of cigarettes and cheap perfume.

When she snuck into the store the kid had gone into, she was surprised to see how long and narrow the interior was. It was a world unto itself: a jewelry store—or ten. Separate glass counters glinting with gold and silver stretched back at least thirty feet. Each counter appeared to be its own independent business. The Asian owners called back and forth to one another, conversing in a language she couldn't comprehend. Herds of customers shuffled from one station to the next, examining the selections of bracelets, earrings, necklaces, and rings.

Near the back, Isabel spotted the kid. He was talking to a curvy young woman about her own age who was wearing a tight red blouse. Not exactly a criminal look. Isabel inched her way closer to them, pretending to be interested in the jewelry. Within a minute, the kid was walking back out the door. He didn't notice her hunched over one counter studying a pair of gold hoops.

But the mysterious woman stayed where she was. Isabel saw that she was saying something to an Asian man at a workstation littered with metal tools. He seemed to be some kind of repairman. Isabel made her way closer, thankful for the first time for her heightened sensory awareness. She stopped at the adjacent counter and asked to try on a silver necklace, all the while listening and stealing sidelong glances over her shoulder. The woman didn't appear to notice her.

She was holding up the ring for the Chinese man to see. Its sparkling fake ruby matched her shirt.

"It's not real, right?" she asked.

The man took the ring and examined it with a special eyeglass, then shook his head. "Costume."

The woman didn't miss a beat. "How much to engrave a date?"

"Twenty dollar."

"Then do July six, 1957. Here, I'll write it down."

She scribbled something on a scrap of paper.

What in the world could that mean? This was getting more and more confusing. In Isabel's ear, Galileo kept telling her to be careful. "Don't get involved . . . just come back . . . the GPS is running . . ."

But, she wanted to respond, *look what I just learned. Your GPS would never have picked up this much detail.*

"Okay, I do now," the Chinese man said, plucking the ring from the woman's French-manicured fingers. His own nails were lined with black grime. "Ten minute."

"I'll wait," she said.

Isabel waited, too. She dawdled, trying on various bracelets and necklaces, no doubt frustrating the proprietor who was catering to her. Every piece reminded her of her mom. She was all right, Isabel knew. They spoke over Galileo's satellite phone every few nights. But she was worried and isolated with Andy in the safe house back in Key West. Their lives, too, had been monumentally disrupted. Isabel yearned for the moment she could tell them her killer was caught. But who knew how long that might take—if ever?

Then a carved wooden jewelry box caught her eye. It was in the shape of a hardcover book laying flat. Horizontal drawers pulled out from its spine. It was perfect for her mother, a voracious reader who sold books for a living.

She haggled the cost from $50 down to $35. Galileo could arrange to send it to her. Isabel was sure it would bring a smile to her face.

Just as she took the plastic bag, she saw out of the corner of her eye that the Chinese man was handing back the newly engraved ring.

"In a new box," the woman instructed. Her tone was oddly firm.

Isabel picked up its subtext right away. The investor suspected that the original box was embedded with GPS, not the ring itself. But still, why did he want it at all? What had happened on July 6, 1957? Nothing made sense.

The woman pocketed the new box, paid in cash, and

strode out of the store. Isabel hurried out in her wake, elbowing through the crowd that clogged the sidewalk.

"Isabel!" Galileo shouted in her ear. "You don't have to do this!"

Up ahead, the woman was disappearing down into a subway station. Isabel followed her down the steps despite not having any idea where she might end up. Galileo's repeated pleas cut out as soon as she got underground. A metallic gray train was waiting in the station.

The woman breezed through the turnstile and hopped on board. Isabel tried to run after her but the turnstile jammed into her stomach. No MetroCard, no ride. She watched helplessly as the doors slid closed and the train accelerated.

A streak of red flashed by before vanishing into the blackness of the tunnel.

When Isabel returned to the ship, Captain the dog was the only one to greet her. Everyone else was busy working. The dog jumped up and licked her leg excitedly, then led her down the stairs to Quinn's lab, where she found Galileo, Richard, and Chris. While Richard was sitting for another blood draw, he and Galileo were glued to a computer screen. She braced herself for an argument as she walked in.

"I'm sorry," she said, "but I wanted to get as much information as I could."

Galileo waved her defensiveness away. "I get it," he said. "I'm just glad you're okay."

Richard was confined to a chair with Chris's needle deep in his inner elbow. Both men chimed hello. She mus-

tered a smile, hardly able to make eye contact with Chris.
When her gaze settled on Richard instead, he tightened
his lips in subtle acknowledgment of her disgust.

"Check this out," Galileo said, gesturing to the laptop
on the counter. Next to it was his black satellite phone.

She rushed to get a better look at the screen. A map of
upper Manhattan showed a glowing red GPS dot.

"The ruby's been stopped there for a while," he said.

"Where is that?"

"Two-fourteen West 104th Street. Some residential
building with a dozen apartments. But that's as specific
as the GPS gets."

"So what do we do now?"

"Someone's going to have to go there and investigate.
So far none of this is adding up. Why take the ring in the
first place if he knew it was fake?"

Isabel sunk her fingers into her hair. "And why have
me drop it off? Then get that random date engraved?"

"There must be a reason." Richard winced as Chris extracted the needle from his arm. "If I know one thing
about Robbie, he never messes around. He's one cunning
son of a bitch."

An hour of discussing possible explanations went by
before the satellite phone rang. It shrieked a high-pitched
note that sounded like a wail. Isabel saw that its flashing
display read *No Caller ID*. When Galileo answered, his
face became grave. He pressed speaker.

"I said, is Richard Barnett there?" a familiar voice
growled. "Hello?"

Isabel gaped at the phone. *How did he get this number?* But then she remembered. Robbie Merriman had

promised to call to confirm the transaction. And the transaction was a fraud.

"Hello, Robbie," Richard said, astonishingly casual. "What can I do for you?"

"You have no idea what game you're playing, do you?"

Isabel, Chris, and Galileo stared at Richard. This time he was on his own. There was no script. He opened and closed his mouth, but no sound came out.

"I didn't think so," the voice went on. "Allow me to fill you in. I entertained your little stunt so that your stupid bitch client would come to New York, so I could set eyes on her myself. Now I know she's alive. But she *was* dead. Impossible, isn't it?"

Galileo made a cutting motion across his throat. Isabel noticed that Chris clamped his fingers tighter around the tube that contained Richard's blood.

"How do you explain it?" the voice demanded.

"Maybe," Richard suggested, "it was a miracle. Divine intervention?"

A snort came over the line. "Christ, spare me."

"Then I don't know."

"Well, I plan to find out. I am an investor after all, and I know a pot of gold when I see one. And only one person who can tell me how to get to it."

Isabel felt a boulder of dread barrel through her. She glanced helplessly at Galileo, but he was fixated on the phone.

"Lucky *Isabel*"—the sound of her name was a sneer— "is going to meet some friends of mine in the projects tomorrow. Tell her to go to 1844 Lex in East Harlem at midnight, apartment four. She better be alone, no cameras, no weapons, no trackers, nothing. She *will* be checked. If she has anything on her or calls the police, it's over. My friends will be expecting a credible explanation. If she cooperates, she'll be let go unharmed. We'll call it even."

"*Even?*" Richard's nostrils flared in rage.

"She did rip me off. And you tried to. Thanks for the ring, by the way. I think it'll actually come in handy."

Isabel was shaking her head so hard her neck hurt. *He can't make me*, she mouthed. Surely Galileo would agree to just push out to sea and leave New York behind forever. Then she'd move her family somewhere far away and forget all about her desire for justice.

"You're crazy," Richard said. "She'll never do that."

"Oh no? I'd think twice if I were her."

"Why's that?"

"You think I don't know about her brother? Or should I say *cousin*?" He pretended to seem hurt. "I hate when you underestimate me, Richard. You know I always do my research."

Isabel sprang to her feet, her heart thudding.

"Someone followed her family when they moved last week," he continued, oblivious to her panic. "Someone who's watching their house as we speak. If she refuses to comply or if they attempt to leave, the feds will be tipped that el Cubano's been squatting here for years." He paused to let the news sink in. "So I have a feeling she'll be there—unless she wants to see him deported."

CHAPTER 34
Joan

New York

Strangely, all the lights were off when Joan got home from the gym. But Greg was supposed to be there—this was his night off from the ER.

"Honey?" she called from the hallway as she pulled off her gloves. Her left ring finger remained starkly bare. Even though the diamond had managed to bring in a cool thirty grand, she couldn't shake her sadness over its loss. She chastised herself for mourning over a mere *thing*, with so many real problems mounting—like the fact that her quest to track down the investor was at a dead end. But every time she caught sight of her naked finger, she felt her heart constrict.

"I'm here," Greg called from inside the apartment. "Come on in."

"Then why are the lights off?"

As soon as she walked into the living room, her depressed mood lifted. Their bland place had been utterly transformed. Dozens of flickering votive candles decorated the living room, the kitchen table, the bookshelves. A fresh bouquet of pink dahlias, her favorite flower, stood in a glass vase on the coffee table. And in the center of the floor, down on one knee, was her smiling husband.

She blinked at him, unsure if she was seeing correctly. He hadn't been romantic in ages, ever since the whole crisis began. A slow grin spread across her face.

"What's going on?"

He produced a small box from his pocket. "I've been feeling terrible that we had to sell your ring. But then I thought of something else you could wear."

He opened the box. Inside lay a dazzling oval ruby surrounded by glittering white gems, set in a thick gold band. "It was my mother's. I'd forgotten about it in the safe. My dad gave it to her for one of their anniversaries."

"Oh my God, it's gorgeous!"

She held out her hand and he slipped it onto her left ring finger. It felt surprisingly solid. "How could your dad have afforded this?"

Greg's father had been a post office worker in Nebraska whose idea of luxury was going out to dinner once a month.

"Oh, it's not real. It just has sentimental value. He even had their wedding date engraved."

She wagged her finger so the scarlet stone reflected the candlelight.

"It's beautiful," she said. "You could've fooled me."

PART THREE

CHAPTER 35
Isabel

The full moon hung low off the river, illuminating the pier fifteen feet below. A chilly breeze whipped at Isabel's cheeks. She was alone on the top deck. She needed to get off the ship—and fast—but there was no way to deploy the general access ramp without waking everyone aboard. So she'd thought of another way.

She eyed the thin metal staircase affixed to the port side in case of an emergency evacuation. In one breath, she climbed over the edge of the deck and gripped the cold railing. Her feet tentatively connected with the first step. The wind hissed in her ears and whipped up the inky black water below. Little eddies swirled and lapped at the rotting wooden pier. If she lost her nerve now . . . *Don't look down.*

Her rubber-soled shoes squeaked as she made her white-knuckled descent. No one tried to stop her. Because no one, not even Richard, knew what she was doing.

It was 11 P.M., exactly one hour before her deadline to show up in the Harlem projects. Per Robbie Merriman's instructions, she wore no earpiece, no GPS, no camera. This time, she was completely, woefully alone.

It didn't matter that Galileo had promised to protect her family. It didn't matter that he was "working on a solution" and had emphatically told her to stay put on the ship. As much as she wanted to lean on him, she kept circling back to his mistake about Chris and his flippant dismissal of the truth. How could she trust a man like that with the people she loved most?

All it took to make up her mind was an image of Andy getting wrenched from her poor mother's arms; Andy getting sent back to Cuba, to a life of privation and misery . . . because of her own failure to act. The horrific thought spurred her on as she hopped down to the pier and scrambled past the other docked ships. No, she would rather confront evil than sacrifice her brother to it—and he *was* her brother, in all the ways that counted. She ran through a deserted parking lot to the West Side Highway, where an empty cab pulled over for her waving arm.

"I have two stops," she told the driver. "First, two-fourteen West 104th."

According to Galileo's GPS, the ruby ring had been stopped at that address for a whole day now. But since Robbie's call last night, Galileo had disappeared into his private cabin with the ship's only phone, Chris remained holed up in his lab, and she and Richard tolerated three more blood draws. The other personnel, meanwhile, were caught up in their own all-consuming drama about whether the X101 could be salvaged. No one volunteered to go out and investigate the ring's address.

But someone had to. Since she was sneaking out anyway, she decided to make a pit stop there on her way to the projects. If this was actually the last night of her life—and she viscerally recoiled at the thought—then every move had to count. If she died tonight, her murderer couldn't get away with it—twice.

Richard would be devastated. But at least she knew he would champion the cause in her absence. He was just as angry, just as hell-bent on justice. As the cab zoomed uptown, she felt a pang of sadness over leaving without saying good-bye. She hadn't even left a note, in case someone found it and tried to stop her. He was the only reason that life on the ship was bearable. Now that she was away, she realized how much she relished his companionship. A sideways glance or a wry smile was often all they needed to exchange a whole conversation.

As the cab zoomed uptown, she found herself missing his face. At first glance, his slightly hooked nose, floppy hair, and pointed chin had seemed terribly average. But since he'd quit smoking and shed a few layers of cynicism, his whole look had transformed, too. A renewed vitality shone through. His smile was warmer, his hazel eyes more earnest. Every day he was regaining more strength. Once he reached peak recovery, his trim body would be pretty sexy after all. She was sorry she had never told him so.

At least, if something did happen to her tonight, he was safe behind. Plus, with him on board, the X101 still had a shot. With his blood, they didn't need hers, so she didn't feel too guilty about deserting the critical research. And she didn't feel guilty at all about deserting Chris. Her heightened senses were starting to fade, anyway, which meant the drug's concentration in her blood was weakening. Richard's was stronger and thus more useful, since he'd received his dose a few days after hers.

If Robbie Merriman's thugs thought she was going to

show up and hand over a map to the drug, well, it wasn't that easy. She just hoped she could escape their retaliation. What if they tried to kill her?

She waited for a bolt of fear that didn't come. After a minute, she realized why. Death itself was peaceful, she now knew. It was total deliverance from suffering. She involuntarily thought of her dad's death in the context of her own, and for the first time, felt a degree of comfort. She imagined him sliding out of his panicked agony into that welcoming blackness. Now that she grasped how complex it was to effectively resuscitate someone, she realized how pointless it was to blame herself for failing to do CPR on her dad. Even if she'd acted sooner and gotten him to a hospital, it would still have been a conventional hospital without the Network's cooling protocol and the X101. So his heart attack would have still likely been fatal. There was nothing she could have done. If only Galileo had been there the way he had for her.

When the cab stopped in front of 214 West 104th Street, she asked the driver to pull over and wait until she returned. With the meter running, she ran up to the stout brick townhouse. It was about six stories high, sandwiched between a dive bar and a smoke shop on a poorly lit street. As she walked toward the front door, she noticed that a window of one of the ground-floor apartments had been smashed in. Its hole was patched over with silver electric tape.

There was no doorman. She pushed open the glass front door and entered a small foyer. Trampled old takeout menus littered the floor. Ahead was another door, this one locked and shielded with a wrought iron security gate. On the left wall was a row of narrow mailboxes and a panel of twelve buzzers corresponding to various apartments. Next to each buzzer was a name.

She skimmed the list: *Slattery, Eisenberg, Chen, Hughes, Wilcox . . .*

No Merriman. Not that she expected it. She knew it was a pseudonym. But someone on this list was connected to him. How could she figure out who? A quick idea wormed into her head. It might never work, but it was worth a try. She rushed out to the waiting taxi and asked the driver for a pen and paper. He scrounged in his glove box and produced a crumpled sheet of yellow legal paper and a black Sharpie.

"I'll be right back," she promised him.

He shrugged. The meter was still running. "Take your time."

She thanked him and raced back. As she entered, a trendy couple in their forties walked out of the building holding hands. Isabel scurried past them into the foyer as though she belonged there. She ripped the piece of paper in half and secretly copied down all the names next to the buzzers as fast as she could. The couple paused in the doorway, watching her. She heard them murmuring to each other.

Then the man cleared his throat behind her. "Can we help you with something?" His tone was cold.

She spun around and smiled sheepishly. "Um, thanks, but I'm okay."

"Do you know someone here?"

"Sort of. A friend of a friend. I lost my favorite ring here the other day, so, um, I was just leaving a note for the whole building." She held up the pen. "In case anyone spots it."

She scrawled out a quick message and showed him:

Lost costume ruby ring, oval stone in plated gold band. Reward $$. If found, please call 413-919-8020.

It was Galileo's satellite phone number.

"Oh," the man said. "Well, good luck." He lost interest and turned to leave, but his wife's attention perked up when she read the note over his shoulder. Isabel was pressing it to the wall, trying to find something to pin it up.

"Is it a big stone?" she asked. She curled her forefinger and thumb into a sizeable circle. "With little diamonds around it?"

Isabel blinked at her. The woman was decked out in a chunky gold necklace, emerald stud earrings, a diamond ring, and a wrist full of metallic bangles. She stared back openly, as though she had nothing to hide.

"How did you know?"

"Our new neighbor was wearing it today," she said. "I even complimented her on her good taste."

"My wife is obsessed with jewelry," the man added with a grimace. "In case you couldn't tell."

She smacked his arm playfully and all her bracelets jingled together.

"Which neighbor?" Isabel asked.

"Oh, I don't know her name," the woman said, "but she's in 1B. Do I get the reward?"

"Katie," her husband groaned. "Come on. You don't need this young woman's money." He pulled her out the door. "Good luck," he said again to Isabel, more sincerely this time.

They stepped out arm in arm, leaving her standing there with her heart slamming against her ribs. She scanned the panel on the wall for apartment 1B.

Hughes.

It was 11:25 P.M.

Far too late to call on a stranger. But her midnight deadline loomed—and after that, who knew if she'd have another chance to come back?

She drew a breath, pressed the buzzer, and waited.

CHAPTER 36
Joan

Joan frowned when the buzzer rang. It was late and she was alone. She disliked being by herself in the apartment, but Greg was working the night shift at the ER and wouldn't be home for several more hours. She waited for the unexpected visitor to go away, but then the noise came again—an insistent second buzz.

She got out of bed, slipped into her velour robe, and trudged to the intercom.

"Who's there?"

Surprisingly, a woman's voice answered. "You don't know me, but . . ." She sounded nervous. "Can I talk to you? It's important."

"What? Who are you? What is this about?"

"I lost something I think you have. A ruby ring?"

Joan inhaled a sharp breath. She looked down at her left finger, where the rich red stone sparkled in the hallway's dim light. The fact that it was a legacy of Greg's mother made it all the more special.

"Sorry," she said into the intercom. "You must be mistaken."

But the strange coincidence jarred her—how in the world did some random woman know about her ring at all?

"Please, just for a minute? I don't have long."

Joan hesitated for a beat until her curiosity won out. "Okay."

She pressed the buzzer, and through the peephole watched a slender, dark-haired woman approach her door alone. She had an honest face. Something about it seemed vaguely familiar. Wide eyes, a delicately sloped nose, pale lips. Her features conveyed the sensitivity of someone who had a soft touch, but her eyes seemed troubled. Joan noticed that she wasn't carrying a purse like most women did. All she had on was her clothes: a faded pair of jeans, sneakers, and a blue Windbreaker zipped up to her chin. A crease deepened between her brows before she knocked.

Joan opened the door. "Hi."

"Hi," she said. She looked young, no older than thirty. Her gaze shifted instantly down to Joan's hands. When she saw the ruby, she gasped.

Then she looked up with a mixture of shock and dismay. "That's it."

Joan shook her head. This poor girl was clearly confused and in the throes of some kind of distress. "I don't think so," she said gently.

"No, that's it, I'm sure of it." She stared at Joan with blatant astonishment, as if trying to make sense of something inexplicable.

"Sorry, but you're mixed up." Joan twisted the band around her finger. "This belonged to my husband's mother."

The woman's eyes grew large. "Your husband—he told you that?"

Her disbelieving tone piqued Joan's annoyance. "Yes, why?"

"What's his name?"

"As if it's any of your business?"

"Mr. Hughes? I saw it on the mailbox."

"*Dr.* Hughes," Joan retorted.

"Is he home?"

"*No*, he's at *work*. Who are you, anyway? And how did you know I had a ruby ring?"

"He's lying," the woman declared. "That ring was bought a week ago in Florida for a very specific purpose."

Joan laughed uneasily. "Okay, you're nuts and I'm closing the door."

"Wait!" the woman stuck her foot in the doorframe. "I'm not crazy, I swear. My name's Isabel Leon and I'm telling you the truth. Hear me out."

Her name with the face suddenly clicked. Joan peered through the crack at her.

"Hang on, you're the one on that show. *Wild Woman* or something on cable?"

"Yes! That's me." She smiled proudly. "On the Outdoor channel."

"I saw one episode over the summer . . . Peru, was it? In the rainforest?"

"Bolivia."

Joan opened the door a little wider. So she wasn't necessarily nuts—though appearing on reality TV wasn't exactly the mark of sanity. She was just sorely mixed up.

"What are you doing here? How did you get to me?"

"I'm sort of on a hiatus from the show." She paused as though considering what more to reveal. "I can't really say much, but I'm working on another project right now . . ." she trailed off.

"Also a survival show?"

She grimaced. "You could say. Listen, I have to run, but you should know: That ring didn't come from your mother-in-law. It's a tool to catch a violent investor who goes by the name Robbie Merriman. He buys up life insurance policies and then goes after victims for their death benefits. I was one of them, and now he's put my whole family in danger."

Joan let out a cry. "Oh my God! You too?"

"What do you mean, *too*?"

"My husband also sold his policy, and then we heard the rumors . . . We've been so afraid . . . I was doing everything to track down the perp, but I've had so little to go on . . ."

Isabel stared at her. "But he gave you that ring?"

"It was a surprise last night."

"I'm sorry, but he's definitely lying. He must have something to do with Robbie Merriman."

Joan crossed her arms. "You have some nerve, coming here and accusing—"

"July sixth, 1957," Isabel cut in.

"What?"

"It's engraved inside, isn't it?"

The words felt strangled in her throat. "How could you know that?"

"I told you." Isabel pointed to Joan's paralyzed hand. "That ring was mine."

CHAPTER 37
Isabel

Isabel checked her watch. It was already 11:35 P.M. Less than a half hour to go.

"I'm sorry," she said, "but I really have to leave now."

The woman in the doorway was fretting at her ring as though it were an alien specimen. "I just can't . . ." she muttered. "How . . . ?"

Isabel couldn't be sure if her bewilderment was genuine. It was possible, of course, that she knew more than she was letting on. But it didn't seem that way. Maybe it was the jaunty blond curls framing her face, or the elegant way she held up her neck, or the warmth in her eyes that projected care and concern—but the sum added up to an air of integrity. Her age and look reminded Isabel of a teacher she'd had in grade school whose uncompromising standards concealed her tender core.

Still, she knew better than to say too much.

"I didn't catch your name," she said as she turned to go.

"Joan." The woman blinked at her in a daze. "But you can't just go. I don't understand . . . aren't you going to explain . . . ?"

Isabel took a few steps back, considering what more to say. Nothing that could compromise the investigation or put Galileo and the Network in danger. As she was about to apologize, she caught sight of a framed picture on the wall behind Joan's head. It was an action shot of her with a striking man in his fifties who had salt-and-pepper hair and the kind of chiseled bone structure that would make a sculptor swoon. They were on some white-sand beach, and Joan was laughing at the camera while her grinning husband carried her in his arms toward the surf. They looked like the Platonic ideal of a carefree married couple.

But the real Joan in front of her was far from happy. She glanced over her shoulder to see what was transfixing Isabel.

"That was last year." The ache in her voice was palpable. "Maui, for our thirtieth anniversary."

Isabel was about to reply when a realization hit her:

She had seen that man before.

The day she went to Riverside Park to drop off the ring. He was sitting on a bench, typing on an iPhone. Like the other strangers in the vicinity, he had appeared not to notice her. But she remembered his face. It was too handsome to forget.

There could be no doubt now: he was involved with Robbie Merriman. Hell, he could even *be* Robbie Merriman.

"What?" Joan demanded. "What's wrong?"

She must have looked stricken. "I can't . . . here." She opened her clenched fist, which held the note she'd scrawled earlier with Galileo's phone number. It wasn't enough to compromise his safety or location. But it was a way to connect with Joan again. There was a chance that if she were innocent and willing, she might be able to help.

"Call this number," Isabel said, "if you want to know the truth."

Then she turned and scrambled out of the building, ignoring Joan's pained shouts to wait. There was no time to waste. She thought of Andy asleep in bed, totally unaware of the danger that threatened him and why. She thought of her mother, who also knew nothing. What good would it do to warn them, when they would inevitably try to escape? According to Robbie's warning, that would trigger the creep who was watching their house to call in the fatal tip. The tip that would send Andy away to the place he feared the most.

She jumped into the cab, whose meter was now over $50. The driver raised his eyes from his e-reader and glanced at her in the rearview mirror. His black turban wound around his head like a coiled snake.

"Where to?" he asked in his thick Indian accent.

"1844 Lex," she panted. "In East Harlem."

He raised his eyebrows. "The projects?"

"Yeah. I'm, uh, meeting someone. Can I borrow your phone really fast? I . . . left mine at home."

He gave her a sympathetic nod and handed over his cell. Whatever she was doing there, he seemed to know it wasn't good.

The taxi squealed away from the curb as she dialed Galileo. His phone rang and rang unanswered. When the message machine beeped, the words tumbled out in one breath: "I went to the ring's address and found a woman wearing it in apartment 1B, Joan Hughes, said her hus-

band Dr. Greg Hughes gave it to her, and get this—I saw
him in Riverside Park when I dropped it off, he has to be
involved somehow, I don't know about her, but I gave her
your number . . ." Isabel paused to breathe. "It's almost
midnight. I know you said not to, but you know where
I'm going now. I have to. I'm sorry. You don't need me
anyway, since you have Richard. I just hope—"

A harsh tone cut her off and a robotic voice droned:
"Message limit exceeded."

She closed her eyes. *I just hope I come back in one
piece.*

The building that housed the projects was a beige
brick monolith that spanned the length of an entire city
block. A few scattered streetlights cast a wan glow on its
crumbling paint and thin vertical windows. Their look reminded Isabel of a jail—which, she supposed, wasn't far
off.

A couple of guys in hooded sweatshirts and baggy
jeans were loitering near the unattended front door,
smoking. As she hurried by, a distinctive odor engulfed
her, and it wasn't cigarettes. Cold stares bored into her
back. She felt about as conspicuous as a gazelle in a
lion's den.

"Hey, pretty mama," one of them crooned after her.
"Slow down, we ain't gonna bite." There was a note of
menace in his voice that kicked her adrenaline up a notch.
She ignored him and quickened her step.

She was ready to fight. All her fitness training, her experience facing down savage environments, her accrued
mental toughness—she was counting on every survival

skill in her arsenal to make it through this night. Though she looked petite, she knew enough karate to wipe out an attacker. Her calves twitched to act. She mentally ran through the deadliest self-defense moves her father had taught her: a side kick to the throat, a knee drop to the heart, a back kick to the groin. Yet her years of practice in martial arts and the intensive training for her show had never been tested in a real-life assault situation, and she still wasn't up to peak strength since recovering from—well, from death. Damn, did that take a lot out of you. It wasn't like a bout with the flu.

She hovered anxiously outside the front door, keeping one eye on the huddled guys who were watching her. On the wall was a list of apartment numbers and corresponding buzzers. She pressed 4B. It was 11:59 P.M.

Maybe no one would answer. Maybe she would wake up from this nightmare and be back in her cozy double bed at home in Key West, with Andy snoring in the next room and the sound of her mom's television trickling in from the hall.

But then the buzzer sounded. She pushed open the door and went in. There was barely a lobby to speak of, just a bank of old elevators next to a stairwell. A few crushed beer cans were piled atop an overstuffed garbage can in the corner that reeked of rotting food. Yellowed cigarette butts littered the floor around it.

The button to call the elevator didn't light up, but after a few seconds, the doors screeched open. Inside the steel car was a putrid mess of what looked like dog piss. Or human piss. She took the stairs. With each flight, her heart pounded harder—more out of mounting fear than exertion. Who was inside 4B and what were they going to do to her?

She could still go back to the ship. She could climb into bed next to Richard and let herself be held. On the top step of the fourth floor, she paused. The temptation beckoned like a siren song. It wasn't too late to turn around. But poor Andy—what would he do if the feds showed up to wrench him away? How could she live with the consequences, knowing she could have done something to prevent it?

She grimaced and kept going, out of the stairwell, down a sparse hallway with about ten doors on either side. From one apartment she could hear the angry shouts of a man and woman arguing. She fought the urge to knock on their door and plead with them to watch her go into 4B. But that wouldn't accomplish anything. The most they could do would be to call the cops, which was strictly forbidden. There was only one option.

She stopped in front of the plain brown door of 4B. No noises came from within—no chatting, no voices, no nothing. But inside, she knew someone was waiting for her.

She knocked. Heavy footsteps plodded toward her and then the door swung open. The first thing she saw was the crumpled limp body on the floor. A man's body. He looked like a thug, with multiple black tattoos sheathing his biceps and a thick gold chain around his neck. A wifebeater hung off his shoulder and his oversized pants sagged. He was curled on his side, knocked out, mouth open. A massive bruise was darkening his puffy eyelid.

Isabel felt a scream rise in her throat as she looked to the left. There, on the ground, another thug was writhing. His front teeth were bashed in. A stream of blood dribbled over his lips and down his chin, pooling on the wood floor where his cheek was pressed. His eyes seemed to roam in and out of consciousness as he let out an anguished moan.

Before she could make any sense of it, a third powerfully built man stepped out from behind the door and fixed his severe gaze on her.

He was Galileo.

CHAPTER 38
Greg

Dr. Greg Hughes smiled modestly as he strode out of the operating room to hearty applause. The surgical staff and the dozen residents watching from the balcony broke into cheers as soon as he repaired the torn aortic valve of the gunshot victim on the table. It was a tricky surgery with no room for error, and once again, he'd proved his coolness under pressure.

He acknowledged the adulation of his colleagues with a mock salute. Then he tore off his gloves and headed out to tell the victim's distraught parents that their son—an accidental victim of a drive-by shooting—would make a full recovery.

There was truly no better high than the power conferred on a surgeon in an emergency. A pop of Vicodin couldn't even come close. In the operating room, he was God. He was a hero. And everyone around him knew it. He thrived on their respectful awe, which negated the black crust of his soul: the sinister fragment he had to keep hidden at any cost.

As he stepped into the hall, his ears still buzzing from the applause, he found himself walking straight toward

Ellis Yardley. Of all the people in this hospital, why did he have to run into the one person who could bring him down faster than the flick of a scalpel?

Ellis's balding hairline glistened, as did his trim gray mustache, and there were dark pit stains under his white coat. He was a sweaty bastard. The beer belly didn't help. Behind his spectacles, his watery corneas were snaked with red lines. He glanced around to make sure no one was watching them. Then his upper lip curled into a sneer.

"If I were you," he said in a low voice, "I'd wipe that shit-eating grin off my face."

Greg stiffened. His tongue itched to retort, but he knew it was too dangerous. Their dynamic was as fragile as a diseased heart, and just as prone to a disastrous rupture.

"Tonight," Greg said. "Everything is going to change after tonight."

"Just like the last time you promised?"

"This is really it," he insisted. "I swear. Just give me until Sunday."

It was Wednesday now. That would leave him four more days to secure his lifeline out of hell. Otherwise, Ellis would burn him alive. If the world found out the truth—if his family found out—he would be abandoned for the rest of his days. The inevitable prison sentence might be bearable—he could find allies, a job, a routine to pass the time. But he could forget his hopes of ever reconciling with his son or knowing his grandkids. And beyond that loomed the thing that scared him the most: life without Joan. Such an existence was impossible to fathom, like a captain without a ship. Her love kept him afloat. Without it, his compass would go awry and the darkness he worked so hard to suppress would engulf him. He might as well be dead.

Ellis blinked, unwavering. He seemed to be relishing Greg's desperation—the pathetic appeal of his onetime friend who'd always been more talented, more popular, and more attractive than himself.

"Please," Greg said, his hatred intensifying at being forced to beg. "You won't regret the extra time. I'll make it well worth your while."

Ellis waited for him to squirm, but Greg lifted his chin in a risky act of defiance. He had already stooped low enough.

"Sunday," Ellis said at last. "By midnight. Not a minute later."

"Thank you," Greg said. It took every effort to keep his tone civil.

They parted without another word. Greg's body felt rigid as stone. His mind darted, as it had countless times throughout his shift, to the event that was taking place a few miles uptown. Tonight, at an apartment in the Harlem projects, the golden goose of all his "lives" was going to come clean about how she survived death.

And then she was going to die again.

Talk about killing two birds with one stone. Tonight was going to be the mother of all double whammies. If she really could lead him to the source of a way to reverse death, the windfall would be copious enough to solve everything. Getting rid of her would be an added quick bonus, providing just enough cash to tide Ellis over until the real prize could be delivered as the ultimate peace offering.

He felt a weak prick of satisfaction at the thought of Isabel Leon's death. She *had* cheated him of hundreds of thousands of dollars by cutting off her breasts. Still, he didn't want to have to get rid of her, just like he hadn't wanted to get rid of blind old Mrs. Ruth Bernstein, rest her soul. Their deaths were necessary evils. But he had saved so many other lives throughout his medical career, and even again just tonight, that he figured his karma was in the black. Sometimes one or two people had to be sacrificed for the greater good. But it wasn't his fault. Unfortunate circumstances had prevailed, so he had to react to the forces acting on him. He wasn't a bad person overall. Far from it.

He was a goddamn hero.

When he arrived home after 2 A.M., his sublime operating-room high was gone. Yardley had killed it, plus there was still no word from his crew uptown. What the hell was happening with Isabel? He had half a mind to swing by and find out, but discretion was key. That part of his identity could never be compromised.

Before he opened the front door, he popped four Vicodin from a prescription he'd written for himself. An illegal maneuver of course, but his nasty addiction had come back with a vengeance since the whole crisis started. He paced on the sidewalk while he waited for the suckers to kick in. Four of them ought to be enough to resurrect the high he chased, that feeling of invincibility. It was a compulsion he'd lived with since he was a teenager, a monster that needed to be fed. Sometimes drugs did the trick, or gambling, or operating, but only for so long. Without those crutches, a twitchy edginess set in, and that was when he could become reckless. That was when mistakes could be made.

No one knew the darkness of his inner depths—his twisted delights and his private pain. As a doctor, he operated not for the honor of saving lives, but for the pleasure of domination, of inert flesh at the mercy of his hands to shape and bend as he desired. It scared him sometimes how little he felt if things went wrong, if the patient slipped away on the table. There was always another one lined up. They blurred together like specimens, though he was able to mimic empathy with learned precision like any other surgical feat. Mostly he lived for the glory when things went right. He could never get enough of that. A good day was about pushing his limits—physical, mental, financial, legal—without ever losing control.

But then, back on earth, there was Joan. Oh, Joan. She was the heart he wished he had. She was the solid ground. In her presence, his compulsions diminished, the darkness receded, and he felt something akin to peace. She had enough humanity for them both. It was as natural for her as water from a spring.

After three decades together, he remained in awe of her genuine goodness. She cheered on his victories in the emergency room and felt real pain at his defeats. She was deeply appreciative of heroism—his own and others'—and its various incarnations could move her to tears. She might weep at Supreme Court rulings that granted freedom to the oppressed; at the sacrifices of soldiers; at the bravery of thinkers who suffered for unpopular but righteous causes. On the flip side, she loathed injustice, and had devoted her former career to exposing crime. She raged when evil triumphed, whether it was in the form of a school bully, a terrorist, or a presidential election.

Her authenticity was effortless. There were no errant pieces that had to be beaten into submission to fit the whole. She was also a thoughtful partner, knowing just when to give him space or attention. Hell, she'd given up her career for his after their son was born. He still remembered what she told him the day she announced her decision to quit journalism: *I might expose bad guys, but you get to save good ones. You win.*

Yet he had won by virtue of having her. Her tenderness as a mother defied his comprehension. During the difficult period after Adam's birth, she never complained about the baby's infuriating tendency to cry for hours straight, or the bleary-eyed stupors that seemed never to lift. While Greg nursed a private resentment toward the red-faced creature that had invaded their lives, she nursed their colicky boy with an endless reserve of patience. He might have hated her if he wasn't so thoroughly hooked on her.

A light rain was falling outside, but he didn't mind because a familiar warmth was starting to course through his veins. He felt his tense shoulders relax. Everything would be fine. It would all work out. That motherfucker Ellis Yardley was not going to bring him down. Because he was unstoppable.

He went inside. The lights in the apartment were off. Joan was in bed on her side facing the wall, with the covers pulled up to her chin. He undressed to his boxers and climbed in beside her.

"Hi, honey," he whispered. "I'm home."

"Mmm," she murmured, without turning to face him.

He spooned her, pressing his body up against hers. Usually she woke up and kissed him when he got into bed. But this time she remained stiff. He let his hand caress her bare stomach, then venture up to her breasts. God, it had been a long time since they'd had sex. Hadn't she complained about their dry spell not too long ago? So why was she now pushing his hand away?

"You okay?" he said softly.

"Not feeling good," she muttered into her pillow.

"Oh, poor boo." He kissed the top of her head and rested his arm around her waist instead. "You need anything?"

She sniffed. "Just sleep."

His head fell back on his own pillow. She could never know what he was up against. No matter how much he wanted to confide everything, it was crucial that she remain ignorant. He knew there was only so far her forgiveness could extend. She had already once approached the point of no return. Thank God he'd figured out a way, on the spot, to satisfy her suspicions without divulging the real answers.

That story about gambling debt hadn't been a complete lie, but the game he played wasn't found in any casino. The additional lie about selling his insurance and fearing for his life had been a stroke of genius. She'd long suspected that the unregulated hedge funds who bought up people's life policies were up to no good. By playing into her embedded fears and making her pity him as a victim, he'd built up her sympathies and made it impossible for her to leave. And he *was* a victim, in his own way. He was a victim of circumstance.

The problem was that she cared too much about protecting him. She had taken it too far, faking those heart pains and then going to the hospital to investigate on his behalf. The nurses knew nothing, but she'd come face-to-face with Yardley—Yardley!

He'd had to scare her away somehow, so on the night of the gala, he'd rushed home between his shift and the fund-raiser, making sure she'd already left by the time he arrived. In the closet, he found an old bat they saved from Adam's high school baseball days, one their son had used to hit a winning home run. Then he took it and smashed the front window to pieces. Not the sweetest message he'd ever left for his wife, but it was a critical one:

Back off.

Before she got too close to the truth.

CHAPTER 39
Isabel

Isabel stared at Galileo in shock. He was panting in the doorway of apartment 4B, his broad face rimmed with sweat. A gash above his left eye trickled blood. One sleeve of his black trench coat was torn at the cuff, and red scratch marks raked across the inside of his wrist. The skin of his knuckles was shredded raw. Behind him, on the floor, lay the two semiconscious thugs.

"How did you . . . ?" she began.

"Come on." He grabbed her elbow, closing the door behind him. "Let's get out of here."

"But what about my family? This wasn't allowed to happen!"

"They're fine," he said. "Come, I'll explain."

Then he jogged to the stairwell she had exited only minutes earlier.

She remained rooted to the spot. "Where are they?" she demanded. "I want to know exactly where they are."

He threw a weary glance over his shoulder. "They're being moved as we speak. You're going to have to learn to trust me. Let's go."

He disappeared into the stairwell. She had no choice

but to follow him down the four concrete flights, skipping steps to keep pace with his brisk clip.

"But they weren't supposed to leave the safe house!" she cried. "That guy watching will see them go and he'll get my brother deported!"

Galileo didn't so much as slow his step. "It's all been taken care of."

His nonchalance infuriated her. Did he not realize how much was at stake?

"Deported," she said again, in case he didn't grasp the weight of the threat. "The feds will find him eventually, and then what?"

"Let's just get in the car."

They exited the stairwell into the trash heap of a lobby, and then out into the bitter cold night. A mixture of rain and snow drizzled from a bank of foggy clouds overhead. The hooded guys she had passed before were still standing in a cluster smoking a joint. She stuck close to Galileo, who at six foot five dwarfed not only her, but also them. They eyed her as she scurried by, but a hard stare from Galileo prompted them to look away. His height combined with his cut-up face and assured stride made him a man no one wanted to mess with.

On the curb, a yellow taxi was parked without its light on. He opened the door for her.

"It's been waiting for us," he said, in answer to her look of surprise. "Get in."

She obeyed. He climbed in next to her and directed the driver to Chelsea Piers on 39th Street and 12th Avenue, where the ship was docked in the Hudson River. As the cab gunned up to speed, he turned to her.

"Do you remember when we met, what I told you about myself?"

She thought back to her first moments after death,

when she'd regained consciousness only to find herself surrounded by medical personnel on a ship. Then he had cleared everyone out and explained to her about the existence of the Network. But he'd been less than forthcoming about himself.

"You're on the most-wanted list," she recalled. "Though no one knows your real name or who you really are."

"That's true," he said. "But I did give you a hint about my past. I'm ex-FBI."

"Right. You're a criminal and a crime fighter in one."

He seemed amused. "Something like that. Anyway, I still have a lot of friends in the Justice Department, old colleagues who think I'm retired—many of them the same people who tried for years to dismantle the Network. In fact, I used to be in charge of the effort."

She raised her eyebrows. "That's crazy."

"It was completely intentional. That way, I could keep my researchers safe while directing the officials to false leads. Eventually I led the government to conclude that the Network had fallen apart on its own, so they closed their investigation. That way, I could retire and focus on it full-time."

Despite her confusion, she had to give him points for sheer brilliance. But he hadn't yet proven that he'd pulled off the most critical feat of all, the one that was more important than all his scientists' breakthroughs put together.

"Okay," she said, "but what about my family? What about my brother?"

"I was just getting to that. When we got the threat from Robbie Merriman last night, I knew I had to get to work exploiting my connections. I spent all day making phone calls and calling in rush favors." His lips tightened. "It's times like these I remember to be grateful for having worked in our illustrious government."

Her heart sped up in spite of his sarcasm. "What kind of favors?"

"These." He reached into his coat pocket and pulled out a folded piece of paper. She opened it up—and gasped. What she was holding could not be paid for. It existed only in fantasy. It was a scanned printout of two formal documents: a U.S. Social Security card and a U.S. birth certificate, both in the name of Andrés Enriqué Leon.

She balked at him. "But these are fake."

He smiled cryptically. "Perception is often all that counts, my dear. Especially when they're perceived in the federal database."

"You did not!"

"I did."

"This is insane!" She gawked at the printout. "But how did you know his name and birthday?"

"I called your mom. Once the documents were finally created, I called her back and explained that she and Andy needed to move to a new place, so right now, one of my professional drivers is taking them to a different safe house in the Keys where no one will be able to track them. They're perfectly fine, and now you guys will never have to worry about his status again."

"Why didn't you tell me?" she demanded. "I never would have snuck out!"

"I told you not to go anywhere, that I was working on it, but I didn't want to overpromise something I might not be able to deliver. This was no walk in the park."

"What did you have to do?"

He lifted one shoulder. "Oh, you know, just greasing the palms of the junior Florida senator, pleading with a couple reps on the House Subcommittee on Immigration, asking my old buddy who runs the Justice Department to turn a blind eye."

"Damn." She stared at him with renewed awe. Here was a man who dared to thunder where others pattered. If people were raindrops, he would be a hurricane.

"I have to say, not many folks could have pulled it off," he said, as though reading her mind. "But when I finally went to tell you the good news, you were gone. I knew there was only one place you could be."

"Thank you," she said, looking him in the eye. "I don't want to think about where I would be right now if you hadn't shown up."

"Those guys were bad news." He wiped a smear of blood off his eyelid. "They weren't expecting me, that's for sure."

"But why go so far out of your way for me?" she asked. "I mean, I've caused you so much trouble already. Wouldn't it have been easier to just . . . let me go?" She winced at her own euphemism. From the look of those thugs and the price of her death, not to mention the drug she wouldn't have been able to deliver, it was all too clear she wouldn't have left that place alive.

"And be murdered?" He cocked his head at her. "Yeah, I guess that would have been easier than a bunch of phone calls."

"Fair enough." She put her hand on his arm. "Seriously, thank you."

He nodded. "You missed one other thing."

"You did, too," she said, thinking about her encounter with Joan Hughes. Now that she was out of immediate danger, a belated thrill kicked in. The lead about Joan's husband wasn't a sure thing, but it was a definite step on the path to unmasking Robbie Merriman.

"You go first," she said. "You look too excited about your thing."

He smiled. "Chris was able to use traces of the compound from your blood to complete a crucial step in the reverse engineering process. He's really getting somewhere, but he needs another sample from you as soon as possible."

She frowned. "What about Richard?"

"It seems his blood contains an excessive clotting factor that's partially obscuring the compound. His concentration may be higher than yours, but it's much more difficult to isolate. So now is when we need you the most."

"Great," she muttered. "I'm there."

"Chris couldn't do this without you. It's just such a damn shame it happened this way." He glanced out the window at the starless sky. "I still can't believe Horatio is actually gone."

She bit her lip. Just when she was starting to believe in his competence, he had to go and remind her of his mistake. Since the rapport between them had grown more comfortable, she was tempted to tell him again about Chris. But he'd already dismissed her accusation once. If he hadn't admitted his error by now, he wasn't going to. Hopefully, she thought, the whole ship wouldn't have to pay the consequences.

Upon her return, she found Richard pacing anxiously outside her cabin as Captain the dog nipped at his heels. At the sight of her coming down the hallway, both of them sprinted toward her at full speed. Captain stood on his hind legs and covered her hands with enthusiastic kisses; Richard was slightly more restrained, but no less thrilled.

He drew her into his arms without hesitation. "You're okay! Thank God."

She rested her head in the crook of his neck. "Thank Galileo."

Richard tilted her chin up with one finger, and then out of nowhere, his mouth was on hers. It felt so natural that she forgot to be surprised. She kept her face upturned, reveling in the tenderness of his lips. That was when she realized she'd been wanting to kiss him for days. It was as clear to her now as the sky after the storm.

After he gently drew back, they stood in a quiet embrace while Captain frolicked around their feet. Exhaustion crept into her muscles. She let her body sag against his chest. For the first time that night, she noticed how bone-tired she was.

"What happened?" he asked after a few moments.

"So much," she said. "And so much that didn't."

"I have time."

"Sadly, I don't." She nuzzled closer into him to escape the duty that was pressing on her. "I'm supposed to go to the lab right now to give Chris another sample."

A guttural noise in his throat expressed the disgust she felt but couldn't confide to anyone else. And the fear. As much as she wanted to feel safe on the ship, with Galileo in control, it was impossible when a killer remained at large.

A killer who needed her blood.

CHAPTER 40
Greg

Greg lay awake next to Joan, listening to her steady, rhythmic breathing. It was after 1 A.M. and still—*still*—his phone had not rung. His repeated texts remained unanswered. What the hell? His guys never failed to get back to him.

Catastrophic scenarios wormed into his mind, but he steeled himself against panic. They just needed a little more time to get the job done, that was all. They were probably in the middle of disposing of Isabel's body. They must have gotten all the info they could out of her, and now they were busy cleaning up their tracks.

As he waited, the memory of Yardley's sneer kept popping into his mind. It was hard to believe how much between them had changed in such a breathtakingly short time. For a decade, they'd been each other's most trusted confidants. Their friendship had grown organically out of sharing shifts in the emergency room and complaining of the various bullshit that entailed. A wide spectrum of human scumbags constantly marched into their ER with righteous demands to be treated, no matter if they were homeless bums, vomiting drunks, gang members, welfare mothers, or undocumented aliens with no intention of ever paying a cent.

He and Yardley couldn't legally turn anyone away, no matter how strained their resources or how overburdened their workloads. Being a doctor wasn't about a glamorous life of money and status like they'd idealized in medical school. It was about sacrifice—sacrifice for society's least fortunate and least glamorous. It was a perversion of everything they'd wanted. Sure, performing surgery might afford Greg the high he chased, but he was often repulsed to think of who was benefiting from his handiwork. On a given day, he might be forced to treat any number of assholes.

But he was better than that. And he deserved better than his paltry low-six-figure salary. After accounting for taxes, his son's private school expenses, his Manhattan mortgage, and Joan's expensive taste, he had to lead a fairly modest life—the opposite of what he'd envisioned. He switched briefly to private practice but that proved no better, because then he'd had to deal with mounds of paperwork and stingy insurance companies telling him how to treat his own damn patients. So he'd reluctantly returned to Roosevelt's ER, where Yardley welcomed him back with a sorry pat. It felt like a regression. To get through the rough patch, he'd started to prescribe himself Vicodin.

Then he learned of an opportunity to consult for an unusual hedge fund that was buying up "lives" in the secondary market for life insurance. The fund needed doctors to analyze the medical records of the potential patients whose policies they wanted to bid on, in order to then estimate the time frame of their deaths. He jumped at the opportunity to supplement his income. For several years,

he shared his analyses with Yardley over beers at the end
of their shift. Yardley would never fail to chime in with
his own expert opinion. When those opinions proved
stunningly accurate, they both came to realize that Yardley possessed a rare talent for assessing a patient's future
mortality. Greg, in thanks, gave him regular kickbacks
out of his own handsome fees.

The arrangement was working out fine until the day
Yardley cornered him in the hospital's empty locker room,
his eyes shining with excitement.

"Screw the middleman," he said. "Why don't we start
our own fund? We'll buy up lives ourselves and split the
death benefits."

"Yeah, right." Greg rolled his eyes. "Buying up a single policy could run a hundred grand or more. And then
we might have to wait years for it to pay off. We have
nowhere near the kind of capital we'd need to invest."

Yardley's plump cheeks puffed out in a conspiratorial
grin. "Oh, but we do."

"We do?"

"Doctors on the Mend."

Greg stared at him like he was out of his mind. Doctors
on the Mend was the nonprofit charity he had founded to
help doctors overcome addiction. He'd recently opened
up to Joan about his own reliance on Vicodin—and she
was appalled. Starting the charity had been a way for him
to prove that he wasn't a total screwup for prescribing
himself pain pills to abuse. As part of his recovery, he was
"giving back to his community," or whatever crap he was
supposed to do to show Joan that he was still a decent
man. It shocked him when the charity attracted stacks of
donor money from hotshot physicians who understood
the perils of addiction and wanted to help other doctors

avoid its traps. After a round of local media, his little charity became downright trendy.

But how could it have anything to do with an investment fund?

"I don't know what you're talking about," Greg said to Yardley, who was standing with his arms crossed, an extension of his smirk.

"You get a shit ton of donations, right?"

"Yeah, but so?"

Yardley lowered his voice. "So why not divert some of them into a separate offshore account just for us? We use those funds to buy up lives, and then we can funnel some of our profits back through the charity as donations. Of course, we also take a nice cut for ourselves—and best part, the whole thing is tax free. No capital gains."

"Come on." Greg eyed him to gauge if he was serious. "Money laundering?"

"It wouldn't hurt anyone. We'd just finally be compensated the way we deserve."

"What about my consulting fees?"

Yardley pretended to spit. "A drop in the bucket compared to what that hedge fund is making off of us. We're being *used*."

"You greedy bastard." Greg smiled at him affectionately. "I must say, I like the way you think."

And so Robbie Merriman, investor extraordinaire, was born. His name was a combination of their middle initials, Gregory Ryan and Ellis Michael. Greg couldn't tell Joan because she was too honest. She would be horrified. When the "lives" started to pay off, Greg told her it was from bonuses and added work from his consulting gig,

which he had in fact left altogether. Now, he was competing with that hedge fund to buy up the oldest and sickest
"lives," the ones that would pay off the fastest. With the
death benefits that soon poured in, he moved them to an
Upper West Side penthouse suite, took Joan on lavish
trips, started a trust for his son, and put a couple cash down
payments on beachfront properties in Hawaii and Florida
that he rented out when he wasn't there on vacation.

He kept his job at Roosevelt all along because it was
his only on-the-books source of income to the IRS. The
rest was all cash from the Cayman Islands offshore account, in the name of SkyBridge Asset Management. Greg
opened an office near his apartment under the auspices of
his charity, but he used the privacy of the space to handle
the fund's business. He hired an assistant to oversee the
actual charity, which the naïve young woman had no idea
was a façade. He and Yardley were the only two people
who knew the truth. Together they were masters of the
universe; it was about damn time.

That was until six months ago.

The crash of the economy abruptly changed everything. His own U.S. bank went under, for God's sake. The
savings account and stock investments he shared with
Joan were wiped out practically overnight. Donations to
the charity dried up faster than dead skin. The vacation
properties he rented out went vacant, leaving him stuck
with mortgages he'd never had trouble affording before,
not to mention the mortgage on his luxury New York
penthouse. The thousands in debt he'd casually run up on
his credit card came due, along with Adam's fancy college and law school loans, Joan's credit card that she
maxed out every month, in addition to the $100,000 do-
nation he'd recently pledged to the Harvard Medical

School Alumni Foundation, so his snotty former class-mates would know just how successful he'd become. No way in hell was he about to back out.

Rather than face financial ruin, he'd turned to the one pristine source of cash at his fingertips: the fund. He drained it of all its liquid assets—about $2.2 million—and paid off his immediate debts. There was one little issue, though: He didn't consult Yardley. He was hoping that by the time Yardley found out, some of their walking "lives" would have died and replenished the fund.

Unfortunately, it hadn't worked out that way. Yardley needed money, too, badly. On top of the financial crisis that had similarly depleted his savings, he was going through a divorce that was draining him dry. With all the legal fees and alimony payments and a dwindling estate to divide with his ex-wife, he was just as desperate for cash. To add insult to injury, their beleaguered hospital cut back both of their ER shifts and reduced their salaries accordingly.

When Yardley found out what Greg had done, he was so furious he almost went to the feds. But Greg promised to come up with some of the money right away, even though all the remaining assets were tied up in "lives." That was when Mrs. Ruth Bernstein came in; she was the easiest target, old and blind, without any close relatives. No one would demand an autopsy. Her death was a nec-essary evil that had tided Yardley over with a $500,000 cash infusion.

But now Yardley's impatience was peaking again. Greg had wronged him, and now he was demanding his right-ful half of the fund's total investments, about $4.5 million to him, so he could walk away from their partnership made whole. He didn't care how Greg went about getting the money as long as it was recouped.

But if he didn't get it *by Sunday*—just three days away—he was really going to rat out the whole setup to the feds this time.

Vindictive asshole.

Since Greg's charity was the money-laundering vehicle, all the blame would fall squarely on him. Yardley's participation had no paper trail. There was no way to prove his involvement and they both knew it.

If Greg didn't come up with the money, his life was over. Plain and simple. Joan would leave him. His son would never speak to him again. He would end up in jail, penniless and disgraced and alone.

But that wasn't going to happen.

First of all, Isabel's death was *finally* going to bring in a desperately needed $2 million. That wasn't enough, but it didn't matter, because that was only the prelude to the much, much bigger cash cow he hoped she would lead him to: the drug that could defeat death.

He knew such a drug was in the works. Everyone in emergency medicine did. Seven years ago, at a conference of the American Medical Association, the renowned Dr. Horatio Quinn had announced his groundbreaking development of a compound that could delay the death of brain cells in rodents. The tantalizing research had the whole medical community buzzing. But then Quinn succumbed to a scandal, something about stealing a colleague's intellectual property, and was fired. After that, he disappeared from the public eye. Greg and Yardley used to speculate about what had become of him and his miracle drug. There were rumors that he had gone to work for a covert organization that recruited cutting-edge researchers. So it was very possible that he was still alive and that his work had progressed.

Since Isabel had been miraculously resuscitated—but not in any known hospital—Greg wondered if there might be a connection. Could she have been saved by the long-lost scientist and his drug?

If so, and if he could get his hands on it, then all his problems would be solved. Yardley could take it and sell it to the highest bidder in the pharmaceutical world. No one else had deeper pockets. Then that greedy jerk would have all the money he'd ever want for the next ten generations. He'd shut up forever. At this point, Greg didn't care about missing out on such a windfall. He just wanted to walk away with his life—and his marriage—intact.

Beside him in bed, Joan had not budged for the last hour. She was an enviably sound sleeper. So he didn't worry about waking her when he got up and tiptoed to the bathroom clutching his cell phone. The goddamn call still hadn't come.

What the hell was happening with Isabel? He knew his guys were loyal, though; they couldn't be blowing him off on purpose. One of them had been a gunshot victim of a gang turf war whose life he'd saved in the ER last year. At the time, the grateful thug offered to repay him however possible. Now, for once, Greg was glad to have operated on a violent criminal. It was funny how life could come full circle.

He shut the bathroom door and dialed the number he knew by heart. The sound of the repeated rings tormented him. He resisted banging his fist on the wall.

Come on, pick up!

But the phone rang and rang, unanswered.

CHAPTER 41
Joan

A shadow blocked the morning light on Joan's face. Her closed lids sensed the change from pink to black, but it didn't wake her. She hadn't been sleeping to begin with, even though she'd feigned slumber when Greg came home around 1 A.M. In fact she'd lain awake all night as her unnerving encounter with Isabel Leon looped over and over through her mind.

Now her eyes fluttered open. Greg was standing by her bedside, blocking the window's rays. He was naked except for a towel around his waist, and despite his exhausted expression, he looked as striking as ever. His face was freshly shaved, and his muscular body smelled of pine. Her first instinct was to reach for him. But her memory pierced a stake through her desire. She stared up at him as if at a stranger.

He put a hand on her shoulder. She stiffened.

"It's after ten," he said gently. "You never sleep in this late."

She pulled the covers up to her chin. "I'm sick," she mumbled.

She shut her eyes again and rolled away from him.

"Do you want anything?" he asked. "I'm off until tonight, so I can take care of you."

His tone was so sweet that she felt the sting of tears. How was it possible that her adoring husband, the father of her son, her partner for thirty years, could be involved in anything sinister? It made no sense.

Yet maybe, horrifyingly, she wondered if it did. The act of speculation alone made her feel like a traitor. But if she forced herself to be as objective as any decent journalist, she saw that her reflexive dismissal of his guilt was a defense mechanism. Sometimes it was difficult to acknowledge incongruous facts when they conflicted with the ones you wanted to believe.

Like the fact that his colleagues had seemed ignorant of a dangerous scheme that pitted Greg as the victim of a ruthless investor—even though Greg had told her that this very rumor was swirling around the hospital.

Like the fact that the front window of their new apartment had been smashed in only a few days after their move. She could accept that someone actively pursuing Greg could have discovered their new address. But now that she was reconsidering everything, an unsettling detail about the incident jumped out at her. There were two windows on either side of their building's front door. The left one was theirs, apartment 1B, and the right one was their neighbor's, apartment 1A. Even if a stranger knew their apartment number, how could he have known which window was theirs? They'd never hosted any guests in the new place, not even Adam. So how could anyone but Greg himself know it was that window? Could *he* have smashed it in? Maybe to scare her away from investigating the truth?

Then there was the fact that they had become flush

with cash suddenly about five years ago. At the time, Greg explained the windfall as a boon from the consulting gig he did on the side for a hedge fund. But was there any vaguer job description than *consulting*? She never drilled him before because the details didn't interest her. All that mattered then was that he was making good money, better than he'd ever made at the hospital. He didn't want to leave the ER, though, because he told her he was "a healer" and "his patients needed him." No matter how rich he got, he wasn't about to quit his passion. And for that, she'd fallen in love with him a little more.

And what about the so-called fact that he'd sold his life insurance policy to help cover their debts? Sure, when people got desperate, they leveraged every asset they had. In recent months, with the crash of the economy, they'd gotten hit hard enough that the notion of Greg selling his own policy had seemed logical to her.

But now that she was pondering it, she realized he wouldn't make a very attractive candidate to a buyer. He wasn't sick or elderly, and his family history was spotless—no cancer, no stroke, no heart disease. He came from hearty Russian peasant stock. Good old-fashioned age had killed his parents in their nineties. With their genes, Greg might live another forty years—not exactly a quick turnaround for an investor. It didn't take a financial whiz to see that his policy wouldn't raise much cash.

The more she thought about his claims, the less sense they made. But then what was the root of all the fear and worry he'd been suffering with these past weeks? He acted like he was a target waiting to be attacked. If she knew one thing about him after thirty years, it was how he handled stress. And he was genuinely freaked out.

She uneasily thought back to the incident their son had gotten so bothered by a few years earlier—Greg's strange outburst of rage when Adam surprised him with a visit to his charity office. *It was like he was a different person,* Adam had told her at the time—a melodramatic assessment she'd easily shrugged off. But now she wondered: If he wasn't the person they knew and loved, who was he?

His hand on her forehead startled her out of her thoughts.

"You're cool as a cucumber," he said. "Do you feel feverish?"

"Not really," she muttered. "I just want to go back to sleep."

"You need fluids. Do you want some tea?"

"Okay."

"English breakfast with a squirt of lemon and half a Splenda?"

He knew her so damn well. How could she barely know him at all?

"Thanks," she mumbled into her pillow.

As he headed toward the kitchen at the opposite end of the apartment, she watched his handsome figure recede. A few drops of water from his wet hair trickled down his smooth back. On a normal day, she would have found herself coyly telling him to lose the towel. She liked seeing his naked body across a room, teasing her by staying just out of reach. She liked seeing his crooked smile and the hunger in his eyes when he couldn't stand it anymore, when he raced over and pinned her to the bed, his mouth on hers.

But today was not a normal day.

There was one more inescapable fact. It was heavy and beautiful, and it was sparkling on her finger. She slipped off the ruby and stared at the date inscribed in the gold band: *7-6-57.* That was the day of his parents' wedding in Lincoln, Nebraska. The ring had to be a family heirloom.

So how in the world could Isabel Leon have known the date?

The ring was "a tool," she'd said, to catch a violent investor who went by the pseudonym Robbie Merriman. So there really *was* a dangerous investor out there—and somehow Greg was involved. But maybe not in the way Joan thought. A horrific idea popped into her mind unbidden:

Was it possible that Greg could . . . *be* Robbie Merriman?

She recalled the terror in Isabel's face: *He buys up life insurance policies and then goes after victims for their death benefits. I was one of them.*

But the man she knew was a healer. The man she knew would never hurt anyone.

Unless the man she knew was a lie.

The piece of paper with Isabel's cryptic phone number was crumpled at the bottom of her purse, though she had the digits memorized. They burned in her mind like a taunt: *Do you want the real answers?*

There was nothing else she wanted more. But what if they unraveled her life as she knew it? She wanted to save her husband, not lose him. The caring doctor and the doting husband threatened to vanish forever if she called that number.

Maybe it was all a big misunderstanding. Greg would be redeemed, the actual criminal caught, and an explanation found to satisfy all her suspicions.

From the kitchen, she heard the teakettle start to whine. Any minute, he would return with a cup. She needed more time.

"Honey," she called across the apartment. "Can you make me something to eat?"

He stepped into the living room so she could see him from the bedroom. He had a knife in one hand and half a lemon in the other. The silver blade glistened with droplets of juice.

"Sure," he said. "Toast with almond butter and some sliced papaya?"

She flashed him a tight smile. It was her favorite breakfast. "Thanks."

He went back into the kitchen. She heard cabinets opening and closing.

It was now or never. He would be home taking care of her the rest of the day. She hopped out of bed, grabbed her cell phone from the nightstand, and tiptoed into the bathroom.

Then she dialed the digits. She expected to hear Isabel pick up, but instead an older man answered hello. The timbre of his voice was deep and resonant, like a wooden bass.

"This is Joan Hughes," she said softly. "Isabel Leon gave me this number. I understand you're investigating my husband?"

"Joan," the man said. "I'm glad you called. We were hoping you would."

"I'm ready." She strained past the lump in her throat. "I want to know the truth."

CHAPTER 42
Greg

Three more days. That's all Greg had until Yardley went to the feds. And Isabel—the miraculous survivor—had survived again. She'd escaped the projects unharmed. He could hardly believe his bad luck. Some might call it karma, but he didn't buy into that mystical crap. This was called getting screwed at the worst possible time. He'd never been more enraged—or afraid—in his life.

He worked on slowing his breath as he buttered Joan's toast in the kitchen. She was sick in bed today and he was staying home to take care of her until his ER shift in the evening. No doubt her immune system was weakened from all the stress he'd already put her through. God, if she knew what was really happening . . .

After an agonizing night of waiting, he'd finally gotten through to his guys in Harlem. Impossibly, unbelievably, they had gotten the shit kicked out of them by some martial arts–trained asshole who'd shown up in Isabel's place. Now one of them was in the hospital with a punctured lung, while the other was hurting from a broken nose, two knocked-out teeth, and a scratched cornea. In the meantime, Isabel had disappeared. Even her family down in Key West was gone. They'd left in the middle of the night, despite the threat of the boy's deportation. The hired thug who'd been watching their house reported that they were hauled away in the back of some slick Dodge Viper that gunned them out of there "faster than a shot out of hell." The thug had no chance in his hulking Ford SUV. He'd lost track of them somewhere along the highway.

If only Greg could get rid of Yardley that easily.

As he sliced up a fresh papaya the way Joan liked it, in square chunks, he imagined each cut of the knife sinking into Yardley's squishy flesh. But that bastard was untouchable. He'd warned that if he or any of his relatives were harmed leading up to the deadline to deliver the money, his lawyer would be prompted to send a sealed letter to the authorities detailing Greg's fraud.

Sweat was forming on his brow. His mouth was dry and his heart felt like it was beating too hard. He set down the knife and counted a slow inhale. *One two three four.* Then out. *One two three four.* He groped for the pillbox he kept hidden at the back of the utensil drawer and popped three Vicodin. Their soothing warmth kicked in after a few minutes.

But his high was an illusion and he knew it.

Now that Isabel was gone, how was he going to find the drug? Without it, he had no chance in hell of raising $3.5 million by Sunday. Slaughtering a bunch of people whose deaths he owned would be far too complicated and messy, not to mention a perversion of his real identity as a healer. Isabel was one thing. She was the golden goose of all his "lives," *and* she'd wronged him by cutting off her breasts. Mrs. Ruth Bernstein's death could also be excused. Old and decrepit, with no one to mourn her, she'd practically been a walking corpse. But killing multiple innocents was taking it too far.

He loaded up a tray with Joan's toast, tea, and fruit,

and carried it in to her, but the bed was empty. She'd gone to the bathroom. He put the tray on her nightstand and waited. A faucet was running. Maybe she was drawing a bath.

Above all else, he wanted to preserve her ignorance so she would never leave him. He wished he could spirit them away to some remote island across the world from the coming explosion. But he *was* the bomb. No matter where he was, Yardley was going to detonate it and she would discover the truth.

His throat caught when he realized that today might be one of their last days together—ever. A sudden urge possessed him to want to sweep her into his arms. He hurried to the bathroom door and knocked.

"Hang on," she called. The faucet was still running on high.

He gripped the doorknob. It was locked. That was odd.

"You okay?"

There was a pause. "Not really . . ."

"Do you need anything?"

"Just some privacy."

"Okay." He stepped back, disappointed. "Anything I can do?"

"No." Her voice sounded strangely sad. "No, I don't think there is."

CHAPTER 43
Isabel

Chris's voice burst through her cabin intercom without warning. "Isabel."

It was the last voice she wanted to hear.

She was lying in her bed next to Richard, with Captain snuggled at their feet. After her encounter with Joan Hughes and her near-death encounter in the Harlem projects the night before, her primary concern today was to rest. She was safe, her mom and Andy were safe, and, thanks to her initiative in finding Joan, Galileo was now away meeting her to assess how she might help them unmask Robbie Merriman.

Isabel was thrilled for the mission's continued momentum, but she desperately wanted a break. Especially since she'd endured a visit to Chris last night to supply him with more blood. Why couldn't he leave her alone for just one day?

She groaned, then extricated herself from Richard's embrace and dragged herself three steps to the intercom. "What's up?"

Chris's tone sounded urgent. "I need you."

She rolled her eyes at Richard. He propped himself onto his elbows and shook his head in annoyance. A lock of hair fell over his broad forehead. He was shirtless, and even with the still-healing gash across his chest from his heart surgery, he was looking stronger every day. His defined biceps and pecs revealed a power that belied his lanky frame, thanks to his hours of physical therapy. The improvements didn't end there. Since there were no cigarettes on board, his breath was better and his habitual cough was on the wane. His sarcasm had softened to a dry wit, and despite his lingering fondness for bad puns, Isabel found herself more and more attracted to him. Men who were sexy and funny, loyal and trustworthy, were as rare as fine gems. She was only sorry it had taken her so long to appreciate him.

"Isabel?" Chris's voice asked. "You coming?"

Screw him, Richard mouthed. He beckoned her with one finger and a coy smile.

She turned to the intercom with an edge in her voice. "I'm in the middle of something. Can it wait?"

Despite sleeping side by side last night, she and Richard hadn't gotten totally naked. They'd been content to kiss and cuddle, distracting each other from the heavier concerns that occupied the rest of their time. Together, in her bed, they discovered a place to get away from it all. He let her set the pace, so she became comfortable enough to remove her shirt and show her reconstructed breasts to a man for the first time since her own surgery. Richard gazed at them—at the fake curve of her implants, at her uneven nipples, at the raised pink scar that ran underneath her breasts. Then, very lightly, he kissed the scar and he kissed her lips. The simple gesture felt more intimate than sex. Now she wanted nothing more than to climb back into bed with him and continue their exploration of each other's bodies.

But Chris was insistent. "I really need to see you."

"Why?"

"Just come to the lab."

The strange excitement in his voice compelled her to agree.

She sighed at Richard. "I'll be right back."

"You want me to come?"

"Nah, it's fine. Captain will go with me, right?"

When the dog heard his name, his silky ears perked up.

"Yes, you," she cooed.

He lifted his head from Richard's foot and wagged his fluffy tail at her. Richard pulled the comforter up to his chin. "Hurry back."

"Oh, I will."

With the dog trailing behind her, she made her way down the stairs to the laboratory deck. The ship swayed ever so slightly on the Hudson, where it remained docked. After days on the roiling Atlantic, the river's gentle current felt almost like land.

In the hallway of the labs, she ran into Dr. Cornell, a taciturn physician-researcher in his seventies who specialized in organ repair. Now that Quinn was gone, he was the oldest and most experienced doctor on the ship. Somehow his presence comforted her, though they'd barely ever spoken. He gave her a friendly nod as she walked past him to the familiar door near the end of the hall.

Its gold plaque still read QUINN. It was startling to see his name there, as if nothing had changed. As if she might walk in and catch him hunched over a microscope, his bushy white eyebrows knotted in concentration.

She traced the plaque's engraved letters. There was nowhere to go to mourn him. No grave, no memorial. This lab was as close as she could get to the resting place of his soul. The finality of real death—irreversible death— was incomprehensible. How could someone you loved dis-

appear suddenly off the face of the earth? It was like trying to picture a rope with one end, or the edge of the universe. But whether she could accept it or not, the man who
had saved her life was gone. Just like her father was gone.
Now all that remained of their kind eyes and reassuring
voices was an ever-fading fragment in her memory.

She closed her eyes for a moment in honor of them
both. Then, steeling herself to face the person responsible
for Quinn's tragedy, she knocked.

Chris opened the door right away. He was grinning.
Patchy stubble covered his chin and lower cheeks, as
though he'd forgotten to shave. His facial hair, burly build,
and thick neck reminded her of a caveman, a repulsive
Neanderthal who happened to be dressed up in a scientist's white coat. But the confidence that had once attracted her was still apparent in his straight back and
squared shoulders. He ushered her inside and closed the
door. A weird squeaking noise was coming from somewhere in the room.

She crossed her arms. Captain sat at her feet.

"What's up? You can't need more blood already."

He shook his head. "Check this out."

She tried not to flinch when he put one hand on the
small of her back and ushered her to the counter along the
far wall. There, in separate cages on separate metal wheels,
were three white rats. Their tiny pink feet trudged from
one rung to the next, as if spinning the wheels took mon-
umental effort. Isabel had seen rats in other researchers'
labs on the ship, so their presence didn't surprise her.

"They look tired," she said. "Are they sick?"

"Actually they're quite well."

"Why's that?"

"They're alive."

She spun around to face him. "You did it?"

He beamed, his top row of teeth gleaming under the fluorescent lights. "All thanks to the trace elements in your blood."

She stared from him back to the spinning rats. "They were dead?"

"Yup." Chris pointed at them one by one. "Drowned, suffocated, and poisoned. I resuscitated them with test doses this morning. Their brains are perfect, but they're sluggish at first, like you were. I expect them all to make a full recovery."

Genuine joy flooded her. "This is amazing! Everyone will be so happy!"

"And get this." He went over to the refrigerator and took out a chilled clear vial that was about three inches tall. He cradled it in his hands as he walked back to her. "I made enough for one human dose."

"You're sure it's the right formula?"

"The rats are alive, aren't they?"

She couldn't stop staring at their plump little bodies. "I can't believe you did it."

"I also developed my own check in the process for quality control, to make things easier from now on."

"Oh yeah?"

"Quinn had this inefficient way of requiring a previous perfect dose to calibrate a new batch, but I one-upped him."

Chris smiled shamelessly and her delight vanished in an instant. His audacity was galling—a sign that he had no idea what she knew.

She swallowed. "What is it?"

He went to the supply closet and produced a glass flask that contained a colorless fluid. Then he heated the flask over a burner. "This is a solution of hydrogen peroxide and sulfuric acid. Watch what happens when it reacts with certain elements in the X101."

Using a pipette, he sucked up one drop of the X101 from the vial. The drop was so small that the level of clear fluid inside the vial barely changed.

"This negligible amount won't affect the efficacy of the dose," he said, as he squirted it into the flask. The reaction was immediate. The drop transformed the entire solution to inky black.

"Cool, right?" He looked at her, awaiting her admiration.

She nodded weakly. "But what if the concentration is off?"

"That's why this works. Only this precise formula reacts to produce black, because of the X101's specific atomic transfer of potassium iodide and sodium thiosulfate. The compounds I made before I got it right didn't cause this reaction."

"I see." Chemistry was gibberish to her, but she wasn't about to ask him to explain. All she wanted was to get out of there.

"Isn't this so much better? Now we don't need any previous doses for quality control!"

"Yeah," she managed. And then, to get past the awkward pause: "Good job."

Her own praise made her want to vomit. She glanced away from his self-satisfied grin and braced herself against a rising tide of nausea. The number of seconds she could bear his presence was dwindling rapidly. She crouched down to pet the dog, who was lying at her feet.

"Does Galileo know?" she asked, without looking up.

"Not yet. He's away for the afternoon. But I wanted you to be the first to know."

He put a hand on her shoulder. She felt herself tense. He didn't appear to notice. Instead he slid his fingers up the nape of her neck and into her hair. She jumped to her feet and whirled around, her heart thudding against her ribs.

She kept her tone casual so as not to reveal her alarm. "What are you doing?"

The lust in his eyes told her the answer. "Celebrating."

Then he grabbed her hand and pulled her body close against his, wrapping his other arm around her waist. His mouth smothered hers with disorienting force. Before she could process what was happening, his hand was somehow already creeping up her shirt, under her bra, to her breasts.

"Get off me!" she yelled, shoving him hard. He smacked against the counter with a grunt as Captain growled and nipped at his ankles.

"Are you out of your mind?" she cried. "What the hell?"

He scrunched up his face. "I thought you were into me."

"Well, you thought wrong."

She bent down and scooped up the dog.

"I don't understand. What about the night we had together?"

"You mean the night Quinn was killed?"

His eyes narrowed to slits. She knew she had said too much.

"Quinn had an accident," he snapped.

She regarded him stonily.

"An accident," he said louder, like she was deaf.

His cheeks had deepened to a frightening shade of pink. It was the color of fury.

She shifted her attention to the door a few yards away,

but he clamped his hand around her wrist. "Did you hear what I said?"

His thumb and forefinger pressed so hard into her skin that she could feel her pulse throbbing beneath his fingertips.

"I heard." She suddenly twisted her wrist upside down in a maneuver that flung his hand off. He stumbled back in surprise.

In her arms, Captain bared his pointy teeth as she flew to the door without a second glance. But her uneasiness only sharpened when she stepped out of the lab, and with a chill, she realized why.

Chris now understood that she knew his secret—and the return of the X101 meant he no longer needed her blood.

He no longer needed her alive.

CHAPTER 44
Chris

Chris sat cross-legged on the floor of his lab, cell phone in hand. He wasn't technically allowed to have one—it was against Galileo's rules—but when the hell had he ever played by the rules? Not as a teenager, when he knocked up his high school girlfriend and abandoned her to a life of small towns and small dreams; not when his parents shunned him for deserting his kid and told him he deserved to fail; not when he took up dealing drugs to put himself through Harvard; not when he undermined his competition in graduate school to study with the master biochemist Horatio Quinn; and certainly not on the ship, when he learned enough about the X101 to no longer need Quinn at all.

He powered on his white iPhone, which he kept hidden under his mattress in his private cabin. There was no call history because he'd never used it before. But for the past seven years, as long as he'd lived on the ship, he knew the day would come when he would need to sneak off—and execute his master plan. All along, he aimed to cultivate a business partner on the outside, someone knowledgeable enough to help him convert the physical existence of the X101 into glory and wealth. Ideally this person would help him get a patent, a prestigious journal publication, and some national press, then help him license distribution to the highest bidder. No doubt pharmaceutical companies all over the world would trample one another for a piece of the drug that defied death. The companies would love that it could be manufactured and sold immediately, without the hassle of FDA approval, because the drug worked on a corpse, not a patient—and there were no rules governing acceptable medication for the dead.

Of course Galileo would never dare come after him. If he did, Chris could expose his illicit routes, members, and allies around the country. The blow he could deliver would paralyze the entire Network. But he wouldn't have to go that far. The power of the threat alone was enough to ensure he would escape without retribution.

He smirked just imagining the look on his father's face when Old Pop realized that the son he'd condemned to failure all those years ago was a celebrated scientist worth millions. Then Pop could no longer be ashamed. Once Chris was a mind-blowing success, his family would have to admit they were wrong to think he was a negligent asshole. They were wrong to tell him to give up his grand ambitions in order to be a young father and husband, trapped in a pathetic conventional life like theirs. They would be horrified to realize how deeply they had misjudged his talent and genius, and they would beg him to accept their apology. And he would, because he was forgiving. He might even agree to meet the son he'd never wanted. The kid probably hated him, but once he got rich, he could write a check to smooth things over. Everyone would have to admit he was a star and they were lucky to dwell in his orbit.

He'd come this far already, putting up with year after

year of painstaking toil in obscurity, not to mention Quinn's ferocious possessiveness. Year after year of cultivating his skeptical mentor's trust—while stoking his paranoia about everyone else. Year after year of keeping his own head down in front of Galileo, waiting for the day it would all pay off. He wasn't about to let some prude bitch get in his way now. She hadn't been bold enough to condemn him outright, but the accusation was plain in her eyes.

It was unfathomable how she could have come to suspect him. Between the raging storm and the fire, nature had handed him the perfect cover that night. In the same moment, he'd recognized his opportunity and seized it. Time was of the essence, since Quinn had been on the verge of giving up the whole secret synthesis procedure to Galileo. Stupid Quinn would have erased Chris's proprietary claim to the knowledge, so thank God that threat was over.

But his new problem was just as worrisome. What if Isabel went to Galileo with her suspicions—and then Galileo kicked him off the ship? So many excruciating years would go to waste, his life's master plan ruined in an instant.

About ten hours had passed since Isabel's unnerving revelation. It was 10:05 P.M., and so far, at least, his worst fears hadn't come true. When Galileo returned from his off-site appointment around 5 P.M., Chris had rushed to corner him before she could. He announced the return of the X101, and Galileo had practically exploded with euphoria. He led a procession to see the resuscitated rats in the lab, where all the other staff cheered and whooped and slapped Chris on the back. Isabel and Richard were the only ones who didn't join in the hoopla, but no one else seemed to notice. Afterward, the party moved to the top deck to celebrate with a feast of the kitchen's best stock—brisket and potatoes, with cherry cobbler for dessert.

Now the rest of the ship had gone to bed, and Chris was back in his lab, alone. Pacing. The ridges of his iPhone dug into his palm. Time was running out to make a sly exit. Any minute, Isabel could be ratting him out. As much as it pained him, he had to let go of his original plan to make as much of the X101 as he could smuggle out. It would take too damn long. He also originally wanted to wait to leave until he had a partnership in place on the outside, someone cunning enough to guide his next steps. But at this moment he knew no one, had no money, and nowhere to go.

All he had was the single vial of X101. He needed to escape with it ASAP.

And he could think of only one person nearby who could help him. It was someone who wanted to profit off the drug as badly as he did. Someone who also played by his own rules. But unlike himself, this person had financial savvy and power and connections. And a common enemy in Isabel Leon.

It was the investor Robbie Merriman.

Chris had memorized his number after having snuck a peek at Galileo's recent call history on the satellite phone. He strode to the lab's door to double-check its lock, then dialed the digits. He noticed that his hands—whose steadiness he prized—were trembling.

The phone rang until a machine instructed him to leave a message at the tone. Chris called back three more times, not caring if he was being obnoxious, until finally someone picked up. A brusque voice hissed in his ear:

"Hey, asshole, you have the wrong num—"

"Mr. Merriman?" he cut in. "I'm Dr. Chris Donovan, and I—"

"How do you know my name?"

He tightened his sweaty grip on the iPhone. "I'm one of the doctors who brought Isabel Leon back to life." The faster his words tumbled out, the faster he paced. "She was a test subject of a new drug that delays the death of brain cells for up to twenty-four hours. There's literally never been anything like it in history. It's going to change the face of medicine."

He paused to breathe. He knew he sounded like a pitchman, but if there was any product that ever lived up to its hype, it was the X101.

Merriman's strident tone softened. "So it is real."

"It's real," Chris said. A grin tugged at his lips. He was about to be a freaking *billionaire.* A sensation. It was so close he could already see the headlines: THINK DEATH IS PERMANENT? YOU'RE DEAD WRONG—MIRACLE DRUG REVOLUTIONIZES EMERGENCY MEDICINE.

What Merriman said next stunned him. "Did you know Horatio Quinn?"

"You've . . . heard of him?"

"I remember the crazy buzz around his research before he dropped away some years back."

"Well, I'm his protégé. He died in an accident and left me his legacy. I'm the only person who knows how to synthesize the drug—and I'm currently holding the only vial in existence."

Actually the vial was in the refrigerator at a perfect 35 degrees Fahrenheit, but it sounded more dramatic that way. He'd always had a flair for drama.

"Why are you calling me?"

"Because I'm trapped right now." Chris touched the

cool metal of one of the rat's cages. The plump white rodent was curled up next to his wheel, exhausted from the ordeal of having died. But he was alive. His little back was rising and falling with the steadiness of his breath.

"Why? Where?"

"In a private lab near Manhattan with Isabel and a bunch of other researchers. They think the drug is communal property and they're going to take it from me, even though Quinn wanted me to license it for the public good. I've got to get it out of here before it's too late, but I need help. I have nowhere to go and know nothing about business. You'd get a cut, of course."

Merriman barely waited a second to reply. "My connections in finance and big pharma would open all the doors you need. I know how to get major deals done fast."

Chris pumped his fist. He had to force himself not to shout. "I figured you're an investor," he said smoothly. "You'd know what to do."

"You're in a lab right now?"

"Yes."

"Show me." Merriman's voice gained a hard edge. "I want to see this vial. I want to see you're the real deal."

Chris gave an easy chuckle. "I promise I am."

"Prove it."

"Fine." He tapped his iPhone to request FaceTime. A couple of high-pitched beeps sounded, then Merriman's face popped up on the screen. It was obscured in darkness. All Chris could make out was the curve of his forehead and a vague outline of dark hair.

"Hi," he said to the shrouded face. "Okay, so, here's the lab." He held up the phone and slowly turned in a circle so Merriman could take in its state-of-the-art microscopes, countertops lined with laminar flow hoods, sinks, centrifuges, and shining chrome equipment that gleamed under the fluorescent lights.

"Here are test rats I've just revived with the drug." He zeroed in on the rodents sleeping in their cages. "And here"—he walked to the refrigerator—"is the vial I put back a minute ago." He swung open the door and carefully plucked the vial from its holder. The colorless X101 didn't look like much, so he rushed to speak before Merriman became skeptical. "It's an extremely precise compound that acts on the brain's calpain enzymes to inhibit the signals to neurons that it's time to die. And," he added proudly, "I've just developed a new test for quality control."

You don't think I'm legit? he thought. *Watch this.*

Setting the phone upright on the counter facing him, he set up a quick demonstration with a heated flask of hydrogen peroxide and sulfuric acid, explaining in detail how the atomic ratios in one drop of the formula reacted with the solution to produce a black liquid upon contact.

But just as he was about to suck up a drop of the compound with a pipette, his hand froze. *What the hell?* Some of the liquid was missing. He'd made exactly 2 milliliters—the amount needed for one human dose. So why was the level now at 1.75 milliliters? A tiny drop or two for the demo wouldn't affect the volume that much.

"Well?" Merriman's voice prompted from the speakerphone.

"Sorry." He shook off his bewilderment and completed the demo. Then he returned the chilled vial to the fridge before it warmed up. "I also have extensive notes about our clinical trial with Isabel and twenty-one other recent corpses whose brains were preserved by the drug, in conjunction with therapeutic hypothermia and other known emergency measures, while doctors reversed their underlying causes of death. The drug's worked on victims of heart attacks, overdoses, poisoning, blood loss, and of course, drowning. Everyone's recovered without brain damage."

"Impressive," Merriman said.

Chris caught a glimpse of white teeth on the dark screen. A smile.

"Thank you, sir." He exhaled a breath, feeling as though he'd just passed the most important exam of his life.

"We just have one issue." There was that harsh edge again.

Chris frowned at his shadowy image. "What?"

"How do I know you're coming to me in good faith? For all I know, you're working with Isabel to trap me. I'm not an idiot. I know what she's after."

"Absolutely not! I'm trying to get *away* from her. She's nothing but trouble."

"That's not good enough. I need you to convince me."

"How?" Chris clenched his teeth. "I'm already running out of time."

"Get rid of her. The sooner the better. Then we can talk."

CHAPTER 45
Isabel

The abrupt knock jarred Isabel awake. She opened her eyes to near total darkness. The sky outside her porthole was black. The only light came from the digital alarm clock on her nightstand. Its glowing red numbers read 12:10 A.M.

She was alone except for Captain, who was curled up behind her head on the pillow. It must be Richard, she thought. He was coming to visit for a late-night rendezvous. She threw off her covers and climbed out of bed. He probably wanted to pick up where they'd left off, before her confrontation with Chris ruined her mood.

Afterward, she'd shut herself in her cabin to brood. Of course Chris had announced his breakthrough with the X101 the minute Galileo returned, before she could get a word in edgewise. But what good would it do to tell Galileo her suspicions for a second time? He seemed as eager to celebrate Chris as everyone else. He hadn't even bothered to tell her yet about his offsite meeting with Joan Hughes. He was too busy calling Chris a savior—without irony. It was enough to make her gag.

She was too agitated to be good company for the evening, so she told Richard she needed some space. He'd kissed her and gone to bed in his own cabin next door. That was three hours ago. Since then, she'd tossed and turned until deciding to lie still with her eyes closed, in the hopes that imitating sleep might quiet her racing mind.

Richard surprising her now was just what she needed to escape the cruel eternity of insomnia. It was perceptive of him to realize that she didn't really want to be alone, even when she said she did. Maybe his senses were still heightened from the X101, or maybe he was just a discerning guy. In any case, she would reward him well. She smiled as she opened the door.

And then she froze. On the threshold, wearing jeans, Converse sneakers, and a black hoodie, was Chris. His big-boned figure filled the doorway and would have unnerved her if not for the contrite look on his face. He bit his lip as he thrust a pink origami rose into her hands. Its paper bud was carefully folded to mimic the unfolding petals of a real rose. She blinked at him without taking it.

"What's this? What are you doing here?"

He gave her a sheepish half smile. "Sorry I couldn't get real flowers. But I had to come by to apologize."

She crossed her arms. "Do you know what time it is?"

"I know, but I can't stop thinking about what happened before. I totally misread the situation and now I feel like an asshole. I'm sorry."

Because you are, she wanted to snap. Her expression must have said it because he winced.

"I mean it," he said. "Can we be cool?"

"Sure, whatever." What was she supposed to say? *No, you're a murderer?* "Well, it's late, so . . ." She trailed off just as Captain hopped down from the bed and padded over to her. Chris bent down to pet him, but the dog didn't wag his bushy tail the way he usually did. Instead he emitted a strange whine that sent a tingle down her arms.

Her stiff tone betrayed her discomfort. "Good night."

She started to close the door, but Chris stood up and blocked the doorway.

"Take this," he insisted, offering her the faux flower again. "I made it for you."

She took it grudgingly, just as she noticed that his other hand was hidden in his back pocket.

"What—"

Before she could finish the thought, his fist reared back and smashed into her forehead. Its propulsive force toppled her backward, pain searing through her skull like a white-hot migraine. She felt herself stumble in the darkness, tried to grab hold of the door to slam it, but he knocked her down and overpowered her with the full weight of his body.

She rocketed into fight mode, thrashing and biting for all she was worth. When her knee smashed into his groin, he cried out and fell to his side, grabbing his crotch.

"Bitch!" he moaned.

She tried to scramble away, but he recovered quickly enough to slam her back against the floor. When he sat on her chest, her ribs felt like they might crack. She shrieked, but he stifled her voice by shoving a handkerchief into her mouth. Captain nipped at his hands until Chris scooped him up and threw him out into the hallway, then closed the door. Now they were alone.

She kicked and bit and flailed with all her strength, but he was impenetrable. It was like trying to injure a bear with a toothpick. He easily pinned down her arms by squashing her hands beneath his weight. Then he reached into his back pocket—while holding her gag in place— and pulled out a coil of gray electrical tape. She kept trying to scream, even just to make eye contact, but he avoided her gaze altogether. His eyes had hardened into a look of dispassionate concentration, like a robot executing a task. Any human warmth or compassion was gone. That indifference frightened her the most, because it meant he was capable of anything.

He unspooled the tape and ripped off a section with his teeth. Then he fastened it across her mouth from ear to ear. Her cries came out like pathetic muffled whimpers. Still sitting on her chest and hands, he whipped out an iPhone from the pocket of his hoodie. An iPhone! No one on the ship had one. Her eyes widened as he dialed a number he seemed to know by heart. He turned on video while it rang and positioned it upright on a nearby chair facing them. A man answered hello, but his face was hard to make out from her helpless position on the floor.

"I told you I wouldn't waste time," Chris said. "Can you see?"

"Yeah. You got the vial?"

She could hardly believe whose voice she was hearing. It was Robbie Merriman.

"In my pocket," Chris said.

"Then make it fast and get out of there."

Chris turned his attention back to her. "This'll be quick."

She glared at him as viciously as she could. But struggling was useless. Her arms were inert and numb. She was beaten. His grubby hands started to constrict around her neck.

An image popped into her mind of her mom and Andy, and how devastated they would be. The pain of knowing she would never reunite with them hurt more than Chris's fingers digging into her throat, pressing against her vocal cords, choking off her breath. A horrifying flashback struck her of being held underwater by the scuba diver, suffocating to death. How could this be happening again before her bruises had even healed? Her head was growing dizzy, the edges of her vision fading to black.

She heard Captain's frantic barking out in the hallway. His high-pitched yap seemed to get farther and farther away. The pressure of Chris's enormous body crushing her chest was how she imagined a heart attack must feel. If only she could gasp for air! But his hand was tightening around her neck like a blood pressure cuff. The rush of blood to her face made her even dizzier. The harder he pressed, the less clearly she could see.

She felt like she was seconds from passing out when she heard, along with the dog's barks, a thunderous kick on her door. She squinted through her blurry vision to see Richard storming into her cabin. He flipped on the light.

"What the hell is going on in here?"

Chris immediately released his grip around her neck and jumped up. His immense weight lifting off her felt like a divine reprieve. She curled onto her side, panting.

Richard took one look at her crumpled body and the tape around her mouth, and lunged at Chris with the savageness of a feral animal. They crashed onto her bed and traded blows to the face, but Chris was too powerful. He was pummeling Richard, pounding him over and over with his giant fists. She ripped off her tape and screamed as loud as she could, and within seconds, her nearest neighbors were in her cabin breaking up the fight.

She looked on as two furious men, Theo and the cardiac specialist Dr. Powell, dragged Chris off Richard. Chris struggled and shrieked expletives at them but the men held his hands behind his back and wrestled him to the ground. He went limp and silent when he finally realized he was defeated.

She gaped at his prostrate figure lying inches from her feet, his sweaty pink cheek pressed to the wood floor. Her head was throbbing, her mind numb.

Theo put a hand on her arm. "Are you okay?"

She didn't realize she was trembling against the wall. But his touch snapped her out of her daze. Poor Richard was doubled over moaning on her bed, holding his left eye with both hands. She stepped around Chris, resisting the urge to kick him in the jaw, and ran the few steps to the bed.

"Oh, honey. Can I see?"

Richard winced as she gently moved his hands away from his face. His battered eye was already turning purple and swelling. Blood oozed out of a nasty cut on his lid. He was keeping his eye open with his thumb and forefinger.

She dabbed at the blood with her nightshirt. "That's going to be a nasty black eye." She glanced at Theo and Dr. Powell, who were working to immobilize Chris's wrists and ankles with his heavy-duty electrical tape. "We need some help."

"On it." Theo sprang to her intercom to call for backup.

Richard was beginning to hyperventilate as he pried open his lid. His breaths were coming out in short rapid bursts. He swung his hand wildly back and forth in front of his nose.

"You're going to be okay." She stroked his forehead. "It's just a black eye."

"No." His panicked gaze darted from his hand to her face. "I can't see."

CHAPTER 46
Joan

Joan anxiously climbed the steps up to Adam's fourth-floor walkup. It was far too late to be surprising him with a visit, but what she had to tell him was too important to wait. If she risked phoning first, he would brush her off, so she'd just decided to show up and hope for the best.

They hadn't seen each other since the day of her grandson's birth and her mortifying encounter with the OB-GYN nurse. Since she'd refused to explain herself, Adam had grown wary and aloof. Now he wasn't returning Greg's calls or hers. Not that she could blame him. Ever since he was a kid in a sandbox, he'd demanded the highest standards of integrity from the people around him. There was no surer way to lose his trust than to steal, cheat, or lie. Joan supposed she could take credit for instilling him with such rigidness. She ought to be proud. Instead she was petrified.

She knocked softly on his door. It wasn't long before she heard quick footsteps approaching. She attempted a half smile for the peephole, pushing a strand of hair behind her ear. The door opened a crack and Adam's weary face poked through. Like any father of a newborn and a toddler, he looked utterly wiped out—his eyelids sagged, his floppy hair was disheveled, his skin oily.

She felt a stab of guilt over the bombshell she was about to deliver. But he had a right to know the truth. She couldn't shield him from evil forever. Especially when the evil was his own father.

"Mom?" His eyes narrowed. "What are you doing here?"

"Hi, sweetie. We need to talk."

"Now? I just put the kids down and I—"

"Now," she said. "This is the only time I have."

Greg's late-night ER shift meant she could steal away for a couple of hours, but tomorrow, Friday, he had the day off and would want to spend it with her.

"Can I come in?" she asked. "It's important."

He hesitated for an awful moment, and her heart constricted—she didn't know if she could handle a rejection by her own son when she needed him most.

"I know you're disappointed in me." She looked him in the eye. "But there's a lot you don't know. I want to tell you—if you'll let me."

He must have read the pain on her face because he nodded. "Okay. But not inside." He stepped out onto the stoop beside her and quietly closed the door.

She winced. Was he too angry to let her in?

"I don't want to wake them," he said. "Getting them both to sleep is a miracle."

"I remember when you were a baby." She couldn't keep the ache out of her voice. Those days were so simple by comparison—full of exhaustion, yes, but also boundless joy. "Whenever you cried, Daddy used to carry you around the house pointing at all the paintings on the wall."

It was the word *daddy* that brought tears to her eyes. Who was that tender loving man and where had he gone? Had he ever even existed in the first place?

Adam folded his arms. He was apparently in no mood for nostalgia. "So what don't I know? Besides the fact that"—he counted out on fingers—"one, Dad's a jerk, two, you put up with it, and three, you got yourself kicked out of the hospital?"

She sank to the top stair and curled her fingers around the balustrade, too nervous to face him head-on. He sat down beside her, his elbows resting on his knees.

"This is going to come as a shock," she said, looking down at her lap, "but your father—it seems he . . . has an alter ego."

Adam raised a dubious eyebrow. "What, like Clark Kent and Superman?"

She grimaced. "Not quite. I only just found out myself, so I'm still trying to wrap my head around it. I should add it's not for sure—we have no solid proof—but it's looking frighteningly plausible. If it's true, it would explain a lot."

"Just spit it out, Mom."

She exhaled a shaky breath. And then out came the whole story. The layers upon layers of deceit and manipulation whose sheer audacity dizzied her. She recounted to Adam how the financial crisis had depleted their nest egg. That much was certain. But after that, things got dicey. Greg gambling away their remaining savings? A lie. Instead he appeared to be running an illegal hedge fund that bought up "lives." Greg fearing he was going to be targeted by some malicious investor who owned his life? A lie. It seemed *he* was the investor. He'd been covering it up with fables about his victimhood so she would stand by him without ever learning the truth. The unspeakable irony was that she'd become preoccupied with tracking down a criminal who was right beside her all along. A criminal he'd led her to believe she might unmask through investigating his hospital. That was why she'd snuck into Roosevelt, which later got her kicked out.

Adam listened in stunned silence. "So Dad's wealth in the last few years came from other people's deaths? I thought it came from medical consulting."

"So did I." She pulled her coat's wool collar away from her neck. "It makes me sick. All those trips we took, the penthouse, your trust fund . . ."

The horror in Adam's eyes gutted her. "But how do you know all this? Obviously Dad hasn't told you himself?"

"Of course not." She held out her left hand, where the ruby lay sparkling on her ring finger. "Because of this."

She recounted the recent events—Greg giving her the ring in a seemingly sweet gesture, then meeting Isabel, finding out it was really a tool, calling the number to find out the real deal, and finally, the encounter she'd had that very afternoon. Meeting a very tall older man with ice blue eyes, who said he was an undercover federal agent—he'd shown her his gold badge—and learning that Greg was suspected to be a violent investor who went by the name Robbie Merriman. The ring had been mailed to the investor in an attempt to find out his real identity—it contained an embedded GPS chip—and lo and behold, Greg was the one who received it. All signs pointed to his guilt. But there wasn't enough evidence to arrest him yet. It was too circumstantial. He needed to be trapped into confessing the truth.

And the agent wanted Joan to help make it happen. Her cooperation was the only way she could prove she wasn't an accomplice. Then she'd be granted immunity from any subsequent prosecution.

"I thought you had a right to know," she finished, picking up Adam's hand. "And I wanted you to understand what I'm facing." Her voice choked up. "I just don't know how I'm going to get through it. It all feels so surreal."

Adam draped his arm around her heaving shoulders. "I had no idea. This is absolutely insane."

She wiped her eyes. "And your dad has no idea I know anything. I hate to think what he would do if he found out."

Adam's tone sharpened. "You think he would hurt you?"

"I hope not. I think he loves me. But before this week, I thought a lot of things."

He suddenly whirled to face her. "Why don't you come away with us? We're still trying to move to Kansas anyway, so what if we all just packed up and went? We could stay with Emily's parents until we figure things out . . . put some distance between you and Dad . . ."

"I wish." She shook her head. "I already promised to help. I'm central to the plan—any minute I could get a call. Plus I'd look guilty if I fled."

"What's the plan?"

"I can't go into it. I signed a confidentiality agreement."

She also didn't share with him the grim temptation worming its way into her mind. She imagined herself peeking over a balcony from the thirtieth floor. Leaning a little farther, testing the resistance of the bars, testing her very sanity. One tumble, and it would all be over. Or one quick gunshot . . . A painless escape from the public dis-

grace that lay ahead, the shame and stigma that would follow her for the rest of her life.

She didn't know she was capable of such warped
thoughts. Realizing that she was terrified her. Did it mean
she might act on them, too? Clearly she didn't know her
husband; did she even know herself?

She clasped her chest to quiet her racing heart.

"I'm here if you need me." Adam rubbed her back.
"You're not alone, okay?"

She managed a grateful smile, then glanced at her
watch, a beautiful mother-of-pearl Omega that Greg had
given her last year on her fifty-sixth birthday. As soon as
she looked at it, she knew she would never wear it again.

"Do you have to get home?" Adam asked.

It was after 1 A.M. Unless Greg got called into surgery,
he would return from his shift soon. "I should," she said.
"But first can you do me a favor?"

"What?"

"Can you let me see the kids for a second? I promise I
won't wake them."

"If it'll help."

"It will."

He got to his feet, pulling her up with one hand. Then
he put a finger to his lips as he opened his front door.
They crept inside the dark apartment, where in an alcove
off the side of the living room, baby Justin and little Sophia
were sound asleep. He lay in a crib on his back, his chubby
arms flung up by his cheeks. She was tucked under her
hot pink twin comforter, her blond ringlets cascading
over her pillow.

Joan tiptoed as close as she dared. The mere sight of
her sweet grandkids was fuel. Soon she would have to
wrench her gaze away, say good-bye to her son, return to

the stranger impersonating her husband. There was no telling what her future held, or how long she might stick around to find out.

But if something were to happen to her, at least—at the very least—one of her final memories would be of the faces she loved the most.

CHAPTER 47
Isabel

Isabel paced back and forth outside the blue curtain that partitioned off Richard's hospital bed on deck 1. After the fight, an ophthalmologist who was on board researching ocular biomechanics had been woken up to look at his injured eye. First Richard's pupil had to be dilated with special drops, which required twenty minutes to take effect. Now the examination was in progress, and then the specialist, Dr. Reynolds, was expected to come out and announce his prognosis.

It was after 1 A.M., but Isabel was jittery with adrenaline. She kept scratching at her throat where Chris had squeezed it. The pressure of his monstrous fingers felt permanently imprinted on her skin. The fact that he'd gotten caught was a slight comfort, but she remained too shaken up to indulge any real relief. She replayed the encounter in her mind: him coming to her door, the stupid fake flower, his pretend apology, the sudden blow to her forehead. A tender purple lump had popped up there, but otherwise she'd escaped relatively unscathed.

As she waited to hear about Richard, she chided herself for falling prey to Chris's bait and switch. She was a survivalist, but yet again she very nearly failed to survive.

If it weren't for Captain barking his lungs off and Richard coming to the rescue . . .

The uncomfortable truth was that when it came to actual survival scenarios, whether on television or in real life, she needed backup. When had she ever come through totally on her own? Even with the white-water rafting episode, she'd counted on the few men in the group to help with chopping wood for shelter and kindling before she made the fire. Completely alone? Never.

She spun angrily on her heel, thinking about how she could have been stronger or smarter. Not that it mattered. The point was that she was okay. And hopefully Richard would be, too. She hated to think where she would be without him.

Chris, apparently, would have taken off with the only vial of X101 in existence—and run straight to the enemy camp: Robbie Merriman. Their surreptitious partnership floored her. At least they couldn't get away with anything together now. Chris was currently subdued in restraints up on deck 3 while his fate was being determined. The only upside to it all was that finally Galileo would have to admit she had been right all along.

Just as she was thinking about what punishment he would impose, she heard his footsteps exiting the stairwell. His catlike stride was unmistakable; no one else on the ship moved as efficiently. She crossed the room to greet him at the doorway to the hospital chamber, which was really the ship's converted formal dining area. The relics of its past life seemed incongruous: the crystal and gold chandelier, the oak-paneled walls, the crown moldings along the ceiling. The whole room was about the size of a basketball court, but the original open-plan style was separated by newly built walls that sectioned off the three operating rooms from the triage area of patient beds, where

Richard was currently being examined. Each bed was cordoned off with heavy wraparound curtains, though they hardly muffled Richard's moans.

Isabel tried to block them out as Galileo strode into the chamber. He looked surprisingly calm for someone who'd just been betrayed by one of his allegedly loyal scientists. Despite the late hour, he was dressed in a pair of ironed jeans, a gray T-shirt, and loafers, and his wavy dark hair was combed back off his forehead. His smooth brow and relaxed shoulders gave the impression that he was doing rounds, not managing a crisis.

"My dear." He reached out his arms. "What a nightmare. Are you okay?"

She let him embrace her. "Not really," she mumbled into his shoulder. "I'm more worried about Richard than anything."

"I was hoping Dr. Reynolds would be done by now."

"Any minute." She pulled away and looked up at him. A smidgeon of resentment crept into her voice. "So you really didn't see any of this coming, huh?"

"Truthfully?" He sighed. "Yes and no."

"What's that supposed to mean?"

He met her frown with a sad smile. "I knew you were telling me the truth before. I just couldn't say so."

"What?" She stared at him, flabbergasted. "Why not?"

"Because of the X101. Chris was the only one with enough expertise to reverse engineer the formula. If I'd punished him any earlier, he wouldn't have cooperated, and Horatio's legacy would be lost for good. I was waiting for him to make a few more doses before I did anything. I just didn't expect him to try to escape tonight, or to go after you."

Her jaw hung open. All the doubt and disappointment

she'd been harboring toward him faded like smog on a clear day. "So you weren't blowing me off?"

"Just the opposite. I installed a camera in his lab to record him working. He never suspected that *I* suspected him, so he never noticed the tiny bulb in the ceiling vent watching him the whole time."

"Seriously? So it's possible to synthesize the drug from a surveillance video?"

His lips tightened. "It's not ideal, but it should work. The key is that we recovered the vial he was trying to steal, so we have an example of a perfect batch. That's absolutely critical for engineering another one at this point. Without that, I don't know if the video alone would cut it. But with the two together, we should be good."

"I'm no expert," she said, "but didn't Chris just develop a chemical check to streamline the process, so you don't need a previous dose to make a new one? He was just bragging to me about it earlier."

Galileo conceded her point with a nod. "He did. And it is pretty brilliant. But it's only useful as a final check once you've got the process down. It's like plugging your answer into an algebra equation. It will tell you if you're right, but it won't tell you how to fix it if you're wrong. That's where the previous dose comes in, for help with calibration. So thank God we got that vial back before it was too late."

"Thank Richard," she said, craning her neck toward his closed blue curtain a few yards away. His intermittent moans were still audible; she wondered how much longer the doctor would take.

They started to walk side by side toward his unit before she stopped and crossed her arms. "I don't get something." Her slim brows knitted together. "If you're so sneaky, why couldn't you have just installed a camera a long time ago to watch Dr. Quinn? Wouldn't that have been easier than waiting years for him to open up? And then his secret process wouldn't have almost died with him."

Galileo's head dipped back as if to say *I wish it were that easy.* "Clearly," he said, "you didn't know Horatio."

"What didn't I know?" Her nostrils flared in defensiveness. "He was kind. He was a genius. He saved my life and Richard's."

"And he was absurdly paranoid." Galileo's tone grew weary. "For years he was convinced I was spying on him, and used to tell me off through the ceiling vent. You think he wouldn't have noticed a camera bulb somewhere?"

She closed her mouth. "Oh."

"I had to build up his trust, not destroy it." The corners of his eyes crinkled in a mournful smile. "We were so close. Man, do I wish things had happened differently."

"I'm sorry. I still can't believe he's gone."

"Death is mind-boggling. One day you're talking to someone, and the next—" His voice broke off. He paused to collect himself, dabbing gently at his eyes.

The visibility of his emotion left her speechless. Normally, his stoic competence was a mask he wore every minute of every day. It came as a revelation to peek behind it—to see that deep down, he was still human.

"You okay?" she asked.

"I don't talk about this much"—he stared off into the distance—"but fourteen years ago, I lost my only child."

Her hand flew to her lips. "I'm so sorry."

"She died at eleven." He shook his head. "And it was all my fault." He stole a glance at her and a tremendous guilt lay bare in his eyes. "She inherited a rare genetic disorder that ran in my family. I never should have taken the risk, but I was young and careless. By the time she was born, it was too late."

She drew a sharp breath. "That sounds unbearable."

They stood in silence for a moment, each absorbed in private thoughts. When he spoke again, his voice was fierce.

"There was an experimental drug that was showing promise in clinical trials. I got her into one, but she was randomly assigned to the control arm so she got the standard crappy treatment. I begged and pleaded, but no doctor was allowed to give her the new drug before it was FDA-approved. She died waiting."

Isabel stared at him in horror. And just like that, the mysterious puzzle of his identity clicked into place. She realized she didn't need to know his real name or where he grew up or any other incidental detail to make sense of who he truly was: A father spurred on by grief.

"Hence the Network . . . all the researchers . . . even me being brought back . . ."

He nodded. "I promised Hallie when she was dying that she wasn't going in vain. That I'd figure out a radical way to end suffering and disease, and no one was going to stop me."

He swept out his arm toward the triage area, hidden behind the blue curtains, and the walls that carved out three world-class operating rooms. "You, too, are part of her legacy. But even after all this time, the loss can still hit me fresh."

She touched his arm. "I understand. My dad dropped dead of a heart attack last year and I think I'm still in shock. If only he'd gotten the X101 . . ."

"I'm sorry." He paused. "But if it's any consolation, you have my word that we're going to keep working on it and testing it until it's ready to go mainstream. Sometime soon, heart attacks will no longer be a death sentence."

"I believe you." She let out a sigh. "You know, the same thing happened to Richard's dad." She glanced longingly at his hospital curtain. "He understands what it's like, too. . . . It's just hard to let go."

"I don't think I ever will," Galileo said. "And I wouldn't have it any other way."

"I wonder if everyone is always mourning someone, even if it's just in the backs of their minds."

He contemplated her with a sad smile. "Perhaps."

"At least," she said, "my mom and brother are safe."

"Oh, I mailed them that jewelry box today, the one you bought in Chinatown." His characteristic grin unexpectedly returned. "I think they'll be delighted to get something from you."

"That's great, thanks." She tilted her head at him. "What're you up to?"

"Me?" he said. "Nothing, why?"

She saw he wasn't going to tell her anything, so she shrugged. "Whatever. As long as they're okay."

"They're fine."

"Do you have a family?" Her own directness took her aback; the question had just slipped out. "I mean, not like it's any of my business."

His smile widened. "In fact I do. You know Theo? He's my stepson."

"Really?" She blinked, assimilating this new tidbit. "I thought he was just another young researcher you recruited."

"Oh, no. I've been married to his mom, Natalie, for a decade. She's a scientist, too."

"Is she on board?" Isabel mentally scanned through

the female researchers on the ship, but none of them struck her as charismatic or sexy enough to attract a man like Galileo.

"Unfortunately not," he said. "She's working at a chimp facility in Namibia at the moment. We were planning to set sail there before we met you." There was no resentment in his voice—just matter-of-factness. "So, a slight detour for now."

"Oh my God!" she exclaimed. "I totally forgot to ask about your meeting with Joan earlier. How did—"

Just then Richard's blue curtain whipped back and out stepped Dr. Reynolds, a slight wisp of a man whose tortoiseshell glasses covered half his face. He pushed them up on his nose as he walked toward her and Galileo. On the narrow bed behind him, Richard was sitting up, swinging his legs to the floor. His left eye was covered by a taped piece of gauze. When he refused to look over at her, she knew the news was bad.

Dr. Reynolds grimly pressed his lips together, then addressed Galileo. "The repeated blows to his eye caused his retina to detach. Unless he undergoes emergency surgery in the next few hours, his blindness will be permanent."

"So what are we waiting for?" she demanded. "The ORs are empty."

The doctor shifted his gaze to her. "I'm not a retinal surgeon. He needs a specialized procedure to implement a piece of silicon called a scleral buckle around his eyeball. He has to get to an outside hospital—and the closer it is, the better, so we don't waste time."

Isabel sprinted to Richard's bedside and pulled him to his feet. "Let's go! Come on."

He rose unsteadily. She could tell the news had left

him stupefied. Another surgery, another recovery. A chance of lost vision for life. No wonder he seemed so reluctant to put one foot in front of the other.

Galileo's commanding voice filled the space. "I'll have Theo escort you to the nearest hospital in midtown. We'll get the ambulance ready right now."

Isabel shot him a grateful look as Richard stopped short, turning to her.

"You stay here. You've been through enough for one night."

"No way. I'm not leaving you."

His one good eye blinked rapidly. "I'm going straight into surgery anyway. You can come in the morning after you get some rest." He kissed the top of her head. "Stay. You're safe here now."

His firmness left her no room to argue. She stood rooted to the spot as he approached Galileo and Dr. Reynolds. "Here I am," he said. "Take me away."

They guided him urgently toward the stairwell.

"First thing in the morning," she called. "I'll be there."

But she couldn't shake her unease as she watched him slip out the door.

CHAPTER 48
Greg

Greg stormed into the empty on-call room and locked the door. It was impossible to concentrate on his patients after the outrageous scene he'd witnessed over video call. Chris Donovan, his eleventh-hour godsend, protégé of freaking *Horatio Quinn*, had almost done away with Isabel Leon at last—and delivered the priceless vial that would solve everything.

How had it all gone so wrong, so fast? One minute Chris's hands were around her neck, and the next he was fighting off some furious intruder, then being wrestled to the ground by a couple of other assholes. Meanwhile, Isabel—living, breathing, two-million-dollar-payout Isabel—watched it all go down from the safety of a corner. Greg saw her on her knees gulping large quantities of air. Then his screen had gone dark. *Call ended*, read the display. No shit. It wasn't the only thing ending, either.

He slammed his palm against the wall of the on-call room hard enough to dent it. He didn't care that he was out of control, that four Vicodin hadn't even dimmed the edges of his rising panic. He felt nothing but the urge to annihilate. Period. Who or what didn't matter. In a few short days, Ellis Yardley was going to turn him in anyway, and after that, his glorious future awaited. Jail, disgrace, divorce.

Someone outside the door jiggled the knob.

"Hello?" a woman called. "Everything okay in there?"

"Fine," Greg yelled. "Be out in a minute."

He recognized her voice as one of the pathetic nurses who always flirted with him. He waited for her footsteps to recede before plunking down on a cot to catch his breath. His fingers tingled with the desire to inflict pain. He knew he had to calm down. The edge of his willpower was eroding—the edge past which his temptations threatened to overpower his rational mind. Then it was all too easy to get sucked into the black hole of his darkest urges. After that, the ugliness inside his core, the rotted part he tried so hard to control, would inevitably burst forth. And then there was no going back. It was frightening to suspect what horror you were capable of—but it was worse not to know at all.

An officious knock on the door came, three loud raps, just as a man's voice barked: "This room isn't supposed to be locked."

Jesus Christ. It was Yardley. His Long Island accent was as grating as his tone.

"I'm busy," Greg called back. It was almost 3 A.M. The ER was practically deserted, most of the doctors already gone for the night. Plus he was the attending physician. He could lock whatever damn door he pleased.

"Open up!" Three more sharp raps. "Come on, I need to get in there."

Greg glanced around at the uncomfortable bunk beds, the wicker hamper, the closet filled with clean scrubs, the full-length mirror hanging on the back of the door. There was no way to escape without facing the person he hated most. He stood, ignoring the sight of himself in the mirror, and unlocked the door.

Yardley pulled it open. His pudgy face always reminded Greg of an allergic reaction to a bee sting—his fleshy cheeks appeared inflated, with his eyes, nose, and mouth clustered in the middle. When he saw Greg, his lips edged down.

"I thought that was you."

No sudden moves, Greg reminded himself. He just had to concentrate on exiting smoothly. Then, after checking on the new admits, he could go home.

"Excuse me," Yardley said, setting foot in the doorway. "I need to change." He was wearing a pair of teal scrubs and shoe covers, a surgical mask that dangled around his neck, and a white paper cap over his hair. Greg was still in his scrubs, too, underneath his white coat, but he wasn't about to hang around changing now.

He stepped aside. "Go ahead." He unclenched his fists, remembering to breathe.

Yardley strolled past him inside as his obnoxious voice filled the room.

"It's no use, you know. I've already made up my mind."

Greg closed the door and leaned against it. "What do you mean?"

"I know I gave you 'til Monday, but I've waited long enough." Yardley turned around to glare at him. "I'm calling the feds first thing in the morning."

"But it's only Friday! You have to give me the weekend!"

"For what? To bang your wife one last time?"

Greg dug his nails into the door. It took every ounce of his self-control not to smash that fat face into an unrecognizable pulp.

His voice came out like a growl. "To come up with the money."

"If you haven't by now, you're not going to. It's over." Yardley snapped his fingers. "Say your good-byes."

"You little—"

"You did this to yourself, Greg." Yardley held up his hands as if to absolve himself of responsibility. "You stole *our* money. I have no other choice."

The worst part was that he was right. If their roles were reversed, Greg would be lording the same punishment over him. But still, he couldn't bear the smug bastard's presence a second longer. Without another word, he walked out and slammed the door behind him. His shift was almost finished. It had been a quiet night—only a few broken bones, two sets of stitches, one nonfatal heart attack, a hypochondriac with a rash. As long as there were no new patients needing his attention, he could turn over the reins to the overnight staff and get out of there. If this really was his final night of freedom, he wanted to hightail it to Joan's side. He would spend every last hour with her until they hauled him away.

A pit stop at the reception desk near the front of the ER supplied him with a list of all the patients who had been admitted in the last several hours. He scanned the spreadsheet of their names, ages, insurance types, and complaints. One line immediately popped out at him: *Richard Barnett, forty-three, Blue Cross, retinal detachment.*

Richard Barnett.

Greg quickly thought back to the scene he'd witnessed over the video call: Isabel being rescued by a furious man. A man Chris had punched in the eye. And Isabel had come up to New York from Florida with Richard Barnett to deliver the ruby ring.

This patient had to be him. It made too much sense not

to be. Roosevelt was the only full-service hospital on the West Side between lower Manhattan and Columbia Presbyterian, all the way uptown. If his injury had occurred anywhere in the vicinity, he would have been rushed here.

Greg stared at the spreadsheet. According to the notes, he'd been admitted an hour and twenty minutes earlier, then undergone emergency surgery. The gold standard treatment for a retinal detachment, a scleral buckle implantation, usually took about an hour barring complications. That meant Richard ought to done in the operating room. He was probably already in recovery. If he'd been accompanied by Isabel, then she could be nearby, too.

Greg's heart kicked against his ribs. The tingling feeling crept back into his fingertips. He still owned both of their deaths. A total of $3 million in cash payouts. But of course, he owed more than that to Yardley—$4.5 million. Even if he did manage to come up with a good chunk of the money, he knew Yardley wouldn't be satisfied.

At its core, their dispute wasn't over the stolen cash. It was over Greg's act of betrayal. So the restitution had to be all or nothing—and *all* meant not only offering every penny of reimbursement, but also suffering some excruciating loss of his own. Yardley wanted to feel that he was digging a spur into Greg's chest before he walked away on top.

Greg could think of no better way to offer him that triumph than to hand over a vial of Horatio Quinn's famed wonder drug, losing all chance of profiting off it himself. Yardley would understand that the currency of defeating death was worth a hell of a lot more than a few million bucks.

If he could somehow still get his hands on it . . .

A brazen last-ditch plan came together in his mind. He signed out of his shift and wished the receptionist a good night. Then he started toward the door that led to the waiting area and the exit, before stopping with his hand on his backpack.

"Forgot something," he announced.

The receptionist, a sour woman who presided over her glassed-in station like a police chief, nodded him back toward the interior hallway. Through there, he could access any of the hospital's multiple wings. He smiled at her and walked quickly to the elevator banks, his rubber soles squeaking over the floor. No one else was around. It was 3:03 A.M.

He took the elevator to the fourth floor, where the post-op outpatients temporarily went to recover after their surgeries. From there, they were monitored for a period of time before being checked out or admitted for longer stays. Because it was the middle of the night, Richard would likely be admitted for a few hours until morning, when the retinal surgeon would return to assess his condition before signing his release.

The fourth floor consisted of a long antiseptic walkway with beds on either side separated by thin paper curtains. Each bed was surrounded by a constellation of beeping machines and flashing displays, so walking down the unit was a little like a tour through a depressing casino, except here the game being played was survival. Everyone was a gambler; some just had better odds than others.

Greg marched up and down, but didn't recognize Richard in any of the beds. He went up to a harried-looking nurse who was tending to paperwork and asked after his whereabouts.

"Richard Barnett?" she said, consulting a chart. "They just moved him out of recovery. He's been admitted overnight for observation."

"So he's in his own room?"

"Number 403."

He flashed her a gracious smile. "Thanks."

Then he strode purposefully down the hallway as though he were still on duty. None of the nurses paid him any attention. Doctors of all specialties came to follow up on post-op patients regularly, so his presence on the floor raised no red flags.

He slipped into room 403 and closed the door. There, in a narrow bed in the center of the tiny room, lay Richard Barnett. Alone. Greg recognized him right away from the video: his lanky arms and legs, his prominent nose and close-cropped blond hair.

He was sleeping on his back with his mouth partly open, an IV stuck in his inner elbow, and a thick gauze bandage covering his left eye from his cheek to his hairline. A square monitor beeped by his side, displaying his blood pressure and oxygen saturation. The numbers looked solid. He didn't wake when Greg approached his side. The powerful sedatives from his surgery were still wearing off. The curious thing about those particular drugs— benzodiazepines plus Demerol—was that they had an amnesia effect; patients under their spell remembered nothing afterward.

Greg smiled down at him. There was a time not that long ago when they had spoken on the phone regularly, though they'd never met in person until now. Greg had even come to respect him. Like any good broker, he drove a hard bargain for his life settlement clients, but he also played straight and fair. Negotiating deals together was a dance they had come to perfect over the years, like longtime partners who knew exactly when to lead and when to step back. Greg was almost sorry their first meeting was happening this way. Almost.

He walked up to the room's only window and peered out over a dark side street. Then he unzipped his private cell phone from his backpack and dialed the number Richard had given him days earlier to confirm the ring transaction. Greg wondered who, if anyone, would answer the line this time—and if that person could get a message to Isabel.

It rang twice before a man answered sounding surprised. "Hello?"

"This is Robbie Merriman," he said. "I'm calling for Isabel Leon."

"What the hell do you want?"

"I want to talk to her about Richard Barnett. It's urgent."

There was a long pause. Greg heard a rustling noise and some static, then Isabel's tentative voice came on the line. "Hello?"

"Isabel," he said. "A pleasure as always."

She said nothing. He went on.

"Richard's nice and sleepy. But if you don't want him to get *too* sleepy, then listen up. You're going to follow my directions."

Still she said nothing. "You there?" he snapped. "I'm not screwing around."

"I'm here," she said softly.

"Good. As soon as we hang up, you're going to come to Richard's hospital room at Roosevelt, number 403, and you're going to bring the vial of Horatio Quinn's drug. Chris had it on him two hours ago, so you must know where it is now. Then you're going to leave it in his room. A drop of it *will be tested*, so don't even think about bullshitting this."

"How?" she demanded.

"Your friend Chris shared his little demonstration with

the heated flask of hydrogen peroxide and sulfuric acid. If you think those chemicals aren't all over a hospital, think again."

She didn't respond, but he could hear her breathing.

"If the flask doesn't turn black," he said, "then Richard will get a little too much painkiller in his IV. So think very, very carefully about your next move."

"You can't!" she screamed. "I'll call the police, you'll be arrested!"

"Who will?" he said calmly. "A voice on the phone?"

Again the line went silent.

"I'm hanging up," he said. "You have thirty minutes. Starting now."

CHAPTER 49
Joan

Joan could hardly believe what her own hands were doing. She watched with a surreal sense of detachment as they opened her closet door and pushed aside the beautiful skirts and dresses she would never wear again. She crouched beneath their silk hems and groped in the darkness for the safe.

Her ruby ring knocked against it. She felt along its cool surface for the keypad. Its four-digit code made her cringe: it was the date of her and Greg's engagement in Central Park thirty-one long years ago. She could still feel the tickle of the grass on her ankles and the way her heart sped up the moment he dropped to one knee. Now her heart was thumping just as fast, but for a very different reason.

The door of the safe popped open. She reached inside and withdrew the .38 semiautomatic pistol Greg had bought after their window got smashed in. She'd never shot a gun before, but he'd shown her how to rack the slide to chamber the first round if the time came. Its metal heft felt solid and powerful in her palm. A feeling of disbelief overwhelmed her as she gripped the handle. Was she really going to do this?

But Greg had left her no choice. The only way through was out.

She tried not to imagine his reaction when he came home from his shift to find her. It was already after 3 A.M. and he wasn't back yet. The shock alone might inflict permanent damage on his psyche. But his well-being was no longer her concern. She couldn't go on telling herself lies about his innocence. Hope to the doomed was nothing but cruel self-denial.

She walked in a daze to the living room and lay down on the couch. Her sweaty fingers clutched the shaft of the gun. Closing her eyes, she lifted up her nightshirt and pressed the cold barrel into her abdomen. The second it touched her skin, her entire body stiffened. She opened her eyes, breathing hard.

In the corner of the ceiling she spied the camera bulb they'd installed to bolster their security system after the window incident. Except for the bulb's dull glass eye, she was alone. She thought of broken promises, of justice and deliverance.

Then she remembered something. She let go of the gun. It plopped against her stomach, rising and falling with her breath. In one quick defiant motion, she yanked off her ruby ring and hurled it across the room. It smacked into a wall and plunked to the floor.

With a trembling hand, she picked up the gun again and thrust its barrel into her skin. She hesitated. Would this be an act of betrayal or bravery? Victory or defeat? And most importantly, would the people who still mattered forgive her in the end?

Her index finger slid into place over the trigger.

In her head, a countdown began.

Three.

But Greg loved her.

Two.

He would be destroyed.

One.

Which was exactly what he deserved.

PART FOUR

CHAPTER 50
Isabel

Isabel stepped out of Roosevelt's fourth-floor elevator, her cheeks tingling from rushing through the cold. Here inside the hospital, the blustery dead of night didn't exist. Harsh fluorescent lights glared overhead. The stale air smelled of disinfectant. Muffled beeps could be heard emanating from various rooms.

A deserted corridor stretched before her like a sterile white tunnel. She hurried past door after door, scanning their plaques for number 403. Clutched under her arm was a leather messenger bag on loan from Galileo. Inside it, chilled within a miniature cooler, lay the glass vial that she hoped would secure Richard's life.

Whether from nerves or the frigid air outside, she was shivering. She tightened her wool coat, praying that Galileo's bold last-minute plan would carry her and Richard through the night unscathed. But it had all come together of necessity so fast that her confidence faltered. Everyone was depending on her—and yet for once, she was utterly alone.

As she hastened down the hallway, she thought of enlisting a nurse or two to accompany her into Richard's room for protection. But what could she tell them? That she suspected the patient was in danger of being murdered, but she had no way to prove it? They would think she was nuts; they might even throw her out. She didn't dare risk that. Anyway, the plan couldn't work unless she was by herself.

Room 403 flashed into view. She stopped before the plain white door and gripped the knob. It turned. She pushed open the door, peering nervously around it.

The first thing she saw was an older male doctor's white coat. He was leaning over Richard's bed with his back to her. His salt-and-pepper hair was thinning at the crown of his head, though his body looked trim and muscular. Relief washed over her like a reflex at the comforting sight of authority. His presence emboldened her to step into the room.

That was when he turned around. A strangled gasp escaped her.

His face was unmistakable: Those light blue eyes, that Roman nose, the chiseled symmetry of his jaw. He was too handsome to forget. She recalled her only previous sighting of him—on a bench in Riverside Park—and the picture of him and Joan together on a beach. But if there was any doubt, the embroidery on his lapel confirmed his identity: *Gregory Hughes, M.D.*

Aka Robbie Merriman.

His eyes remained deadly serious as his mouth twisted into a smirk. A kind of feverish menace radiated from his gaze. Six feet away, she tensed under its spell. But the second she stepped back to run, she noticed what lay hostage in his grip. Horror struck her as the balance of power between them shifted in his favor. He acknowledged her recognition of it with a haughty lift of his chin.

He was holding a fist-sized pump attached to a tube that split off in two directions: one branch led up to a fluid-filled bag that hung on a pole, while the other snaked down to a needle that disappeared inside Richard's elbow. Richard, whose left eye was taped over with gauze, appeared to be sleeping comfortably, unaware of any danger to his life. The heart monitor beside him beeped at regular intervals.

"You can't!" she cried. "You won't get away with it!"

"Quiet," he snapped. "Do you really want to test me?"

She gave him the dirtiest look she could manage, but closed her mouth.

"Now take that chair in the corner and push it against the door." He waited while she reluctantly obeyed, hauling a heavy solid oak armchair into place to block the door; apparently hospitals didn't have locks inside patients' rooms.

"Good," he said.

She dared to take her eyes off him for one moment to scan the ceiling for a camera. If she gave it her most pleading expression, then maybe someone on the other end would notice and come to help.

"Looking for that?" He tilted his head up at the far left corner of the room, where a white camera was positioned to capture both the patient's bed and the door. There was only one problem: a black handkerchief obscured its lens.

"No one will notice for a bit, probably not until morning," he said. "So it's just you and me. Sorry babe."

She crossed her arms, glaring at him. His smirk stretched a little wider. He seemed to be enjoying her imposed silence.

"You know, you're not quite as annoying as I thought

you'd be." His gaze shifted to the messenger bag under her arm. "A present for *moi*?"

She remained stock still, her hatred rising by the second. His amusement morphed into a snarl with astonishing speed. He wagged his thumb above Richard's pump.

"Just hand it over. Hurry up."

Barely taking her eyes off his thumb, she slid the bag from her shoulder, unzipped the mini cooler, and lifted out the chilled glass vial. She cradled it in both palms like a fragile bird, making sure not to jostle it—or, God forbid, drop it.

"Very good," he said. His tone had regained its glee, but an ominous edge lingered. "Now I thought we could run a little experiment together."

Still holding the pump with one hand, he reached underneath Richard's bed and produced a glass flask filled with clear chemicals.

"Still warm," he noted. "My lighter came in handy."

He blew on the top of the mixture. A whiff of hydrogen peroxide and pungent sulfuric acid floated her way. Her nose wrinkled. He snickered at her obvious dismay.

"You didn't think I was gonna run the test? But I promised I would. I always keep my promises." He set down the flask on Richard's nightstand and beckoned to her. "Bring me the vial."

Her pulse throbbed in her temples. She felt totally helpless, a chess piece trapped in checkmate. Any step would be the wrong one—backward, forward, sideways. Frustration and fear swelled within her: Nothing short of Richard's life hung in the balance. Yet again she was failing, and this time he wasn't about to rescue either of them.

"I said, *bring it to me.*" Greg's nostrils flared with impatience. "Are you deaf?"

She started to walk toward him. Then, forcing herself to take the unthinkable risk, she opened her mouth. The words streamed out at the pace of an auctioneer's spiel.

"I have to tell you—"

"Shut up!" he interrupted. "What did I say?"

In the same breath, he jabbed the button on the IV pump.

Richard's head lolled to the side on his pillow. His sleeping eyelids fluttered and a string of drool dribbled out of the corner of his mouth. A sudden drop registered on his heart rate monitor, but after a few seconds the number stabilized.

"There's more where that came from," Greg warned.

His arrogant little smirk was back again.

She regarded him with a look of pure loathing—and terror.

"Come put the vial at my feet," he commanded. "Right now."

She had no choice but to comply. She approached him defensively in a side stance, with her elbows sticking out, the vial still cradled in her palms. When she was two feet from him, she crouched down to set it on the floor.

He let go of the pump to kneel and grab it, but just as she stepped back, he caught hold of her wool coat and jerked her toward him. She sunk her teeth into his hand as hard as she could, but he didn't release her. Instead he shoved his hand farther into her mouth, gagging her screams, and wrestled her onto her back in spite of her flailing limbs. His substantial weight felt like a bear crushing her chest. All she needed was a split second for him to let go of her mouth so she could scream, and then surely someone would hear and come to help.

She let her body relax, as though she were giving up, and as soon as she felt the pressure of his body ease up, she jerked her foot up into his solar plexus. But instead of him falling backward like she expected, he actually smiled, his hand hardly budging from her mouth.

"Tough cookie," he muttered, almost to himself. She tried to catch his eye—to make him reckon with her agony— but he was focusing on something inside his coat. . . .

He kept her pinned with his knee and fist, while his left hand reached into his front pocket and withdrew a long needle. Her eyes widened; she gave a last desperate jerk and scooted her head an inch away from the needle just as he depressed the plunger. Clear fluid spurted out onto the floor beside her face. "Dammit!" he snapped.

She caught a glimpse of his enraged face before he jammed the remaining solution into the back of her neck.

The needle stung like a hundred bees. She let out a wail, but his rigid hand remained clamped over her mouth. Almost immediately, she was overcome by the sensation of her insides hardening. Her legs, arms, abs, neck, face— every bit of her seemed to be suddenly turning to stone. After five seconds, she couldn't even blink her eyelids. A coherent thought broke through the plume of her rising panic: How was this even possible?

But then the panic expanded like a gas throughout her entire skull, nullifying all thought—it felt like insanity, a frenzied protest of every fiber of her being at once. Neurons fired urging her arms to punch, her legs to kick, her teeth to bite, but all she could do was emit a silent shriek that died in her throat before it had even begun. The urge of her lungs to gulp all the air in the room resulted in a pathetic wisp of a breath.

She remained completely motionless.

"That's better." Greg stood up with an approving nod.

"Now," he said, "we can get down to business."

CHAPTER 51
Greg

"You're probably wondering what the hell just happened."

Greg sank to his haunches in front of Isabel, who sat gagged and bound to a dusty wooden chair in the corner of Richard's room. It had taken a ridiculously small amount of effort to scrape her limp body from the ground and tie her up with a couple of double-knotted pillowcases. Then he'd stuffed a chunk of cloth in her mouth and secured it with a strip of white medical tape. She offered zero resistance, of course. Unless you counted the venomous look she was managing to communicate in spite of her frozen state. If she'd gotten the whole damn dose of the drug, she wouldn't even be breathing right now, let alone staring at him with pure hatred.

He ran his finger along the needle before dropping it back into his white coat.

"Succinylcholine," he said. "My favorite untraceable drug. It's used to paralyze anesthesia patients before intubation. But don't worry, it wears off real fast. In the meantime"—he bustled around collecting the chemical flask and the glass vial off the nightstand and the floor—"I'm going to run my little experiment."

The only response came from Richard—a nasal snore. Greg glanced over at him lying on the bed. His mouth was wide open and his only visible eyelid was twitching in deep sleep. Good. The extra boost of painkiller on top of sedation had knocked him out solid. Greg never could have gotten away with actually killing him—his monitors would sound the alarm and the nurses would burst in with a crash cart—but Isabel didn't know to call the bluff. Perception always mattered more than the truth.

Double-fisting the flask and the vial, he returned to crouch before her. She stared at him without blinking, a lock of hair hanging over her eye. Inside her ugly woolen coat, her body remained inert—hands fastened behind her back, each ankle secured to a leg of the chair.

"First, though, I owe you a thank-you—and an apology." He set down the flask near her feet, still clutching the ice-cold vial. Its clear liquid sloshed a tiny bit, and he was surprised to notice that his hand—his steady operating hand—was trembling.

"I appreciate your compliance," he said to her. "This means everything to me, assuming it's real of course. But"—he paused, staring at a spot above her head, then back at her—"even if it is, I can't let you out of here alive. You know too much."

Her eyelids lifted ever so slightly, and in that almost imperceptible movement, he could read the intensity of her panic. He could also see that the quick half-life of the succinylcholine meant it was already beginning to wear off.

"It's nothing personal," he went on. "You're in the business of survival, so you of all people should understand."

Her brows flicked, a mere twitch, but he recognized her attempt at a challenge.

"How would I get rid of you without getting caught?

Simple." He pointed to the window. "No one would be the wiser if you happened to jump to your death in that dark alley in the middle of the night."

She lowered her gaze to the floor. Her feet began to squirm against her restraints, the soles of her sneakers scuffing the linoleum. A spot of wetness appeared on her lower lids.

"You know," he said, "the fastest growing demographic with mental illness is young women." He shook his head. "It's really a tragedy. I'd hate to come of age in this era. Your generation just got the shit end of the stick.

"Anyway." He turned his attention to the flask not far from her jerking feet. "Let's do this." He held up the glass vial, regretting the fact that he hadn't thought to locate an eyedropper. His goddamn hands had to stop shaking so he could pour out a tiny drop; he literally could not afford to spill.

He tried to focus on holding the vial steady, but the continual scraping of her squeaky shoes against the floor was driving him insane. She seemed to be doing it for that sole purpose, too, because there was no way she was actually going to break out of her restraints.

"For God's sake!" he snapped. "Cut it out."

But she only escalated her speed, tapping and scraping with apparently desperate urgency. There was only one thing that annoyed him more than distraction, and that was disobedience. He fished in his breast pocket for the red Swiss Army knife he carried around—it came in handy quite often—and whipped it out in front of her face. He peeled back one of the crisp silver blades.

"Don't make this messier than it has to be. I *said*, hold still."

She had the gall to ignore him. But, he saw, most of

her body actually was motionless. She wasn't struggling to free her arms or get up from the chair. In fact, not even both of her feet were moving. It was just her right foot. When he focused on it, she grew excited—nodding her head in an exaggerated motion and moaning into her cloth gag. Her gaze kept switching from his eyes to her ankle, back and forth.

That was when he noticed something odd. Her foot kept scraping the ground in the same way over and over. What he'd thought was a deliberate attempt to aggravate him instead seemed to be some sort of frantic message. The longer he watched her foot, the faster she pumped out the pattern. He inched closer to get a better look.

He watched the downward swoop of her toes, their slide to the left. Then an oval. A triangle. And an upside-down *u*. Over and over, the exact pattern repeated.

What the—

A glimmer of comprehension dawned on him. They were letters.

The first one was indisputably *j*. Then *o*.

Holy Fucking Christ. She was spelling *Joan*.

But that was impossible. To her, he was Robbie Merriman. He was a voice on the phone. An anonymous ghost. He didn't have a wife named Joan.

A cold shiver tore through him. He ripped off the tape over her mouth.

"Where did you get that name?"

It took a few seconds for her to cough out the cloth, find her tongue. When she finally did, it wasn't to scream or to curse. Instead her soft voice came out resigned.

"Your wife knows everything. I tried to tell you before but you wouldn't let me."

"Bullshit." His ears buzzed with static. Joan knowing

the truth was as absurd as an alien materializing in the room. He'd spent the last five years covering every possible track.

"No, I'm serious." Isabel glared up at him. "You're going to kill me anyway, why would I make this up? She knows all about Robbie Merriman and what you did to me."

He smacked her hard across the face. "You're lying."

Her eyes watered but she didn't back down. "Your address is two-fourteen West 104th Street. The ring had a tracking device inside it. I went and told her everything last night and she totally freaked out. She said she was going to help me get you arrested, but tonight I tried to reach her like twenty times and there was no answer. I just feel like she might be in trouble."

Greg suppressed a rising scream. Before she could say another word, he was scrambling to pull out his iPhone and call his wife's cell—they didn't have a landline—but her phone rang and rang, then went to voice mail.

Something was seriously wrong. She always slept with her phone charging on her nightstand in case of an emergency. He tried again but got voice mail.

Isabel's frown deepened. "Is there any other way you can check on her? I didn't mean to cause any harm . . . I just wanted her to know the truth . . ."

He drew a sharp breath. The security camera. They'd recently installed one connected to a subscription app so they could check on their home in real time from afar.

He brought up the app on his phone and quickly typed in his password. It went black for a few moments while a progress bar loaded. He saw nothing; felt nothing; not even the glass vial still in his hand. His entire existence compressed down to the blue bar at the bottom of the screen.

After a ten-second eternity, a bird's-eye view of their living room popped up.

There, on the couch, lay his beloved wife—eyes closed, face white, the gun he bought for protection resting in her unmoving palm.

Her nightshirt was soaked through with blood.

CHAPTER 52
Greg

He stared dumbstruck at the screen.

The woman on the couch had Joan's blond bob and olive skin and delicate bone structure. She had the same brown mole above her lip, the same long eyelashes, the same petite figure. She was even wearing Joan's favorite silk nightshirt and pajama pants.

But this woman looked dead. This woman could not be Joan.

"Let me see," Isabel said. Her shoulders wriggled as she tried to free herself from the chair. "What is it?"

He looked up in surprise, having almost forgotten she was there. He blinked. Words deserted him. Sound dimmed and space receded, stranding him on his own silent plane of agony. The unbearable image flashed before his eyes no matter where he looked.

His expression must have revealed the news, because her face crumpled in horror. "No. No."

He turned the phone to show her.

She let out a cry of anguish. "Oh my God." Her eyes squeezed shut. "I never should have told her . . ."

A sliver of Greg's consciousness urged him to go on a

rampage, to crush her skull between his bare fists, this stupid bitch who had destroyed everything instead of dying weeks ago like she was supposed to—but he was too shaken to do anything except flip the phone back around to stare at his wife's lifeless body. The red stain was dark and wet against the soft cloud of her nightshirt. He could almost feel its silk between his fingers, he knew those pajamas so well, had caressed her in them countless times over the years.

Isabel's lowered chin jerked up. "Let me see that again."

Too shaken to resist, he obliged. The time warp in his mind was dragging out each moment to an insufferable hell. If only he could call Joan, she would know what to do.

"Closer," Isabel instructed. He inched the screen toward her face.

She studied it for a few seconds before looking up at him, her eyes suddenly blazing with excitement. "It might not be too late—it looks like she bled out from her stomach, but that could be repaired in surgery if she gets treated in time!"

"In time for what?" he cried. "She's dead!"

"Yeah"—Isabel flicked her bound ankle at him—"and you're holding the drug that could save her!"

In his trembling left hand, the clear fluid splashed up the insides of the vial. He gaped at it, and at her. If she was right, then everything he knew about emergency medicine and the permanence of recent death—everything he'd learned thirty years ago in medical school about brain hypoxia and the limited scope of resuscitation—was wrong.

But she had to be right. She herself had survived.

"The X101 stops the death of neurons," she said, as though reading his mind. "If we can get it to her ASAP she might still have a chance."

Greg felt his heart banging inside his chest. "Do you just inject it straight into her brain?"

"No, she needs this whole precise protocol, I don't know all the details, but it involves cooling her body down, detoxifying her blood, injecting lines into her shoulders and knees—"

"But this ER isn't equipped for that!" he interrupted. "No one will know what to do!"

"It's okay," she said, "I can get her to the doctors who saved me. They work on a ship docked in Chelsea Piers. They have everything she needs, including their own ambulance. I can call right now."

She tried to wrestle her hands free, but they were still tied behind her back.

"What's the number?" he demanded.

"I have to do the talking," she said, "or else they won't cooperate. But first you have to release me."

In a striking flash of clarity, he saw his life collapse. There was no way he was going to hand over the drug as payment for Yardley now, no way he could escape the wrath of the feds and the inevitable prison sentence. Which meant Isabel's existence no longer posed a threat. She was beside the point. His freedom was beside the point.

The only point, the only thing that mattered, was Joan.

He reached into the front pouch of his white coat, deposited his phone, and withdrew his sleek little folding knife. Flipping open the sharpest blade, he lunged at Isabel—she gasped in alarm—but he avoided her altogether, slicing instead through the knotted cloth that bound her wrists to the chair.

"Thank you," she said gratefully, shaking out her arms as he also freed her ankles. "If you let me live, I swear I won't tell anyone that you're Robbie Merriman. I just want to go home."

"It doesn't matter anymore. It is what it is." He slipped the knife back into his pocket and shoved the phone at her. "Just make the call."

She wasted no time getting through to whoever was on the other end, described Joan's emergency in a few words, and told them to send the ambulance to 214 West 104th Street, apartment 1B, *stat*.

"I'll meet you there with it," she said into the phone. "Yeah, I have it . . . I will."

When she hung up, she leveled her gaze at the vial in Greg's left hand. Her tone grew stern. "Be very careful with that. She needs every last drop."

He tightened his grip around the cool thin glass. Nothing short of an army could make him part with it now. "No shit. Are they coming?"

She nodded. "They're on their way. Let's go."

He turned on his heel and practically sprinted to the door. She trailed behind him, pausing at the threshold to glance back at Richard, who was still fast asleep.

"Come on," Greg hissed to her. "We have to go."

They rushed through the empty corridor, down four flights of stairs rather than waiting for the elevator, and out through the lobby into the freezing windy night. He barely felt the cold, but Isabel buried her chin in the collar of her wool coat as he hailed the first yellow taxi that drove by.

She jumped into the backseat and scooted away from him to the far window. He stepped in carefully so as not to jostle the vial too much, even though its cap was tightly secured, and commanded the driver to gun it to his address.

"It's an emergency," he panted. "Please, as fast as you can."

The car zoomed away from the curb. It was after 4 A.M.—the streets were empty except for a few other stray cabs and the streetlights stayed green for an eternity. He and Isabel didn't trade a single word. Each stared out their respective windows at the dark buildings outside. His own impatience spiked with each passing block.

"I said to hurry," he snapped to the driver after three minutes. "Come on, man."

The guy hit the gas and the car accelerated faster up West End Avenue, a straight shot to 104th Street, before finally pulling up next to Greg's dingy townhouse.

With his free hand, he grabbed a twenty from his wallet and flung it through the gap to the front seat. Then he darted out of the cab and scrambled to his front door, Isabel following a couple steps behind.

"Where's the ambulance?" he demanded, looking up and down the street.

"I'm sure it's almost here," she said. "They're not that far."

He unlocked the building's door, rushed down the short hallway to his apartment, jammed the key into the lock. He felt his throat tighten in anticipation, wasn't sure he could bear the sight, but knew he had to go in and try to stanch the bleeding, try to stay calm, try not to completely break down . . .

He pushed open the door.

And came face-to-face with a strange, grim man. A man holding out handcuffs.

Behind him, wiping a dark red smear off her stomach, stood Joan.

Joan, on the verge of tears, very much alive.

CHAPTER 53
Isabel

A few feet behind Greg, Isabel watched his final moments of freedom unfold.

He stood rigid in the doorway, still holding the vial he was so sure was the X101, but was really just 2 milliliters of ice water. Galileo never would have let her remove the real vial from the safety of the ship.

Greg stared at Galileo's unsmiling face, then at Joan's. No one moved. The air felt too stifling to breathe. The steady tick of a clock could be heard from somewhere inside the apartment. Each loud second was a testament to Greg's complete and utter shock. Isabel wondered if he had ever been rendered so speechless in his life.

Galileo stepped forward to cuff him right as he snapped out of his daze and flung up an elbow to delay the inevitable.

"I can't fucking believe you," he spat at his wife. "How could you do this to me?"

She looked him straight in the eye, her voice shaking only a little. "I've been thinking the exact same thing."

"But I gave up everything for you!" he cried.

"All right buddy, time's up." Galileo advanced, dangling the silver cuffs. At six foot four, in his black trench coat and heavy combat boots, he possessed the severe authority of a general at war. The smile that lived behind his eyes was gone. Isabel had never seen him look so intimidating.

Greg brought the vial close to his chest. "Who the hell are you?"

"I'm the guy taking you into custody." Galileo clicked open the cuffs. "Thought that was pretty obvious."

Greg whirled around to face Isabel, still clutching the vial. "You little bitch! You knew the whole time."

Emboldened by Galileo's presence, she reached into her wool coat and pulled out the covert wire stuffed into an interior pocket. It wasn't an actual clumsy wire; Galileo had hooked her up with a more sophisticated device from his time in law enforcement—a radio frequency transmitter with a self-contained wire built into a tiny box with an antenna. The discreet thing was not much bigger than a matchbook. On his end, Galileo had the audio receiver that had recorded her entire confrontation with Greg: His confirmation of his alter ego. His threats to her life and Richard's. Every last damning word.

She watched the livid realization cross his face. A flush darkened his cheeks, his lips went slack, his nostrils flared. A crazed look crept into his eyes, the look of a man with nothing left to lose. He stumbled back around as Isabel felt her stomach plummet.

She shouted in warning—against what, she didn't know—just as Greg flung the vial to the ground. The glass shattered at Galileo's feet, and in the moment that he was distracted, Greg snuck a hand into his white coat and yanked out his folding knife.

Isabel and Joan screamed in unison as Galileo looked up from the broken glass, but it was too late, the razor edge was already tearing through the air, its momentum unstoppable. Galileo had only half a second to register horror before the blade plunged into his stomach. He cried out, doubling over, as Greg withdrew the bloody knife and impaled him once more.

He collapsed to the floor with a sickening grunt.

Greg spun on his heel and ran.

CHAPTER 54
Joan

Joan charged after her husband with a blood-pumping rage she had never before felt. But she had also never witnessed an assault as shockingly brutal. Now the federal agent was sprawled out clutching his abdomen, a dark red stain pooling beneath him, and Greg was storming through the doorway about to barrel past Isabel.

"Stop him!" Joan screamed, three feet behind. "Don't let him get away!"

But Isabel was already planting herself directly in his path, her pink face scrunched up in fury. With sheer animalistic force, she rammed her knee up between his legs. Greg's moan was instantaneous. He bent over as his hands flew to his groin. Before he could recover, Joan saw her opportunity.

She grabbed the open handcuffs from the floor where they had fallen, sprung at Greg's feet, and clicked the cuffs around one hairy white ankle, then the other. By the time he twisted around in surprise, she was rising to face him with the shiny silver key in her hand.

"What the—?" he sputtered.

Joan slapped him so hard that her palm stung. "You're not going anywhere."

He tried to lunge at her, but she stepped back and let him trip over his bound-up ankles. With an added shove from Isabel, he crashed to the ground on his hands and knees. He scrambled toward Joan, but Isabel kicked him again in the groin, this time from behind. Grunting, he curled in on himself. Then Isabel and Joan together grabbed his arms and wrenched them behind his back. He flailed against their efforts for thirty seconds before Joan remembered the gun she'd left behind on the couch, a prop for the camera.

She bolted into the living room, got the gun, and ran back into the foyer aiming the barrel at his head. As soon as he saw it, his brows shot up and he immediately ceased struggling. His arms went limp in Isabel's grip. She shot Joan a look of exhausted gratitude and dashed to the poor injured agent a few feet away.

"If you move," Joan warned, "I shoot."

Greg stayed on his stomach and dropped his arms to his sides, lifting his chin off the ground in disbelief. "You wouldn't."

She approached him with her index finger on the trigger. "Don't test me."

He must have registered the seriousness of her threat because the last shred of defiance vanished from his eyes. He lowered his cheek to the floor.

On the other side of his body, Isabel wiggled out of her wool coat and threw it over his legs to prevent the loss of body heat. At the same time, she was desperately trying to plug the agent's wounds with her bare hands.

"Get me a phone!" she shouted. "Hurry!"

"I'll call 911," Joan said, running backward to grab her cell from the kitchen without taking her eyes—or her aim—off Greg. "Don't you dare get up," she warned.

He didn't.

"No!" Isabel hollered. "Not 911. Just bring me the phone!"

Joan obeyed despite her confusion. There was no time to ask questions. She got her phone and sprinted to Isabel's side, leaping over Greg on the floor. The poor agent had fallen unconscious. His lips were parted and his face was pale, and the pool of blood beneath him was expanding alarmingly fast. It was seeping into the cracks between the wood panels, staining the knees of Isabel's jeans, streaking her hands red.

She snatched the phone from Joan and dialed a seven-digit number.

"Get me Theo," she cried into the mouthpiece. "Put someone else in charge of Chris, it's an emergency! . . . Hi, no, you need to come right away, Galileo's been stabbed . . ." She jabbed two fingers against his inner wrist. "Barely . . . Two-fourteen West 104th, 1B. Hurry!"

She set down the phone and returned to trying to stop his bleeding. Without a word, Joan ran into her bathroom and unearthed an old first aid kit from a cabinet. It was ridiculous even to her, but as she was rushing back, all she could think about was how she wished Greg were there to help—the caring, loving Greg he had embodied just for her. He was an ER physician—he would know what to do—but the real Greg remained inert on the ground, silent but watchful, his mouth a thin mean line.

That was when she realized he had never really given a damn about his suffering patients. He was no healer. He didn't care whether they lived or died. He only pretended to care. And she'd fallen for it. She'd fallen in love with a lie. On her way past him, she restrained herself from spraying a gob of saliva at his face. Her spit was too good for him.

Instead she crouched beside Isabel, opened the first

aid kit, and removed a hunk of gauze. It wasn't much, but she handed it over and Isabel pressed it against the bigger wound. The blood soaked through it in less than two minutes.

"Shouldn't we call 911?" Joan said. "I mean, he needs to get to a hospital . . ."

Isabel shook her head, trading out the drenched gauze for a new piece. "He will."

"He will?"

"Yeah." She hesitated. "He belongs to a . . . group with special facilities. Trust me, it's better than what he would get otherwise."

"Oh. Is it just for top brass or something? He told me he was an undercover agent, but I got the sense that he's someone really high up."

Isabel gave a cryptic shrug. "Something like that."

Joan could see she was trying not to cry, so she quit asking.

Isabel grabbed his wrist again. "His pulse is so faint."

"How many beats per minute? Here—" Joan held up her wristwatch with its ticking second hand. Isabel stared at it as she counted silently for a minute.

Then, her voice trembling: "I think around twenty-one."

Right at that moment, they heard the distant wail of an ambulance. Both of them tensed, listening, hoping it was the right one. And sure enough, the siren got louder and louder until it pulled up to the curb outside, lighting up the street blue and red.

"Thank God," Isabel said. She was still pressing the hopeless gauze against his abdomen. Blood was dripping from her wrists.

Joan jumped to the front window to see two somber

men approach the building with a stretcher. She buzzed them in and threw open her apartment door.

"In here," she called to them.

They ran inside as Isabel stood up to move out of their way. The second they spotted him, limp and unconscious in a frightening amount of blood, their mouths fell open. But after a split second, their professional efficiency resumed—they sprung into action and lifted him carefully up onto the stretcher. As they maneuvered him through the doorway, the audio receiver fell out of his trench coat. The proof of Greg's monstrousness.

Joan picked it up. "I'll give this to the cops," she promised Isabel, who was following in the hallway behind them.

She looked over her shoulder at Joan. "You can take it from here?"

"Yep." Joan waved her off. "You go ahead."

"Thank you," she said. Then she turned and fled to the stretcher and out onto the sidewalk. In a matter of seconds, the ambulance and its flashing lights were gone.

Joan went back inside, almost surprised to notice that the gun was still in her hand. Greg hadn't moved. She shut the door and walked in front of him so he could see her with it, in case he decided to try anything stupid. But he seemed to have given up.

He lifted his head to look wearily at her.

"Can I at least sit up?" he asked.

"No."

He sighed. "I'm still your husband, you know."

She raised an eyebrow. His audacity never failed to astonish her.

"Everything I did was for us," he insisted, his voice pathetic and shrill.

She didn't dignify him with a response. They were beyond pleas, explanations, and apologies. The gap between them had yawned into an irrevocable chasm that rendered all words pointless. A tiny shake of her head was all she needed to communicate a diatribe of regret and disgust—made even more pointed by her refusal to say any of it.

He lay his cheek back on the floor and closed his eyes.

She wiped the sticky blood off her cell phone and dialed 911 on speaker.

An operator answered after one ring. "Nine-one-one, what is your emergency?"

"Yes, hi." The deceptively simple question left her searching for a way to explain; from a certain perspective, her whole life was an emergency. But hidden underneath the panic and the agony was the first inkling of peace she had felt in months. Because her quest for the truth was finally over. No more lies. No more pretense. From here on out, for the first time in three decades, she was on her own. And that didn't sound so bad after all. She steadied herself with a deep breath.

"There's a murderer in my house," she said into the phone.

"Are you in any danger?"

Greg opened his eyes to await her answer.

"No." She stared straight through him. "He's no longer a threat."

CHAPTER 55
Isabel

"He's flat-lining!" Theo screamed through the partition. "Hurry!"

Up front at the wheel, Isabel slammed her foot on the gas. The ambulance howled like a frightened wolf, its red and blue lights reflecting off the windshield as she careened down the West Side Highway toward the dock.

Her heart felt like it was pumping hard enough to power the engine. She was quivering so badly, she was practically levitating. There was no time to look over her shoulder at the chaos in the rear, not while she was edging toward ninety-five miles per hour, dodging cars so much slower they looked like they were standing still. But through the open partition, she could hear a shrill, sustained beep that told her everything she needed to know.

Almost immediately came the accordionlike groan of the automatic chest compression machine, amid the shouts of Theo and Dr. Cornell, one of the ship's general surgeons who had come to assist. Isabel knew the solemn doctor only by sight because he was often ensconced in his lab, cloning organs, but Galileo spoke of him highly.

Galileo. Oh God. The violent scene replayed in her

mind as if to force her to believe the unbelievable: the knife sinking into his stomach, his shell-shocked face, the blood spouting from his torn flesh. Too much blood. Brownish smears had dried on her own hands like scabs; she was too preoccupied to notice.

She zoomed into an empty lane, trying to tune out that horrible steady beep of the heart monitor, the men's frantic voices, and the rustle of equipment—the slam of a compartment door, the pop of a line injection, the whirring of the ECMO machine. The word *dead* hovered at the gates of her consciousness, but she refused to let it in. *He's going to be fine*, she thought. *He can survive. I did. Richard did.*

Yet there was one crucial difference between their plight and Galileo's: Dr. Quinn. How well could Dr. Cornell and Theo compensate for his absence? Cornell's specialty was organ repair, not resuscitation. At least Theo had been training under the master, but he was still an apprentice. Isabel couldn't help cringing at the thought that Galileo's life was resting in less-than-experienced hands.

It would all come down to the X101, Quinn's legacy, the greatest gift he could give to Galileo from beyond the grave. She pictured the beauty of the real glass vial, the liquid compound as clear and pure as baptismal water.

Above the monitor's high-pitched beep, Theo's shout pelted her eardrums: "Can't you go any faster?"

"Almost there," she hollered over her shoulder, jerking the wheel to bypass a sleepy truck in her lane. The orange digits on the dashboard read 4:37 A.M. Outside the window, the Hudson River snaked along the highway, its blackness barely distinguishable from the sky above.

At last the road was clear. She crushed the pedal all the way to the floor. The ambulance blasted ahead, its engine whining as though it might combust. Soon they were zipping past the cavernous warehouses that comprised the parking lots for Chelsea Piers. The whole area stretched for dozens of blocks to accommodate all the private and commercial boats that stopped off in Manhattan.

Isabel kept her eyes peeled for the blocky white numbers of Pier 41. As soon as she spotted it, she turned sharply off the highway and zigzagged through the parking structure to the dock. There, the stately white ship rose high off the river like a tribute to grandness, a throwback to an era when greatness mattered. No lights shone through any of the portholes. The loading ramp lay unfurled against the flat wooden pier.

Isabel drove straight up to the ramp's edge and slammed on the brakes. As ambulance squealed to a stop, Theo's ashen face thrust through the partition.

"Go get the X101 and bring it back stat!"

She popped open the door. "Is he . . . ?"

"Just go, his neurons are already starting to die!"

She jumped out and scrambled up the ramp into the belly of the ship, beelining past two worried nurses down the stairs to deck 2. The drab hallway was empty. Of course no one was working because it was the middle of the night. She was shocked to realize that almost everyone else on the ship was still asleep—that they had no idea what was happening, despite their high stakes in the outcome.

She panted up to Dr. Quinn's lab, refusing to attach any other name to the space—though she had only ever seen one man working there. The door was carelessly left open, against protocol; all labs were supposed to be locked overnight in case of a security breach. She peered warily around the door frame, but no one was there, so she bolted to the refrigerator. A vision rose in her mind of the single precious dose that lay chilled inside at a perfect 35 degrees.

She whipped open the door and reached out—

The plastic tray was empty. The vial was gone.

She rubbed her eyes, then stared again at the spot where the vial had been a mere two hours earlier. She'd seen it herself, because when Greg called to blackmail her into bringing it to the hospital, she'd compared the real one with the fake one she'd prepped instead.

A plume of cool air wafted into her face. She shut the fridge. Her fingertips felt numb with fear . . . and rage. There was only one person besides Galileo who knew the code to unlock the number pad on the door.

A person who was supposed to be under tight supervision.

Deck 3, she remembered, that's where he'd been taken after his attempt on her life. Her fingers fluttered up to the base of her neck, where his rough hands had left her sore and bruised. Each swallow prompted a stab of pain.

She sprinted at full speed up to deck 3. It was eerily quiet and dark along the corridor. Doors lined it on either side, leading to researchers' private cabins. She stopped in front of Chris's and banged loudly. If Theo was no longer in charge of him, who the hell was?

No one answered. She kicked open the door—and gasped. On the floor, curled next to an overturned chair, lay Dr. Powell—the heart specialist who, with Theo, had pried Chris off Richard hours before. The bridge of the doctor's nose looked broken, bright red blood trickled from both nostrils, and his broken glasses hung askew across his face. Chris was nowhere to be seen.

Dr. Powell moaned as she fell to her knees beside him.

"Where's Chris?" She gave his shoulders a gentle shake. "Dr. Powell?"

He trained his dazed expression on her, appearing to have trouble focusing. After a few seconds, his eyes closed.

"Do you know where he went?" she demanded.

He nudged his head a tiny bit from side to side.

A sob rose in her throat. Galileo's brain was perishing with each passing second. She jumped to her feet and ran up to deck 4, then deck 5, scouring the kitchen, the gym, the dining room, the glass-walled lounge, the captain's quarters—but no Chris. Not that she expected to find him; she knew she was too late.

Tears spilling freely, she raced back outside down the ramp, past the anxious nurses, to the waiting ambulance. Her head throbbed as she approached its closed rear doors. They loomed like the finish line of some failed race in which the most deserving contestants came in dead last.

Just as she was about to open the doors, a familiar sharp bark traveled downwind on the breeze from some-where above her. She glanced up, confused.

There, on the roof of the ship, stood Captain, his rigid little body a pop of white against the blackness of the sky. His ears were perked, his tail stiff, and he was barking with the audacity of a much larger animal.

Isabel's eyes darted to the object of his anger: Chris.

He was scrambling over the edge onto the evacuation ladder, then down the rungs as fast as he could with only one free hand. The other was raised in triumph as if bearing a torch, his fingers curled around something so clear it was almost invisible.

Silhouetted against the predawn sky, he hopped onto the end of the narrow jetty, about twenty feet out from the ambulance. The frigid river gurgled all around and behind him. He broke into a run toward land, but the moment he saw her, he gave a startled cry and stopped short.

She was standing defiantly in the center of the dock—arms crossed, stance wide—blocking his path to freedom.

CHAPTER 56
Isabel

At first neither of them moved. Ten feet apart, they traded venomous stares. Isabel narrowed her eyes at the vial in Chris's fist, excruciatingly aware of each passing second. She wanted to scream, to charge at him with all the force she could muster, but knew she was no match for his gorilla strength. He could overpower her with devastating ease; he already had. And this time, there was no one to rescue her. No backup.

Blood rushed to her temples in a hurricane of panic that rendered her motionless. Her tough girl stance felt like a charade—the posture of a scrappier version of herself that existed only in fantasy—and any moment Chris was going to see right through it.

She was about to turn away in defeat when Galileo's voice popped into her mind: *Perception is often all that counts, my dear.* The memory of his words struck her with a sudden insight that no amount of preparation could have enhanced.

She lifted her chin like she had all the time in the world. "Didn't think we'd meet again, huh?"

Chris glared at her as he stormed over the jetty's uneven rocks to close the gap between them. He clasped the vial to his chest. "I can go around you or through you."

A few feet in front of the ambulance, she gave him her best impression of bored annoyance—head tilted, arms crossed, lips tight. He was fast advancing on her, his face twisted into an imperious sneer.

"Go ahead." She smirked at him. "You're getting exactly what you deserve."

"The hell I am!" His knuckles whitened around the vial. "I made it and no one's gonna take it away."

She turned on her heel toward the ambulance, as if his fleeing were inconsequential. "Then it's too bad Galileo already did."

"What?" He leaped from the edge of the jetty onto the floating wooden dock; it groaned under his weight as he stalked closer to her. "I have it right here."

She rolled her eyes as though he were woefully unsophisticated. "You really think Galileo would leave the only vial of X101 anywhere near you after what you did to me?" She shot him a withering look. "He's not an idiot, you know. He replaced it in your lab with a fake—and thank God, because now he needs it way more than you do."

Without waiting for his reaction, she threw open the ambulance's rear door and scrambled inside to reveal an alarmed Theo and Dr. Cornell leaning over Galileo's body on the stretcher. A tube was jammed down his throat; his naked torso was stuck with wires and lines leading to various machines; an automatic compression device was pumping up and down on his chest; ice packs lined his limbs; bloody bandages covered his stomach wounds. The heart monitor still displayed a single flat line.

"Where is it?" Theo demanded. "What took you so long?"

She shook her head, squeezing past him and Dr. Cornell and Galileo's stretcher to get to the compartment in the ceiling. The same compartment from which, only two weeks ago back in Key West, she'd watched Chris withdraw a vial of X101 to resuscitate Richard. Those few milliliters of the drug were gone, of course. But the vial was not.

"Play along," she hissed, reaching into the compartment and grabbing the cooler where the empty vial was still stashed. She quickly tore open a spare bag of saline in the cooler and dunked the vial in. Already she could hear Chris's voice bellowing louder as he thundered toward the open doors.

"What the hell is going on?"

Isabel thrust the full vial at Theo just as Chris jumped inside, his biceps flexed, eyes blazing. Dr. Cornell shrank out of his way against the wall while Theo and Chris gaped at each other in a split second of mutual shock. If Chris registered Galileo's peril, his expression betrayed no sympathy—nothing but raw, vessel-bursting rage.

"Hurry!" Isabel shouted at Theo. "Before he can stop you!"

She threw herself at Chris with all of the momentum she possessed as Theo connected the phony vial to a line inserted into Galileo's shoulder.

"That's mine!" Chris roared. "Don't you dare!"

Isabel rammed her head into his broad chest, but her resistance was too weak to stop him. He let go of his own vial as he shoved her against a window, then lunged at Theo. The real vial plunked to the floor and rolled along the rubber mat; her hand immediately shot out to snatch it up. Only Dr. Cornell noticed; he was cowering on his haunches, but his spine straightened as a look of understanding crossed his face.

Theo shrieked at Chris to get away, hovering protectively over his own vial, but Chris threw himself at it with reckless abandon. They traded violent shoves until Chris emerged from the scuffle victorious—or so he thought. As soon as his fist closed around the new vial, he bolted to the rear doors and leaped out onto the dock. Isabel pressed the real one into Theo's outstretched palm, then stampeded after Chris for good measure.

"Stop!" she yelled, her sneakers pounding the dock. "Come back!"

He sprinted away at top speed without ever looking back. She chased him all the way down to the parking structure, panting and shouting. Her last glimpse was of his hunched shoulders as he scurried, ratlike, into the shadowy void.

When the echo of his footsteps faded, she ran back to the ambulance to find Theo and Dr. Cornell almost finished draining the X101 into Galileo's tube.

They both stared at her in awe as she climbed inside.

Theo offered her a helping hand. "I had no idea you could act."

A weary smile tugged at her lips. "Well," she said, "I was a TV star."

CHAPTER 57
Isabel

Forty-eight nerve-wracking hours needed to pass before Galileo's prognosis would become clear. Isabel knew this, but like everyone else on the ship, she couldn't resist lining up outside the ICU on deck 1 for an opportunity to glimpse his lifeless body and pay her silent regards. During the first few hours, the line stretched out the hospital door and backed up to the stairwell.

All the researchers, doctors, and support staff had woken up that morning to the staggering news of his death, along with Chris's betrayal and escape. More than thirty people deluged Isabel's cabin at 7 A.M. to drill her—some furious, others in tears—about what had happened during the night. She groggily related the entire sequence of events, from Richard's punched eye and the hospital confrontation that culminated in Greg's vicious knifing to Chris's theft of the X101 and her desperate last-minute retrieval.

"It should work," she declared to the anxious crowd. "I mean, he wasn't dead long enough for his whole brain to die, right?"

Her statement was met with a troubled silence, and Isabel knew what they were all thinking: The X101 came with zero guarantees. It hadn't yet been tested on someone who'd died of blood loss. Even though Galileo had received the necessary injection, been cooled down to 70 degrees, and undergone a blood transfusion and surgery to repair his gutted stomach, he was still dead—in the clinical sense, if not necessarily in the permanent, irreversible sense. So far, his monitors registered no heartbeat and no brain waves.

Isabel sensed there was also something else upsetting the group, making them trade anguished looks: Galileo had used up the very last dose of X101. And Chris, the only one who knew how to make it, was no longer around to engineer it from scratch. The video surveillance of him in the lab would not be enough by itself to enable them to synthesize the formula. Those precious few milliliters had contained a sacred promise—to fund the Network's costly experiments as long as everyone working there was alive. The painful realization descended on the researchers like a collective sucker punch: Without a perfect sample left to analyze, the drug—and their future security—was lost.

Isabel could offer them no comfort. They stumbled out of her cabin with a shattered stupefaction she recognized all too well. She'd experienced the same feeling after her father's sudden heart attack: It was the struggle to reconcile yourself to your hellish new reality. No matter how strenuous your denial, the truth waited like an unavoidable snake, ready to sink its fangs into your flesh at every turn.

Seven hours into the waiting period, around 11 A.M., Richard was discharged from St. Luke's. When he returned in a taxi, Isabel was the only person there to welcome him. He emerged onto the dock with a wry smile and a black patch over his injured eye. His cheekbones seemed to have grown sharper and his step slower, lending him an air of tired dignity. She ran down the ramp to throw her arms around his neck.

"Ahoy, mate," he joked, hugging her tightly. His musky odor combined with the pungent smell of the hospital's antibacterial soap.

She planted a kiss on his lips. "I'm so glad you're okay."

It felt almost foreign to smile, as if her facial muscles had forgotten how. She linked her arm through his and led him back up the ramp into the ship.

"Me too," he said. "They took off my patch this morning and I could see—it was blurry as hell, but I'll take it."

"Will it get any better?"

"In time, yeah, once all the inflammation goes down. Apparently I lucked out with one of the city's top retinal surgeons."

"It's about time someone around here caught a break."

He frowned at her dejected tone. "Did I miss something?" They were heading through the deserted dining area, past clusters of tables that were usually set for lunch by noon, but today remained bare. "And where is everyone anyway?"

She sighed. "They're visiting Galileo . . . on deck one."

"As in, the hospital?"

Maybe it was the sincerity of his worry or the depth of her own, but that was when she broke down. Right there, in the middle of the dining hall, she fell against his chest and sobbed. He embraced her without a word, cupping the back of her head and stroking her hair. After a minute, the whole story poured out amid her hiccups and sniffles.

His good eye widened in horror throughout, especially during the violent parts with Greg, and when she finished, she felt as drained as if someone had deflated her down to two dimensions. She exhaled a shaky breath.

"Well," he said gently, "there's nothing we can do but wait." He pushed a stray curl behind her ear. "We might as well get some rest. You haven't slept in two days, have you?"

She shook her head. The heaviness of her eyelids startled her; she hadn't noticed until now. But since he'd mentioned it, she realized that a fog of exhaustion was clouding her brain and permeating her bones. She hadn't felt so fatigued since . . . well, since her own death.

"Come," he said, taking her by the hand. "I'm putting us to bed."

The ship was rocking underneath her when she woke up later that evening. The clock on Richard's nightstand read 10:09 P.M. She'd passed out beside him for a solid ten hours, longer than she'd slept at a stretch since her college days. She ran a quick calculation in her head: They were more than eighteen hours into the waiting period for Galileo. That meant less than thirty to go.

Richard was still snoring softly; Captain lay curled up on his pillow, their noses an inch apart. She tried not to wake either of them as she crept out of bed to look out the porthole. The sky was surprisingly pitch-black, which it never was in Manhattan. She saw no outlines of buildings, no pointy spires lighting up the distant skyline. The ship must have disembarked from the city.

Her stomach was growling. She tiptoed out of Richard's cabin and made her way up to the dining area to rummage around for leftovers. That was, if the service crew had even bothered to make anything. The rigidity of their schedule seemed to have collapsed along with their leader. Sure enough, she found nothing in the refrigerator but some raw chicken, an unmade salad, and a two-day-old platter of meatloaf.

As she set about heating up the meatloaf in the microwave, she heard footsteps approaching the kitchen. She poked her head out to see Theo trudging toward her, wearing the same sweatpants and black V-neck he'd been in since the previous night. His tight shoulders and morose expression mirrored her own.

"Hey, you," she said. "Hungry?"

He nodded. "Starved."

"I'll warm you up a plate." She gestured to a stool in front of the counter island. "Take a seat."

"Thanks." He offered her a limp smile, his cheerful dimple noticeably absent.

"So where are we?" She gestured toward the kitchen's circular window; outside, a multitude of stars glittered across the sky like spilled sequins. "Clearly not New York."

"We're about fifteen nautical miles off the coast, in international waters. We couldn't risk staying."

"Because of Chris?" The microwave dinged. She removed the plate she'd prepared for herself and served it to Theo instead.

"Yeah. He's a liability now."

"I'm just glad he's gone. I couldn't take seeing his little smirk ever again."

"Amen." Theo thrust his fork into the meatloaf as she warmed another slice.

She let him eat in silence for a minute. When the microwave beeped again, she couldn't help noticing the clock on the display.

"Twenty-nine more hours."

"I don't know how I'm gonna wait that long." He sank his fingers into his disheveled hair. "I feel like I might explode."

"Any change?"

"His heartbeat's back now. Real faint, though."

"That's great!" She slid onto a stool across from him with a grin. "Isn't that a really good sign?"

Theo shrugged. "Yeah, but still no brain waves. But he's only at 87 degrees at the moment, so it's still too early."

"They warm him a quarter of a degree Celsius an hour, right?"

"Exactly. Good memory."

It was discouraging to think that even though his heart was beating again, he was still dead—legally—as long as his brain was gone. If someone went crazy and pulled the plug, it wouldn't be murder.

"What if he stays brain-dead?" she blurted.

Theo winced, and she immediately regretted asking.

"We don't have to think about that," she said. "Never mind."

"I'd authorize them to . . ." He lowered his gaze. "I'm his next of kin. I know he wouldn't want to be kept on machines."

"Well, let's wait and see. I think he has a real shot." Of course she had no idea if he did or didn't; the complex chemical interactions of the X101 with dying neurons was far beyond her comprehension, but what else could she say?

When Theo looked up at her, his lips were curved in a grateful smile. "I meant to tell you," he said, "good job before. You really came through there."

"Thanks." Her heart lifted like a helium balloon, lighter than air. "You have no idea how much that means to me."

* * *

With eight hours to go, the anxiety on the ship was festering like an actual living organism. It seemed to exist of its own accord: thickening the air, wrinkling people's foreheads, shutting down their stomachs, closing all the labs.

To distract herself, Isabel used the satellite phone to call and check up on Joan. When she answered, her voice sounded tired but also buoyant, as if some great invisible hurdle had been cleared.

"Isabel!" she exclaimed. "Thank you for calling. How's our agent friend, is he okay? I've called all the local hospitals but no one knows a thing about him."

"We took him . . . out of state. He's still critical, so it's touch and go right now."

"Oh. I'm so sorry, I still can't believe what my—what Greg did."

The recollection of the unspeakable moment made them both go quiet.

After a few seconds Isabel hazarded a follow-up: "Is he in custody at least?"

"Of course, he's already been arraigned and entered a guilty plea. I'm sure he'll end up in prison for the rest of his life."

Isabel felt a weak satisfaction at justice served, but more than that, she was overwhelmed with sadness for Joan.

"Do you need help or anything? I mean, where do you go from here?"

"Oh, honey, don't worry about me, I'll be okay."

"For real? You're not just saying it?"

"I've still got my son and my grandkids and my mind, and I've come to realize that's pretty much all I need. Anything else is gravy."

Her sincerity filled Isabel with both admiration and relief. It was astonishing how strong some people could be in the worst possible times. In the truest sense, she thought, Joan deserved the title *survivor.* They both did.

"That's good to hear," she said. "We should keep in touch."

"I would like that very much." Isabel could hear the smile in her voice. "You know, I owe you a thank-you."

"You do?"

"I was blind for so long. Thank you for helping me see the truth."

At 4:15 A.M., just a few minutes before the forty-eight-hour mark, the entire population of the ship gathered around Galileo's bedside in the ICU. Isabel and Theo sat closest to him, on either side of his head; Richard hovered behind her with a hand on her shoulder. The several dozen researchers, doctors, service staff, and nurses completed the tight cluster.

Galileo lay with his eyes closed underneath a white sheet. The monitors connected to his chest and forehead were beeping in quiet, regular intervals. There was no longer a tube down his throat, now that he could breathe on his own, and the recent MRI of his brain had come back clean, but Isabel knew better than to celebrate just yet. One horrific scenario was still possible: even if his brain had recovered function, his time without oxygen might have left his nervous system paralyzed—so he could be left locked in, unable to speak or move, but fully conscious. She could imagine no worse fate.

Nobody spoke. The only motion was the gentle swaying of the ship beneath their feet. Each minute seemed interminable. Every five to ten seconds, Isabel glanced up at the plain white clock on the wall above Galileo's head. She was too nervous to squirm, as though any movement might disrupt the fragile chance of his recovery. Across from her, though, Theo kept cracking his bony knuckles and sighing.

She found her mind briefly wandering to thoughts of her mom and Andy. She couldn't wait to see them again. But even when she returned home, she intuited that her life would never be the same. For one thing, she had Richard now. She reached up to cover his hand with her own. Her old job in reality television would be waiting for her, but she knew with a sudden certainty that she couldn't return to do a second season of *Wild Woman*. It would feel too much like a charade to "survive alone in the wild" with a whole production crew just out of sight. It also seemed pointless now to spend all her energy entertaining couch potatoes. That mission wasn't enough anymore.

Her next thought materialized like a distant glimmer: She would put her survival skills and newfound confidence to use fighting evil in the world, like her father had. Her true calling felt so right that she was shocked not to have recognized it sooner: she would apply to join the FBI. She would make Galileo proud.

An excited murmur swept through the crowd; her attention snapped to his face.

His eyelids were fluttering open.

No one dared breathe. Isabel felt her own lungs expand to capacity, her heart thumping in her throat. Richard gave her shoulder a tight squeeze.

After a few dazed seconds, Galileo's intelligent eyes appeared to take in the crowd. His gaze shifted from one familiar face to the next. Everyone seemed to understand not to speak right away, to give him time to adjust. He touched his face, then lowered his hand to feel across his stitched-up stomach. At first a shade of confusion wrinkled his brow, but only for a moment. Then his eyebrows lifted and one corner of his mouth spread into a crooked grin.

"It's quite boring to be dead," he said. "I don't recommend it one bit."

CHAPTER 58
Isabel

An instant cheer rose up from the crowd. A few of the nurses were dabbing their eyes, and many of the researchers clapped. Isabel applauded along with them, laughing through her own tears. She and Theo exchanged a look of ecstatic relief as Galileo weakly pushed himself up to a sitting position.

"I take it you missed me," he said, half smiling. "It's good to be back."

The left side of his face wasn't moving at all and his words slurred a bit. He didn't seem to notice, but Isabel and everyone else certainly did. She caught the concerned frown on Dr. Cornell's face as he whispered something to another doctor standing beside him.

Sharp as ever, Galileo caught their looks, too. "Oh, this?" He gestured to the frozen side of his face. "I can live with it. No big deal."

"But no one else has been paralyzed after the X101!" Theo cried. "This isn't supposed to happen!"

Isabel buried her face in her hands. "None of this was supposed to happen," she said, surprising herself with an outpouring of the secret guilt that had been torturing her for two days. "It's all my fault. If you had never met me, you wouldn't have gotten hurt trying to help me. And now the last dose of the drug is gone." She peered through her fingers, wincing at him and at the crowd. "I'm so, so sorry."

Several of the more antisocial researchers glared at her, but many murmured that it wasn't her fault or shook their heads to absolve her of blame.

Galileo cleared his throat. The effort it took to speak through his fatigue was apparent. "Trust me, will you?"

Everyone stared at him. Isabel hesitated; maybe he hadn't understood her? She never should have blurted out the bad news about the X101—it was too soon to upset him in his delicate state. She was silently berating herself when his matter-of-fact voice surprised her.

"I didn't receive a full dose," he slurred. "I'm sure that's why I ended up this way."

"You didn't?" Theo said. "But I gave you every last drop in the vial!"

He turned to Theo with his trademark smile of mischief. "You did fine, don't worry. There wasn't a full dose to begin with. I stole a quarter of a milliliter right after Chris finished making it and sent it ashore."

A chain of gasps circled around the room amid dumfounded exclamations. Isabel could only shake her head in wonder at the fact that she had ever underestimated this man.

"Where?" Theo asked in disbelief.

"Somewhere safe," he promised. "Somewhere secret, so no one can ever blackmail anyone to get it." His attention shifted to Isabel and Richard.

"Now, my dears," he said, "tell the captain to head south. Let's get you home."

CHAPTER 59
Isabel

Key West

Isabel raced up to the porch of her mother's bungalow, inhaling the glorious scent of the yard's coconut palm tree. Since there was no longer a need for the Network's protection, her mom and Andy had been transferred from their safe house back home. Now they were eagerly awaiting her arrival and the details of her journey; she'd promised to tell them the whole story face-to-face. There was just too much to pack into a single phone call; the two weeks of her absence seemed like a short lifetime. She felt like a different person, and in some ways, she was.

As she bounded toward the door, the light breeze on her skin felt like a revelation: never again would she take Florida's mild winters for granted—or, for that matter, any day of her life.

On the threshold of reuniting with her family, she paused. It felt good to savor the moment of anticipation, and to utter a silent thanks to everyone who had made her continued existence possible. Dr. Quinn. Galileo. Richard. A great tide of awe and fondness washed over her, permeating her core deeply enough never to be forgotten.

Captain licked her calf, reminding her of his presence. He was a final gift from Galileo, who'd come to accept the tightness of their bond. And anyway, as Isabel had pointed out, Captain could enjoy life as a dog much better on land than at sea. He was a pet now, not a test subject. She couldn't wait to introduce him to the beach.

But first—she knocked on the door. Captain barked as it swung open, and her mom and Andy immediately bombarded her with hugs and kisses. They ushered her inside on a crest of affection, Captain excitedly circling their feet.

"You're home!" her mom squealed. "Finally! We couldn't sleep all night!"

"Oh my God." Andy dropped to his knees in front of Captain. "You got a dog? This is the best day ever!"

She laughed, drinking in the sight of her scrawny little brother and her beautiful raven-haired mom. A pang struck her when she noticed they both looked paler and more exhausted than she remembered, but they were beaming so happily it was impossible not to do the same.

"Just for you, bud," she said to Andy. "His name's Captain."

Andy scratched his ears as her mom hovered near her, rubbing her arm. "So, how are you? Are you hungry? You look thin."

"I'm fine. How are you guys? Did I miss anything?"

"I got to skip school for two weeks!" Andy exclaimed. "We stayed in our own huge house and it was awesome."

Her mom cocked her head as if to tell Isabel, *Awesome isn't exactly the word I would choose.* Isabel understood: their separation had been not just excruciating, but terrifying. She took her mother's hand. *I'm home*, she said via a quick squeeze. *And this time, I'm here to stay.*

"I'm glad you guys were well taken care of," she said. "Galileo promised me you would be."

"It was very nice of his . . . group. Speaking of them . . ." Her mom ran into the kitchen and brought back a miniature cooler that Isabel didn't recognize. It was a sturdy white box made out of what looked like indestructible plastic.

"A courier came by the other day to deliver the jewelry box you got me. It was really pretty and unexpected—but the guy also brought this. He told me to keep it in the fridge until further notice."

She held out the cooler for Isabel to open.

Inside was a tempered glass vial that contained a few drops of a clear liquid.

Isabel gasped. Her mom stared at her, mystified.

"You know what it is?"

"I think," she said, smiling, "I have one hell of a guess."

ACKNOWLEDGMENTS

I am greatly indebted to certain people whose support helped me realize my ambitions for this book:

My agent extraordinaire, Erica Silverman at Trident Media Group, whose friendship I cherish and whose guidance I can always trust.

My insightful editor, Michaela Hamilton, who granted me a dream assignment to write this book and whose valuable comments have made it the best it can be.

The entire team at Kensington Books, for their passion and expertise in production, design, marketing, publicity, and distribution.

Dr. Sam Parnia, for giving me a tour of the emergency room at Stony Brook Hospital and answering all of my nitty-gritty questions about resuscitation. His book *Erasing Death* was indispensable to me.

Dr. Robert Klitzman, my adviser at Columbia University and head of the Bioethics Program, for helping me to gain a deeper grasp of the ethical issues I raise throughout the book.

The late Dr. Michael Palmer, for talking me through the early stages of idea development. His mentorship was a precious gift I deeply miss.

My parents, for their unshakeable belief in my writing ability.

Susan Breen, of Gotham Writers' Workshop, for reading my earliest drafts and providing spot-on evaluations every time.

My sidekick pup, Wally, the inspiration for Captain, who warmed my lap during a cold, long winter of writing.

My husband, Matt, my first and favorite reader. This one's for you.